# A MATTER OF

Ginger Kolbaba & Christy Scannell

# A MATTER OF
# WIFE & DEATH

AUTHORS OF
*DESPERATE PASTORS' WIVES*

A NOVEL

SECRETS FROM
LULU'S
CAFE
SERIES

HOWARD
*Fiction*
A DIVISION OF SIMON & SCHUSTER
New York   London   Toronto   Sydney

Our purpose at Howard Books is to:
• *Increase faith* in the heart of growing Christians
• *Inspire holiness* in the lives of believers
• *Instill hope* in the hearts of struggling people everywhere
*Because He's coming again!*

Published by Howard Books, a division of Simon & Schuster, Inc.
1230 Avenue of the Americas, New York, NY 10020
www.howardpublishing.com

*A Matter of Wife & Death* © 2008 by Ginger Kolbaba and Christy Scannell

Library of Congress Cataloging-in-Publication Data

Kolbaba, Ginger.
  A matter of wife and death : a novel / Ginger Kolbaba & Christy Scannell.
    p. cm. — (Secrets from Lulu's Café ; 2)
Summary: "In this sequel to Desperate pastors' wives, a retreat for pastors' wives turns out to be anything but peaceful when one pastor's wife doesn't return home, causing the other wives to reevaluate their callings and their lives"—Provided by publisher.
1. Spouses of clergy—Fiction. 2. Wives—Fiction. 3. Female friendship—Fiction.
4. Coffee shops—Fiction. I. Scannell, Christy, 1967– II. Title.
  PS3611.O5825M38 2008
  813'.6—dc22                                    2007025638

10 9 8 7 6 5 4 3 2 1

ISBN 13: 978-1-4165-4388-6
ISBN 10:    1-4165-4388-0

For information regarding special discounts for bulk purchases, please contact Simon & Schuster Special Sales at 1-800-456-6798 or business@simonandschuster.com.

Edited by Ramona Cramer Tucker
Interior design by Jaime Putorti
Cover design by Kirk DouPonce

Unless otherwise noted, Scripture quotations are taken from the *Holy Bible, New International Version*®. NIV®. Copyright © 1973, 1978, 1984 by International Bible Society. Used by permission of Zondervan Publishing House. All rights reserved.

Isaiah 25:7–8 is taken from the *Holy Bible, New Living Translation*, copyright © 1996, 2004. Used by permission of Tyndale House Publishers, Inc., Wheaton, Illinois 60189. All rights reserved.

# Meet the Pastors' Wives of Red River, Ohio

*Lisa Barton* is an at-home mom with two kids: Callie, fourteen, and Ricky, thirteen. Her husband, Joel, has pastored Red River Assembly of God for nearly four years. Lisa's parents pastor the Assembly of God in nearby Cloverdale.

*Felicia Lopez-Morrison's* husband, Dave, pastors the First Baptist Church. They have one child, Nicholas, who is four. Felicia is a high-powered public relations executive with an office in Cincinnati. The Morrisons came to Red River nearly two years ago from Los Angeles.

*Mimi Plaisance* is a former teacher who now stays home with her four children: Michaela, ten; Mark, Jr. (MJ), eight; Megan, five; and newborn Milo. Mark, her husband, has pastored Trinity United Methodist Church for several years.

*Jennifer Shores* is married to Sam, pastor of Red River Community Church, where she is the church secretary. They have been married ten years and do not have children.

*Katherine "Kitty" Fleming Katt* is the wife of Norman Katt, who pastors First Presbyterian, the largest church in the county (as Kitty constantly reminds everyone!). She leads the Southwest Pastors' Wives Fellowship and always wears yellow.

# A MATTER OF
# WIFE & DEATH

# Lulu's Café

*Tuesday, January 16*
*12:01 p.m.*

Mimi Plaisance groaned as she pulled her green Freestar minivan into a parking spot in front of the friendly but divey Lulu's Café in Southwest Ohio's Cheeksville. The other women's cars were already there. She hated to be late, especially for these get-togethers—the one point of sanity in an otherwise chaotic existence. Mimi prided herself on being punctual. Even while rearing three children—now five, eight, and ten—she had succeeded at keeping it "all together." Well, almost. Last year had been a bust. And this year looked to be more of the same. Worse, actually.

All because of baby Milo. The child who refused to cooperate.

Well, she wasn't about to miss her lunch date with her three best friends, Jennifer, Felicia, and Lisa—all pastors' wives, like her, from churches in her hometown of Red River, forty miles from where they secretly noshed every other Tuesday. It was their only chance to get away from their nosy, busybody town.

Because Mimi gave birth to Milo on December 22—the day of her church's live nativity and Christmas sing-along—the four women had dis-

1

cussed canceling their biweekly gathering at Lulu's, at least until things settled down for Mimi. But they'd all quickly agreed: Their time together was worth juggling holiday schedules and maneuvering snow-covered back roads. Mimi was grateful; she desperately needed to get away and spend some time with adults. Being alone all day with a screaming, colicky baby and a whiny, ornery five-year-old in the afternoons was enough to make her pull out strands of her blond hair and tie their mouths shut.

But packing up Megan and her newborn brother and getting them settled at the baby-sitter's was a real trick. Not to mention trying to avoid the snoopy comments and questions from Gladys, the nearly-seventy-year-old who watched the kids for her.

Gladys had never before asked where Mimi dashed off to every other Tuesday. But now that Mimi had Milo, who was less than a month old, the upraised eyebrow and less-than-subtle judgments began. "It's not good for you to drive in this kind of weather—especially since you have another baby . . . Is Pastor okay with you runnin' off like this? . . . It must be somethin' mighty important for you to leave these babies every other week . . ." And on and on.

Mimi tried to be as noncommittal as possible without being rude. Where she went was nobody's business—even though the members at her church, Trinity United Methodist, tended to think otherwise. The one good thing about Gladys was that she didn't blab. Mimi's secret was safe. At least she hoped so.

Mimi glanced at the dashboard clock. *12:02.*

*Well,* technically, *I'm on time.* She pulled her red angora scarf tight about her neck, just in time to see one of her "favorite" people come out the door of Lulu's.

"Oh, great." She groaned and ducked to the side, hoping Katherine Katt, the notorious Kitty, wouldn't see her.

*Tap, tap, tap.*

*Maybe if I ignore her, she'll go away,* Mimi thought, even though she knew there was no escaping Kitty.

*Tap, tap, tap, tap.*

2

Mimi inhaled deeply, pasted her best pastor's wife smile on, and turned toward the window. There stood Kitty in her trademark bright yellow coat and gloves, both with black fur trim. With her black bouffant hairdo, Kitty resembled a giant bumblebee more than the pastor's wife of First Presbyterian, the oldest and largest church in the county.

"Oh, hi, Kitty!" Mimi said as she opened the door to get out, acting as if she'd just noticed Kitty standing there.

Kitty smiled her big, toothy grin. "If I didn't know you better, Mimi, I'd think you were trying to avoid me." She laughed and pulled her faux fur collar closer around her.

"Not at all, Kitty." Mimi reached over, grabbed her purse, and held it up. "I was just getting this. It's nice to see you." *God, forgive me*, she thought as she uttered this obvious lie.

"Ah, yes. Well, I was just having a little *chat* with your girlfriends." She pursed her lips, as if just saying the words left a bad taste in her mouth, like sucking on a lemon.

*Well, it would match her outfit,* Mimi thought.

Mimi knew Kitty hated that the four pastors' wives got together routinely without involving—or inviting—Kitty. It gave Mimi a silent thrill to know that it must be eating Kitty alive not to have her hand in all things PW. The thought made her smile brightly—genuinely, this time.

"Speaking of, I should probably get in there. I don't want to keep them waiting." Mimi shut the car door and stepped toward the curb as Kitty's hand reached out and grabbed her sleeve.

"You may want to talk to them about the pastors' wives' retreat coming up. I mentioned it, but coming from you . . ."

*Was that a slight sign of defeat?* Mimi wondered.

"Well, it's never too early to plan," Kitty continued. "I know you'll all want to be there. It will mean so much to your churches and husbands, I'm sure."

Leave it to Kitty to cop a superior attitude with a raw comment. Mimi knew where Kitty's line was going and mentally finished it. *After all, you and the others have so much you can learn from me, since I* am *the pastor's wife of the largest and most respected church in the area, and your churches are, well, significantly smaller and less known.* Kitty never could pass up a chance to remind the other pastors' wives how unimportant they were in comparison to her.

The snow was now falling in large flakes, covering Mimi's blond bob and dark-colored peacoat. "I'm sure we'll all be there. We wouldn't want to miss it."

"I have exciting things planned for this year's retreat."

"Something to look forward to," Mimi said, working her way toward Lulu's.

"I'm almost dying to tell you, but I wouldn't want to spoil the surprise."

"Definitely. We wouldn't want that. 'Bye now." Mimi slipped through the door into the brightly lit café before Kitty could say anything else. The warm air rushed from the vents above the door and *swooshed* around Mimi. It felt wonderful, even if she did feel flushed from her Kitty encounter. She shook her head and brushed off her coat, which appeared to be covered with dandruff.

In their typical booth toward the back right-hand corner of the café sat Mimi's three friends: the PWs, they called themselves. They'd first received that honorary title from their waitress, Gracie, who discovered that they were all pastors' wives. The name stuck.

"Ha!" Jennifer said, pointing and laughing. "She got you, too."

Mimi shook her head slyly.

"I liked your little football tackle move to avoid her," Jennifer continued. She ducked first one way, then another. "Whoo! Haah!"

"You know that never works with Kitty," Felicia said. "I've tried that move several times. Always backfires."

"Well, I saved it by grabbing my purse as my excuse," Mimi defended as she tossed her coat into the next booth and scooted in next to Felicia.

Felicia was, as usual, dressed in a business suit—dark mauve this time—since she'd joined them from her public relations firm in Cincinnati.

"Yes, I've even used that as an excuse," Felicia continued. "It's like hope springs eternal, you know? I keep thinking, *This time it will work. This time I'll be able to avoid her."*

"Who are you avoiding this time?" Gracie, their waitress, said as she came from behind Mimi and plopped a large glass of milk in front of her.

"You, if you keep pushing that homemade apple pie at me." Felicia laughed.

Gracie snorted and eyed Mimi appreciatively. "Look at you, girlie. How'd you get the pregnancy weight off so quickly? It's only been a month."

"With you taking off work, nobody's been here to feed me properly," Mimi joked. Mimi knew Gracie took off a month to visit her sister in Florida who'd recently been diagnosed with breast cancer. She hoped that Gracie's brush with mortality had made her more open to the spiritual side of things. Mimi and the other pastors' wives had been working on Gracie since they first started meeting together for lunch here nearly two years earlier. Gracie had always told them she had no interest in anything spiritual, but a few times had mentioned that knowing the PWs had made her appreciate their faith. "Keep working, ladies," she'd told them. "Maybe one of these days . . ."

"Gracie," Mimi now said, "how's your sister?"

"She's okay. They took both her buddies, so she's mourning that. But they gave her a good prognosis."

"Buddies?" Lisa asked, seemingly bewildered.

"Breasts," Jennifer whispered.

"Oh!" Lisa nodded.

"We've been praying for her," Felicia told Gracie. "*And* for you."

"Keep it up, girls. Keep it up. Your food will be up soon. I went ahead and ordered your usual." Gracie tapped the table and winked at Mimi before she plodded off to her other customers.

"Am I that predictable?" Mimi said to her friends.

"Naw," Jennifer replied. "Only every other Tuesday. You look great, by the way."

Felicia and Lisa chimed in immediately with their agreement.

Mimi held up her hands. "Thanks, but I don't feel great. Obviously you aren't noticing the huge black rings around my eyes. Nor have you noticed the large, baggy clothes to hide the pooches. See?" She pinched her oversized cranberry sweater.

"Well, you still look great," Lisa said. "After having my two kids, it took me forever to lose the weight. Actually, twelve years later and I'm *still* trying!" She laughed.

"I'll loan you my four monsters," Mimi replied. "That should do the trick."

"I don't get it," Jennifer cut in. "You said four *monsters*. How can a sweet little baby be a monster already? I mean, with your other three I get the connection. But Milo?"

"Girlfriend, sweet little babies can be the worst!" Felicia said.

"Oh, Milo's sweet when he sleeps, which is *never*. The kid eats and poops and cries and cries. And that's it. I've never experienced a baby like him. My other kids were great. They were sleeping through the night within weeks. Not this one. The kid's got the lungs of an opera singer."

"Or a pastor!" Felicia joked.

"I wouldn't be surprised," Mimi continued. "I'm going deaf. I haven't slept since we brought him home from the hospital, and my breasts feel like I have a twenty-four-hour udder pump attached to them. I swear that kid's going to be the death of me." She lifted her glass of milk in a cheer.

"I remember those days," Lisa said. She touched just above her breasts. "I was so tender!"

"I guess the one good thing is that Mark's also so exhausted he hasn't had any energy to mess around. After this baby, though, I think I'd shoot him if he tried to!" Mimi remembered how they'd ended up with Milo. She'd been too exhausted to say no when her husband, Mark, gave her The Look. It was more like she'd simply asked him, "Do I have to do anything other than just be there?"

"Just keep reminding yourself," Lisa said, "this is only for a season."

"Yeah, well, I've got a name for this season: PK chaos." Mimi watched the girls nod in sympathetic agreement.

"Okay, now stop," Jennifer whined good-naturedly. "You're going to make me stop wanting kids."

"Any news on that front?" Felicia asked.

Jennifer shrugged and ran her fingers through her wavy strawberry-blond hair.

"Come on!" Mimi said, knowing instinctively that Jennifer was up to something. Jennifer had wanted a baby so badly that when Mimi had announced her pregnancy with Milo, there had been some tension between the two friends.

Jennifer sighed. "Okay, well, we have an appointment with Dr. O'Boyle on Friday afternoon. I'm getting tired of these fertility drugs, so I'm hoping he has another idea for us."

"So Sam's going with you then?" Felicia asked.

Mimi could tell that Felicia was trying hard to be compassionate, but she knew it was as difficult for her as it was for the rest of them. They loved Jennifer dearly, but her infertility struggles wore thin on them.

"What kind of idea do you think he might have?" Mimi asked hopefully.

"I really don't know." Jennifer hung her head. "I think all that's left is IVF."

Lisa crinkled her forehead. "Why am I so out of it today? Now what is IVF?"

Jennifer glanced up. "In vitro fertilization. You know, test-tube babies."

Silence covered the table. Mimi suddenly felt Jennifer's desperation for a baby, and she felt horrible for ever complaining about Milo.

Lisa smiled brightly. "Well, Jennifer, this just means we'll double up our prayers for you. God will clearly show you the direction he wants you to go. And he'll make it work out."

Coming from somebody else, those words would have sounded like platitudes. But not from Lisa. Mimi knew Lisa *would* double up her prayers for Jennifer. And Mimi knew Lisa really did believe that God causes all things to work for good.

"Lisa's right. God has something planned for you," said Mimi. "We just can't see the big picture yet. But he's putting it together."

Jennifer smiled softly. "Thanks, guys. I know that's true. Sometimes I just need to be reminded—and not from church members full of unsolicited advice."

The women laughed easily at that.

"Speaking of children and church members," Felicia said. "You know, I thought it was bad enough to have hassles from the church family. I figured my home family should behave. But my own pastor's kid can be a real challenge."

"Ah, yes." Lisa nodded knowingly. "And how is Nicholas's biting coming along?"

"Thank God today was our day to get together, that's all I've got to say," Felicia answered. "With yesterday being Martin Luther King Day and Nicholas home all day, he had nothing better to do than practice his biting skills."

"Is he *still* doing that?" Jennifer said. "I thought you and Dave had controlled it."

Felicia shook her head. "Yeah, well, apparently not. He's at it with gusto."

Mimi joined Lisa and Jennifer as they *tsked* at the recurrent problem and settled into the booth a little deeper. She sighed contentedly as she surveyed her friends. It felt good to be there—even though making the trip was difficult. The PWs had been meeting together now for almost two years and Mimi knew they all felt those lunches were a lifesaver. Of course, they had to sneak out of town to meet, but it was well worth the risk of discovery.

These friends had talked at length about how difficult being a pastor's wife was. They each loved the ministry and felt passionate about what God was doing through their families. But still, even with the feeling of being an instrument of God, it didn't make dealing with other Christians in their churches any easier. And even the other pastors' wives in the region had been difficult to connect with. Mimi wasn't sure if it was because of some sense of competition or just a fear of becoming too vulnerable, but the other pastors' wives would go only so far in their relationships. Everything was always "fine" when she'd talk to one of them.

That's what made their foursome so special. Lisa, Jennifer, Felicia, and

Mimi, all in their thirties, had each taken a chance to truly open up to each other. To speak honestly about how difficult being in their position was. In the "Lord's business," you never knew whom you could trust. You always had to fight against other people's expectations of what you should be and do—as well as fighting against your own. At times the pressure could become overwhelming. Then the one thing you wanted to do most—other than tell somebody off—was to run away.

She thought sadly about the pastor's wife who'd been in the news for shooting her husband. She didn't know what the situation was but felt terrible that this woman had had no one to turn to. No other pastor's wife. No one in the congregation. That was typical, Mimi knew. Church members wanted perfect people in their pastors' families. And it was a pastor's duty to make sure his family fit the bill. It didn't matter that that wasn't real life. It just made life's messiness even more messy and difficult. It's no wonder pastors and their families were leaving churches in droves. She'd considered it on many occasions. If it just wasn't for that whole "feeling God's call on their lives" thing . . .

But when things at the church were good, they were very, very good. The world was sunny and bright, and God was in control. Evil was being conquered, lives were being changed, and they felt the smile of God on them. Most of the time that seemed to happen, too, on every other Tuesday at Lulu's Café.

Mimi shook her head to clear her thoughts—and to wake herself up. It felt so comfortable and warm in the back of the café.

Felicia was in the middle of telling a story about Nicholas biting her ankle when she told him he couldn't watch any more TV.

"What did you do?" Lisa asked, holding her iced tea glass in mid-sip.

"I yelped and was about ready to read him his last rites when I thought, *WWSND.*"

Mimi blinked. "Huh?"

Felicia broke into a bright smile. " 'What Would the Supernanny Do?' Supernanny would send him to his naughty corner and say, 'That is unacceptable.' " These last words were spoken in a rather bad British accent that got the women giggling. "So that's exactly what I did. I sent him to his naughty corner. Oh, did he have a fit."

"I'll bet," said Mimi, who thought of her kids—especially her second child, Mark Jr., or MJ, as the family called him. If she instituted a naughty corner, he'd basically end up living there. She could set up a small cot and etch the words MJ's NAUGHTY CORNER right into the wall.

"If we could only have a naughty corner for ornery church members . . ." Jennifer said conspiratorially, with a mischievous smile.

The women sighed in agreement.

"Speaking of *ornery*, was Kitty on her way to her son's?" Mimi felt odd saying *son*. It was only a few months ago that the women had discovered Kitty's secret: She'd had a son when she was a teenager and had given him up for adoption. She'd reconnected with him recently and visited him regularly in his apartment across the street from Lulu's. But her husband, Norm, still didn't know about Kitty's son's existence.

Jennifer nodded. "She picked up a carry-out order and was on her way there. You know, she now comes precisely at the time we're here so she can insert her way into our company."

"She almost had me pitying her, until she pulled that little stunt," Felicia said.

Mimi remembered that day well. The women had confronted Kitty, thinking she was having an affair, until they got her to confess to having a son. Lisa had done a great job showing compassion and understanding and mercy with Kitty. *Like a true pastor's wife*, Mimi had thought at the time. It was love in action and it had worked. That is, until Kitty regained her nasty composure and turned on the women. Her last words had been that she didn't have a problem, and they'd do well to remember that.

Lisa's eyes grew sad. "Really, we should still pity her. Imagine what it's like being her, living with the insecurity. I mean, she's living under grace, yet living so far from it. Every time I think of her or see her, I pray that God would make himself real in her life."

Mimi and the others grew silent. Lisa was right, Mimi knew. And Lisa was the one who always brought a sense of mercy and balance to everything. Besides Mark, Lisa was the one Mimi knew she could always count on to pray for her.

"What would Supernanny do for teenagers?" Lisa asked, seeming to want to change the subject.

"Take away their video games and cell phones!" Jennifer laughed. "Don't tell me your two angels are flirting with the dark side."

Lisa shook her head, then moved her mouth back and forth as if unsure about whether to open up. Finally she said, "Ricky's fine. He's a good kid. But Callie concerns me. I'm starting to see a bit of attitude toward God and the church. And toward her dad and me."

"That's normal," Jennifer said. "Kids that age all go through some form of rebellion. It's worse for pastors' kids."

"Maybe," Lisa said. "Callie's always been strong-willed and opinionated—but in a good way. But we've been having some trouble brewing at the church. It's affecting Callie, I think."

*Trouble brewing.* The words sank in deep with Mimi, and she knew instinctively it was hitting Lisa and Joel hard, too.

"What kind of trouble?" Felicia asked quietly. "Trouble like, 'We don't want to change the color of the carpeting because it's always been rust-colored shag' trouble?"

Lisa fidgeted in her seat.

"Here you go, ladies," Gracie interrupted, setting down a large round tray filled with plates of hot food.

Lisa grabbed her napkin and spread it over her lap, as if glad for the interruption.

They got their plates and prayers squared away, and immediately the conversation went back to Lisa.

"What kind of trouble, Lis?" Jennifer asked.

Mimi was afraid to hear—almost like it was a bad omen . . . not that she really believed in those things. But she and her husband had been in the ministry long enough to know that when one church was struggling, other churches would feel the tremors, too. And when a church was struggling, inevitably the worst hit was the pastor and his family.

"Several people in our church—two in particular—have started a campaign to commit mutiny." Lisa pushed back her shoulder-length brown hair, still with the red highlights the girls had made her keep up after they took her for a makeover last year, then she stabbed a fry with her fork.

"Lord, have mercy," Felicia whispered.

The table grew quiet as the women focused on their food and allowed Lisa's words to sink in. There was definitely trouble brewing.

# Jennifer

Jennifer jumped a little as Dr. O'Boyle burst into the exam room. Even though she was comfortable around her ob-gyn, it always startled her when a doctor came through the door.

This time, though, she didn't need to worry about keeping the paper gown wrapped around her because she was in her regular clothes as she sat on the examining table. Across from her in the small room was her husband, Sam, his eyes glued to the floor.

"Posters bothering you?" Jennifer had just asked him. She was used to the medical illustrations of women's genitalia and breast tissue in a gynecologist's office, but knew it probably would be uncomfortable for a man to be surrounded by them.

Sam had shrugged and just started to speak when Dr. O'Boyle whooshed into the room. "Hello again," the doctor said cheerfully. He set Jennifer's chart on the counter and shook Sam's hand, then stood in front of Jennifer with his hands lightly on her knees. "Well, love, what do we do now?" he asked rhetorically.

Jennifer felt tears coming to her eyes until she glanced at Sam. She knew he was mentally repeating what Dr. O'Boyle said, and his fascination with the doctor's Irish accent made Jennifer smile. She knew she'd be hearing his words later from Sam in a makeshift Irish brogue.

"Well, now, I'm glad to see you're keeping up a good spirit," said Dr. O'Boyle, easing himself onto a rolling stool and reaching for the chart.

Jennifer stole a glance at Sam, who was mouthing the doctor's words in what she knew in Sam's mind was a Bono sound-alike. She flashed big eyes and a hand wave at Sam in an effort to make him stop, but she really was glad he was there to bring some levity to an otherwise grim situation.

"I think we've pretty much come to the end of the road, haven't we?" Jennifer asked while the doctor paged through the top of her chart. "We've done the IUI and the meds and everything. Well, everything but—"

Dr. O'Boyle raised his head. "But in vitro."

Sam's ruddy face turned serious. "Doctor, is that really our only option at this point? There aren't any other procedures we can try before we get to that? I'm just not sure I'm ready for a petri dish baby." He pushed his glasses back on the bridge of his nose, a nervous habit.

Jennifer was glad to hear Sam express himself—he rarely did to her— even though she was concerned about his reticence to do anything and everything to have a baby.

The doctor cleared his throat. "Sam, we can keep trying the meds and the assisted impregnations, but to be straight with you, I don't think it's fair to continue pumping Jennifer's body with those medications."

Both men eyed Jennifer. Even though her heart was broken over her failure to become pregnant, Dr. O'Boyle was right about her spirit. Rediscovering the Lord last year had buoyed her through all the testing and the injections and the numerous times she'd had to present herself in a most undesirable way on Dr. O'Boyle's procedure table.

"Whaaat?" she responded playfully to the two sets of eyes searching hers. "Just because I'm a loony-tune half the month because my body is about to explode from hormones? What excuse will I use for being crazy if I go off the meds?"

They appeared relieved at her answer, but a second glance between Jennifer and Sam told her Sam knew she was putting on a good front.

The doctor closed her file. "My recommendation is to go off everything for now and keep trying naturally. I had one patient who went through the same stuff you've done and then gave up. She was only twenty-four then and her husband was thirty-four, so they adopted a boy and a girl—brother and sister. Then, would you believe, nineteen years later she became pregnant at forty-three years old? You want to talk about out of the blue."

Jennifer gasped quietly. Sam shook his head in astonishment. Although the doctor's story was inspirational, she knew she didn't have anywhere near nineteen years of fertility left—if she had any at all.

"Doctor, what about the in vitro?" she asked, curious as to why he hadn't been more proactive about explaining it.

"Jennifer, in vitro is expensive and—" He stopped and turned to Sam, then back to Jennifer. "As a Christian, I have some moral and ethical problems with it. I'll give you the name and number of the place we send people who want to pursue IVF, but as a fellow Christian I suggest you two spend some time researching it. And some prayer time, of course."

Jennifer took the paper on which Dr. O'Boyle had written the IVF clinic's name and phone number. She glanced at Sam, who appeared to have a head full of questions.

The doctor stood, causing Sam to rise, too. "Doctor, I appreciate your caution, but can't you just tell us what about this in vitro you've found to be inconsistent with Christian teaching?"

Dr. O'Boyle reached for Jennifer's hand to help her slide off the exam table. "Sam, I would really rather you discuss this with . . ." He chuckled. "Well, I started to say with your pastor, but since you are the pastor, that might be difficult."

Sam put an arm around Jennifer. "That's okay . . . we have people we trust for counsel."

*Yeah, right. And who would that be?* Jennifer thought glumly. She wasn't too eager to share their infertility questions with anyone, except the PWs of course.

After they said their good-byes to Dr. O'Boyle, Jennifer and Sam made their way silently to the elevator—through the gauntlet of hugely pregnant women in the waiting room—and then down to their car. Jennifer reasoned that Sam might wish he had people he could "trust for counsel," but she knew he would never discuss such an intimate matter with their church members or another pastor for fear of causing dissension over their decision.

Even though Sam didn't say it, Jennifer knew he would depend on her to find out what about this procedure was wrong or right. And besides informing him, she knew he would expect her to keep the whole thing to herself.

# Lisa

"Callie!" Lisa Barton yelled upstairs toward her teenage daughter's room. "Let's go. We're leaving in five minutes."

"Hey, Mom," a voice called from the kitchen. "Where's the Cheerios? I thought you bought some more."

Lisa turned her attention toward her thirteen-year-old son, now standing in the hallway, dressed for church in a beige sweater and khaki pants, holding a gallon of milk and an empty bowl. "It's next to the Grape-Nuts."

"Nuh-uh." Ricky turned back toward the kitchen, as if beckoning his mother to follow so he could prove her wrong.

Lisa was used to her son not being able to find things. *He takes after his father,* she often thought. For some reason, neither Ricky nor Joel, her husband, could ever find anything—unless, of course, it was the remote control. They seemed to have a homing device on that thing.

She could picture exactly where that box of cereal was. And she also could envision Ricky standing in front of the cabinet, holding the door wide open, and staring blankly at the boxes of food without seeing any of it.

"Callie, let's get a move on!" Lisa called upstairs once more before heading down the hall.

She stepped into their eighties-style kitchen with its dark wood cabinets and beige linoleum floor. The morning sun, reflecting off the newly fallen snow, gleamed through the window over the sink. Lisa peered into the open cabinet and reached to the top shelf to grab the box of Cheerios sitting next to the Grape-Nuts and an assortment of pastas and crackers. "Here. And eat fast. We're leaving in five minutes." She wasn't really sure why she told him to eat fast. The kid didn't eat; he inhaled. If she could plug his eating habits into his cleaning habits, her house would be spotless all the time. She glanced toward the digital clock on the microwave: *8:35.* "And don't forget to brush your teeth when you're done."

"Mom!"

Lisa pointed at him accusingly. "Don't 'Mom!' me. I know you'd rather chug mud than do your teeth. They're going to all rot out if you don't take care of them." She glanced again at the clock. "What's your sister doing? I haven't heard a peep out of her room."

Ricky shrugged. "Maybe she was abducted by aliens or something. Or"—he seemed to brighten—"maybe she tripped and fell and is in a coma."

"Would you be nice, please? That's a horrible thing to say."

"Well, I didn't say she died or anything," he said defensively, as if that made it so much better.

"What's a horrible thing to say?" Joel pushed through the back door, stamping his boots on the rug to clean off the excess snow caked on them.

"Your son is wishing ill on his sister again."

"Huh." Joel half smirked. "Well, that's a first. Could you try to can it, at least for this morning? We're on our way to church, you know." He glanced appreciatively at Lisa in her long-sleeved green-and-white fitted dress. She had recently lost five pounds and was able to get back into the dress that had been relegated for several years to the back of the closet. Even with those extra pounds gone, she could feel herself flush by his look, and she sucked in her stomach. "Nice" was all he said. But it was enough. That Joel had noticed at all made her feel wonderful. The last several years had been difficult on their marriage and only recently had they made amends and rekindled the flames of their relationship.

"It's cold out there this morning," he said as he pulled off his black gloves. "I've got the car warming up, but it barely started. I hope it holds up through this winter."

Lisa nodded and turned toward the coffeemaker. They had to get to church for him to unlock the doors. Hopefully Gus, one of the church trustees, was already there plowing the parking lot. "Are you finished with this so I can turn it off?" She held her hand near the electric outlet where the coffeemaker was plugged in.

"No, let me get a quick cup."

She grabbed a nearby mug she'd set out earlier for him, poured his coffee, then unplugged the Mr. Coffee and pushed it toward the back of the counter.

True to form, Ricky, who'd inhaled his cereal as if his mouth were a vacuum, tipped the bowl up to his lips to suck down the leftover milk, then dropped the bowl into the sink. "Okay, I'm ready to go," he said, wiping his mouth.

"Are we forgetting something?" Lisa crossed her arms, half frustrated that Ricky constantly pushed the envelope where dental hygiene was concerned.

"I don't know. Are we?" Ricky broke into a wide smile and nodded happily, obviously enjoying the pleasure of driving his mother crazy. "Oh, yeah. My coat!"

Lisa pulled her lips over her teeth and smiled wide, like a crazy woman with no teeth. "This is you in twenty years."

Ricky furrowed his brow. "I get the toothless part. But I become a woman, too?"

"You stinker," Lisa said, laughing. "Get upstairs!" She shook her head in mock exasperation. "He's your son," she said to Joel. "On your way up," Lisa told Ricky as he was walking toward the stairs, "check on your sister. She should be ready by now."

"Right. Like Miss High Maintenance would be ready on time for anything."

Lisa ignored Ricky's comment and walked to the hall closet to get her and the kids' coats. *What is up with that girl?* she thought. *Is she sick?* But Callie hadn't been ill the night before. She'd stayed up late talking on the phone to her best friend, Theresa. The two of them could chitchat more than anybody Lisa had ever known. She had no idea what they could talk about for so long, but apparently, it was "life-or-death" kind of stuff, because Callie was totally absorbed in it.

When she didn't get any response from Ricky on what Callie was doing, she said to Joel, who was sipping his black coffee, "I'm going to check on Callie."

At the top of the stairs, Lisa passed Ricky's bedroom. Disaster zone was more like it. She could barely stand to peek inside. He'd left the overhead light on. Again. *That boy thinks we're made of money,* she thought as she reached in and switched off the light. *We should start charging him part of the electricity bill.*

Next she walked across the hallway to her fourteen-year-old's room and knocked on the door. It was covered with signs that read, Keep Out, Callie Avenue, and Girl Power.

Silence.

Lisa knocked again. Still nothing. She quietly turned the doorknob and pushed the door slightly ajar. It was dark and still inside. A knot tightened in her stomach. *Callie must not be feeling well.* A large lump was curled up under the blankets. She crept to the side and leaned over to touch Callie's shoulder.

"You all right?" she asked gently.

Callie didn't answer, except to turn away.

"Can I get you something? You want me to stay home with you?"

Callie shook her head, her straight brown hair flying off the pillow with static.

"Okay, sweetie. Get some rest. You sure you don't want me to get you anything?"

"No." Her daughter's voice was bland and quiet.

Lisa placed her hand on her daughter's forehead. It didn't feel warm or feverish. Maybe it was a headache or cramps. She knew Callie could get horrible cramps during that time of the month. She bent down and kissed Callie softly on the forehead, then headed for the door. "Is it cramps?"

Callie shook her head.

Ricky banged on Callie's door with a quick, "Move it, Princess," then Lisa could hear him plod down the hallway and downstairs.

"A headache?" Lisa asked.

Callie took after Lisa in that department. They both could get terrible migraines that could wipe them out for days.

"No." She wasn't sure why, but Lisa felt as if Callie's one-word answer held a twinge of exasperation in it. She decided not to push the matter. If Callie wasn't feeling well, she wasn't feeling well.

"Okay, well," said Lisa. "Love you, baby girl. Feel better."

As Lisa closed the door to her daughter's room, she had a sinking feeling about going to church. *Maybe I should just stay home.* But she knew Joel had been dealing with some touchy church members and she wanted to be there to support him. *I'm sure she'll be fine,* she tried to convince herself. But her motherly instincts tugged at her.

As Lisa walked down the hall, she knew Ricky and Joel were probably now already in the car or at least headed that way. Joel was Mr. Punctual where church was concerned. She threw on her coat, grabbed her Bible and purse sitting on the kitchen counter near the back door, and raced out toward the waiting Taurus.

Lisa still wasn't convinced she shouldn't stay home. At least if Callie needed something, she wouldn't be alone. "Callie's not feeling well. Poor thing," Lisa said, clasping the top of her coat to keep warm and shifting into the car seat, trying to get comfortable as she pulled on her seat belt. Joel nodded and started to back out of the drive.

"So she's still alive," Ricky mumbled from the backseat.

"Ricky, that's not nice." Lisa glanced back at her son, who was smiling widely. "Did you even brush your hair?" she asked, noticing his dishwater blond locks were ruffled in a mop shape.

"Hey, be glad I brushed my teeth."

"Yes, I know," she said, rolling her eyes. "We'll have a medal waiting for you after church. Do you have a quota on how many things you're allowed to brush?"

"Yeah, I do."

Lisa shook her head and chuckled, in spite of herself. "He's your son."

"Yeah, you keep saying that," Joel said good-naturedly.

As they pulled away, she glanced up once more with concern toward the second floor, where Callie's room was. Lisa narrowed her eyes. Callie's bedroom light was on.

# Felicia

*Monday, January 22*
*6:30 p.m.*

"Here, eat this." Dave tossed a red apple from the kitchen counter to where four-year-old Nicholas was sitting on the family room floor playing with Legos.

"Dad, you have to cut it first. That's what Mom does," Nicholas said breathlessly as he chased after the apple, which he had failed to catch and was now rolling under the big-screen TV stand.

Without looking up from the laptop balanced on her knees as she perched on the edge of the family room couch, Felicia pleaded, "Can you two hold it down? I just have a few more minutes here and—"

"Why don't you try biting into that apple instead of into your mother and me?" Dave told his son. Clearly he hadn't heard Felicia's plea for quiet.

Nicholas reached his stubby arm beneath the oak TV cabinet. Felicia saw the TV sway in her peripheral vision. "Nicholas, watch th—"

Like they were on springs, Felicia and Dave flew to rescue their son. Dave grabbed Nicholas from behind and lifted him away as if he had just

23

recovered a fumble from his UCLA football-playing days while Felicia spread out her arms to balance the TV on the stand.

"Ow!" Dave dropped Nicholas, who landed like a cat on his feet and took off running.

Felicia let go of the now-steady TV and checked on Dave, whose intense blue eyes were pinched in a wince, then returned to the couch to pack up her laptop for the night. "Did he get ya again?" she asked as she bent down and noticed a run on the left leg of her hose, a casualty of brushing up against the TV cabinet too sharply.

"Yeah. Man, he almost drew blood this time."

Felicia walked over to Dave with her laptop case in one hand and her other outstretched. "Let me see the boo-boo," she said in a mock mommy tone.

Dave, a fake pout on his face, presented his reddened forearm.

"Ew, that is a pretty nasty one," she said in her normal voice.

Dave sighed. "What are we going to do with this kid? He's going to get kicked out of day care again. And I'm guessing there's some sort of reporting system between the other day cares in Red River."

Felicia laughed. "You mean like a kiddy blacklist?"

"Well, yeah. I mean, I know we were able to make it work last fall with baby-sitters and all, but it *was* a hassle. If he bites and gets kicked out again . . ."

Felicia set her laptop case by the back door. "Well, the good news is Melinda said he hasn't been biting at Happy Times since she let him back in. And that's been almost three weeks."

Dave pulled Felicia close as she tried to pass by. "That is good news, as long as it lasts." He kissed her, then glanced over her shoulder at the clock. "Okay, give me another kiss, *mi amor.* I'm off to Brew-Ha-Ha for comedy night. Think you can hold down the fort with our little beaver boy?"

The "beaver boy" comment made Felicia laugh as they kissed, which resulted in a funny snort sound that made her laugh again.

"I think we can manage," she said as they pulled away. "Maybe I'll order a pizza so he can have something to sink his teeth into."

Dave pulled his winter coat off the peg by the door, put it on, and tossed his cell phone into his pocket as he unlatched the door's lock. "If he doesn't watch it, he's going to be the only kid in kindergarten next year who has to gum his lunch!"

"Ha, not funny," said Felicia, playfully pushing him out the door into the cold Ohio night. "Be careful driving," she called after him. "They said there could be ice on the roads tonight."

Felicia closed the door and locked it, but not before the cold air whipped its way around her, causing her to shiver. She pulled a melon-colored velour throw off the back of the couch and wrapped it around her petite frame.

Even though the frigid Midwestern winters would never be to her liking, Felicia did feel a sense of satisfaction when she thought about how far her life had come in the last several months. She and Dave still had their spats, but they seemed to have come to terms in their expectations for each other. She figured that was helped by the fact that church attendance had been steadily increasing, in part because of the new singles' ministry started at Brew-Ha-Ha Pub. And as she'd gotten more involved with Tonya's working women's Bible study group—and made herself more visible at the church—she'd sensed a new respect among the eyebrow-archers who had questioned her viability as a pastor's wife with an outside career.

Felicia hunkered down on the couch, still cozily wrapped, and closed her eyes. *Thank you, Lord,* she prayed, *for giving me such a full, fulfilling life. I praise you for all you have done to make this family—*

"Mom!"

Felicia jerked her head up. She was so absorbed in her prayer, she hadn't heard Nicholas come into the room.

"Why are you sleeping? We haven't even eaten dinner yet. And I'm starved!"

Felicia slid the throw off her shoulders and hopped up. She started to explain to Nicholas that she was praying, not sleeping, but instead she just plucked the cordless phone off its holder and hit speed dial 4.

She heard a click on the other end. "Domino's Pizza. Can you hold?"

"Mmm-hmmm," she answered, but deeper inside she felt a flutter. *Oh, help us hold, Lord. I want to hold right here, where life is easy and good.*

# 5

# Mimi

*Thursday, January 25*
*8:57 a.m.*

Milo was in an uncooperative mood.

Mimi's five-week-old baby had been crying nonstop for the past two weeks. The pediatrician called it colic. Mimi called it annoying, disrespectful, and cranky. She couldn't remember any of her other children being this way. And she didn't like that she couldn't control the situation. Not one bit.

She had tried everything she could think of to get Milo to calm down. This morning she'd started by rubbing his back, then by feeding him. He seemed to like the feeding. But as soon as he was finished, he went back to crying. His little face had turned almost purple as he worked himself into a fit, wailing and hiccupping. And so loud.

*How can a baby have such lungs?* she wondered as she tried bouncing him and pacing around her living room. *If I cried and screamed myself into a tizzy like this, I'd lose my voice. Why doesn't he lose his voice? Or I lose my hearing?*

She continued to bounce him in her arms as she sashayed widely into the kitchen, where she glanced at the rooster clock hanging above the sink. *Nine o'clock.* Five hours of Milo's aria. Five *long,* painful, angst-filled hours.

It was bad enough that Milo was keeping her up all night long—he was making the rest of the family cranky, too. Mimi's husband, Mark, had complained that he couldn't work on his Sunday message. And her other three children, Michaela, MJ, and Megan, had whined that they couldn't hear themselves think. Eight-year-old MJ had taken great advantage of the situation and had claimed he was unable to do his homework. Mimi realized they all had to deal with Milo.

But she wasn't really in the mood to give them sympathy. Especially since they could leave. Mark could go to the church, and Michaela and MJ to school. Even five-year-old Megan could escape to kindergarten every day or hop over to her friend Ethan's house down the street. But not Mimi. Nope, she was Mother. She got to deal with Colicky Baby. She got to go Sleepless in Red River.

Mimi cringed to think that this may be a sign of things to come and was tempted to ask God what she had done to deserve Milo's temperament.

Holding this soft, pink-bodied, brown-fuzzyheaded child who had been given eternal lung capacity, she could sympathize with stressed mothers who finally out of desperation shook their babies to quiet them. She knew she wouldn't do that, but she also knew she was going to have to do something. Soon.

Megan had taken their cockapoo, Buster, and holed up in her room, with the door shut, listening to *The Little Mermaid* on the small CD player one of the church members had given her for Christmas last year. Mixed with Milo's cries and Buster's howls, the sounds of Megan's voice singing "Under the Sea" caged Mimi in a cacophony of noise.

Tremors began to shake her body as she walked upstairs past Megan's closed door to the nursery, where she laid still-bawling baby Milo in his crib. She lifted her chin and, marching in tune to his wails, left the room like a rat abandoning a sinking ship. On the other side of his door, she breathed in deeply, trying to get ahold of herself. Then, as calmly as she possibly could, Mimi returned downstairs to the living room, where she carefully closed all the blinds, straightened one of her beige and mauve lampshades, and, inhaling deeply, proceeded to scream at the top of her lungs.

She'd read somewhere once about the importance of giving oneself permission to let loose with a primal yell when stress seems overwhelming. Well, the Geiger counter was making a lot of racket, and it was telling her she was overwhelmed.

When she ran out of breath, she bent over, closed her eyes hard, and then stood again to let loose once more. She yelled. She stamped her feet. She flailed her arms. She balled her fists and released them. *If only I had something to punch. One of those Yogi Bear children's punching bags.* Spying the couch throw pillows, she strode to the middle of the room, knelt beside the couch, and thumped the pillows with blows that would rival Oscar de la Hoya's.

"Mommy?" came a small voice from upstairs. Mimi stopped mid-blow, puffed a tousle of blond hair from her eyes, and popped up.

"Coming, sweetie," she said as she strode to the stairs. There, at the top, stood wide-eyed Megan, gripping the rails, her face poking through the banister. Her towheaded locks were chopped short, most of it standing straight up from the static electricity, as if she'd just placed her finger in a light socket. She was wearing her favorite Tweety Bird shirt, which was faded, stained, and had a hole near the collar from continual wear. Beside her sat Buster, whose black snout and puffy dark face were sticking through the banister beside her. They were almost the same height.

Immediately Mimi stood and pulled down her red cable-knit sweater, straightening it, and smiled brightly. In her tantrum, she hadn't noticed that Megan's music had stopped.

"Hi, swee—" She broke into a coughing spell. "Uuuh," she said as she rubbed her aching, raw throat.

Motioning for Megan to join her, Mimi walked into the kitchen in the hope that a glass of water would ease her throat. She could hear Milo's wails emanating from the second floor as Megan and Buster raced down the stairs.

*Thank God it's winter and the windows are closed, or the neighbors might think we're beating him.*

"He's still crying," Megan stated matter-of-factly and grabbed Mimi's hand.

Mimi sighed. "Yep."

"Can we put a plug in his mouth? My glue stick will make it stay."

Mimi squinted slightly. She really wanted to say, "Okay, let me consider that." Instead, she grabbed a bottle of water from the fridge and sipped quietly, trying to think of what to do next.

"Go grab your coat," Mimi said determinedly. "We're going for a ride."

"Are we taking Milo?"

"Yes, we're taking Milo."

Megan cringed. "Do we have to?"

"Yes, we have to," Mimi said, turning Megan toward the living room and patting her bottom to push her out of the kitchen. "Go get your coat and boots."

There was only one more thing she could think of to help Milo and to keep her sanity. She only prayed it would work.

———

*10:52 a.m.*

The sounds of Baby Einstein floated through the Freestar as Mimi slowed to a stop at the red light at the corner of Main and Hope Streets. She had spent the past hour and a half driving around, hoping the gentle sway of the vehicle and the calming classical music would finally lull Milo to sleep. A silent, deep slumber that would last, oh, a week.

Finally, after about an hour of driving through Red River and out past snow-covered cornfields, Milo had settled into sleep, giving Mimi her first moments of peace. Even Megan and Buster had dozed off. Exhausted, Mimi headed home.

She pulled up to the red light and, to celebrate the silence, closed her eyes. The music was soothing her. *Just for a minute,* she thought.

She inhaled deeply and licked her lips. It felt so wonderful to have her eyes closed and to absorb the serenity of silent children. Her head slowly dropped toward her chest, which jerked her awake in time to get a glimpse at the light. Still red. She closed her eyes again and leaned back against the headrest.

She thought she heard what sounded like a horn blaring but simply responded by yawning.

A siren blared in the background. Mimi blinked her eyes quickly to focus on the light. Red. She glanced into the backseat to check on Milo and Megan. Still asleep. Seeing the light hadn't changed, she settled into her seat and let her heavy eyelids close. *If Milo would only sleep for the next twelve hours, life would be so good. Then I could sleep. That would be so—*

*Tap, tap, tap.*

She shook her head slightly. *If he were only like the other ki—*

*Tap, tap. Tap, tap, tap.*

Eyes still closed, Mimi furrowed her brow, annoyed.

From a distance, she heard a muffled, "Ma'am. Ma'am! Hello?"

*I thought Milo had knocked out my hearing, and now I can even pick up conversations on the street, through the closed window.*

Mimi let her left eye pop open to check the signal light. Red. *This is quite the long light.*

Her eyes had just returned to their restful state when a violent tap at her driver's side window caused her to spring up, nearly choking herself on her seat belt. Turning, Mimi caught sight of a slim black club. She followed the club up to who was holding it. There stood a displeased thirty-something police officer. His face and neck were beet red, as though he'd been out in the cold too long. She wasn't sure if that was just his natural reddish complexion, frostbite, or an angry flush, and she sure wasn't going to ask.

Her stomach doing flip-flops, she opened her eyes wide and tried to give her best innocent smile as she rolled down the window.

"Have a nice *nap?*"

The officer stood straight and close to the van, causing Mimi to have to lean slightly out the window and crane her head to see him. She noticed a small muscle in his jaw twitching.

"I'm so sorry," she whispered, hoping her small voice would put him in a better, or at least merciful, mood. "I was driving around, trying to—"

"What?" he barked.

She exhaled slightly and pointed toward the backseat, then leaned over and again whispered, "I was driving around, trying to—"

"No." He cut her off. "You weren't driving. You were sleeping."

"I can expla—"

"You can do all your explaining over there," he said, pointing across the street to the 7-Eleven parking lot.

Mimi felt the panic rising, making her whispers come out more strained. "But every time I looked, it's been red!"

"Lady, you didn't even budge when I finally used the siren. Now pull through the intersection. That is"—a sneer crossed his face—"*if* you can stay awake that long."

Mimi gritted her teeth. What was she going to do? she wondered. Her hands had gone clammy and were shaking. She wasn't sure which she was more afraid of—getting a ticket or waking Milo. But besides the fear, a tiny surge of anger welled inside her chest. *He didn't have to be so snotty. He has no idea what I've been going through.*

Mimi pulled into a space at the far end of the parking lot and waited for the officer to approach the van. "Please, God, don't let this guy give me a ticket," she breathed. "And please, *please* don't let Milo wake up." She glanced in the rearview mirror to see if Megan was still asleep and how Milo was doing. His face seemed crunched, uncomfortable, but at least his eyes were closed and his little rosebud lips were pursed with tiny bubbles gurgling out.

*He is beautiful,* she thought, momentarily forgetting what a pain he could be when he was awake.

She noticed then that the officer had gotten out of his squad car—lights still flashing—and was approaching her side of the minivan. In order to make sure the officer didn't wake Milo, Mimi opened her door and threw her arms in the air to show she didn't have a gun. Unfortunately, she'd forgotten her seat belt was buckled, so instead of stepping free from the van as she'd planned, she flailed aimlessly, all of her extremities hanging out of the van while her torso remained put.

"What are you doing?"

She pulled her legs back in and dropped her arms. "I don't have a gun or anything," she said meekly.

Mimi's response seemed to lighten his mood a little, for she noticed a slight twitch to his lips.

"Cop shows, right?"

She smiled slightly and shrugged.

"Just give me your license and vehicle registration," he said, moving closer.

"Oh!" she responded, her hands shaking. *Nerves.* She mentally berated herself for being weak. Quickly and quietly she grabbed the registration from the glove compartment and picked up her large purse (which was really a disguised tote bag—she couldn't fit everything she needed in a purse these days). She decided to riffle through it outside. This time she unfastened the seat belt and hopped out of the van, gently closing the door—*Please don't wake up; this is bad enough*—and trying to appear somewhat normal.

*Calm down,* she told herself as she picked through pacifiers, notepads, tissues, and packs of gum, trying to find her license, *or he's going to think you're on drugs or something and take away your children.* She knew her fears were probably unfounded, based on all those cop shows she'd seen recently—what else was there to watch in the middle of the night when Milo wouldn't go down? But what would they do to someone who fell asleep at the wheel? Would she be charged with neglect? Would they take her to jail? She could see the headlines now:

**PASTOR'S WIFE ARRESTED FOR SNOOZING ON THE ROAD**

With half the contents of her purse now splayed out on the van's hood like goods at a yard sale, Mimi noticed to her relief that the officer was no longer holding his club but a clipboard, with what she assumed was the paperwork for her ticket—or, maybe, a warning? *Do they still do that?*

*Never on TV! Please, please, please?* Her hands kept shaking, trying to find her wallet.

"I only closed my eyes for just a minute," she tried to explain, hoping he wouldn't notice her hands. Or hoping he *would* notice her hands and feel sorry enough for her *not* to issue her a ticket. "I checked the light. It was red."

The officer pushed up his standard-issue cap and scratched his forehead. Tendrils of caramel-colored hair peeked out from underneath. "You timed it perfectly, then. I was sitting behind you, tapping my horn every time the light turned green. Four times."

She ignored that revelation. "You see, I've been driving around, trying to get my baby to fall asleep."

He glanced into the minivan. "Well, he seems to be asleep now. But he wasn't driving. You were."

As if on cue, Mimi saw Milo start to stir. Wide-eyed, she froze. "No," she mouthed, as much to Milo as to the officer.

She peered at the officer's nametag. *Officer McCarthy.* Then she glanced down at his left hand to see if he was married. No ring. *Maybe he just doesn't wear one. Or maybe he's an uncle,* she rationalized, hoping that he would understand about children, particularly colicky ones.

She tried to smile but knew it was a poor attempt. To cover her discomfort, she tucked her blond hair behind her left ear. "This kid is driving me crazy."

The law-and-order man just stared at her blankly.

"I haven't slept in days."

No compassion registered on his face.

"He has *colic*." Mimi pushed the word, hoping that would get her off the hook. Still nothing. "It's a condition that—"

"Yes, ma'am, I know what colic is."

"Oh!" She giggled nervously. "I just . . . well, I . . ." And she was off and running. Shockingly, appallingly, she dumped her story on him. It was as if she had swallowed the Energizer bunny. She just kept going and going and going, chattering on about everything—she even told him how her pregnancy with Milo had been a surprise because "I was just too tired to say no, you know?" and how ill she'd been during those early months, vomiting all over the place, including on Kitty Katt's shoes at the annual Red River July Fourth picnic.

Mimi watched Officer McCarthy's eyes glaze over as he listened to her babble, but she felt powerless to stop.

"Ma'am." He raised his hand. "I appreciate the background story, but really, I'm just interested in your license and registration." He held out his hand for the two things she'd been holding during her confession.

"Right. Right. Sorry about that." *You dope! What'd you do that for?* She felt like duct-taping her mouth. Recovering, she started to hand the driver's license to him, then noticed it was smeared with some unknown substance from inside her purse—*Cereal? Lipstick? No, I haven't worn that in weeks*— so she wiped it off on her dark peacoat and handed it to him along with the registration slip. She watched him move back to his squad car with its red-and-blue lights flashing like a Kmart special.

Slightly hopping from one foot to the other, Mimi wanted to keep waiting outside the van to avoid opening that door again and rousing the kids, but she was feeling the cold seep into her bones. She considered joining Officer McCarthy in his car—*Should I get in the front or the back? No, I can't do that.* It was a dilemma: freeze or wake the monster-mouthed child. Finally, she opted for the squad car.

Slowly she walked to the back of the van, lifting her hands again to show, *See? Still no gun.* Then she dropped them quickly, feeling silly after that first exchange. She tapped politely on his window to get his attention.

"What?" he said, attempting to cover the paperwork.

"I'm so cold, and I don't want to wake my kids. Would it be all right if I just sat in the back while you finish what you're doing?"

His face went blank. Slowly he smirked, then chuckled. "If that's what you want."

"I'd really appreciate it." *Not to mention it's a moment of respite from my children.*

She had just settled into the backseat, uncomfortably noticing the bars placed between the back and front seats, when she saw Martha and Bud Magruder pass by and spot her. The Magruders attended Trinity, the church where her husband was pastor.

*Great. I love small towns,* she thought as she ducked down. She figured the news would travel through Red River, and everybody would be chattering on about Mimi's "police record." *If the news hasn't already gotten around . . .*

She could just envision the chairman for the Sunday service getting up and announcing, "We have a convict in our midst this morning. Ha, ha, ha." She hated people knowing her business—not exactly something a pastor's wife has much control over, she knew. She hated the fact that she'd been stopped at all!

Mimi prided herself on being a law-abiding citizen. Especially since her father was a convict. Not really, but he had spent a few nights in the county jail. Mimi knew her father hadn't meant to shoot his next-door neighbor in the tush with a BB gun when Mimi was eight years old. But when her father would start drinking, which was most of the time, he would do, well, *things.* Like the time he got into an argument with their neighbor over whether the fence in their backyard was on their property or his. Her father, to settle the matter, had walked inside their house, dusted off the BB gun from the basement, walked outside, and shot their neighbor square in the left buttock. It had mortified Mimi and the town. And their church.

Fortunately their neighbor, who was squatting over his prized rosebushes, thought it was a bee sting. Until his wife saw it and called the police, that is. When the police arrived at Mimi's house, they'd scared her with their brisk tones and harsh faces, guns holstered to their hips. She remembered hearing them converse with her father, who argued with them, telling them the neighbor made it up, but he would be more than glad to pop them one, too. Mimi had been hiding behind the door to the basement, peering through the crack, and watching the policemen's faces squint in anger before they turned her father around and handcuffed him.

From that point on, Mimi didn't want anything to do with the police. She barely wanted anything to do with her *father,* even though she loved him and prayed for him daily to find God's grace and forgiveness.

Now here Mimi sat in the warm interior of the squad car, with a policeman who had it in his power to lock her up if he chose to. He was taking so long finishing, she began to wonder if he was going to handcuff her and take her off to the Red River police station. She knew it was absurd to think that, but she couldn't help it. Officer McCarthy would run a background check, see her connection with her father, and then *bam!* Away she'd be carted. She bit her lip in angst. Just then Milo's vocal cords started to awaken. Amazingly enough, she could hear him that far away. *Well,* she thought trying to calm herself, *if I do get arrested, I might get a full night's sleep.*

"I should probably get back to the van and check on Milo."

"Yup" was all the officer said.

Mimi opened the side door to the van to try to calm Milo when Megan started to cry. "Why are you crying?" Mimi asked her sleepy-eyed daughter in a statement more than a question. Mimi's eye caught Officer McCarthy as he stepped out of his squad car and walked toward the van. And then she spotted the Magruders' car pass by again, with Martha and Bud both craning their necks to get a better view.

*11:13 a.m.*

Mimi's husband, Mark, was standing in the driveway when Mimi pulled in. She'd called him on her cell phone as soon as Officer McCarthy had left her. *Don't cry,* she told herself silently. *Just don't cry.* She sucked in her lips, pressing firmly on them, hoping that would keep her eyes from leaking like a garden hose on a hot summer day. Then she blinked hard. *Crying will not help the situation.*

She watched her tall, dark-haired husband walk around her side of the minivan and open the door for her.

"Hey, how ya doing?" he said gently. He sounded so sympathetic and kind, so pastorly. And that was all it took. She started to sob in gasps and hiccups, making her sound almost like Milo. Trying to form words, she couldn't capture enough breath for anything other than a whelp, as from an injured animal.

"It's okay," Mark told her, helping her out of the car. "It's not the end of the world."

"I ca-can't believe he ga-gave me a *ticket!*" she bawled. She mentally kicked herself for letting her tears gush.

Mimi had never gotten a ticket, not even for speeding. Not even in college when all her friends were getting parking tickets for not paying for campus parking passes. Mimi always went by the book. She couldn't believe the police officer wouldn't even consider just writing her a warning. No, Mr. Law-and-Order had to go straight for the ticket. Even after he heard Milo and Megan's cries. No compassion. He'd offered no sympathy. Just passed her the ticket for impeding traffic, returned her license and registration, and said, rather snarkily she thought, "Maybe you should invest in a good pair of earplugs."

The only bright spot was that he apparently hadn't run the background check and didn't haul her off to jail.

"He wasn't even sympathetic when I told him Milo is colicky—and he *heard* Milo crying. It's not like I'd make up that screaming," she complained to Mark, who'd started to take Milo out of the vehicle. She flung her arm toward the again-wailing baby in the car seat, as if to say, *See? That kid will not shut up!* She went to the other side of the car to get Megan. "What is *wrong* with people? Have they no compassion and sympathy for mothers? For the *sleep deprived?*" Mimi wiped her eyes with her palm and lifted Megan out of her car seat.

"Well, honey, you were asleep out in the middle of the street," Mark said.

"Don't take his side!" she wailed, droplets of spittle flying from her mouth toward Megan's face. She watched, embarrassed, as Megan flinched.

"Hey!" Megan yelled crankily and wiped her face. "Eew!"

"Go inside, Megan."

"I'm not taking his side, Mims," Mark said, walking with the wailing

Milo toward the back porch. "I'm just saying, try to see it from his side. Compassion has nothing to do with it. You could have been drunk or on drugs, for all he knew."

"Well, all he had to do was look at me!" she said defensively. Then she remembered how she probably appeared—sleepless, showerless, lifeless— and felt a tinge of gratitude that he hadn't.

"It's not that big of a deal, really. And better that you fell asleep at a light than while you were actually driving."

"I wouldn't have!"

Mark shrugged in a noncommittal way that caused a surge in Mimi's growing frustration.

"And anyway, it's not just that," she pushed on with her argument. "Probably the whole church and town know what happened by now. The Magruders drove by. Twice."

She could see Mark's lips twitch up in a slight smile.

"Oh, sure! Laugh at my expense. Have yourself a really good—"

"Whoa! Hang on there, Annie Oakley. I didn't do anything, so don't turn your frustration on me, okay?"

Mimi huffed and could feel the tears beginning to swell again. She stared at her ticket.

"Usually," Mark said, touching the back of her neck as they walked toward the back steps of the house, "you can go to driving school and get the offense taken off your record. No big deal. Okay?" He gently shook her. "Hey. Okay?"

Reluctantly she nodded.

"Just take a few breaths, let's go inside, and I'll make you some hot chocolate." He leaned close to her left ear and whispered, "With marshmallows." Then he elbowed her jokingly, something he always did when he was trying to cheer her up. "I'll tell you what. How about I draw you a bath and I'll take Milo Patrol."

Mimi's mood brightened slightly. Mark seemed always to have that effect on her. "I don't know," she drawled. "I may end up falling asleep in the tub and drown. Then you'd have to take care of all the kids all the time."

Mark shuddered jokingly and chuckled.

"Oh! I forgot my purse." She jogged back to the minivan to retrieve it, then watched Mark walk into the house. A wave of love toward Mark warmed her. *He's a good guy.* But she still hated that he could be so logical and rational. She hated that he didn't have five zillion post-pregnancy hormones coursing through *his* body, making him crazy. And she especially hated that her nose wouldn't stop running—both from her crying jag and from the cold January winds.

She stomped over the sprinkling of snow on the ground. "He still didn't have to give me a ticket," she muttered under her breath. "Hey!" she yelled out at the thought that popped into her brain. "We could find out where Officer McMeany lives and drop off Milo for an evening of babysitting extravaganza."

Mark held open the back door and laughed. "Now you've got the right idea."

# 6

# Lisa

*Sunday, January 28*
*7:14 a.m.*

"Callie!" Lisa stood at her daughter's closed bedroom door and knocked. It was beginning to feel like déjà vu all over again. "Let's go. Up and at 'em. We need to get to church early since your dad and I are singing, and we need to practice with Brenda."

Silence. Again. There had been a lot of silence lately when Lisa tried to talk to her daughter.

Lisa sighed and spied Ricky coming out of the bathroom he and his sister had to share. His hair was in its typical mop shape. "Heard of a hairbrush?"

Ricky just grinned and shook his wet hair at her like a dog coming in from the rain. "Don't make me have to get a brush, boy," she said, laughing. "Or better yet, the scissors. You really need a haircut." Ricky was a good kid, Lisa knew. He was passionate about the Lord and video games. He loved hugs and pizza and belching out the alphabet during church potluck dinners. Okay, so that was a little embarrassing. Well, a lot embarrassing. But he also loved to pray. He'd said many times he wanted to be a missionary pilot. That or play drums in a rock band, depending on the day. Lisa smiled as she watched him enter his room across from Callie's. Within a few seconds she could hear the loud pounding of Third Day playing from his stereo.

Growing impatient, Lisa burst into her daughter's room. Callie was in her bed, nestled under the covers, just as she had been the previous Sunday. Lisa flipped on the overhead light, grabbed the edge of the covers, and pulled them off Callie's body.

"Hey!" Callie yelled, grasping at the blanket, trying to pull it back over her.

"Time to get up. We have to be at church early this week."

"Fine. Go." She yanked the covers, pulled them over her head, and turned toward the far wall, away from Lisa.

Lisa's stomach tightened. She hated fighting with Callie. But right now a fight seemed inevitable. "I know you're not sick two weeks in a row. I let last week slide. But don't push it. Now get up."

"I'm not going."

*No way,* Lisa thought. *If I have to go and face those troublemakers at the church, you're certainly going.* "This isn't a democracy," she said, fighting the urge to crawl into bed beside Callie and not go either. But she was a pastor's wife. Of course she wanted to go to church. She could think of nothing she'd like more than to sit in the worship service and watch helplessly as church members made critical statements about the way her husband was leading them.

"I don't care. I hate church."

*Amen. Me, too.* "Fine. You don't want to go, take it up with your dad. Shall I get him now?"

"Whatever," Callie spit out.

Lisa held her tongue. The father-daughter relationship wasn't so hot right now. She wouldn't exactly call it volatile, but it certainly wouldn't make for sweet talk if Lisa brought Joel into this situation. He was already frustrated that Callie wasn't pulling her weight as a pastor's kid. The pressure on Joel to have a "good" (read: perfect) family was extremely taxing. And even though no one ever named that thousand-pound gorilla in the room, it was always there. Breathing down their necks. Lisa had tried to play peacemaker—after all, she herself had been a pastor's kid and felt the weight of that pressure on her all her life. But it was different watching as her babies were forced to go through this.

Lisa thought of what her mother, the picture of a perfect pastor's wife, would have said—or done!—to Lisa if she had thrown this kind of tantrum or spoken this way when she was a teenager.

"I don't appreciate your talking to me this way, Callie. I know you've been dealing with some things lately, and I'd love to sit down and get to the bottom of this with you. But right now, we don't have time. So I need you to hop out of that bed, take your shower, and be ready to go in a half hour." The unspoken, *Please, do this for me, so we don't have to bring your dad into this,* hung heavy in the air.

Callie didn't respond.

"Callie, I mean it. Get up. You're going."

Lisa turned to leave but stopped at the door when she heard Callie mumble something. "What did you say?"

"Nothing."

"If you have something to say, say it."

Lisa could see Callie's face poking out from under the sheets. It was set hard and angry.

"When you get in the shower, try to clean up your attitude, too," Lisa said and walked out of the room. As soon as she shut Callie's door, she closed her eyes tightly and clenched her fists. *I do not need this.*

Ricky walked out of his room, stopping at the sight of his mother. "You okay?"

*No.* "I'm fine. I'm glad to see you brushed your hair. Sort of."

---

*7:46 a.m.*

Lisa stood in the kitchen finishing her coffee. She glanced at the clock on the microwave. The showdown was on. Would Callie obey her? The entire situation with Callie was confusing and frustrating. Yes, Callie was a hand-ful, but she had been a good kid. She loved God and grew up talking ener-getically about her faith. Lisa had seen Callie's gift of mercy and evangelism. But Callie was changing. And Lisa didn't like it.

Callie was going through adolescence and dealing with all the raging hor-mones and whatever else. And Lisa also knew that pastors' kids had a tough road—and many of them rebelled against their families, the church, and God. While growing up, Lisa had known too many PKs who'd gotten into drugs, alcohol, or promiscuity. It had always been a shock to the congregation—even to her parents—but not so much to Lisa. Lisa understood. Pastors have a lot of pressure on them. And a pastor's wife has pressure to be perfect, plus the added pressure of watching helplessly while church members denigrate and take ad-vantage of her husband. But pastors' kids had a whole set of additional issues. They didn't sign up for the tour of duty. They didn't ask to be dumped into the hardship of serving God and meeting everybody's expectations.

Had she failed Callie somehow? Was this what Callie's attitude shift was about? Was Callie under pressure at school? *What is it? What can it possibly be?* Lisa wondered again as she took a final sip of her coffee.

A few moments later Lisa heard the tromping of her daughter's footsteps down the stairs. *One battle averted,* she thought, relieved that she wasn't go-ing to have to go back upstairs and drag Callie down. But with one glimpse, she realized she'd averted one battle all right, but here stood the potential for another.

Callie stormed into the kitchen, arms folded, hatred sprawled across her bespectacled face—at least, what Lisa could see of Callie's face, since Callie's brown hair was hanging straight down into her piercing hazel eyes and almost touching her nose and chin. An old Cincinnati Bengals T-shirt and faded jeans—the ones she wore when she had to clean her room—were apparently the preferred attire of the morning.

Joel walked into the kitchen humming the song he and Lisa were going to sing and did a double take at Callie. "What are you wearing?"

Callie puckered her lips as if she were sucking a lime and narrowed her eyes, but remained silent.

*The standoff continues.* Lisa sighed inwardly.

"Get back upstairs and put on something appropriate for church," Joel said in a barely controlled but calm, low voice. "Right now." Lisa didn't like it when he used that tone; she knew it meant he was really ticked off. And that was the last thing he needed on a Sunday morning before he went into his own battle with mutinous church members.

"If I have to go, I'm going to be comfortable," she said to her father as she glared at Lisa.

"I will not have my daughter dressed like that at church," Joel said, turning to Lisa. "She has an obligation, a responsibility as a member of the pastor's family."

*Oh, boy, we're in trouble now.*

He continued to glare at Lisa as if she were the one wearing the get-up. What did he want from her? Did he want her to drag Callie upstairs and dress her as if Callie were still three? If she could, she would. But she knew she couldn't do that. It would only exacerbate the problem. And all Lisa wanted right now was some tranquility—especially since she doubted she was going to have much of it at church.

"Can't we all just get along?" she wanted to rail. Instead she said, hoping to avert any more of a flare-up, "We're going to be late for practice, and Brenda's probably there right now, sitting out in the parking lot. Let's just go. Callie's the one who should be embarrassed that she looks that way. It has nothing to do with us." Secretly she hoped her last statement would make Callie feel guilty or, indeed, embarrassed. But Callie didn't change her expression.

"Get your coat, Callie," Lisa said coldly.

Callie stood for a moment, staring a hole through her mother. Lisa didn't know whether Callie would make a move toward the car or if she really wasn't going to church and this was her way to prove it. She knew Joel would pick her up and bodily carry her to church—no member of his family was going to miss without being sick. Period.

*Please don't push this,* she pleaded mentally.

"Did she not hear you?" Joel asked Lisa tensely. "Tell her to get her coat."

Callie jutted her jaw but turned toward the hall closet, slamming doors and hangers until she had wrestled out her pink coat and put it on.

Ricky bounded down the stairs and stopped mid-step after one look at his sister. "Did the Ugly Fairy stop by your room last night?"

"Shut up," Callie muttered.

"She's not wearing that, is she?" Ricky stepped toward Joel, as if Callie's dress would somehow affect Ricky's church "coolness" factor.

"Get your coat, Ricky," Lisa answered. "We're going to be late."

"But she looks like crap."

"Takes one to know one," Callie fired back at him.

"We do not use that kind of language," Lisa said. "Both of you, get on your coats and let's go."

"I'm going to the car," Joel said.

"Hurry up, let's go." Lisa picked up her purse and Bible. "Ricky, make sure the door's locked when you leave."

"What is her problem?" Joel whispered, once Lisa entered the car.

"I don't know." Lisa sighed, frustrated.

Ricky and Callie scooted into the backseat, with Ricky still pouring it on about how terrible Callie looked, but adding, "Actually, now everyone will see what I have to deal with, and they'll feel sorry for me."

"Shut up, moron," Callie snapped.

"That's enough." Joel yanked on his seat belt. "I don't know what your problem is," he said icily, as he turned and pointed at Callie, "but you need to get over it. Quickly."

Lisa heard Callie mutter under her breath in a mimicky tone, "I don't know what your problem is, but you need to get over it."

Gigantic mutant butterflies began to crash into each other in Lisa's stomach. She knew she needed to say something, but what? What could she possibly say to a rotten, bitter, adolescent girl? One who was making her and her family's life miserable—and who wasn't helping their situation at church?

"You're grounded, young lady," Lisa said, staring straight ahead. "No phone calls to Theresa. No televi—"

"What? You can't do that!" Callie yelled.

"And you'll take over your brother's chores this week," Lisa continued as if she hadn't been interrupted. Out of the side of her vision, she caught Joel giving her a surprised but pleased expression.

"Yes!" Ricky laughed and smacked the ceiling of the car.

"I hate you," Callie said tightly. "I hate this family."

"Awww," Ricky cut in. "Boo-hoo-hoo. Poor little Callie girl's got it so rough."

"Ricky," Joel said strongly, but not in the same angry tone, "you're on thin ice. Cut it out."

Lisa could hear Ricky still chuckling. He was obviously enjoying this moment that Callie was being forced to endure.

"You don't hate us, Callie," Lisa said, feeling deeply hurt but being careful not to show it.

"Yes, I do. Don't tell me what I feel."

"Well, Callie Ann," Joel said, "maybe you should take this up with God. Or do you hate him, too?"

Lisa wished Joel hadn't said that last part; she was afraid of what Callie would say. What if she said, "Yeah, I do hate him. So what?" She and Joel had been so intentional in teaching their children to love God. How could they succeed with others, yet fail with their own children? She couldn't bear to think about that.

This was tough love, she knew, but it hurt her more than it hurt Callie, she was sure of that. She just wanted to curl up into a fetal position and cry. She loved her children and she desperately wanted them to love her, to like her. But it didn't seem to matter what she did lately, she couldn't win with Callie.

*How did Mom deal with this?* she wondered as she thought about her own mother. Deep down she knew her mother didn't care. Or at least that's what it had always seemed like. Her mother had another agenda: being a perfect pastor's wife. And her mother certainly would not put up with an unruly, rebellious child. Instinctively, Lisa had always known that, so she had never tried that route when she was growing up.

But Callie was different. Callie didn't care how it appeared to the church. She was so emotional and . . . a brat. Her daughter was a brat! Well, if she wanted to act like a baby, that's how they'd treat her.

"You're already grounded for a week," Lisa surprised herself by saying. "Another word or mutter under your breath, and we'll make it two. Are we clear?"

*11:55 a.m.*

Lisa barely heard a word though the service. Her mind was a football field of thoughts all charging into one another. *I'm the worst mother. She hates me. Where did we go wrong? Was it something I did or said? Maybe this is just a phase. But what if it isn't? What if she really starts to rebel? Or has she already? What's the church going to think? Will they kick Joel out? Great, I'm a failure. How can I lead a church when I can't even handle my own child?*

On and on the accusations and worries flooded over her. Her insecurities about being a good mother and a good Christian were out in full force. Involuntarily Lisa lifted her hand to her temple to try to remove the dull ache that had started. *Great—now I'm getting a migraine on top of everything else.*

It had been so much easier when the kids were little. She could decide everything for them, and they would just do it. People had said babies and toddlers—those terrible twos—were difficult. But Lisa thought those years were a breeze compared to the terrible fourteens. If she could only just tell Callie what to do and watch her do it obediently, excited to please her mommy. *Oh, for those days . . .*

She knew Callie's newfound rebellion was bothering Joel, too. He'd made that *very* clear. But he seemed to manage it all by yelling at Callie and storming out or by yelling at *Lisa* about Callie and storming out. He wanted Lisa to "fix" it when his yelling didn't do the trick. But Lisa couldn't. Lisa had tried to talk with him about it. She guessed that was just the way he handled the sense of helplessness—by bullying his daughter into behaving. But deep down, Callie was a sensitive girl—and Lisa knew that bullying her would do more harm than good.

As she sat in the powder-blue cushioned pew, half hearing the church sing, "I'm going to hold to his hand, God's unchanging hand," Lisa worried about what the congregation was thinking about her family. Would they judge her harshly as a parent because Callie was dressed in faded, torn blue jeans and a T-shirt?

She tried to glance casually back at her daughter, who had plopped herself angrily onto the back pew. Earlier, during the special music when Joel and Lisa sang, accompanied by the trusty pianist/organist Brenda, Lisa had seen Callie's scowling face. Her arms were folded tightly in an "impress me, if you dare" pose. Lisa desperately wanted to shout, "Will somebody, some other mother who's dealt with this parenting phase, come over and offer me encouragement?" But she didn't. And no one came.

Lisa knew they would come, however. Not to offer encouragement, of course. To offer tsks and other sounds or demonstrations of disapproval. Or they would offer parenting advice—like the good-natured, "Huh, I'd think your being so much closer to God, you'd have this parenting thing figured out, so you could be a model for the rest of us. Maybe you should get your kid under control."

She could just hear the comments now about how Callie was dressed and how inappropriate that was. Why not? They were already up in arms about how Joel wasn't doing anything right. They might as well just add this fuel to the fire.

At the end of the service, during the benediction prayer, as she did every week, Lisa grabbed her purse and slipped toward the back where she could stand with her husband and greet people.

On her way toward the doors, she noticed Callie was missing from her seat. *Where is she?* Lisa wondered and glanced over the congregation to see if Callie had changed seats. If she was there, she was hidden well.

Just as the worship leader was saying *Amen,* Lisa walked past Joel, shaking her head, and darted to the parking lot.

Without a coat, purse dangling from her right hand, Lisa stood outside the doors to the church and gazed toward their car in the spot marked PASTOR. It was right next to three handicapped parking spaces. An irony that wasn't lost on her.

Sure enough, inside in the backseat sat a bundled-up Callie. It was as if Callie were doing everything possible to keep herself in a riled state, including sitting in a cold car in the middle of an Ohio winter.

If it weren't for the situation, Lisa would have thought it was funny. Girls that age could be so melodramatic, wearing their feelings on their sleeves, never taking time to think rationally or logically about anything. Just committing 100 percent to their "feelings." And Callie's feelings were all about making a statement to her family, to the church, and to the world, apparently. Lisa thought that statement might be, "I'm an angry teenager because of some injustice done to me." But the other part of her statement was obviously "I'm insane for sitting in this below-freezing weather when I could be just as angry inside where it's warm."

For a split second, Lisa wanted to run to the car, turn it on, and talk to her. At least Callie could be warm in her protest. She wanted to get some answers from her about why she kept acting this ridiculous way. Even more, she wanted to shake some sense into Callie and stop all this nonsense.

Lisa took a step toward the car, then stopped. *What am I doing? Will this make Callie forget her anger and thank me? Will I be the hero, the great mother?*

She knew the answers. She was in a no-win situation. *Okay, so the choice is: I enable her and her rebellion, and then lose because she still hates me. Or I leave her there, stewing in her own anger, and then she gets really cold, which feeds her bitterness, and I lose and she still hates me. So, basically, I come out the hated one either way.*

Her mothering instincts shouted, *Warm her up! She's your baby.*

She wondered what her mother would do in this circumstance. She knew right away. *She'd leave me there to learn my lesson. If I wanted to do something stupid like that, so be it.*

*Of course,* her mind raced on, *if I leave her there, nobody would get a second glance at her outfit or attitude. This could be a blessing in disguise.*

*Why does she have to hate me?* her mind whined back.

"What are you doing out in this cold without a coat?" A woman's hand touched Lisa's shoulder. Lisa turned to see Brenda and her husband, Eric, standing behind her. People were either milling around inside talking or heading to the parking lot.

Lisa smiled, hoping her face didn't give away her inner arguments. "I was just running out here to warm up the car." And with that she pulled out her key ring, clasped onto the remote car starter Joel had surprised her with for Christmas, and pushed down on the button. Immediately the parking lights flashed.

As she thanked Brenda for accompanying Joel and her in their song, she heard the car engine sputter and then rev to life.

Her decision was made. She knew it probably wouldn't ease Callie's attitude—although she could always hope!—but to her motherly mind, it would at least warm Callie's body.

Fifteen minutes later, Lisa extricated herself from a conversation with the Newburys, a couple who'd been attending the church for about a year, to check on the car. She knew the car wouldn't run indefinitely; it was supposed to turn off after about fifteen minutes. Sure enough, it was no longer running. She casually pointed the remote starter outside and pushed the button again, then watched the parking lights blink, indicating the engine would start in a few seconds.

Lisa turned back toward the remaining families who were still visiting and noticed her husband wasn't in his usual place by the sanctuary door. Figuring he was in his office, where he went before heading to the parking lot after the service, she decided to walk down and meet him. Plus, she knew she still had to find Ricky, whom she assumed was hanging out with his friend Steve, talking about video games and football.

"Well, this is a problem, Joel. As usual," a harsh voice said behind the closed door of Joel's office as Lisa drew near. She paused, not wanting to interrupt but also wanting to eavesdrop. She immediately recognized the gravelly voice of Tom Graves. *Please don't let this start again,* she half prayed. *Not today. Not with everything that's going on with Callie.*

"Tom." Joel spoke evenly, but Lisa could tell by the clipped way he said the man's name that he was feeling tense. Or maybe he wasn't, but Lisa was feeling tense herself and projected that tension onto her husband. Either way, she knew the conversation couldn't be good. "I appreciate all you've done for the youth group," Joel continued. "But this is getting out of hand. You can't go in and take over just because you don't like the way Kevin is handling the kids. Why don't we discuss this at the board meeting next Thursday night? If you still have an issue, we can deal with it there."

"Oh, you can count on that, Joel."

Lisa sensed the impromptu meeting was ending, so she quickly knocked on the door and opened it a fraction. "Honey, I don't want lunch to burn. You ready? Oh, hi, Tom. Sorry to interrupt." She hoped her proactive movement in announcing that she was there seemed innocent.

Tom brushed past her without saying a word, leaving Joel standing with an outstretched hand, apparently waiting for a handshake.

"What now?" she asked, almost afraid of his answer.

Joel just slightly shook his head in a motion that Lisa took to mean, "Later."

"Dad?" Ricky burst through the slightly ajar door like a Rottweiler chasing a cat. "Mom," he said, seeing her but it barely registering, "can I go to Steve's house? He just got the new X-Men video game and his mom said we could try it out. Please?"

Joel started to object, so Lisa quickly interrupted. "I think that's a great idea," she said, still focused on Joel. "Do you want us to pick you up later?"

"Naw. Can they just bring me with them to church tonight? Mrs. Markins already said it was okay," he said, referring to Steve's mom.

"Sure she can handle you that long?" Lisa said, smiling. She loved to tease her son about his boyish antics.

"Hey!" Ricky flung out his arms in mock protest. Then, in a humorous attempt at an Italian accent, he said, "We'll be quiet as mouses in the houses. Capisce?"

Lisa rolled her eyes and groaned.

"Try to act human so you don't embarrass your family," Joel said, and in his own Italian accent added, "Capisce?"

"Thatsa my papa!" Ricky said.

"What are you, the men of many accents?" Lisa said, shooing them all out of the office.

"He would be," Joel said, shaking his head, "if they didn't all sound alike."

Ricky simply proffered a wide smile.

"Okay, go," Joel said. "Don't stare too long at the computer screen. Try to take a few breaks every now and then."

"We will," Ricky called as he ran toward the front door. "Thanks!"

Joel and Lisa stood still for a moment, watching their son disappear. Finally Lisa wrapped her arm through his. "Well, that's one down. Now, to Callie." She only hoped Callie was still in the car and hadn't disappeared.

---

*12:11 p.m.*

The ride home from church was like the calm before a tornado. Lisa wished Callie would yell or spit out hateful comments—anything but the thick tension that hung heavily in the car. Callie didn't even emit the long, heavy, melodramatic sigh used by most teenage girls.

Lisa assumed Joel was quiet not out of retaliation but because his mind was still on the scene with Tom. Did he even notice what was—or *wasn't*—happening in the car? Well, she noticed. Oh, how she noticed. And she knew Callie was saying a mouthful with her silence.

Callie was building a case against her parents. Fortunately for Callie, Lisa figured, Callie was not only the prosecuting attorney, but also the judge, jury, bailiff, news reporter, and jail warden.

Lisa yearned to say something. To break the ice—or some heads. It didn't matter which. But what? What to say? What to do? It was that pro-verbial rock and a hard place she found herself between more and more frequently. As a pastor's wife, she had come to accept that dealing with unhappy people at church was part of her job description. But now it was in her own family.

More than anything, she wished she could call her mother and ask for advice. But after more than three decades of experience, she knew that would do no good. Her mother was long on well-meaning platitudes, but woefully short on genuine compassion or good advice. And she couldn't go to her mother-in-law, since she'd passed away more than five years before.

And going to someone in the church? Lisa chuckled to herself at that thought. As if she didn't already feel the weight of unmet parenting expectations.

She loved the PWs, but none of them had children Callie's age. All their kids were younger. *At least I can be there for them when their kids become teens,* she thought ruefully. *Let's face it. There is no one. You're on your own, kiddo.*

She'd often joked with Joel and her PW girlfriends that she wished parenting came with a *Worst-Case Scenario* handbook. Pop out a baby, and the hospital hands you a delivery bill for several thousand dollars, along with a coveted parenting manual for the ages of newborn through twenty-five.

And all the parenting magazines—those were all for parents of young children. She really needed a parenting magazine for mothers of rebellious teens. Something like *Parents of Teens* or *The Terrible Teens* or, better yet, *Rude and Ready.* And any contests the magazine put on would be things like "Plan your dream life—without the sighing, whining, griping sounds of teens." The grand prize would be an all-expenses-paid trip for the child of the parents' choice to a sod farm in the Upper Peninsula of Michigan. No cell phones, no television, no fast food.

*Okay, Earth calling Lisa. Back to reality. What are you going to do with the child in the backseat?*

Joel pulled the car into their driveway. But before the car fully stopped, Callie hopped out, slammed the door, and stomped to the back porch.

The door slam seemed to wake Joel. "What's her problem?" He asked that question almost every day now, but it kept coming out as if it were the first time he'd uttered it.

"I don't know," Lisa returned the same answer. Then all of a sudden, as if a thunderbolt had struck, she paused. "I don't know, but I have an idea."

# Felicia

*Monday, January 29*
*8:58 a.m.*

Felicia trudged through the slushy snow from her car to the office building door, carefully carrying her shoes in one hand and her briefcase in the
other. Her laptop bag strap was slung over her shoulder, causing one side of
her red wool coat to hang awkwardly.

She knew she looked disheveled, and it made her anxious. Felicia prided
herself on appearing pulled together, especially at the office, where she felt
she needed to set an example for the other employees. But she'd learned last
year, her first there, that Ohio winters were the great equalizer when it came
to sloppy versus savvy.

Normally she set down all her bags as soon as she was safely inside the
building's lobby, where, to the obvious amusement of the doorman, she
would robotically strip off her snow boots, throw them in a plastic bag, take
off her coat, pull out her mirror, and fix her hair and reapply her lipstick.
Once she felt she was "in place," she'd hoist all of her belongings and head
for the elevators.

But today was different. There was no time to regroup and refix. When

55

she'd dropped Nicholas at Happy Times, he'd refused to go in. Sweet encouragement turned to desperate force as Felicia finally dragged him into the preschool classroom. She saw Melinda give her an uneasy eye, which frustrated her even more, but she had no choice—she had to get to work.

*Wonder how many he's bitten so far today,* she thought as she tapped the button for the fifth floor, sure that his early-morning acting-out would result in his chomping on anything in sight.

The elevator ferried her to five and Felicia headed down the hallway to her office suite. She was relieved to see her assistant, Delores, already there, answering the phone.

"It's Ted from LA," Delores whispered, holding her hand over the phone receiver. "He's called twice already."

Felicia calculated the time difference in her head. "It's only six there," she mouthed worriedly to Delores and pointed to her office so Delores would transfer the call. She tossed her stuff in a side chair, kicked off her snow boots, and took a deep breath as she padded in stocking feet toward her desk chair. A call from her boss so early couldn't be good news.

She picked up the receiver. "Felicia Lopez-Morrison."

"Ah, Felicia! How's the weather?"

Felicia gritted her teeth. Her LA colleagues got such a kick out of their perception of the California girl living in the tundra.

"Hey, Ted. How are the housing prices? And the commute? Oh, and the air quality?"

Felicia bit her lip. Her hassle with Nicholas had her on edge, which made her come across a bit harsher than she'd intended.

Ted laughed, but Felicia sensed a nervous tone to his chuckle. "Yeah, well, you'd better get used to that commute again."

Felicia felt her heart jump into her esophagus like a Sea World whale show. "Wh-what do you mean, Ted?"

Ted cleared his throat. "We're closing the Cincinnati office, Felicia."

She nearly fell into her chair. "What? Why?"

"That location just isn't proving profitable for us anymore. We can handle the whole region from the Chicago branch."

*Chicago? But what about my twelve employees in Cincinnati?*

"We'll provide a nice severance package for your folks there," Ted said as if reading her mind. His laissez-faire attitude made Felicia instantly bitter. She hadn't worked so hard all these years for a few thousand dollars in severance.

"And, Felicia, this closure is going to benefit you. We're not letting go of you—we want you to head up the Chicago office. You know Jane is retiring, and we need someone we can count on to step in and keep that machine rolling." He chuckled. "And now that you're used to that weather—"

For the first time in months, Felicia heard the screeching sound of the airplane in her mind. "Chicago? But we live here."

Ted's tone brightened in a condescending sort of way. "I know your husband has that little church there, but Chicago has plenty of churches. Surely he can find something—"

Felicia silently pounded her fist on her desk. She saw Delores watching her from the outer office. Turning to avoid her, she glanced down and saw a run in her hose near her ankle. *Ugh.*

"Ted, we can't just pull up and leave here. We've set down roots. We have a life here . . ." Her voice drifted off. She knew she was not sounding too convincing. The Midwestern idea of a settled family life was anathema to LA's movers and shakers. Ted, a nominal Jew whose greatest achievement was getting reservations at the French Laundry in Napa to surprise his latest trophy girlfriend, would not understand her argument.

"And Felicia, Brown & McGrory is prepared to offer you a very generous package for your trouble. In fact, your husband could probably give up his church thing and stay home to raise your ankle-biters."

*Biters.* Yeah, she definitely had one of those, she thought. Maybe it would be good if Dave could stay home. Then they wouldn't have to worry about Nicholas getting kicked out of day care. And they could have a second baby without hiring a sitter. It might be an easier life if one of them were home full time.

Felicia snapped back to reality. She reached up with her free hand to smooth her silky black hair. "Ted, there is no way. Dave's pastorate is just as important"—clearly more important, but Felicia felt sure Ted wouldn't understand why—"as my career. I can't ask him to move to Chicago now."

Ted seemed prepared for her answer. "Okay, well, let's just table it for now. I want you to come out to the home office in a few weeks for some meetings anyway. We'll talk more about it then. And we'll discuss how you want to announce the Cincinnati closure."

*How I want to announce it?* Felicia's emotions spiked. *It's his decision. Why can't he announce it?*

Instead she put on her best PR/pastor's wife voice. "Certainly, Ted. When would you like me to be there?"

"We'll start with dinner on Wednesday the fourteenth, so take the early flight that day. I'll send a car for you to LAX."

Felicia agreed and hung up, then consulted her calendar. February fourteenth—Valentine's Day. On a day when everyone is celebrating love, she'd be 2,400 miles away from her husband, plotting how to keep her job and not lose her family. Great. Just great.

# Lulu's Café

*Tuesday, January 30*
*12:24 p.m.*

"And so I go on and on telling the policeman the whole story about Milo having colic and blah, blah, blah, and he looks at me as if I'm speaking Greek!"

Jennifer and Lisa's clattering laugh at Mimi's tale of her run-in with Officer McCarthy jerked Felicia back to the lunch table and away from thoughts of how she was going to save the Cincinnati office.

"So did he still give you a ticket?" Jennifer asked, leaning her head on her clasped hands with her elbows on the table.

"Yep . . . and then I cried on Mark's shoulder about it. Boo hoo hoo." Mimi pretended to wipe her eyes while the others—including Felicia this time—chuckled. "Y'know, those hormones and all," she explained. Then she added mysteriously, "But that's not the best part."

Lisa forked a piece of cantaloupe and shook her head, obviously wondering what else there could be to Mimi's incredible story.

"Oh, no, tell me someone from your church didn't see you getting the ticket," Felicia asked, wide-eyed.

Mimi drained her milk glass and nodded as she set it down next to her empty burger plate. "You got it. There I was, sitting in the back of the squad car to keep warm while he wrote my ticket, and I see this couple from church, the Magruders, drive by not once but *twice*."

"Had to make sure it was you," Jennifer said knowingly.

Felicia pushed away her nearly empty salad bowl. "Did they say anything when they saw you at church that Sunday?"

"Did they say anything?" Mimi repeated. "No, *they* didn't say anything, but Yvonne Loomis, Martha Magruder's best friend, came up and asked me in an oh-so-concerned voice, 'Is everything okay, Mimi?' When I told her I was fine, she said, 'You know, if you ever need help with the children or anything, be sure to reach out to someone in the church before it gets out of hand.' The whole time she was talking she was staring at me as if I was that woman from Texas who drowned her kids."

"Maybe the word will get out at church that you're loony-tunes and everyone will be afraid to mess with you," Jennifer offered. "Could work to your advantage."

Mimi tossed her used napkin in her cleaned plate. "The way I've been looking lately from lack of sleep, they probably think that anyway. No matter what I do for that kid, he will not go down for more than a few hours at a time. And when he's not sleeping, he's crying. I always thought I was a pretty good mom with the other three, but I'm really failing with this one. Maybe the others were just easy, and Milo is proving I'm a terrible mother after all!"

While she was speaking, Mimi's face was like a window that was gradually being shrouded by a curtain, closing off the sunlight.

Felicia could empathize. She'd often wondered if Nicholas's biting was insurmountable. "Aw, come on, Mimi," she said encouragingly. "We can't be judged on our parenting yet. Let's see how they turn out, then decide where we messed them up!"

Mimi perked up, but Felicia noticed Lisa's strange expression, as if someone had sucker-punched her. "Lisa, did I say something wrong?" Felicia asked.

Before Lisa could answer, Gracie stopped by to pick up their plates. "You gals having anything else today?"

Felicia checked her watch. "I need to get going soon, but we're still not caught up, so maybe you could bring us another round of drinks?"

Loaded down with plates and halfway turned from the table, Gracie nodded and asked, not waiting for an answer, "Will that be draft or bottle?" She chortled as she walked toward the kitchen.

The table was quiet, Felicia's question still hanging in the air. "You didn't say anything wrong," Lisa said finally. "It just reminded me about this situation with Callie. She's saying she hates us now and doesn't want to go to church. So when you talk about knowing what kind of mother you've been by the way your kids turn out, it makes me wonder what I did wrong and how I failed her. She'll be grown in just four years, you know."

Jennifer uncrossed and recrossed her legs. "She's just in those bizarre teenage years," she said matter-of-factly. "You can't judge anything by that. I mean, when I was her age I was already in all kinds of trouble. At least you don't have that to deal with."

Lisa's eyes told Felicia that Lisa wasn't so sure what she was dealing with.

"And it took me awhile to get out of it—I call those my 'wilderness years'—but look how I turned out," Jennifer continued with a chuckle. "A pastor's wife even! Who woulda thunk?"

The possibility of her daughter making the leap from church hater to pastor's wife seemed to lighten Lisa's spirit.

"Besides, you're not Callie's only parent. She is Joel's daughter, too," said Felicia, thinking she was adding to Lisa's resolve but realizing when she saw Lisa's face fall that she'd caused another slump.

"Yeah, well, he doesn't see it that way," Lisa said quietly. "He just tries to avoid the whole thing by talking to her through me, or yelling at her and leaving the room. I guess with all the problems at the church he doesn't have anything left to give at home right now."

Gracie arrived with two diet Cokes, a milk, and an iced tea pitcher. She filled Lisa's glass with tea, then reached into her apron pocket and pulled out a check, which she left at the end of the table. Lisa busied herself with adding sugar and stirring. Felicia sensed that Lisa didn't want to delve further into Callie's issues, at least not at that moment, so she dropped the subject and instead reached across and grabbed the check.

"Wha—" the other three said in near unison.

Felicia held up her "stop" hand. "You'd better let me pick up this one. I might be unemployed soon," she warned.

"No way!" Jennifer said, turning quickly to face her. "I thought you were the star of that company!"

Felicia smiled at her compliment. *I am the star, or at least I will show Ted I am.* "They want to close the Cincinnati office and move me to Chicago."

"That's a long way to drive for lunch," Mimi joked. "I guess we could meet you in Indy or something."

Lisa wasn't so amused. "You're not going, are you?" she asked urgently.

"Of course not!" Felicia assured her. "But I am going to try to drum up some business and save that office. It's killing me, but I'm about halfway there. I figure if I can show even a little movement by the time I get to LA next month, my boss will let the office stay."

"But what if he doesn't?" Lisa asked innocently.

*Don't let yourself think that way.* "I guess I'll become the best pastor's wife in the world," Felicia said, circling her hand in the air as if to say, "Ta-da."

"But you already are!" Jennifer said, her arms out as if she were presenting Felicia.

"No, *you* are," Felicia said, nudging her playfully with her elbow.

"I think *you* are," Mimi chimed in toward Lisa.

Lisa grinned and shook her head. "No, Mimi, *you* are the best."

After a few more go-rounds, the women collapsed in giggles.

# Lisa

*Friday, February 2*
*12:22 p.m.*

"Hi, Mom," Lisa said as she slid into the seat across from her mother. She was glad her mother had arrived early enough to get them a coveted booth in the center of the crowded, noisy restaurant, where it was the warmest.

Lydia Jenkins, Lisa's mother, was nursing an iced tea. At sixty-four, she had a mature, formal manner. Her salt-and-pepper hair was wrapped in a neat bun at the nape of her neck. And her pronounced crow's feet around her hazel eyes were more from wearing a stern look than from laughter.

Lisa noticed there was another tea sitting across from her mother. The ice had melted. There were no menus.

That didn't matter to Lisa. Actually, she barely noticed, since she wouldn't use it anyway. They both always ordered the same thing whenever they met for lunch at Breaker Hill Pancake House. Lisa, a tuna-salad sandwich on pumpernickel, with a side of fries and fruit. Lydia always went with a Denver omelet, well done, with a side of salsa, hash browns, and an English muffin, hold the butter. They both got iced tea—one sugar, no lemon.

"I already ordered for you," Lydia said by way of greeting.

63

"Thanks." Lisa pushed her shoulder-length hair back, then picked up her straw and dunked it into her drink.

"Do you need more ice? It melted."

"No, I'm fine. Thanks." Lisa knew this was Lydia's back-door way of saying, "You're late."

"How are things at the church?" Lydia asked.

It was always the same question. They always ordered the same meal, then Lydia started the conversation the identical way.

"The same," Lisa answered, sipping her tea.

"Still having those problems with the church members?"

"Yes. You'd think they'd be more respectful, especially concerning a man of God, but they don't seem to care."

"Well, Jesus had the same problem. We can't expect not to suffer if our Savior himself did."

*Spoken like a true pastor's wife.*

"Yes, you're right." It was better not to debate with her mother.

"How are things with Dad?"

"Oh, you know your father. Always involved with some committee or evangelistic program. The church has been growing. We had three new families come last week."

"Wow. That's great." Somehow things never really got too personal between them. She'd asked about her father, and it ended up going to the church. She'd been through this same scenario for decades, but it still bothered her. Joel always told her to let it go. But that was easier said than done.

Joel respected and admired her parents. After all, Joel had learned how to be a pastor from her dad, growing up under his leadership at the Cloverdale Assembly of God, in the town next to Red River. Then after Bible school and seminary, Joel returned there to be an associate pastor and youth leader. It was a great moment for both Joel and Lisa when Joel accepted his first senior pastorate at Red River Assembly several years ago. And he continued to talk with her father about all things ministry. At least *they* were able to connect.

"Mom, can I talk to you about something?" Lisa started tentatively. She didn't want to dwell on the church and its problems. She had a bigger issue to deal with. She only hoped this conversation would go well. The last time she'd tried to open up to her mother, it had ended in disaster for Lisa. That had been almost a year ago when she and Joel were having marital problems—Joel seemed to be married to the church and ignoring her. His neglect of his marriage almost ended it for them. Lisa had tried to talk to her mother about the problem, but her mother refused to hear about it, instead saying that it was Lisa's responsibility as a pastor's wife to support and encourage her man. Period, end of story. Now Lisa sat again opposite her mother in the same restaurant—only this time it was to talk about Callie.

They were interrupted by the waitress, carrying their meals. Lisa waited patiently until everything was settled, they said grace, and her mother started to pour the salsa onto her omelet.

"You were saying?" Lydia finally said, cutting the omelet and taking a bite.

"It's about Callie." She waited to see if her mother would register any surprise or any feeling. When there was nothing, Lisa continued. "She seems to be going through a phase."

"Phase? What do you mean, 'phase'?"

"Well, you know she's going to be fifteen soon. She's going through adolescence and she's just having some difficulty with it all."

Lisa was met with a blank stare. "Um . . ." Lisa rubbed her forehead. "She's . . . well . . ."

"She's giving you trouble?"

"Yes," Lisa breathed out in relief.

Lydia only nodded.

"She has a terrible attitude. She's mouthy. Her grades have been slipping at school. And now she's fighting us about going to church." Lisa held her breath. Was her mother going to judge her, too? Was she going to say, "Well, you know, Lisa, I never had that problem with you and your brother. What are you doing wrong that you've lost control of her?" *Please don't say that. Please don't say that.* Besides that fear, Lisa was also worried her mother would just float out some spiritually pat answer: "You're not pray-ing enough." "You just have to give it up to God." "You don't have enough faith. Faith moves mountains."

Those were the things her mother said when she moved into what Lisa called "pastor's wife mode," the sort of spiritual self-assuredness that her mother had perfected. It was the manner in which she listened politely, thoughtfully, and compassionately. But then no matter what the situation or story, she always responded with a catch-all platitude. It always seemed to work for other hearers. But Lisa had grown up watch-ing it and having it doled out to her, too. It wasn't that her mother was insincere or without genuine compassion. It was just that her mother was more of the legalistic kind of Christian: If you live a holy life—no smoking, drinking, cussing, or going to movies—you'll be blessed. If you're having trouble in life, then you must not be living close enough to God.

Lisa watched her mother purse her lips. She took that to be a good sign, so she pressed on. "Joel and I don't know what to do with her. We've yelled, we've grounded her, we've prayed for her . . ."

"You have to continue to be firm," her mother finally said. "If you're not, children will run all over you. And you can't afford that being in a pastor's family. The church expects certain things from you. And one of those things is that you and Joel have your family under control."

"I know, Mom. That's why . . . well, Joel and I were . . ." Lisa started to play with her drink, swishing the straw around in the brown liquid. "We were hoping you could . . . take her for a while."

"What do you mean 'take her'?"

"We both think she would do well being under your leadership for a while. Just a week. Her spring break from school is coming up. Maybe you could do a sort of grandparent-grandchild bonding thing?"

"You want us to do your job for you." It was a stinging statement, but her mother had gotten to the heart of the matter.

"Well, I don't think I'd put it that way."

"But that's what it is."

Lisa started to fidget with her napkin in her lap. This was going terribly.

"Lisa, do you think you can send us Callie every time she gets mouthy? Yes, she could stay with us for a week, but we're not going to fix her, if that's what you're hoping."

"No, it's not that," Lisa said defensively, hoping instead she was sounding calm, relaxed. "We just think that maybe some time away from us, from all the stress and tension she's been apparently dealing with, will do her some good."

Her mother nodded, deep in thought, and took another bite of her omelet. "I'll have to talk this over with your father, of course. And she'll have to be told she doesn't get a pass on going to church like she apparently does with you."

That smarted. But Lisa accepted it—if it would get her what she wanted. "Yes, absolutely. I wouldn't have it any other way."

"Fine, then. We'll plan on having her stay with us over her spring break."

"Thank you, Mom. I—we—really appreciate this. We think it will do Callie a world of good."

Her mother said nothing but continued to eat. They remained silent for a few moments until her mom furrowed her brow. "You know, frankly, Lisa, I'm a little disappointed in you and Joel. That you can't handle your own daughter . . ." She shook her head slowly and took another bite. "Maybe if you had a little more faith and were committed to praying for her . . ."

# 10

# Jennifer

*Saturday, February 3*
*10:08 a.m.*

Bending down on the park sidewalk to retie her tennis shoe, her straw-berry-blond ponytail falling to her shoulder, Jennifer felt a disparate mix of relief and dread as she got ready for her walk in the park. She'd made the big mistake of acquiescing to the bloat caused by the fertility medication and had for the last few months been eating anything she wanted. But now that she had been off the medication for a few weeks, she felt the puffiness gradually dissipating. So she decided to buy into that, too, and try to drop a few pounds. She'd even invested in a new jogging suit—gray with lime trim—as an incentive, but as she bent over, she realized the size fourteen was a bit tight.

Walking had always been her favorite exercise, but walking in Ohio in February was not the easiest task. When she'd gotten up that day, she was glad to see sunshine illuminating the frozen ground. What snow they'd had in January was pushed into small piles along the city park's asphalt sidewalks.

Standing up, she reached into her jacket pocket and pulled out her iPod, a Christmas gift from Sam. When she'd opened it on Christmas morning, she thought it was something she'd never use, but now she wondered how she'd ever lived without it. She carried it with her everywhere—even to the church office, where she'd sometimes slip in the ear buds, as Sam had suggested, to avoid hearing him counseling someone in the next room. Although he hadn't said so, she figured the iPod was a bit of a bribe to get her back to the church office as secretary. If he'd only known—she had decided to return anyway. The months home alone had made her inability to get pregnant even more pronounced.

As people walked, ran, and biked past her—she clearly wasn't the only person who'd rejoiced at this crisp yet dry Ohio Saturday—Jennifer touch-tuned the iPod to Amy Grant's greatest hits. Some of the women in her church had tossed their Amy Grant CDs and albums when Amy got divorced in the 1990s, but Jennifer had kept all of hers. Amy's was the first Christian singer's CD Jennifer had bought when she turned her life over to the Lord.

*Just because she messed up doesn't change the message of her music,* she thought defiantly as she stepped off for the first of three miles. *If we threw away everyone who sinned, we'd all be gone.*

She was just beginning to break a sweat—humming along to "Every Heartbeat"—when she felt a tap on her shoulder and spun to see a runner slowing down alongside her.

"Pastor Scott!" she said a little too loudly—she'd cranked Amy pretty high to get motivated—causing the two women walkers in front of her to turn and frown.

Simultaneously she reached down to click off her iPod and stepped to the side of the pavement so others could pass by.

"Jennifer, how are you?" Father Scott asked exuberantly, wiping his forehead with a small towel he'd pulled from his pocket. "It's been, what—"

"Oh, six months at least."

"Any news?" He glanced down at her abdomen. *Why do people always do that?* she thought in frustration.

"No, no, this is all me." Jennifer sighed. "That's why I'm here. The doctor took me off the fertility drugs, so I decided it's time to lose some weight along with that puffiness."

"Ah, I'm sorry to hear that, Jennifer." He motioned her over to a bench.

"What, that I'm losing weight?" She laughed. She was tired of people feeling sorry for her.

Father Scott rolled his eyes and smiled. "So what's next for you two? Will you consider adoption? I have some great contacts at a mission in Guatemala."

Jennifer hadn't let herself think about adoption. It felt like "giving up" to her. "Actually, we have one more thing to try. You've heard of in vitro fertilization?"

Father Scott leaned back against the bench and nodded, his mouth clamped in a straight line as he stared at the pebbles mixed with slush beneath their feet.

Jennifer knew his nonverbal moves did not bode well. "What?" she asked, then remembered he was a slow responder. He'd practically driven her nuts with his turtle-paced answers when she was seeing him for counseling last year, until she'd recognized how wise his advice was—definitely worth the wait.

"Jennifer, what does your church say about this?"

She thought for a moment. Her church didn't have anything to say about it that she knew of. Then again, she hadn't inquired.

"Nothing, I guess." She shrugged.

Father Scott hesitated again. Jennifer glanced at her watch. She'd told Sam she'd be back by 11:30, and she still had two miles to go.

"Oh, that's right. Most nondenominational Protestant churches don't really have doctrinal guidelines on things like this, do they?"

Jennifer decided to speed up the process. She didn't know what he meant by *guidelines*. "Well, Pastor Scott, you clearly have something to tell me, so why don't you just say it?"

Father Scott chuckled at Jennifer's forthrightness. "I'd forgotten how eager you are to cut to the chase."

Jennifer realized how much she'd missed their conversations. Not having a father of her own, she felt that talking with this Catholic priest gave her a sense of what it was like to lean on a dad.

Father Scott bent forward, putting his forearms on his thighs. "Well, here's the deal as far as we view it in the Catholic church. Married couples make love, not babies. If a baby is conceived by that act of love, that's wonderful. But intercourse is not some sort of manufacturing process with children as 'products.' Replacing marital relations with IVF is exactly what that does."

Jennifer nodded. She'd spent the last few evenings reading about IVF online. Father Scott's description resonated with her—the more she'd read, the more she'd felt that the procedure was overly clinical and not loving. Still, it did have a positive result: a baby! What could be wrong with that?

Father Scott continued. "Now, as you know, IVF involves creating children in a petri dish: the father's sperm is put in the dish with the mother's egg. Because it is all so expensive and the couple wants to get pregnant on the first try, the doctor injects the mother with drugs so she creates many eggs. So the result is several embryos."

Jennifer thought she knew what he was going to say next, so she interrupted. "I know. Then they choose the embryos they want to implant and then either destroy the rest or freeze them. But what if we agree that we will implant all of the embryos, regardless?"

"Jennifer, the point here isn't that your desire is wrong. You are right to want to be parents. But that's just it—the Catholic Church's view is that by taking it as far as IVF, you are manipulating the entire process. We are made in the image of God. No humans can 'create' that image. But with IVF, all of the decisions fall on people. Instead of a child being begotten, as the Bible teaches, the child is 'made' by technology. That's not how God intended it."

Jennifer got tears in her eyes. "It's all very dehumanizing, isn't it?"

Father Scott placed a light hand on one of Jennifer's gloved ones. "Oh, Jennifer. You have suffered so, haven't you?"

She nodded, afraid if she spoke she might burst into a flood of tears.

Father Scott grasped her hand securely. "Let's pray about it, okay?"

She turned to face Father Scott more closely. But just before they bowed their heads, she felt the stare of a passing walker. The person's shoes were the first thing she saw, yet they told her everything she needed to know.

Snapping her head up, Jennifer saw the wearer of the unusual shoes, Kitty Katt, gliding by, her lips pursed in judgment and eyes narrowed as she observed Father Scott's hand clasping Jennifer's. Kitty and Jennifer's eyes met silently for a millisecond, then Kitty was gone, her yellow Nikes carrying her down the sidewalk in a fast clip.

Jennifer looked back at Father Scott, who had bowed his head and was starting to pray. Sure, she knew she was sitting on a park bench receiving counseling from a Catholic priest, but all Kitty would have seen was her holding hands with an attractive older man in a running suit. A man who wasn't her husband.

*Wonder how this will come back to bite me?* she thought before quieting herself to join Father Scott in prayer. But she couldn't get the picture of Kitty's glower out of her mind.

# 11

# Felicia

*Sunday, February 4*
*8:27 a.m.*

Becky set a platter of blueberry pancakes on the table just as Felicia walked into the dining room. Because Sunday was the most hectic of all days in the Morrison household—with Dave doing last-minute sermon preparations and Felicia getting herself and Nicholas ready for church—Felicia had asked her once-a-week Jewish maid, Becky, if she could start coming earlier on Sundays to make a hot breakfast for everyone. She'd even suggested some possible menu ideas because she wasn't quite sure what to expect after Becky's matzo ball soup surprise last July.

But as she saw the set table and steaming pancakes, Felicia felt more guilt than satisfaction. Surely other pastors' wives didn't have this luxury. Was there something wrong with her that she couldn't even make a decent breakfast for her family?

"Cool! Pancakes!" Nicholas said, running into the dining room and climbing into a chair. His startlingly blue eyes shone from his olive face. Becky started to fix him a plate, but Felicia stopped her.

"That's okay, Becky. I can handle it from here," she said, forking a pancake onto Nicholas's plate and trying not to sound defensive.

Becky slunk back into the kitchen. Felicia wondered if she'd offended her. She hadn't meant to—she just needed to assert her place as mom in the house. Even though it was a relief to have Becky cleaning and now cooking, Felicia didn't want to be stripped of all her "duties."

"Wow, that smells good," Dave said, joining them at the table. Felicia again felt a twinge of inadequacy, but it disappeared as she watched her two guys plow into the sea of maple syrup they poured on their plates.

Nicholas exuberantly stuffed his mouth full and labored to chew.

*At least he's a good eater,* Felicia thought. *If only I could get him to stop biting into* people. Although the "people" seemed to be just her and Dave these days—she got only good reports from Melinda at Happy Times, which made her even more curious about her son's motivation.

"So are you finishing up your grace series today?" she asked Dave, admiring his gray suit set off by a scarlet tie. *Of course, I should like it since I picked it out. If he knew how much that tie cost . . .*

"I was going to, then I checked the calendar and decided to split my last sermon for that series so I'd end it next week. That way I can start something new when I get back."

Felicia set down her coffee cup, trying to keep her intense brown eyes in check. "Get back from where?"

"The Baptist pastors' conference." Dave swallowed a bite of pancake. "I leave on the fifteenth. Did you forget I'm going?"

"Uh . . ." Felicia had been so wrapped up in trying to find a way to save the Cincinnati office and avoid the LA trip that she had completely forgotten about Dave's conference. She hadn't even told him about Ted's call because she'd hoped to make it all go away before any changes happened.

Dave eyed her suspiciously. "You *did* forget, didn't you?" He smiled. "Well, I hope you can get by without my unfailing wit and staggeringly good looks for a few days."

Felicia knew she had to tell him. "I've got to go to LA on the fourteenth," she said sheepishly.

"What? And you're just telling me now?"

"Well, I was hoping to get out of it, but it's not looking like I can. Ted wants me there for some meetings."

Dave sighed. Nicholas was swirling his fork in the butter and syrup before him, oblivious to the adult negotiations occurring at the table.

"Can't he move it to the next week?" Dave asked. "I'll be back on the nineteenth. And there's no way I can get out of going. They want me to give a report on the Brew-Ha-Ha outreach."

"Dave, I can't ask my boss to change his meeting schedule to accommodate my husband," Felicia said with a hint of spite. She shifted her pantyhose-clad legs under the table and noticed her previously cold, shoeless feet were now tinged with angry warmth.

Dave turned more serious. "This isn't about accommodating your *husband,* it's about caring for our *child,*" he spat, obviously frustrated. "Maybe I could get Nancy Borden to pitch in."

Felicia wasn't sure if he meant that last comment as a joke or a jab, but she didn't like the implications either way. Dave had innocently allowed Nancy to nearly become his surrogate wife last year, but he had put the kibosh on it once Felicia pointed it out to him. Being reminded of this—a situation brought on by Felicia's inability to balance work with home, a situation she had worked hard to resolve—caused her to scowl at Dave.

Becky reappeared and quietly set a plate of cut fruit with a dollop of yogurt in front of Felicia. "I figured you wouldn't want all those carbs," she said meekly.

Felicia transformed her aggravation to gratitude as she turned her eyes from Dave to Becky. "How incredibly kind of you," she said, and she meant it. How did Becky know she'd rather have eaten nothing than succumb to pancakes with butter and syrup?

Becky stayed in the dining room but took a step back. "And I couldn't help but overhear about your . . . problem. If it's a babysitter you need, I'd be glad to take Nicholas for a few days."

Felicia's mind raced at Becky's offer. Could she trust her son to a woman who barely spoke to her? Was it right to hand off her child so she and Dave could go do "business"?

She had no choice, and she knew it. But before she could answer, Nicholas weighed in with his own preference.

"Mom, please?" he pleaded eagerly. Becky had seen Nicholas's toy horses in his room once and told him her husband's brother had horses. Ever since then, Nicholas had begged Dave and Felicia to take him to see the horses.

Felicia eyed Dave, who shrugged in consent. She smiled. "Becky, do you think you might be able to take him by to see the horses for a few minutes?"

Nicholas practically leaped out of his chair in excitement, causing his plate to tip his milk glass. Dave grabbed it just in time.

"Of course," she said calmly. "Nicholas and I will have a good time, won't we?"

Nicholas nodded. Dave reached over and tousled his chocolate brown hair.

As Becky turned to go back into the kitchen, Felicia got up and followed her. As she walked, she inspected her legs for any runs—she had the worst luck with hose, and church was the last place she wanted to be with ripped-up stockings that would get people talking. "I need to warn you about something," she said once they were out of Nicholas's earshot. "We've been having a terrible problem with Nicholas and biting. He's not doing it at day care anymore, but he still lashes out at Dave and me sometimes. I keep hoping he'll grow out of it, but—"

Becky patted her shoulder. "Don't worry, Felicia. I raised two of my own. Eli and I will take good care of him."

Felicia was surprised at Becky's confidence, which put Felicia at ease. What a great find this woman was—a multiple problem-solver all wrapped into one person.

Now if Becky could only help Felicia deal with Ted so she could save her job in Cincinnati.

# 12

# Mimi

*Sunday, February 11*

*11:47 a.m.*

"Well, don't you look terrible."

Mimi's hand tightened ever so slightly as she shook April Rainer's—*ugh, that name*—in the Meet and Greet line after church. But Mimi's smile remained smartly in place. She was a pastor's wife, after all. And if there was one thing she knew how to do perfectly, it was to smile no matter what anybody in her husband's congregation said to or about her or her family.

Today proved especially challenging since she hadn't slept all night. Again. Milo had gotten quite a reputation at the church in his new, young life. From everywhere in the church, people could hear him screaming non-stop in the nursery. Fortunately the sanctuary had doors, so that helped ensure the quiet and sanctity of that room. But most of the nursery volunteers couldn't handle his screeching, so they had recruited (read: guilted and forced) Mimi to do nursery duty for a period of, well, until Milo got over the colicky thing, or until he graduated into the Junior Church preschool class—whichever came first.

Mimi had not been pleased with this new development. She'd hoped that at least at church she'd be able to get a little peace and quiet. But how could she say no? She knew only too well that *no* was not a word she was good at uttering. So she'd agreed to the arrangement. Through gritted teeth, of course, but the nursery workers didn't seem to notice that little detail. The only thing she *could* finagle from the nursery troops was for them to watch him while she greeted church members after the service. But now with April's tactless comment, she wasn't so sure she was getting a better deal than them.

"I mean," April pressed, "bless your heart, you look a mess."

"Thank you, April." *Thank you for pointing out that important detail, Ms. Weird Name. And might I say the same about you, with your roots showing.* She smiled again, feeling guilty for what she'd just thought. *Okay, that was completely not nice. I'm sorry,* she mentally prayed.

Mimi tried politely but firmly to lead April's hand toward Mark's outstretched one, the smile plastered all the while. The line to greet her husband and her was especially long this Sunday, because it was "Bring a Friend to Church" Sunday, and she didn't want to hold it up by getting into a conversation about how bad she was already aware she looked. But April didn't seem to take the hint.

"You know, concealer does wonders under the eyes."

"Yes, so I've heard."

"And maybe a little more blush would help."

"I'll keep that in mind."

"And if you went with a slightly darker shade of—"

"April!" Mark interjected just as Mimi envisioned herself jamming her fist into April's gut. "Good to see you this week."

*God bless my husband.* Mimi was shocked at her violent feelings toward April. Normally, she let the congregation's words roll off her. Okay, not really. Sure she became frustrated and hurt by them, but she'd never before actually wanted to take a potshot at one of the church members. Mimi glanced at Mark as he appeared completely immersed in what April was saying about the depth, or lack thereof, of his sermon.

She stole a glance down the line and inwardly groaned. She'd tried to remind herself not to notice how long the line was, because it was always too long. But today she couldn't help herself. She tried mentally to wish them all away. She wanted nothing better than to curl up on one of the padded pews in the sanctuary—with a blanket would be nice—and make like Sleeping Beauty.

With that wish not granted, she focused on the next people in line and, with pasted smile, thanked them for coming and made the other acceptable comments one made during the weekly Meet and Greet: "How's the family?" "It's so good to see you." "See you next week!"

To be fair, Mimi knew she usually enjoyed this part of the job responsibilities. She loved the members of their church and wanted genuinely to know about and be part of their lives. Just not today.

And it was all Milo's fault. *Everything* lately seemed to be Milo's fault.

She had known that having another baby, in addition to the other three, was going to be an adjustment. She was aware that she'd experienced sleepless nights and frenzied days during the three others' infancies. But Milo seemed determined not to give her *any* peace. Mark had once jokingly referred to Milo as Rosemary's Baby. She called him the little demon child. Or was that MJ? She couldn't remember now. It didn't matter.

Milo was the crankiest baby she'd ever known. She knew babies cried and fussed. Every baby did that at times. Although she used to think with pride about how her three other children were the easiest babies. Very complacent and peaceful. Slept through the night soon into their new lives. They'd complied with Mimi's need for order. But Milo didn't. He hadn't even been a calm, quiet baby in her womb. He'd given her terrible morning sickness—"More like twenty-four-hour sickness," she'd often said, wincing, to Mark. MJ seemed to get great pleasure in announcing, "Mom's puking again!" every time Mimi would run into the bathroom because of the nausea. He'd shout it out wherever they were at the time: home, church, Kroger's.

Milo had kicked and moved constantly. He seemed to tap-dance on her bladder and do somersaults at two a.m.

When the other children had kicked in the womb, she'd just turned on some Mozart or said in a firm voice, "Mommy doesn't like it when you kick, Baby Plaisance. So calm down." And amazingly enough, they had. But not Milo. He just seemed to kick more. He wouldn't even listen, she'd been stunned to discover, when she'd had Mark speak into her womb and tell Milo, "Baby, this is your father. Cool it in there." Of course Mimi knew Mark didn't take that stuff seriously, but she was grateful that at least he'd played along. Which was more than she could say for her newborn.

"Thank you for coming." "It's so nice to have you here." "Welcome to our church. We hope you'll come again." It was becoming rote as she passed each person down the line.

Turning slightly to the next body, Mimi's mouth had already formed the word *Thank,* when the sight of the tall, bulky, thirty-something man stopped her cold. Her eyes widened, and she could feel her hands grow clammy. She would never forget this man. And here he stood at her church, on her territory, wearing a huge, goofy grin.

"Officer McCarthy, what a"—she started to say "pleasant," but caught herself—"surprise. What a surprise this is."

"Done any more sleeping on the road?" he chuckled, seemingly good-naturedly.

"Ha," she said, trying to sound nonchalant and halfway polite. "Not lately. If you tune in, as a matter of fact, you can hear our baby yelling. Hold on a few seconds, and I'll get my little opera singer and let you drive him around for a while."

He threw back his head and laughed. "Hey, no hard feelings, right?"

She only lifted her eyebrows and grinned.

Mark stepped forward with his hand outstretched. "Well, hello there, sir. My wife and I are so glad to see you here this morning."

Officer McCarthy glanced slyly at Mimi, then chuckled. "Maybe *you* are. I'm not so sure about the missus." He leaned toward Mark and in a loud whisper said, "I'm the fella who signed a certain ticket a few weeks back."

Mark blinked, then broke out into a wide smile. "Knowing that makes me twice as glad you're here this morning. Who brought you? Or did you feel the Lord's arresting hand?" He winked and chuckled at his pun.

The officer groaned but gave him a thumbs-up. Then, putting his arm around a frail, silver-haired woman standing next to him and drawing her toward him, he announced, "My Aunt Vera invited me." She tripped slightly over her own feet as she stood before Mark, but smiled joyously and nodded.

"I just moved to town after Christmas because I transferred into Red River's police force to be closer to family," he explained. "Aunt Vera's been bugging me to come to church with her and she finally wore me down. But I liked it. You're a good speaker. I'll be back, definitely."

Mark patted Mr. Cop on the back. "That's what we like to hear. We'll look forward to seeing you next week."

Mimi couldn't believe what she was seeing. Her husband, who was *supposed* to be her loyal supporter, was schmoozing with the cop who'd ticketed her. She wanted to stomp on both their feet, like a three-year-old holding a world-class temper tantrum. *You just wait till you get home, mister,* she mentally promised him.

---

*12:21 p.m.*

"Why did you have to be so nice to him?" she demanded as soon as they pulled out of the church's parking lot.

"Who?"

"You know exactly who I'm talking about." Mimi folded her arms over her dark peacoat, the one she'd been wearing when she got the ticket. Feeling something sticky on one of the sleeves, she uncrossed her arms, making a mental note to get that "unlucky" coat to the cleaners. And maybe leave it there.

"The guy needs Jesus. And he's obviously interested in coming back. What did you want me to do—ban him because he gave you a ticket?"

"Yes!" Mimi sighed. "No. But you didn't have to be *so* chummy."

Mark's deep brown eyes pierced hers. "I'm wondering something about you."

"Hmmmph. What?"

"For a woman who prides herself so much on being in complete control, why are you letting this guy get under your skin? Why don't you just forgive him?"

"Yeah, Mom," MJ piped up. "What's up with that?"

"This doesn't concern you, young man." Mimi shot a warning glance into the backseat. Michaela and Megan hardly ever seemed to care about Mark and Mimi's conversations, but MJ was always listening. They had to be careful about what they said in front of him unless they wanted him to blab all of their behind-the-scenes talks to what Mimi called the "kid gossip chain." MJ would tell some of the church kids, who would tell their parents, who would then tell more adults, and so on like a perverse game of Telephone. One time MJ told a friend his parents were going to France—with the expected results from tithing parents who eventually heard it—when they'd actually been talking about a quick trip to Paris, Kentucky, to see Mimi's cousin Kim.

"The guy was just doing his job. He gave you a ticket—which in the scope of eternity really doesn't mean all that much," Mark continued. "I don't think you're going to go to hell for getting a ticket. Or"—he paused, a little too long for Mimi's comfort—"is this more about a damaged ego?"

"What's an ego?" Megan asked from her car seat.

"It's your pride," Michaela, ten, the eldest Plaisance child, said. "Now be quiet while Mom and Dad fight."

"What's 'pride'?" Megan ignored her sister.

"We're not fighting," Mimi called to the back of the minivan. "We're discussing."

"They're fighting," Mimi heard Michaela and MJ say to each other.

"Hey, Mom," MJ said, "I think it's kind of cool you got a ticket."

"Mark Junior," Mimi snipped. She pursed her lips and pushed her bobbed hair behind her ears, then lowered her voice to Mark. "Okay, yes, I'm glad he's seeking spiritual guidance. Of course, I want him to find God. And I'm more than willing to forgive him. But does he have to seek God in *our* church? It would be much easier to forgive him if he went to, say, the Katts' church."

Mark snorted and shook his head. Mimi shifted uncomfortably. She hadn't meant that to come out so nasty. Maybe she was being too tough on the guy. Mark was right. She *should* be glad that he was attending church and that he wanted to return. She was being selfish—putting her own issues before the officer's spiritual needs. *Shame on me,* she accused herself. But she just couldn't shake the dislike.

"Hey, Mom, maybe you've got postbottom depression," MJ yelled out helpfully.

"It's post*partum,* MJ," Mark said. "That may be true, Mims. You've been under a lot of stress—especially with four kids."

"I am completely under control," Mimi announced, annoyed. "I have never struggled with postpartum, and I don't intend to now. Would you *please* stop tailgating that car?"

"I'm *not* tailgating."

Mimi narrowed her eyes at Mark. "Really? Hmmm. Because I think I can have a conversation with the folks in that backseat ahead."

"I'm just saying," Mark said as he shrugged, "you've been in a bad mood a lot lately."

"Well, maybe if I didn't have a crying baby to deal with and I could get a little sleep and a little more help, and maybe if a certain cop hadn't given me a ticket, then had the nerve to show up in church, oh, I don't know, maybe I wouldn't be so cranky."

Mark stared silently ahead but slightly backed away from the car in front of them.

Mimi felt terrible about what she'd just said. *What am I doing? I am cranky!* She couldn't stand to have any tension between Mark and her. And she knew she was going to have to be the one to break it. "It's just . . ."

"Maybe it's that he reminds you some of the police who arrested . . ." Mark paused, glancing in the rearview mirror. She knew he was checking to see if the kids were listening. She glanced back, too. Of course, they were. She couldn't believe he'd gone there in the conversation. Was it that obvious? And why now? Why was this affecting her like it was *now?*

Slowly she nodded. "I know it's not right. But lately . . . I feel so out of sorts. It doesn't make sense, I know that." She bit her lip that had begun to quiver.

Mark caught her eye.

"I think something's wrong with me," she managed to whisper.

"What?"

"I don't know. I've never felt this way before."

Mark wove his fingers together on the steering wheel, obviously trying to think through something. Finally he said, "Maybe you should give Dr. O'Boyle a call tomorrow and talk with him."

Her eyes widened at his words. She had never had postpartum depression. Overwhelmed, yes. Stressed, sure. But not depressed. Depression to her was a weakness. She'd talked to women in the church who'd experienced depression, and although she had compassion for them (obviously they felt they were going through something real), she'd had a difficult time understanding them. She'd often thought, *Just snap out of it.*

But now here she was. Completely unable to snap out of what she was feeling—unlovely, unable to stop feeling an overwhelming sadness, edgy, weepy. She couldn't explain it, control it, or understand it. And she certainly didn't like it.

"I just want some peace," she finally said.

He nodded, as if trying to understand. "That would be nice, wouldn't it? If you want, I can go with you to see the doctor."

Mimi twisted her mouth in thought, not liking that idea. She didn't want to go see the doctor *at all,* with or without Mark. What if the doctor said she did have depression? Or worse, what if he said something else was wrong with her? What if it wasn't postpartum? What if she was having a nervous breakdown? Or what if she had a brain tumor, and that's what was causing her to feel like she was losing it? She'd seen the shows on the Discovery Channel. Subconsciously she reached up and touched the top of her head to feel for any lumps. *I have to stop watching so much middle-of-the-night TV.*

As they reached their house, she noticed that Mark wasn't braking to make the turn into their driveway.

"Dad, where we going?" MJ asked.

"The Clucker House. Your mom's had a tough day. She could use a break from cooking."

For some reason, her family loved the Clucker House, a local fried chicken joint. She'd tried numerous times to "give them some culture," which was not the Clucker House, she was certain. But her attempts never worked. They just kept migrating back there. So it wasn't exactly what she would have had a taste for, but at least she felt Mark was trying to ease some of the tension. She had to give him credit for that.

Mimi placed her hand on Mark's arm. "Truce?"

He smiled gently at her. "Of course. But I'm not the one you really have the problem with."

"What's that supposed to mean?"

Mark shrugged. "I think you know."

# 13

# Lulu's Café

*Tuesday, February 13*

*12:17 p.m.*

"Gracie, you forgot the Caesar dressing," Felicia reprimanded good-naturedly. She picked through her salad with a fork for effect, as if she expected to find a dressing-filled ramekin.

"Caesar dressing." Gracie shook her head, off-loading Mimi's burger plate, Lisa's tuna melt, and Jennifer's turkey and swiss. "Whatever happened to plain old Thousand Island?"

"Can't make a Caesar salad with Thousand Island," Mimi said with an elbow to Gracie's hip. "Then you'd have a—"

"Yeah, yeah, I hear ya. Fancy salads . . . phooey." Gracie rolled her eyes at Mimi, then walked away, muttering, "I'll be back with your Caesar, Cleopatra."

"Speaking of queens, I had quite the encounter this week," Jennifer said after swallowing her first bite of turkey sandwich.

"Do tell," Felicia encouraged as she twisted around to remove her navy blue suit jacket. Lisa watched her and thought, *She looks beautiful as usual. I wonder how long it takes her to get ready in the morning?*

"Well, a week ago Saturday I was over at the park by my house," Jennifer began. Lisa could tell by her energetic tone that this was going to be a good story. "While I was there I ran into Pastor Scott—you know the priest I went to for counseling last year?"

They nodded.

"Well, I was filling him in on our need to make some decisions about having a baby—the whole IVF thing I was telling you about a few weeks ago?—and he offered to pray with me."

Mimi gulped some milk. "That's so much nicer instead of him just saying, 'I'll pray for you.' I think a lot of people say that and never do. But you hardly ever get someone who will just drop right there and kneel with you."

Lisa was eager to get to the meat of Jennifer's story. "So then what happened?"

"Okay, well, we were sitting on the park bench, and he put his hand on mine for prayer, when guess who comes prowling by in yellow Nikes?"

Mimi drummed her feet on the floor a few times in excitement. "The Katt!"

Jennifer nodded.

At the confirmation, Felicia gasped, her brown eyes electrified. "Did she say anything?"

"Nope, she just glowered at our hands and then at me and kept walking." Jennifer shrugged. "But I know I'm going to pay somehow, someway. You know Kitty never passes up an opportunity to contribute to someone's demise."

They sat quiet for a minute. *How dare Kitty treat Jennifer like that when we've been so honorable in keeping Kitty's son a secret,* Lisa thought. *You would think she'd reciprocate.*

"So did Pastor Scott have any good advice for you on the baby front?" Felicia asked.

"As a matter of fact, he really helped me confirm my thinking on IVF," Jennifer answered. "Sam and I talked about it—I didn't mention that some of my ideas came from Pastor Scott—and decided we would keep trying the natural way. And if it doesn't happen, it doesn't happen."

Although Jennifer appeared to be relieved at her decision, Lisa suspected that her outward casing hid a broken heart.

"I had a little surprise of my own on Sunday," said Mimi. "Remember that cop who pulled me over for sleeping on the road?"

The others nodded.

"Mark and I were doing the Meet and Greet after church, and wouldn't you know, here comes Officer McCarthy along with Vera Archer, one of our longtime members, who's his aunt, of all things." Mimi shook her head, clearly put off by this encounter.

*So what's the big deal?* "Was he rude to you?" Lisa asked, trying to get to the source of Mimi's disdain.

Mimi shot Lisa a look that said, "Why is this so difficult for you to understand?" then answered, "No, he wasn't rude to me at all." She crunched a fry in two. "It was just having to see him again, that's all."

"So you were embarrassed then?" Felicia didn't seem to know what Mimi was getting at either.

"No!" Mimi jumped a bit as she answered.

Felicia peered across at her. "Mimi, what on earth has you so riled up about this cop?"

Everyone stopped eating and stared at Mimi, who avoided their eyes. "I don't know. Maybe it's just hormones. Mark thinks I should go see Dr. O'Boyle about postpartum. I haven't exactly been feeling myself lately."

"Our Dr. O'Boyle always makes me feel a little better, even with all I've had to deal with," said Jennifer about their shared ob-gyn.

Felicia put on her soothing voice. "I think your problem might be lack of sleep. You're tired, Mimi, and it's affecting everything you're doing. The mind can play all kinds of games on you when you don't get enough rest."

Mimi seemed defeated. "You're probably right."

Lisa decided to change the subject. "Speaking of game playing, I'm getting ready to send Callie to jail and she will not be able to stop at Go or collect two hundred bucks."

Jennifer laughed. "Jail? You're kidding, right?"

Lisa wiped her mouth with her napkin. "Depends how you look at it.

For Callie, spending her spring break at my mom's will be jail. But I figured it might do her some good to be around a strong disciplinarian."

"I can't even imagine how difficult it must have been for you to ask your mom to do that," said Jennifer. While her mom and Lisa's mom seemed completely different on the outside, in comparing notes they'd found some peculiar similarities between them, such as their inability to comfort their own daughters.

"It was. I had to take it on the chin, but if it will help Callie, then I'm willing to do whatever it takes," said Lisa. "I love that girl, even though she seems to have no use for me anymore."

Mimi reached into her purse and pulled out three small white envelopes. "Your saying 'love' reminded me. Here's a Valentine for each of you, hand-made by Megan. I told her my lunch friends would appreciate them."

Lisa unfastened her envelope and pulled out the tiny card. The front said, "Love is . . ."

She opened it. The inside was colored purple around a white heart in the center with the word *God* written on it.

Lisa got tears in her eyes. Just a few years earlier, Callie had made her a similar card for Valentine's Day. But that was back when Callie still loved.

# 14

# Felicia

*Wednesday, February 14*

*8:58 a.m.*

Felicia nestled into her first-class seat. Ted was really pulling out all the stops. Not only had he arranged for a car to pick her up at LAX, he'd sent one all the way to Red River to ferry her to the Cincinnati airport. And then she'd arrived at the airport to find he'd upgraded her ticket, too.

"May I take your jacket, miss?"

Felicia sat forward and removed her navy suit jacket, then handed it across the empty seat to the perky young flight attendant. Felicia had already stuffed her winter coat into her checked luggage, figuring she wouldn't need it in LA, even in February.

"May I get you something to drink before takeoff?"

Felicia glanced across the aisle and saw two men drinking beer—at 9 a.m.? "Just some water would be nice," she answered. *I could get used to this . . . but I'd better not. Pastors' wives don't fly first class. Well, unless you're Victoria Osteen.*

The flight attendant—"Lacy" according to her badge—reached in to place a bottle of water on the arm divider, then backed away so the man behind her could take the empty seat next to Felicia. Before he sat, he silently removed his suit coat and handed it to Lacy, who dutifully whisked it away and into the closet.

"Thank you, and could I get a ginger ale?" he called after her, then glanced over at Felicia as he scooted his large frame out of the aisle and into the blue leather seat. Felicia noticed that his brownish-red hair was perfectly combed, and he was wearing an appealing cologne.

"Whew," he said, buckling his seat belt. "Didn't think I was going to make it in time."

Felicia normally didn't talk to people next to her on airplanes. One time she'd made the mistake of asking a woman reading *Purpose-Driven Life* what she thought of it and had suffered the next four hours of Chatty Cathy's monologue—all the way from LA to Cincinnati.

But she thought she might risk it in first class, especially with a guy in what she recognized as an Italian suit that cost well over a thousand dollars. Surely he would have more sophistication than to chew her ear off the whole flight. And with her job on the line, a chance to network was always good, too.

"Oh, did you have to come a long way?" she asked, averting her brown eyes and trying to sound nonchalant, even though she was really curious about him.

"Just flew in from Boston. We were late getting out of there. Snowed last night."

"Oh, yeah, I saw that on the weather report this morning. So do you live there, or is LA home for you?"

"Neither. I came up from New York a few days ago, did some work in Boston, and now I'm stuck in LA for the next week." Lacy handed him a napkin and a glass brimming with ginger ale. He took a sip. "Trade shows. How about you?"

"I live here. I'm going to my company's main office for some meetings. But I'm originally *from* LA." Did she add that last part so he wouldn't think she was some sort of bumpkin from Ohio?

"Huh, lucky us, I guess. Getting to leave winter for a while. But I have to say, I can't stand Southern California. So fake."

Felicia was saved from having to answer because Lacy came by to swipe their glasses, then the preflight instructions began. While the plane was taxiing and launching into the sky, she remembered Dave's parting words to her that morning: "No matter where you go, *mi amor,* you will always be my Valentine."

She felt bad leaving him on Valentine's Day—and Nicholas, too—but she couldn't help but be excited to get back to LA for the first time in months. The meeting schedule would give her a chance to visit with her parents and sisters, plus time for shopping and relaxation in some longed-for sunshine and clear skies.

Once they were in the air, Lacy and the other flight attendant began passing out trays with omelets, fruit, and cinnamon rolls on them. When Felicia and her seatmate received theirs, Felicia decided she might as well continue the conversation with him.

"I'm actually going there to try and save my office," she said between bites of cantaloupe. "My boss wants to close the Cincinnati branch and move me to Chicago."

The man nodded. "Chicago! Wouldn't that be an improvement over Cincinnati?"

"No. Well, maybe. But my husband is a pastor, and he's just getting the church turned around and growing again. So I can't ask him to move."

"Oh, so you're a pastor's wife." He chuckled.

Felicia smiled carefully. "What's so funny about that?"

"Nothing, except you don't usually think of an Ohio pastor's wife as a hot Latina sitting in first class and wearing a Ralph Lauren suit with Armani pumps."

Felicia wasn't sure whether to be offended or complimented by his description. Judging from his tone, she chose the latter. "Wow, you really know your women's clothes. Do you shop for your wife?"

The man handed his tray to Lacy, then reached over and handed off Felicia's napkin-covered tray as well. "No, not married. But I'm in the clothing business. I saw a version of that suit you're wearing almost a year ago in the New York shows."

Felicia's interest was immediately piqued. Clothes, especially designer brands, were her favorite guilty pleasure. "Yeah, well, this might be my last suit if I can't keep a job. You're right about pastors' wives—we normally don't wear designer labels. We can't ask the church to include a clothing allowance in the budget."

The man laughed again and extended his hand over the seat divider. "Randall Simons, by the way."

Felicia shook his hand and smiled. "Felicia Lopez-Morrison."

"Oh, and she's a hyphenator, too," Randall said in mock appall. "You must have caused quite a stir coming to Cincinnati with all of your LA sensibilities."

*If only you knew,* Felicia thought. "Mmm, well, it was a challenge at first. But I'm really settling in now. And you'll love this: We don't even live in Cincinnati. We live in a small town about forty miles out called Red River."

"Red River! Sounds very *Little House on the Prairie.*"

"It can be." The more she talked, the more Felicia felt herself letting go of the Midwest and yearning for California. Had she merely convinced herself that everything was okay in Ohio when in fact her heart was still in Hollywood?

"So how do you hope to save your job? You planning to beg at the feet of your boss?"

Felicia got a kick out of Randall's forward New York style. It was fun to talk with a guy who understood the business world. She and Dave used to talk business, but once he became a pastor, it was all about "worship styles" and "ministry outcomes." A sort of business, for sure, but not one related to her work world. "No, but I do have a surprise for him. I nailed a huge account last week. I'm hoping it will be the boost we need to keep the Cincinnati office open."

"Account?" Randall shifted in his seat. "You in advertising?"

Felicia realized she'd never said what her business was. "No, public relations."

They went on talking for a few minutes, sharing office war stories. Then Randall said, "Excuse me," and slipped out of his seat. Felicia figured the conversation was over, so she reached down to her bag on the floor to pull out some work folders and a legal pad.

When Randall returned from the bathroom, he popped open the overhead, slid out some folders of his own, and hunkered back down into his seat. "Felicia," he said leaning over slightly to get her attention, "what would you think about coming into the clothing business? We're expanding, and we could use a savvy PR person. I suspect you might be just the ticket. And you wouldn't have to leave Cincinnati—I mean, Red River—but you would need to travel some. The rest of the time you could work from a home office."

He handed Felicia a job description. As she read over it, she could feel the goose bumps on her arms and legs. Had the Lord brought Randall to her with this job offer?

Felicia continued parsing the document and asking Randall questions. Soon she was making notes on her ledger. Before she knew it, the pilot announced that the plane was preparing to land. With this opportunity in hand, Felicia felt like rebooking her flight back to Cincinnati and skipping the LA meetings. But she did want to see her friends and family.

Felicia and Randall continued talking as they walked off the plane. Once they were in the terminal, Randall set down his briefcase and pulled a business card from his pocket. Felicia reached into her purse to do the same.

But when she raised her head, she saw him writing on the back of his card. "Here's my cell number," he said, handing her the card. His eyes dropped to her legs and crept slowly up her body until they met hers. "I'll be here 'til Tuesday. Why don't you call and we can get together?"

Randall's tone had changed from business to anything-but. Felicia felt herself shaking as she handed him back his card and returned hers to her purse. "Maybe you misunderstood me, Randall," she said as she flung her purse over her shoulder, "but I am *married*."

As she quickly walked away toward baggage return, she heard him say, "So? Hey, come back. What about the job?"

*I'm on my way to find out,* she thought, determined more than ever to maintain her hard-won success at Brown & McGrory.

# 15

# Jennifer

*Thursday, February 15*
*5:45 p.m.*

*I should have come when it was still light out,* Jennifer thought as she pulled her car to the curb and parked it with the engine still running. She flipped on the dome light and rechecked the directions to Jessica Graham's new apartment.

*Just two streets over from Mother's. Maybe I should . . . no. Why bother? After all these years, if Mother had wanted to get in touch with me, she would have. She knows I married the pastor of the church. She could have found me if she'd wanted to.*

Jessica's street address in her mind, Jennifer steered her car back onto the crunchy, icy road. *They just had to find Jessica an apartment in this part of town.* Her mind strained to remember the last time she'd been in the south section of Red River. Could it have been since she left home at eighteen to escape her mentally ill mother and abusive stepfather?

Even in the dark, just driving past familiar old stores and Sigmund Elementary polluted Jennifer's memory with images of her growing-up years. The sour feeling in her stomach was why she'd avoided this area of town for so many years.

And now here she was, pulling back the curtain on her tragic childhood because she was making a visit to pregnant Jessica, a client of the women's shelter where she volunteered. Jennifer had taken a special interest in Jessica because she'd been at the shelter the night Jessica had arrived. Barely pregnant, Jessica was estranged from her abusive cop husband, and her young face was already haggard from what she'd endured. Jennifer saw a bit of herself in the girl as she remembered her own years of abuse at the hands of her stepfather and then the boyfriend she lived with before finally escaping to the shelter herself and later becoming a Christian.

"I can do all things through Christ who strengtheneth me," she sang aloud, preparing herself for seeing Jessica.

Pulling into a parking space in front of the plain, run-down apartment complex, Jennifer buttoned her coat and then reached across the seat for the grocery bag she'd packed at home. She figured Jessica would make good use of the boxes of ready-to-mix pastas and a few pastries she'd culled from her kitchen in an effort to diet.

"Jennifer!" Jessica said in her Kentucky drawl, her brown hair blowing back with the breeze upon opening the door. "Stella said you might be by tonight. I can use the company, girl."

Jennifer stepped inside. *Is that cigarette smoke I smell?* "Well, I brought you some treats. You know, since you're eating for two and all."

"Oh, Jennifer, you have no idea. I'm just eatin' everything in sight these days. The guys down at the garage said I'm like one of those animals with the long nose, an . . . what're they called?"

"Anteater?"

Jessica set the sack on the coffee table and nodded, easing herself onto the sofa. While Jessica pulled boxes out of the bag, Jennifer sat next to her and took a moment to glance around. The apartment, rented jointly by the shelter and by Jessica to help her get on her feet after she left Ron, her husband, was spartan but clean. Still, that smoke odor . . .

"Now how far along are you again, Jess?"

Jessica stopped foraging and sat up, proudly rubbing her growing abdomen. "About two more months. She'll be borned around the end of April, the clinic doc says."

"And how's the job going?" The shelter had also gotten her a position as a customer service rep at a muffler shop down the street.

"Great! You know, some of those guys who work there are hawwwt." Jessica giggled and pointed at her stomach. "But they'd never pay me no never mind with this big ol' belly a-stickin' out there. Kinda like cold water on a hot fire, ya know?"

*Good grief,* Jennifer thought in contrast to her smiling nod, *here you are pregnant by a husband who beat you and living partially on assistance, yet you're still thinking about getting it on with every guy you see.*

Her disgust showed slightly in her tone when she asked, "Uh, Jessica, do I smell cigarette smoke in here? I'm sure your doctor's told you it's not healthy for your baby if you smoke—"

"Oh, that wasn't me," Jessica said, stuffing a Pop-tart from Jennifer's snack sack into her mouth.

"Well then, you should ask your friends not to smoke when they come over." Jennifer fancied herself a sort of obstetrician after all she'd read on fertility and pregnancy. "Even secondhand smoke is harmful."

Jessica looked away and finished chewing. Because she'd been working with her through the shelter since late August, Jennifer knew Jessica's facial expressions well. She didn't like what she was seeing this time.

"Ronny don't take no for an answer if he wants to light up," Jessica said in a near-whisper, her right hand nervously fingering a small heart pendant around her neck.

Jennifer jumped up off the couch and faced Jessica, her hands on her hips. She'd been trying to adapt the shelter director Stella's calm demeanor, but cool and composed were not members of Jennifer's personality team. "What? Ron was here? Jessica, he's not even allowed closer to you than five hundred feet, let alone in your apartment! How does he know where you live?"

Jessica hung her head. Jennifer could see the tears trickling down. She started to admonish herself for overreacting, then reconsidered. Ron, a police sergeant, had beaten Jessica numerous times before she finally came to the shelter in an effort to save her baby. How could Jessica allow him near her now?

Jessica lifted her head, her face flushed and wet. "I know, Jennifer. I know. Please don't be mad at me. I shouldn't have let him in. But he was outside cryin' and tellin' me he loved me. I didn't want the neighbors to hear."

Jennifer came back around and sat on the couch with Jessica. She pulled a few tissues from her purse and handed them to her. "But why did you tell him where you live?" she said in a more compassionate tone. "Now we're going to need to move you again to keep you safe."

"Oh, ol' Jamal told him. You know, the guy I—"

"That other cop you slept with to get back at Ron?"

"Yeah, that one. He was always so nice to me, so I just called him to see how he was doin', ya know? We talked about what I'm doin' now and that I got my own place. But then he said he wanted to get back together. When I told him I didn't think that was a good idea right now, he got mad at me and hung up. The next day Ronny shows up here, knockin' on my door like some kind of grovelin' ol' puppy dog. I didn't think he'd ever want anything to do with me again after he found out I had slept with a black guy. But he said that didn't matter anymore."

She smiled. The false sense of security that Jessica was obviously feeling alarmed Jennifer. Volunteering at the shelter, she'd seen the pattern again and again: Women had returned to "promising" husbands, only to be beaten even more severely. And she knew firsthand what those beatings felt like. But she had been one of the fortunate ones. After escaping to the shelter, she got a job at the church and eventually became a Christian. It was at that church that she met and married Sam. So she knew women could rise from the depths of those terrible relationships, but she also knew many continued in the cycle until they were physically incapacitated from their injuries—or killed.

"Jessica," Jennifer said gently, shifting on the sofa to better see her, "he *will* hit you again. And you have two people to consider now, not just you."

Jessica shook her head. "No, I don't think so. The police kicked him off the force when that Sergeant Steph reported him." Stephanie was a formerly abused wife who'd become a police officer and the city's primary domestic violence enforcer. "But he got hired by the county sheriffs. They told him he couldn't get any more dings on his record, though. So he's bein' good."

*Yeah, for how long?* Jennifer thought, but decided not to push the issue. She could see Jessica was blinded by whatever love she felt for Ron. She tried a different tactic. "Okay, well, until you know for sure if he really has changed, why don't you agree to meet him in public places only? Like for dinner or a movie or something. I mean, it *is* good that he wants to be part of your life, with the baby coming and all."

Jessica considered her curiously. "This baby ain't gonna be one bit helpful to us gettin' back together. But I hear what you're sayin' about seein' him where there's people around. I'd feel a little better about that, too."

Jennifer stood to leave. "He'll come around about the baby, Jessica, if he really wants to make this work and stop abusing you. I don't know how anyone couldn't be excited about a new baby." She knew her words would sound hollow if Jessica knew that Jennifer's own dad had ditched her mother before Jennifer was born because he didn't want kids.

She noticed Jessica giving her another odd look but she didn't say anything about it, instead instructing, "Make sure you lock the door when I leave. And don't let Ron in again. Okay?"

"Okay." Jessica nodded, walking behind her to the door.

Back in her car, Jennifer decided a zip by her mother's wouldn't hurt anything. She was interested to see if the place had completely fallen down by now—her mother was always too sick to keep it up, and her stepfather too lazy. She remembered the day she'd left home. The first step off the porch had broken as her foot fell on it, which she'd taken as an ominous sign about returning.

*Let's see, there's the Morrows', and the Zeldamans', and . . . wait, is that it?* Jennifer pulled her car alongside her old house. It was almost brand-new! Sure it was dark out, but she could see the house had been sided and it had all new windows. The front porch light illuminated little heart decorations on the windows for Valentine's Day. For a second, Jennifer thought maybe the house had been sold, but she saw her mother's old beat-up Toyota in the driveway, so she knew it was still hers.

Driving away, Jennifer felt a battle raging inside her. Optimism and pessimism were duking it out. Ron was so consumed by anger that he beat his pregnant wife, and her mother was a complete disaster as a parent because she took drugs she didn't need instead of the medication that would help her. Now Ron was being all lovey-dovey with Jessica, and her mother was living in a nice house. Could people really change that much—or is it just easy to fix up the outside while the inside is a powder keg waiting to be ignited?

# CHAPTER

# 16

# Felicia

Felicia could smell the carne asada from the moment she opened the taxi door. As she was handing her fare over the seat to the driver, she heard a squeal from the front of her parents' house.

"Mija," her mom called with open arms. "Come here and let us see you."

Felicia smiled broadly as she hoisted herself and her luggage out of the car, shut the door behind her, and scampered to where her mom stood in the middle of the yard. She wrapped herself around her petite but rotund mother. "Oh, Mama, it is so good to see you."

"Lupita, let the girl breathe," Felicia's dad chided gently as he joined them outside the house. Felicia broke her embrace with her mother to snuggle into her dad's ample arms.

"Papa," she said affectionately.

Soon the modest front lawn was filled with Felicia's family, who spilled out of the house. First came her younger sister, Maria, with her husband, Javier, and their daughter, Estella. Then her older sister, Gina, appeared, holding the hand of an Asian man Felicia didn't recognize.

"And who is this?" Felicia asked eagerly after hugging Gina. Felicia's mom was worried that Gina, who was thirty-eight, was never going to marry, so Felicia wondered if this was a new prospect.

"We just met him tonight, too," Lupita said in what Felicia thought was a hesitant tone.

Gina shot her mother a look, then turned back to Felicia. "This is Li, Felicia. We've been dating for a few months now."

Felicia noticed her mom shaking her head as she trekked back into the house to check on dinner. "Fifi, you have a run in your hose," she called behind her as she walked, using her pet name for Felicia.

Felicia inspected them—*What's new?* she thought as she, resigned, dug through her purse for a replacement. By the time she looked up again, everyone had followed her mother, leaving Gina, Li, and Felicia outside.

She smiled at Li and shook his hand. "Listen, Li. You should have seen the reaction when I brought Dave home—he was the first non-Mexican guy any of us had ever dated. They'll get over it."

Li appeared noticeably relieved as he let go of Felicia's hand and put an arm around Gina, who was slightly taller than Felicia but shared her glossy black hair and fit form. "Well, it's not like we're heading to the altar tomorrow or anything."

Gina rolled her deep brown eyes, which were almost identical to Felicia's. "The altar? Ha! I'm way beyond that."

Felicia wasn't sure where Gina's sudden disdain for marriage was coming from, but Gina had always been the one in the family who rebelled against any rules, so this was probably just one more way to voice her distaste for the family's traditional values. Their mom had mentioned to Felicia on the phone that she'd been worried about Gina's behavior lately, but Felicia had taken that with a grain of salt. Her mom was a champion worrier.

The trio made their way into the austere house—the same one Felicia and her sisters had grown up in. Surveying the room, Felicia wondered how they all had managed to live in that tiny house for so many years. Only two bedrooms and one bathroom for five people! Her Red River house had four bedrooms and three bathrooms just for her, Dave, and Nicholas.

Felicia tossed her purse on the floor and slipped off her shoes, then threw her suit jacket on a chair. She hadn't had time to return to the hotel after her last meeting, so she was noticeably overdressed, which made her uncomfortable. She always tried hard to fit in with her family and not shove her financial success in their faces.

"Can I help?" she asked after deciding to skip changing her hose. She slipped behind the pulled-out dining room table set for eight and into the kitchen. Maria and their mom—both wearing aprons—were scurrying around the small kitchen pouring pots of spicy delicacies into bowls and chopping last-minute onion and tomato garnishes.

"No . . . oh, look out there. See what I mean?" Felicia followed the point of her mother's paring knife out the kitchen window to the backyard, where Gina was sitting on Li's lap, kissing him passionately. He held a lit cigarette in one hand, while his other arm—tattooed with a Chinese symbol—was wrapped tightly around Gina's waist.

Javier snickered. "Good thing your dad's not seeing this," he said to Maria.

Felicia thought Maria was the image of their mother at her age, with her chunky midsection and her sticklike legs, her black hair piled on her head in a clip. Maria peered out the window as she was pouring a pot of posole into a serving bowl and shot her eyes back to the pot. "That's just gross," she said with a disdain even Felicia found off-putting. Felicia wasn't thrilled to see her older sister's display of affection, especially for a tattooed smoker, but she was willing to give the relationship the benefit of the doubt.

Once the table was full of food—nearly groaning, Felicia thought— Lupita convinced her husband to turn off the Lakers game and join them at the table for dinner. Everyone clasped hands in preparation to give thanks, as they always had.

Felicia's dad turned to Li, who had his right hand intertwined with Gina's but the left one barely touching Javier's. Javier, a stocky butcher with a buzz cut, didn't seem too excited to be holding hands with Li either, which amused Felicia. Why were men so afraid to touch each other? "Li, we like to pray our thanks to God before we eat in this house," Felicia's dad said hesitantly. "I don't know what your religious beliefs are but—"

"Papa, just pray!" Gina interrupted with a nasty tone. "The food's getting cold, and we don't have all day for a speech on religion."

Felicia was taken aback at her sister's outburst. She was glad they could bow their heads to put some space between them and Gina's hateful words.

Felicia's dad had just said "Amen" when Felicia heard her cell phone ringing a few feet away in the living room. She popped up, but her dad motioned for her to sit again. "We don't answer the phone during dinner," he said, as if she were sixteen.

She ignored him—igniting a triumphant laugh from Gina—and slid behind Maria's chair to grab the phone on its last ring. "Hello?" she answered, out of breath.

"Hi, Felicia?" It was Becky.

"Oh, hi, Becky. We were just sitting down to dinner and—"

"Well, I'm sorry, but I'm putting Nicholas down for the night so I thought you might want to talk to him first."

Felicia saw everyone sitting quietly at the table. Among the many Lopez family rules, one was no one could eat until everyone was seated. "Uh, Becky, I do want to talk to him, but can you just keep him up about twenty more minutes? We're getting ready to eat and—"

"No, I'm sorry, Felicia. It's nine o'clock, and that's bedtime. Here, Nicholas, talk to Mommy."

Felicia couldn't believe Becky's firmness. When did her skittishness morph into resolve? "Hi, Mommy!"

Felicia's heart leapt at hearing Nicholas's voice. "Hi, my boy. How are you doing? Are you having fun with Becky and Eli?"

"Uh-huh!" Felicia could hear the excitement in Nicholas's voice. "Today was . . ." she heard Becky whisper a prompt in the background, "Shabbat." He treated the Hebrew word delicately, as if it might break.

She suddenly remembered that Friday night and Saturday are the Jewish Sabbath.

"Oh, Shabbat," she repeated casually as if she knew what it meant. She didn't want to scare him. "And how was that?"

"Well, Becky let me help her make this really cool bread in braids," he said excitedly. "And then at dinner she lit some candles and let me blow out the match."

That didn't sound so bad. "Well, looks like you're learning some new things," she said encouragingly.

"Yeah, and tomorrow we're going to"—she heard Becky whisper to him again—"sin-a-dog."

Felicia laughed, matching the muffled guffaws she heard from Becky. "I think you mean *synagogue*, Nicholas." Then the panic of what that meant returned to her. "I think it's your bedtime and I need to talk to Becky again. So you be good, and I love you. You know that, right?"

"Mm-hmmm. *Laila tov,* Mommy."

She asked, "What?" But he had already handed the phone over to Becky, whom Felicia could hear saying, "Good, Nicholas! Now go brush your teeth, please."

"That's 'good night' in Hebrew," Becky said into the phone. Felicia wasn't sure whether to be happy at her son's new skill or not.

"Oh. Well, I need to run, Becky." Her family did not appear to be waiting patiently. "But about synagogue—"

"Don't worry. They have a kids' class, so he won't actually be in with us. And I promise not to make him a Jesus-hater before you get back."

Felicia felt bad that Becky had picked up on her doubt. "Becky, I didn't think that at all. It's just that he's so young. I don't want to confuse him." She sighed and decided to drop the subject. "But how is he with the biting? Has he tried it on you or Eli?"

"Not once. I keep watching for it, but nothing."

"Good, good, good!" Felicia was relieved. Maybe he was finally over this "phase."

After thanking Becky profusely and saying good-bye, Felicia turned off her phone and slipped it back into her purse. When she returned to the

A MATTER OF WIFE & DEATH

table, everyone started filling their plates as if someone had flipped a switch and juiced their batteries.

"Everything okay back home?" Maria asked, tearing a tortilla into small pieces for Estella.

"Yeah. I just hate being away from him, though," Felicia said.

Javier handed her the ceviche, and said, "So how were your meetings? Did you save your job?"

Felicia dropped her shoulders and looked at her mother, who must have felt Felicia's eyes but didn't meet them. "Mom, I told you that in private. Dave doesn't even know."

Her mom handed the carne asada platter to Li, ignoring Felicia for the moment. "This is beef, Li," she said somewhat condescendingly.

Gina picked up her mother's tone right away. "Mom, he didn't just get off the boat. Li was born in LA, too. He's eaten Mexican food before."

Lupita moved from one anxious daughter to the other. "Felicia, Dave is 2,200 miles away. He won't know what we know."

*That's not the point,* Felicia thought, but she kept it to herself. One contentious daughter at this table was enough.

"Why don't you just answer Javier and we'll all agree it's our secret?" her father inserted calmly. Felicia always thought she got her PR skills from her dad, who was the family's peacemaker.

Felicia nodded. "Yeah, okay. Well, the short story is that he gave me a formal offer to take over the Chicago office." She dipped a forkful of meat into some salsa. "But when he did that, I showed him the $500,000 contract I'd negotiated with National City Bank."

Javier whistled through his teeth. "Whoa! How did you get that?"

Felicia finished chewing, then said, "A new guy at our church is their retired CEO, but he still goes up to Cleveland to golf with the current CEO. When he heard the bank was shopping for a new PR firm, he suggested they give Brown & McGrory a try. And I took it from there."

Felicia's dad beamed. He and Lupita were Mexican immigrants who had opened and run a small but steady bakery for forty years, so he was clearly pleased at his daughter's business success. "Did that make your boss happy?" he asked simply.

"It better have!" She laughed. "But he wouldn't make me any promises. He said he'd run the numbers and give me a call next week. I feel pretty confident that it did the trick, though."

Estella started to cry, taking the focus off Felicia while Maria and Lupita both attempted to soothe the two-year-old.

Hearing Estella shifted Felicia into mommy mode and made her long for Nicholas and Dave. As much as she had been enjoying LA's weather, restaurants, shopping, and especially seeing her family, she was surprised at how much she missed Red River and her life there.

*Please, Lord, show Ted how to make Cincinnati work for the company. Please.*

# Lisa

*Saturday, February 17*
*2:47 p.m.*

For the past couple of weeks, Lisa had felt guilty about Joel's and her plans to send Callie to her grandmother's for spring break. She'd doubled up on her prayer efforts, asking God to soften Callie's attitude, to make her more open and loving. But God was silent—either because he wasn't listening, or he was listening but just didn't want to answer right away. At least that's how it felt to Lisa.

Callie seemed to be slipping further and further from her family. She spent endless hours in her room with her door closed, usually on the phone with Theresa—when she wasn't grounded—or listening to music.

While Joel and Ricky had gone to the church to play some basketball in the fellowship hall/gymnasium, Lisa decided to bake a batch of Callie's favorite Snickerdoodle cookies to break the ice. She took the still warm cookies along with a Cherry Diet Pepsi (she knew Callie would gasp at the thought of drinking milk) to Callie's room and knocked softly on the door.

"What?" Callie said in a clipped tone from her room, not even bothering to walk to the door to open it. Such a common courtesy was apparently too much of a strain for the almost fifteen-year-old. Bless her heart.

"I have something for you."

"What is it?"

Lisa was determined to be patient, but what she really wanted to do was pull the door from its hinges, as if that might somehow stop Callie from shutting her out—both physically and emotionally. Instead she answered calmly, "Cookies. Your favorite."

There was a pause, in which Lisa wasn't sure Callie had heard what she'd said. Finally, Callie opened the door just enough for her to reach through and take the plate Lisa held out for her. But as Callie reached out, Lisa pulled back the plate. "Can I come in? I'd like to share these with you."

A heavy, melodramatic sigh escaped from Callie's mouth. The kind of exhale only a professional teenager can accomplish. "If you have to," she said, leaving the door and walking across to a small desk at the far side of the room.

Lisa entered slowly. *What a dump,* she thought as she spied the piles of dirty clothes strewn about the room, flung over a desk chair, or just dropped wherever Callie removed them. Her dresser was covered with jewelry, bottles of perfume, makeup, and a huge collection of lip gloss. The bed looked as though the sheets had not been changed since Moses parted the Red Sea. Lisa knew this because, of course, the bed was unmade. *Too bad all those hours she spends up here aren't put to good use, say, by cleaning.*

"They're still warm." Lisa passed the plate to Callie. "And . . ." She held up the soda. "I know they probably won't taste all that great together, but you can have it for later."

Callie took the can, then lifted a cookie off the top of the pile and began to nibble on it. Lisa wondered if Callie was secretly pleased about the treat but couldn't say anything because it would break her mean-girl cover.

Lisa grabbed a cookie and laid the plate on the desk next to one of Callie's textbooks. "How's history coming?"

"Fine."

"What are you studying?"

"The Civil War."

*Ha. A house divided against itself cannot stand. I wish she'd study the civil war she's engaged in right here.* "I always liked reading about the Civil War. Do you enjoy it?"

"It's okay."

*Just talk to her. Be honest.* "What's your favorite part?"

"I don't know."

"I always liked studying about Gettysburg. Have you gotten to that battle yet?"

"Yeah."

*Talk to her!* "Have you read Lincoln's Gettysburg Address?"

Callie sighed again and finished her cookie. Looking bored, she replied blandly, "Yeah."

Lisa picked a lint ball off her sweater. *Stop avoiding and TALK TO HER!*

"When do you think you're going to get around to cleaning this room?" Doh! Totally the wrong thing to say! Lisa watched Callie make an exasperated face. "Sorry," Lisa said quickly, trying to smooth things over. *Way to go, Lis. Real good.* She grabbed another cookie. "Listen, Callie, we haven't talked for a while. We used to talk all the time. Want to tell me what's bothering you?"

Callie responded by picking up *Seventeen* magazine from one of the piles on the floor and beginning to flip through it.

*Okay, this is going well.* "It's just that I'm . . . we're . . . concerned about you."

Callie's eyes remained glued to the glossy pages, but she did huff slightly.

"You just seem so unhappy," Lisa pressed. "And if I could help you . . ."

"Right," Callie muttered under her breath.

Lisa grew exasperated herself—even though she didn't make the face that went with it, which Callie had perfected. "Well, the fact is, something needs to change. We'd like you to talk to us about what you're going through, but if you don't want to, that's your choice. What isn't your choice, however, is the level of work you'll do for school." Lisa tapped the history book. "You know, if you want to pull this attitude act with us, that's one thing. But when your grades suffer and when you feel you don't have to go to church anymore, then we really have a problem. Since you don't want to listen, and you're not interested in communicating with us, you leave us little choice about our next option."

Callie stiffened but still didn't say anything.

"We've grounded you. And that didn't work. We've given you extra chores, and that didn't work. We've tried to be patient and gracious. But frankly, we are all tired of walking around on eggshells because of you. So your father and I have decided that for spring break, you're going to stay with Grandma and Grandpa Jenkins."

That did the trick. Callie whirled around in her seat. "What? You can't do that!"

"Actually, Callie, we can, and we did. It's already settled, and they're expecting you."

"I don't want to spend *my spring break* with them."

"Sorry."

"Yeah, I bet you are. And where does *sweet, precious Ricky* get to go? Camping with Steve? Hawaii?"

Callie's fury, leveled at her brother, surprised Lisa. "Ricky doesn't concern you. And anyway, he doesn't seem to have the attitude issues that you do."

Callie rolled her tear-filled, angry eyes. "Right. So what you're saying is that if I were more like my brother, I wouldn't be punished."

*Where is this kid getting this stuff?* Lisa wondered incredulously. "Callie, this isn't about Ricky. And believe me, we're not comparing you to him."

"And you're also not sending him to stay with Grandma and Grandpa."

Lisa wasn't going to get into the tangled argument any further. "Look on the bright side," she said, trying to bring the conflict back around. "You'll be rid of us for a week."

"Yeah, that's great. I get rid of you and get an even worse place to be."

Lisa chuckled inside. She had to admit she agreed with her daughter—although she would never acknowledge it. At least not to Callie. And certainly not right now. "Well, consider it a character builder. I'll leave the cookies for you." Lisa turned to go, fully expecting the girl to spew some mean comment, such as "I hate you," which Lisa had now heard several times with such passion. But Callie didn't say anything.

Lisa had just gotten to the door when Callie said, "Maybe I'll just run away."

Before Lisa could think, she spun around and her words just popped out. "Fine, but you'll need to leave everything here, including those clothes, since your father and I bought all those, so technically they're not yours. Take only what actually belongs to you, that *you* bought. That stash of lip gloss is yours for the taking."

Not waiting for an answer, Lisa turned and walked out. She heard a guttural *ugh,* then a loud *crrrack* as Callie's foot connected with the door to slam it shut. Lisa kept walking. She'd let Joel handle that one.

# CHAPTER 18

# Felicia

*Thursday, February 22*
*7:48 p.m.*

*Make a matzoh, pat, pat, pat.*
*Do not make it fat, fat, fat.*
*Make the matzoh nice and flat.*
*Bake the matzoh just like that.*

Felicia rubbed her forehead with her hand. She'd retreated to her home office—something she tried not to do on weeknights—to get away from Nicholas and his singing Play-Doh act, but he'd followed her into the office anyway. A few days with Becky and he had become Tevye from *Fiddler on the Roof*, it seemed to Felicia.

"Nicholas, why don't you go do your thing on the dining room table?" she suggested. If she didn't get some quiet to finish her report on prospective clients, she wouldn't be able to e-mail it to Ted before morning. He'd given her until April 1 to come up with an additional $250,000 in accounts in order to keep the Cincinnati office open, so she was scurrying nearly 24/7 to piece them together.

"Dad said I can't be in there cuz he's reading some dumb book," Nicholas responded as he smashed down balls of dough on the hardwood floor.

"Well, how about the family room then?"

"I can't do Play-Doh on the carpet. You said so, Mom."

He was right: She had forbidden Play-Doh anywhere near their new carpet. The stuff was like colored mud when it was mashed into carpet fibers.

Felicia sighed and hit Save on her computer, then spun around to face Nicholas on the floor. "Okay, then," she said sternly, "you can stay in here, but you need to be quiet. No singing."

Nicholas was unmoved. "Mom, you have to sing the song when you do this. Becky said so."

"Nicholas, you don't have to sing."

"Yes, you do."

"Well, sing it in your head then. To yourself."

"No."

Felicia had had enough. The pressure to get so much new business in such a short time was weighing heavily on her. Plus, Dave had returned from the pastors' conference even more energized to grow the church, so he'd been at meetings the last three evenings, leaving Felicia to entertain Nicholas instead of tackling the extra work she needed to do.

She catapulted out of her chair and grabbed Nicholas by his little arm, intending to deposit him next to Dave.

Instead, Nicholas reached around and clamped his mouth on her wrist. The impact caught her off-guard—he hadn't bitten her or Dave since returning from Becky's a few days ago—and she let go. Nicholas took the opportunity to run to his room and slam the door behind him.

Felicia pushed up her sweatshirt sleeve and checked her arm. He'd broken the skin! *Good thing it's winter, and I'm wearing long sleeves to work or someone might think I'm a battered wife.*

She crouched down and scooped Nicholas's Play-Doh into the corresponding colored cans. *I shouldn't have pulled him so hard, but he has to learn he can't just say no like that,* she reasoned.

Standing up, Felicia gathered the cans in her arms and went out to the living room. "Your son just bit me again," she said with an "If you were doing your part, he wouldn't have done this" tone.

"What do you want me to do about it?" Dave asked, clearly not wanting to be bothered.

It didn't take much to push Felicia's buttons these days, but Dave's lack of interest infuriated her more than the bite. She was already preparing herself for potential failure at work, so the thought of enduring yet another dismal period in her marriage—as she had last year—was more than she could bear.

"How about playing with him for a while so I can get some work done?" she snapped. "You've been gone for the last three nights being a pastor. It's your turn to be a parent now."

Dave ran his hand through his blond hair. "It's not like I'm sitting here reading *Sports Illustrated*, Felicia. I'm skimming this book for part of my sermon."

"I thought you did sermon prep on Fridays."

"Normally I do, but I have a full day of visitation tomorrow because I was gone last week. And Saturday I'm going with the youth on their snow-shoveling fund-raiser."

Felicia shifted the Play-Doh from the bitten arm—which was starting to sting—to the other one. Dave still didn't know about the prospect that her office would be closing, and she wasn't about to tell him when he was so stressed about the church. "Well." She softened her tone. "He's probably cried himself to sleep by now anyway. Maybe he'll sleep for the next four days."

Dave started to smile in agreement, then Felicia noticed the grin slip away and a serious look return. He jutted his chin, indicating something behind her.

She spun around, nearly losing the Play-Doh cans, to find Nicholas standing quietly, near tears, behind her.

"I wanna go to Becky's!" he yelled, then turned and ran back to his bedroom, where Felicia could hear him fling himself onto his bed and sob into his pillow.

# 19

# Lulu's Café

*Tuesday, February 27*

*11:58 a.m.*

Jennifer eased into the booth, purposefully early. She wanted to be the first there so she could prepare her little "skit" for the girls. But she had to figure out a way to wipe from her face the smile that had been firmly in place for the past twenty-seven hours.

"What's got you all bright-eyed and bushy-tailed?" Gracie asked as she dropped off four mini glasses of water. "You look like one of those TV preachers—you know the ones who want your money for some piece of junk coin or prayer cloth or something?"

Jennifer bit the insides of her cheeks to make her mouth dissolve into seriousness. "Gracie, don't let them know you saw me smiling, okay?"

Gracie studied her with the usual mix of road-worn pessimism and simple compassion. "Whatever you say, whatever you say."

She continued on to take the next table's order just in time for Jennifer to see Mimi and Lisa enter. Before they could get a gander at her expression, she hung her head.

"Hey, why the long face, cupcake?" asked Mimi as she slid across from Jennifer. Lisa climbed into the booth next to Mimi.

*Stay sullen.* "Uh, I'll explain once Felicia's here."

She could feel Mimi's and Lisa's eyes on her, but she kept her gaze downward for fear of meeting their eyes and revealing her true emotions. No one said anything, although she could sense Mimi and Lisa giving each other questioning looks.

About a minute later, Felicia came in and sat next to Jennifer. Felicia must have seen the other two faces and Jennifer's posture and assumed something was wrong, because she put her arm around Jennifer. "Jen, what's the matter?" she asked.

*Lift your head but don't give it up yet. Sad face.* "Well, I found another pregnancy test in our medicine cabinet at home. It must have been left over from when we were doing the infertility stuff."

Lisa gazed perceptively across at Felicia.

*They're already preparing their "You still have time to try again" speeches,* Jennifer thought as she continued. "So I figured I might as well use it—no use keeping it around forever."

Mimi reached across and rubbed Jennifer's forearm. "More bad news?"

Jennifer dropped her head again and bounced her shoulders a bit as if she were softly crying. *Forget this pastor's wife thing, I should have been an actress!* "No," she said in a barely audible voice.

Lisa, who obviously couldn't hear Jennifer but assumed the answer anyway, started to say, "Honey, I'm so—"

"Wait." Felicia suddenly turned and reached over to pull Jennifer's face up where they could see it. "What did you say?"

*Let it shine!* "I said no." Jennifer smiled. "No! NO! No bad news! Good news! I'm pregnant!"

The eruption from Booth 17 made everyone in the diner turn and stare at the trio of women who were leaning in on Jennifer, screaming and hugging her and practically dancing in the aisle.

The commotion provoked Gracie to come bobbling over. "Good gravy,

PWs, what is it now?" she asked as they continued carrying on. "Did you win the lottery or something?"

Mimi, back in her seat, beamed. "Tell her, Jennifer!"

Jennifer finished her hug with Lisa, who returned to her seat and allowed Felicia to reclaim her spot next to Jennifer. "I'm pregnant," Jennifer said, throwing her hands in the air.

"Well, it's about time, missy," Gracie said, hands on her hips. "It's about time."

The waitress was still her abrasive self, but Jennifer could tell the woman was genuinely happy for her.

"I just hope you know what you're doing," Gracie warned. "Those rug rats can be a pain in the—"

"Gracie! We're celebrating here," Mimi interjected. "She has time to learn all about the dirty side of parenting later."

Shaking her head as usual, Gracie ambled off toward the kitchen.

"So when did you find out?" Lisa asked.

Jennifer took a sip of water. The excitement had left her with a dry mouth. "Just yesterday. I hadn't had a period since I'd gone off the fertility drugs last month, so I thought maybe my system was just messed up from all that. But then I found the pregnancy test—"

"So *that* part is true," Felicia chided.

Jennifer nodded and smiled. "And I decided I might as well give it a shot. When it said yes, I thought it must be faulty. So before I even said anything to Sam, I ran out and bought several more tests to make sure."

Mimi threw back her head. "That brings back memories," she said about the handful of pregnancy tests she'd taken when she'd conceived Milo but couldn't convince herself it was true. "Yeah, those tests are *never* wrong."

"What did Sam do when you told him?" Lisa asked. Gracie returned to their table with their usual beverages, passed them out, and left.

"He thought I was joking at first—as if I'd joke about something like that!"

Felicia reached over and put her arm around Jennifer again briefly, squeezing her close. "I am so excited for you. You know we all prayed for you that the Lord would bless you, and it looks like he certainly has. So when are you telling your church?"

"This Sunday . . . that is, if Sam hasn't told the world already."

"Wow," Lisa said, leaning back against the bench. The four sat quietly for a moment, absorbing the happy news.

"Okay, okay, enough about me—if I don't stop gushing about it, I'll *never* shut up!" After they stopped laughing, Jennifer turned to Felicia. "So how was your trip? Did your boss agree to let you keep the Cincinnati office open?"

Felicia folded the napkin in her lap. "We'll see. I told him about that National City Bank account—the one the guy in our church helped me get—and he said I need to secure another $250,000 in accounts to justify Cincinnati."

"Whew," Lisa said. "That's hard for me to wrap my mind around. Our church's budget is less than that!"

"What's going on there anyway?" Mimi turned toward Lisa. "You haven't said much about that whole thing lately."

Just the question made Lisa's expression shift from joyous to strained. She hesitated. Then, as if she knew this was the one place she could share her anguish, she launched into it. "When we took this church almost four years ago, Joel noticed in the church history that most of the pastors left at about five years, but when he questioned it, the board seemed to have valid explanations for each one."

Gracie arrived with their food—their usuals—and everyone took an undeclared chat break while ketchup was passed and salt was shaken.

Once everyone was settled, Lisa continued. "Anyway, Joel has started to make some changes. Or tried to anyway. But apparently the church doesn't want a leader pastor. They want someone to visit the sick, do funerals, and preach nice sermons. But they want to keep control."

"Why would they want that?" Felicia asked innocently.

Mimi snorted. "Ooh-ooh-ooooh! Me! Me," she said with a lifted hand, mimicking Horshack on *Welcome Back, Kotter*. "They started the church, and they want to retain control. They want a trophy pastor. Someone who looks good and does what they want but doesn't make any waves and certainly doesn't try to usurp power from the founding members. Am I close?"

Lisa groaned. "You have no idea. It's gotten really bad in the last several months, since Joel has actually tried to make some strong decisions for the church."

"Like what?" Mimi asked.

"Things like reaching out to young families and youth and the unchurched."

"If you ask Kitty, First Pres has *all* the young families in Red River, so good luck," Mimi joked.

Lisa rolled her eyes. "Yeah, there are still a few out there. But sometimes I look at my family and at the ministry and wonder if the sacrifice is too great. We're doing all this for God's kingdom . . . but, in the process, losing our daughter. Is it worth it? Is this really what God had in mind? I don't know. People actually called and complained when Callie wore jeans to church. I wanted to yell at them, 'I'm fortunate I was even able to get her into the building!'"

"But of course, you couldn't say that," Felicia chimed in, nodding knowingly.

"Right. I just took a deep breath and let them run on . . ."

After a minute of silence, Jennifer could tell Lisa was done with the topic, at least for now. So Jennifer slid in a topic-changing question—she didn't want "her" day, the day she'd been awaiting for ten years, to be a downer. "Hey, you guys, are you excited about the conference in a couple weeks?"

Mimi did a little jig in her seat. "You mean the St. Patrick's Day pastors' wives' retreat?" she asked in a fairly decent Irish brogue.

Hearing Mimi's accent made Jennifer think of Sam. *Wonder if he'll talk to the baby that way. I can't wait to get home tonight so we can start planning . . .*

"Speaking of which, would it be okay if we skip our March 13 lunch since we'll be spending that weekend together?" Felicia asked. "I could use that day to get caught up on work before I go."

Everyone agreed. After all, they'd have plenty of time to relax and catch up at the Peaceful Pines Christian Retreat Center.

# 20

# Mimi

*Wednesday, February 28*
*1:40 p.m.*

Mimi pulled up to Hemmings Elementary School with a load of still-warm chocolate chip cookies. It felt good to be able to get out and do something again—something that wasn't church related. She'd enlisted Mark's help at home, so he was doing parental duty while she went to the school to attend the monthly PTA meeting. Even though she'd lost the PTA presidency to Gloria Redkins last year, she'd made it a point to encourage and support Gloria however she could. Especially since Gloria had been so kind to her during her pregnancy, checking up on her, and bringing her soup and homeopathic nausea-relief remedies.

"Hello, Mimi." The principal, Phil Horvath, was a tall, attractive forty-something man. He had wavy chestnut hair and a dimple in his right cheek when he smiled. He held open the door as Mimi entered the school. "Those look great," he said, eyeing the cookies as if she held a treasure. "As do you. You seem to be holding up well after just having a baby."

Unable to control herself, Mimi felt a blush cover her face and neck. *If he only knew.* "You're too kind, Mr. Horvath." She reached into the plastic-wrapped tray and pulled out a cookie. "You're just saying that to steal one of these."

He lifted his eyebrows as if he'd been caught. "How can a man resist your temptations?"

His fingers brushed hers as he took the sweet treat.

Her heart jumped into her throat. *He's talking about my baking. Isn't he?* She wasn't so sure, and she was slightly uncomfortable with the tingly feeling she felt from his touch. She hadn't felt that sort of electricity in a long time—since before she'd had kids, when she and Mark were first married. *It's the hormones,* she reassured herself. She knew she should say something to alleviate her awkward feelings—something neutral would be best. She blinked, trying to get her thoughts together. Finally she blurted out, "They're chocolate chip!" Inwardly, she groaned. *No kidding, dodo.*

"So I see." He chuckled.

*Okay, think. Think. Say something halfway intelligent.* But all she could think to say was, "I'm going to the PTA meeting." *So much for intelligent.* "Are you coming?"

He didn't seem fazed by her nonwitty repartee. He didn't even seem to notice at all.

"Hopefully," he said, drawing the cookie toward his mouth. "That is, as long as I don't have to put on my disciplinarian hat and tend to unruly students."

She laughed, feeling better that she was on neutral, safe ground again. *Yeah, it's all in my mind. I'm making this into something it isn't.* "Okay, okay. You can just name him. I know MJ has a special seat assignment in your office."

Phil rubbed his chin and grinned. "Reminds me a lot of how I was at that age."

"Really?"

"Yep. So, see? There's hope for him yet," he said as he reached over and playfully squeezed her shoulder. There was that tingly feeling again. His touch seemed to linger on her senses even after he removed his hand.

"Well, it looks like my prayers have been answered then." Was she *flirting?* With her son's *principal?* She shook the thought, unwilling to entertain it. No, she told herself. They were just engaging in friendly chatter. But why was she feeling so flushed? And why did it feel so thrilling to have him notice her appearance and to have him touch her?

She stole a glimpse of him as he escorted her to the gymnasium where the meeting would take place. He was good-looking, that was for sure. The girls in their church's youth group would call a man with those looks "hot." Of course Mimi was pretty sure they wouldn't think of their principal that way. Principals were not "hot." They weren't even "warm." They were just, well, principals. But Mimi had always thought he was good-looking. Why was it so different now?

*It has to be the hormones.*

She felt Phil walking closely beside her. There seemed to be an energy between them, even though that thought sounded kind of New Agey to her.

Almost shyly she looked at him again and caught his gaze. They smiled. Awkwardly, she thought.

Mimi liked him. Genuinely liked him. He was a great principal. He had a strong character and was great with kids. He was a leader. And besides, he always laughed at her humorous comments and complimented her baking. She recalled that he'd once even told her he was jealous of Mark: "He's got quite a wife in you. I wish my wife could bake half as well as you do. Or take half an interest in my work. Or be half as interesting to talk to." To which she'd replied, "Yes, but she gets you home on weekends and evenings. My husband's on twenty-four-hour call. The only thing he's missing is a home-to-parsonage hotline for our church members to reach him. Plus you sit with your spouse at church. I've never sat with mine."

Mimi shook her head at the memory. Phil held open the gym door for her and placed his hand on the small of her back, leading her into the large room. Mark was the only one ever to place his hand there. She'd always liked it when he did that. It made her feel cherished and honored. But with Phil, it made her feel conflicted. How was she supposed to react to that? She decided just to say, "Thank you," and move away quickly. She didn't really want to; she wanted to stay close to him and continue talking. He had such a wonderful way of making her feel good. Nice. Important. Things she hadn't felt for a while. Things she hadn't realized she'd missed.

"Hi, Mimi!" Gloria Redkins called out from the tables where the meeting would take place. She was dressed in her usual baggy shirt and slacks. Mimi knew it was an attempt to hide her plump figure, but Mimi didn't care what Gloria looked like because she knew Gloria had a beautiful heart. How different her view of Gloria was now, she realized quickly, ever since last year when they'd had a heart-to-heart about their feelings of inadequacy. "How's Milo?"

"Colicky as ever," Mimi replied.

"Still?"

"Yep."

"Hmmm. I wonder if something else is going on with him."

Mimi shrugged. "We've been to see the pediatrician so many times, we've got our own parking space."

"Well, I hope it gets better soon."

"Me, too. I need the sleep. Actually, I'm only here so I can get a nap in. Would you make sure the meeting runs *really* long and is *really* boring?" Mimi winked playfully toward Gloria and placed her cookie tray prominently toward the front of the dessert and coffee table, then walked toward the meeting tables. Gloria and a few other parents had taken four tables and placed them in a rectangle so everyone could face one another. Judy motioned for Mimi to join her on the far side.

"I can't believe you still brought a dessert!" said Judy, a slender mother of five who was the PTA's secretary. "I swear I don't know when you can find the time."

"Oh, that's easy now. Since Milo had me awake in the middle of the night, I just went downstairs and popped some cookies in the oven." But she knew the real reason she was baking was to avoid filling her mind with late-night TV nonsense. It had been infringing on her sanity, she thought.

Mimi tried to engage in conversation with Judy, complimenting her on her clothes (Judy always wore the best-looking outfits, which she claimed she got from Wal-Mart). But inside, Mimi was well aware of this new attraction sitting across from her, who also, she noticed subtly, was conversing with the parents seated around him.

Even through the meeting, Mimi had a difficult time concentrating, trying *not* to think about Phil. *What is wrong with me?* she wondered. *I'm a happily married woman. I'm a pastor's wife, for heaven's sake. He's just a nice-looking, funny, intelligent man. Nothing more.*

Her brain switched to real time when Phil stood to make an announcement about recruiting for the town's annual spring parade. "As you know," he said, "we ask parents to help build the school's float and to help out during the parade. But this year it would be nice, too, to have a crafts sale simultaneously to raise some money for the new computer lab. Ideally, we'd like to purchase ten more computers."

Mimi couldn't believe she was nodding and volunteering to help out. She knew Mark would *kill* her when he found out she'd taken on another responsibility. Like she had the time. But she couldn't help herself. Her overcommitment had been an ongoing problem she'd been dealing with her whole married life. And even though it had come to a head last year and she'd promised to lay off, she felt like an alcoholic convincing herself that one more sip wouldn't hurt and comfortably slid back into her old habit of pleasing people. But a tiny thought nagged at her. Before, she'd always said yes because she was hoping to fill an underlying need for peace and serenity. This *yes* seemed to have more to it. Did it have anything to do with the man who was making the request?

She noticed Phil's surprise when she raised her hand to volunteer with the others. But his lips turned up slightly as he nodded in her direction. She quickly looked away, feeling exhilarated.

*Okay, stop it,* she berated herself. *This is for my children. Nothing more.* But she felt herself sitting up a little straighter in her metal chair, sucking in her stomach, and casually trying to flip her bobbed hair semi-seductively.

*3:16 p.m.*

On the drive home after the meeting, Mimi replayed the events of the past few hours. She'd always thought Phil was attractive—she'd have to have been blind not to notice his chiseled chin and jawline, the sexy dimple, the twinkle in his blue-gray eyes, his confident swagger. But this was something more. She felt swayed by his charming demeanor and by the way he asked for her opinions on things. And the way he laughed and engaged her in conversation. He was interesting and . . . she couldn't put her finger on it exactly. It was just . . . something.

Mimi pushed back her hair behind her ears and bit the inside of her cheek.

She'd always thought certain men were attractive—she knew her eyes wouldn't dull to beauty just because she was married. For instance, she'd always liked Harrison Ford. And Kiefer Sutherland, he was a cutie. And Tommy Johnson, her coworker in Kentucky when she was newly married. And the guy at the post office—he was a looker.

So why did this feel different? And why was it—whatever *it* was—even there?

Did she feel a stronger attraction to Phil because something was missing in her marriage? No. She shook her head. She knew that wasn't it. She wasn't unhappy in her marriage. She adored Mark. They were good together, and he treated her well. He was a good lover, father, and friend. Sure, they had conflicts and he could annoy her—the kinds of things that all couples faced—but those things weren't insurmountable. So what was going on with this newfound crush?

Maybe it was nothing to be concerned about. Just a passing phase brought on by the post-pregnancy hormones. But what if it wasn't? What if it started innocently and turned into something more?

She would never cheat on Mark. She would never break up her family. Would she?

The thought stopped her cold. She knew *never* was a strong word—even if she felt committed to her marriage and children.

*Of course not.* "No," she said definitely. "No."

But she also knew she wasn't gullible enough to believe that just because she said *no* didn't mean she was immune. She'd known lots of women—Christian women, *pastors' wives*—who'd gotten themselves into those kinds of situations. Those women took the subtlety of sin too much for granted. It was that slippery slope syndrome. She *didn't* want to find herself in that same position.

"Oh, this is ridiculous," she said aloud, as if defending herself to someone sitting in the passenger seat. "I'm attracted to the man. Big deal. That's all there is to it. We're not going to have an affair. He's my children's principal!" *And anyway, I'm sure he doesn't think that way about me.*

But as soon as the thought came, her mind flipped back through the fresh memories. He'd complimented her looks; he'd squeezed her shoulder. And there was that firm connection as he placed his hand on her back . . .

*Was* there an attraction on his side? And if so, how would she respond? And most important, would she say anything to her husband? Would she say anything to *God*?

Still shuffling through her thoughts, Mimi had turned onto Mercer Street, two streets from her home, when she noticed flashing lights in her rearview mirror. Her heart began to pound as she pulled to the side of the road, thinking the police officer would drive by on his way to apprehend a robber or some con-artist salesman. But her eyes widened fully when she watched the police car pull neatly behind her.

*What'd I do? What'd I do? What'd I do?* she thought frantically, clenching her teeth and mentally trying to replay the last mile of her driving. Nothing. She could think of absolutely nothing she'd done wrong. Maybe she'd run a stop sign, busily thinking about Phil? She couldn't remember!

She leaned back her head and told herself to breathe.

*Tap, tap, tap.* There was that obnoxious sound that Mimi was really growing to hate. Keeping her eyes forward, she rolled down the window and waited.

"Hi, Mrs. Plaisance." A familiar voice floated down to her, causing her to jerk her head in the direction of the officer. "You can breathe." He chuckled. "You're not in trouble. Unless you've been sleeping again." He seemed to think his comment was funny, because he laughed. "Actually, I saw you pass and just wanted to tell you again how much I enjoyed your church several Sundays back. I've had to work the last few Sundays, but I'm requesting that my sergeant give me Sunday mornings off so I can start coming regularly." He paused awkwardly and explained, "Y'know, it would please my aunt Vera."

All Mimi could do was gasp out her breath. Her whole body was on adrenaline overdrive, and now it had to calm itself, which annoyed her even more.

"Officer McCarthy, you scared me half to death." Mimi didn't even try to cover her annoyance.

The officer grinned widely. "Yeah, I know. It's a thing I have. I'm working on it. Didn't mean to scare you. And you don't have to keep calling me Officer McCarthy. You can call me Dan."

Mimi wasn't sure she wanted to call him *Dan;* that would make him more "human." And she wasn't ready yet to let those bygones be bygones. *The hormones again,* she thought, getting as much mileage out of that excuse as she possibly could.

Mark's words slammed back into her brain. *He needs Jesus. Don't be selfish. Don't let your pride keep you from showing someone Christ's love.*

Exhaling deeply, Mimi observed him. The truth was that she wanted not to like him. It made her life so much easier not to. But as she narrowed her eyes, she noticed how lonely he looked. *The guy just pulled you over to tell you he liked your church! Maybe he's crying out for help. But why to me?* She hated to admit it, but she felt a twinge of pity and guilt. "So you're really just coming to church to please your aunt?"

He pushed up his hat and rubbed his forehead. "Between you and me, I think she's trying to get me sold-out saved."

"Sold-out saved? Wow, I've never heard that one before."

They both laughed, easing some of the tension.

*Let it go,* she told herself through mentally gritted teeth. "Maybe you're coming to church because it's something deep inside you know you need?"

He nodded thoughtfully, then shrugged. "Well, anyway, I just wanted you to tell your husband." He tapped the door, then started to walk away.

*Don't let him leave yet,* Mimi felt a small voice inside her whisper.

"Hey!" she called out. "Can I ask you a question?" She waited for Dan to step back toward the car. *Okay, God, what do I say?* A thought quickly entered her mind. "Maybe you've been in this profession and have seen a lot of bad stuff and you want something in your life that brings a little hope?"

She watched him swallow hard. Then he smiled. "Maybe," he said and touched the tip of his hat in a salute.

"Uh, wait!" she called again. "Thanks for stopping me. I'll say a prayer for you."

He just nodded.

"Hey, Dan." Her voice stopped him again. "By the way, if you ever stop me like that again and just about give me a heart attack—" She stopped herself. *Don't be rude.* "Well, I'll just have to put you under citizen's arrest."

"Fair enough. See you later. By the way, you've got a taillight out."

# Felicia

*Friday, March 9*

*1:22 p.m.*

Felicia picked up her office phone to dial Becky's number. She knew she'd see her that Sunday, but she wanted to talk with her when Nicholas wasn't around, just in case.

"Hello?" came Becky's timid voice from the other end.

"Hi, Becky. It's Felicia."

"Oh, hi, Felicia." Her voice sounded more confident. "Do you need to cancel for Sunday?"

"No, actually I was wondering if you would do us a big favor." Felicia reminded Becky that Nicholas had been wanting to stay with her again.

Becky chuckled. "Yes, I know. He reminds me every time I'm at your house." She seemed pleased at his fondness for her. "Do you need me to watch him again? We loved having him last time."

It warmed Felicia's heart to hear her child was wanted. There were days lately when even she felt overwhelmed with him. "I'm glad to hear you say that. How would next Friday through Sunday be?"

"Sure!"

"I have a pastors' wives' retreat, and Dave will be home but he's got such a full plate right now . . . I thought it might be a good time to feed two birds with one grain and let Nicholas have some time with you so Dave doesn't have to play single parent all weekend."

Becky was silent for a moment. "Felicia, there's just one thing."

*The biting. Ugh, I knew it.* "What's that?" Felicia asked, trying to sound light.

"Friday and Saturday are our Sabbath. I know last time you weren't too excited about us taking him to synagogue, then Nicholas told me you yelled at him for singing the 'Make a Matzoh' song."

Felicia saw Delores motioning her that she had a call holding. "Becky, I didn't yell at him for singing that *particular* song, just for singing." As soon as it was out of her mouth, she knew it didn't sound right, but she was in a hurry to get to the waiting call. It could be new business.

Becky was quiet again. "Uh, okay then. I promise not to teach him any more songs."

"No, no, Becky, that's not what I meant—"

Delores came into Felicia's office and signaled that it was Ted waiting on the other line, to which Felicia held up a "just a minute" finger.

She didn't have time to explain to Becky about disruptive singing. "Becky, let's talk on Sunday, okay? I've got an important call holding that I have to take."

After she said good-bye but before she clicked over to the other line, Felicia realized she'd just implied that her call with Becky wasn't important. She mentally kicked herself, then pushed the line 2 button.

"Ted! How's it going out there in paradise?" She was trying a new tactic to defuse his glee at pointing out Ohio's less-than-desirable winter weather.

"You mean out here with the traffic and the high cost of living?" He laughed at copying what she'd said before. "It's just grand."

Felicia relaxed at hearing he was in a good mood. Certainly that was a positive sign. Wasn't it? She smiled and readjusted her crossed legs. *Is that a run I feel?* she thought as she reached down with her free hand. *You've got to be kid—*

"Felicia, the reason I'm calling is I'd like you come out again at the beginning of next month. We're going to have Jane's retirement party, and I have some other things I'd like to talk with you about."

She struggled inwardly with whether to ask any questions or wait. Her impatience won out. "So Ted, does that mean you've decided to hold on to this office?" Might as well approach it from the positive.

"Let's talk about it when you get here," he said. "You know how I hate talking on the phone."

Felicia felt uneasy with his reluctance to commit. But she knew he did indeed dislike phone conversations. He preferred the personal touch, which is what he had trained all of his managers to do, and what made Brown & McGrory the most thriving PR firm in the country.

After she hung up, Felicia flipped the page on her calendar to write in the two-day trip. In her anxiety over Ted's lack of assurances, she'd completely forgotten the significance of the first week of April. She shook her head as she perused the dates.

April 5: Maundy Thursday
April 6: Good Friday
April 8: Easter

*Maybe I can fly back late Friday or early Saturday*, she assured herself. But she knew telling Dave she had to go to LA on Easter weekend was going to be a tough sell. Like a fishmonger trying to sell off green, smelly salmon.

CHAPTER

# 22

## Mimi

*Saturday, March 10*

*7:34 a.m.*

Mimi was right. Mark was pretty heated when she broke the news to him that she had volunteered the next several weeks or so to help paint the school's float for the Red River spring parade. And the first workday was in an hour and a half.

"What were you thinking?" he demanded. "With what time? I mean, seriously, Mimi. Didn't we—not too long ago—have a long discussion about how cramming everything in and not saying no was *not* the path that leads to peace for you? I'm supposed to watch Milo and the kids while you run out and do something that other parents can cover? You just had a baby, Mimi."

"Yes," she answered defensively. "A baby who never stops crying. Maybe my peace could come by getting away for a few hours and doing something that doesn't require earplugs and nipple cream. It might be nice to be around a few folks who aren't crying and nagging me about something. Who talk to me like an adult! You know, outside conversation? Stuff you get at church during the workweek? My deepest conversations come at two

134

o'clock in the morning. And they're to the dog. Or, oh! No, I'm mistaken. I can talk on and on richly and profoundly with Bob and Larry, the veggies," she snapped.

Mark threw down the mail he'd been holding, letting it scatter across his desk. "Fine. Go. But it concerns me that you're starting in on these old patterns that have caused us a lot of trouble."

"It's only a few times. It's not as if I signed up for the National Guard."

"But it's those 'few' times that start the slide. 'Only three weeks.' Then it becomes, 'It's just this one project.' 'This one opportunity.' 'They need me.' Just be careful, Mims."

"Well, you could come, too. It's not just for moms." She knew he wouldn't go for that, plus, selfishly, she really didn't want him there. She tried to convince herself it was to get away for some peace and quiet. But the truth was, she knew Phil Horvath would be there. And she wanted to talk to him, to talk about something other than her children and their exploits. She longed to talk about social things, culture, politics even. Something where she could be seen as someone other than her labels of *wife* and *mother*. Was that really so wrong?

Mark shook his head. "If you're going back down that road, you can go it alone. You're not dragging me along so you can feel justified."

She felt her face drain, then the color flooded back as her indignation rose. *I can do what I want! You're not going to stop me. This is for a good cause.*

"Oh, by the way," Mark said as Mimi turned to leave his study, "I have that board meeting this morning, for my *job*, which you obviously forgot about. You know, the meeting for which you volunteered to make the egg-and-bacon casserole? So I can't stay home to watch our children. I guess you'll have to take them with you or hire a babysitter."

Mimi clenched her teeth. She wanted to say, "Hmmm. I guess *volunteering* to bake for the church is still all right, then?" But she held her tongue, knowing that would only add fuel to the fire. "Fine. I'll call Callie and see if she's available to watch the kids."

"Who's Callie?" Mark looked skeptical.

Mimi cringed. She'd forgotten that Mark still didn't know about the biweekly get-togethers with Lisa, Jennifer, and Felicia. How would she explain that she knew Callie through her mother, Lisa? It didn't matter; she'd just tell him the truth. "Callie is Joel Barton's daughter from the Assembly of God church. And I'm sure she'd love to earn a little extra spending money."

*8:47 a.m.*

Mimi wandered into the empty school gymnasium and glanced around. She knew she was early, but she thought somebody else would be there. Strewn against the far wall and around the plastic tarp-covered floor were the materials and paints for the school's parade float—sort of an Under the Sea theme with a mermaid, schools of fish, and a coral reef.

"Hey, beautiful." Phil's quiet voice floated from behind her. Turning, she saw him holding a box of grocery store doughnuts in one hand and a cup of coffee in the other. His jeans and old T-shirt announcing Army of One added to his charming appeal.

She decided not to acknowledge his flattering greeting. "Hi! So we're the first ones here, huh?"

"Looks that way. I brought some doughnuts," Phil said, pushing the box toward her. "They aren't homemade like the ones you always bring, but at least it gives you a break." His smile warmed her, and she fought the urge to giggle like a schoolgirl. Mentally she breathed a sigh of relief that she'd checked her reflection in the driver's side visor mirror several times before she'd entered the school, so she knew she didn't have baby spit on her cheeks or any other number of disgusting things her children had been known to deposit on her. Especially Megan. Mimi remembered once when Megan was about three, she'd been the runniest-nosed kid. Mimi had attended a national Methodist conference and had spent the day, unbeknownst to her, wearing Megan's dried yellow snot brightly displayed across her left cheek for all to see.

Instinctively Mimi pressed her hands against her cheeks, just to do the snot check one more time, but also to partially cover her warm face.

"Doughnuts from Kroger's are good, too," she said, taking the box. "But no coffee?" She chose a chocolate old-fashioned.

"Guilty. Didn't have enough hands."

"Well," Mimi said, all of a sudden awkward at their being alone together—and unsettled about being there at all, especially after his use of the word *beautiful*—"should we go ahead and get started?"

Maybe Mark had been right. She hadn't needed to be there. But there was a part of her, repulsive as it may have been, that wanted to enjoy Phil's company. Just for a little while. Innocently. Not to play with fire, necessarily, but maybe to get a little close to it. *I'm not doing anything wrong. There is nothing that people could see that would cause them to question me or Phil. . . . Okay, am I justifying here?*

Phil handed her a paintbrush and suggested they start by painting the mermaid, which was at the top of the float. In keeping with the sea theme, Phil had already painted the sign that read:

CHICKEN OF THE SEA . . . TUNA OR CHICKEN?
REASON #48 THAT A GOOD EDUCATION IS PRICELESS.
HEMMINGS ELEMENTARY

"We might as well have a little fun." Phil laughed when he showed Mimi his handiwork.

"When did you paint that?"

"Last night. I was here 'til past midnight."

"Really?"

Phil nodded. "Yep. My wife is out of town visiting her sister. Again." To Mimi, his slightly tense way of saying *again* felt intended to signal her that he was having trouble at home.

For a split second, she pondered his attempt at opening an intimate conversation about his marriage. *I'm just enjoying this man's company, but what if he really is interested in something deeper?* She decided to avoid the whole scenario and not engage him on that topic.

"Well, you did a mighty good job for painting so late." Meticulously rolling up the sleeves of her oversized denim painting shirt, she walked toward the paint cans. "I'm not much of an *artiste*, but I'll give it a go."

"You know, I appreciate how dedicated you are, helping out here," Phil told her as they tackled the mermaid's tail with blue and green paint. "A lot of parents won't get involved. Or they say they will, but then don't show up."

"Well, I used to be a teacher, so I understand how difficult it is for schools."

"You were a teacher?"

"Yep. When Mark and I were first married, he pastored a church in Kentucky and I taught third-graders. That was before we had kids, obviously."

"You just get more and more interesting." He pointed his dripping brush toward her, then began to laugh.

"What's so funny?"

He patted his right cheek with a finger, then directed the finger toward Mimi.

Sure enough, feeling her face, she produced aqua fingers. "I can't even be away from my kids and stay clean!" she half whined, half groaned.

Two mothers entered the gym as Phil and Mimi were laughing. "Hi! Sorry we're late," said one of the mothers, whom Mimi knew only slightly.

Phil immediately stood to greet the women and pointed out a few options for them to start on. Mimi felt her heart drop a bit at having to share Phil with the others, then reluctantly scolded herself for having such a ridiculous reaction.

*You're just another mom to him, Mimi. He's friendly like that with all the parents.*

As evidence, the rest of the day went by quickly, without any more meaningful interactions between Mimi and Phil. But she was satisfied just to be there, enjoying his presence. She'd suppressed the nagging thoughts that she might be pushing some boundaries. She didn't want to go there. Instead, she just accepted what she had. It was safe and exciting without being wrong. At least that's what she told herself.

# Jennifer

*Saturday, March 10*
*1:25 p.m.*

Jennifer tapped on the cordless phone receiver as she sat on the sofa and contemplated what she was about to do. She hadn't been able to get the vision of her mother's sparkling house out of her mind. And now that she knew she was pregnant, she really felt the Holy Spirit prodding her to make that phone call.

She turned the phone over to the dialing pad. *I assume it's the same number if it's the same house.* Just dialing those digits for the first time in nearly eleven years—since she'd called her mother to tell her she was getting married, a ceremony her mother did not attend—felt strange.

"Hello?" The voice sounded bright, nearly cheerful.

Jennifer's throat tightened. "Hi, Mother. It's Jennifer. Your daughter." She'd never called her mother *Mom* because that seemed to her like a moniker for a caring parent, not the raging lunatic who "raised" her.

Without missing a beat, her mother said, "Well, I certainly *hope* your name is Jennifer if you're my daughter. You're the only one I have." She chuckled. "That I know of, anyway." *When did she get a sense of humor?* "How are you, sweetie? I didn't think I'd ever hear from you again."

"I just wanted to call to tell you I'm pregnant." Jennifer was never one to mince words. "I thought . . . you might want to know."

"Well, that's nice, but I assume by now this isn't your first baby. Why call now? You've been married what, nine, ten years?"

"Almost eleven. But this is my first pregnancy. We've . . . had some trouble."

"Oh, I see." *Was that compassion in her voice?*

Both women were silent for a moment. Remarkably, more than eleven years of not talking had left them with nothing to say. But Jennifer had some unfinished business. "Mother, I was over on your side of town and I drove by your house. It looks really nice. Did Monty fix it up?"

She knew her stepfather found it difficult to get off his lazy rear end and get to work at his security job, let alone put siding on a house. But she figured she'd play along.

"Monty! Sheesh, he's been gone for more than five years," her mother said. "Once I got my act together, I told him the show was over and kicked his butt out. Haven't heard from him since, thank God."

Got her act together? "So . . . does that mean you're back on your meds?" Jennifer asked hesitantly.

"Not only back on *them*, I've gone back to school and gotten my *degree*, Jennifer," her mother said proudly. "I am a college graduate! Of course, it's just the little tech school, but I sure was happy to get that diploma. Now I'm making my own money keeping books for a few businesses in town. Hoping to start my own company some day."

*Wow, a college degree. I can't even say that.* "That's great, Mother." Jennifer was still careful—she'd seen her mother try to pull the wool over people's eyes before. "But about the meds—"

"Jennifer, I *told* you. I am taking my lithium every day. Some days are a little more high or low than others, but I manage."

Jennifer didn't need to be reminded about the high and low days. She remembered well what it was like cleaning up after one of her mother's manic "oil painting" phases or bringing her food in bed (and feeding it to her) when she was in one of her low periods. It was the only way she really knew to relate to her mother—as a project.

Now that her mother seemed in control, Jennifer wasn't sure where to take the conversation. She'd fully expected, when she phoned today, to get the woozy woman she'd talked to before her wedding . . . not the confident, relaxed one she heard on the other end.

"Well, maybe we should get together some time," Jennifer suggested. She couldn't tell if her mother was glad to hear from her or not.

"I'd love that, Jennifer," her mother replied immediately. "You two want to come for dinner next weekend?"

Did she dare drag Sam over there until she saw how her mother really was? "Uh, I'm afraid we can't next weekend. I have a pastors' wives retreat to go to. How about we meet for lunch the following week?"

"Sure, you just call me and tell me when and where, and I'll be there."

Jennifer felt like she was making plans with one of the women from church. She couldn't help but remind herself that this was her mother, Jo Jo Lawson, the one who'd made her childhood a living hell.

After they said their good-byes and hung up, Jennifer wished she hadn't sent Sam to the grocery store so she could talk in private. She wanted him there so she could share her misgivings with him, and figure out what she should do next. He was such an active listener—it didn't surprise her when people from their church spoke to her so glowingly about his counseling efforts. That's why his silence over their infertility problems had been so deafening to her.

*Do I pretend like nothing happened and move on?* she wondered about her mother. *Forgive and forget? Or should I confront each issue with her?*

*Why should she get off so easy anyway? She knew Monty was harassing me and saying terrible things about me. Why didn't she do something?*

*Didn't she care that I moved out at eighteen with hardly a word? Did she ever care?*

Pop. Jennifer heard the trunk on the car in the driveway open. She had never been so glad to hear Sam come home. Quickly she pulled on her rubber boots so she could help him carry in groceries. But as excited as she was to share the good news, she couldn't help but feel troubled at the pain she knew was facing her.

# Peaceful Pines Christian Retreat Center

Lisa leaned against the lodge door to open it as she kicked her "suitcase"—one of Ricky's gym bags—though the entryway. She hadn't realized until she got ready to pack for this pastors' wives' retreat that she didn't have a proper suitcase, and she was certainly in no financial shape to be investing in one now. So she'd grabbed a red, white, and blue duffel bag from Ricky's closet, and that fit the bill. But all her things made the bag too heavy to carry, so she'd had to drag it to the car, from the car, and now into the retreat center.

Fortunately, Jennifer was already inside. Lisa saw her make eye contact and hustle over to help.

"Good grief, woman, did ya bring Callie in there with you?" Jennifer said as she grabbed one end of the bag and motioned for Lisa to lift the other.

Lisa chuckled and hoisted her end. "Huh—not a bad idea. Who knows what kind of trouble that girl will get into while I'm gone."

They lugged the duffel into one of the dormitory rooms. From Lisa's glance around, the so-called retreat center was really just a big central room with two sleeping areas off to either side. Several other pastors' wives were already enjoying coffee and sitting around tables covered with green plastic "tablecloths." Glittery shamrocks were posted on the walls, and a banner across the kitchen area read WELCOME SOUTHWEST OHIO PASTORS' WIVES.

Inside the bunk room, Jennifer led them to an empty bed, where they let the bag drop with a thud.

"Wow, this place isn't what I expected at all," Lisa said quietly, massaging her overworked hand.

"Tell me about it," Jennifer responded as she scanned the room to see if anyone was listening. "When something is advertised as a 'retreat,' you'd think there'd be some personal privacy. This is like a kids' church camp with all these bunk beds in one room."

Lisa fished some lip balm out of her purse. "Yeah, I know this location was cheap because of the off-season and all, but I'm really surprised that Kitty would go for this dorm type of thing. Do you think we'll get to see her without makeup?"

Jennifer lifted a finger in the air while she giggled over her obvious knowledge. "Are you kidding me? Kitty has taken over the 'leader's room' off the back of the kitchen. She has her own bathroom and everything! I heard her telling Sarah Baker—you know, the PW from that new Church of Christ in Mason—that she felt justified in using that room because she's 'working so hard to see that this event is a *quantifiable* success.'"

Lisa played along gallantly. "Well, let's get at it then. I don't want to stand in the way of Kitty's success!"

Just as they were walking into the main room, Felicia burst through the door, chattering in a business voice on her cell phone, which was in one hand, and pulling a designer-looking roller bag with her other. Lisa knew Felicia saw them because she held the phone out and made a sour face at it, then smiled.

Felicia was, as usual, dressed as if she'd just stepped off the runway. Her purple wool suit hung perfectly around her lean frame, and her cream-colored blouse was as crisp as if she'd ironed it before walking in the door. Lisa admired Felicia for always looking so put together, but she knew she wasn't always so well ordered on the inside.

Still, she couldn't help wondering what it would be like to have those clothes and that house and not a single worry about money.

"Hey, girls, has the party started?" Felicia said after snapping closed her cell phone and rolling her way to Lisa and Jennifer. She raised her hands and briefly punched her fists in the air. Lisa knew she was kidding—none of the PWs expected this retreat to be much of a party.

Jennifer reached out to hug her. "It has now that you're here!" Her eyes darted around the room. "But I wonder where Mimi is?"

Lisa peered out the window. It was dark outside, but she could make out Mimi's bouncy figure coming up the sidewalk to the retreat center. "There's Mimi now," she said. "Jen, you show Felicia where we're bunking"—Lisa noticed Felicia wince at "bunking"—"and I'll help Mimi get in."

The door had just closed behind Mimi when Angela Arthur—the wife of Kitty's church's music minister—announced over the din of chatty women, "Ladies, please take your seats. Kitty asked me to get us settled because she has a surprise for us."

Mimi leaned over to Lisa and whispered, "Poor Angela. She's had more than her share of surprises, huh?"

Angela's "surprise" a year earlier had been the revelation that her husband, leader of the church's huge Living Christmas Tree chorale and other musical extravaganzas, had been arrested for propositioning an undercover vice cop. Of course he'd denied it, claiming he was framed and just helping a "damsel in distress"—and the church fell for it and allowed him to remain in his leadership position, even though he was sentenced to 150 hours of community service. When they'd read about it in the newspaper, Lisa and Joel had felt bad for the church, but they couldn't quite muster sympathy for Ken Arthur, who'd always treated them with a holier-than-thou attitude because he considered his church's music "classic" while, he said, the Assemblies' churches were "denigrating" hymns with their happy-clappy approach.

Jennifer and Felicia reappeared and patted a couple of seats next to them as Mimi quickly dumped her bag in the bunk room and joined them and Lisa at the circle of chairs. Angela waited until everyone was seated, then she pushed the button on a small portable CD player. But just as the music started and the door to Kitty's private room flew open, Mimi's cell phone rang loudly. The ringtone "Girls Just Want to Have Fun" made several of the women giggle and turn their attention away from the open door to a red-faced Mimi.

Although Lisa couldn't see Kitty, she heard her sigh loudly from behind the door.

"Angela, start it over," Kitty yelled in an annoyed tone. "And everyone please turn off your cell phones. This is a retreat, after all."

Meanwhile, Mimi mouthed "sorry" to no one in particular as she rushed from the group to just inside the bunk room to answer her phone.

The music started again. Lisa saw that Mimi was obviously distressed as she talked in the phone while plugging her free ear with a finger.

Just then Kitty's door burst open again to reveal something Lisa couldn't have imagined. Out strode Kitty—as if she had just been named Miss America—wearing a costume so garish and ghastly that Jennifer laughed out loud, Felicia gasped, and Lisa wondered if she had made a big mistake in spending money on this retreat.

*Oh, but who could put a dollar figure on this kind of entertainment?* she assured herself, then leaned back to see Mimi still talking on the phone but with a face that said she was as perplexed by Kitty's presentation as the others.

Kitty walked to the center of the circle, where Lisa could see that Kitty was actually wearing a green-dyed toga with shamrock stickers on it. *That looks like she borrowed it from her church's living nativity costume closet!* Lisa thought incredulously. Topping her perfectly coiffed head—which had been sprayed with green glitter, a product Lisa recognized from Callie's makeup kit—was a plastic headband with two shiny foam shamrocks bouncing above it on springs. Her usual yellow pumps were covered hastily with green felt. While Lisa was sure Kitty meant to be festive, she couldn't help but picture her as a poor man's Glinda the Good Witch.

"Is this supposed to be in honor of Saint Patrick's Day or something?" Felicia asked, aghast.

Lisa only shrugged. *Joel will never believe this when I tell him.*

By the time Kitty made it to the center of the circle, the CD's musical introduction had ended and a familiar accompaniment started. Lisa recognized it as "When Irish Eyes Are Smiling," but Kitty began singing lyrics as strange as her sparkly getup:

> *When pastors' wives are smiling,*
> *They bring joy to everything . . .*

As Kitty pranced around the room, Lisa saw her reach into the gold-painted bucket hanging from her wrist and begin to hand each woman a small net bag full of gold coins. She presented them as if she were touching each woman with a magic wand.

"Chocolate," Jennifer said knowingly when Lisa shot her a questioning glance.

Meanwhile, the song continued,

> *In the depth of their devotion*
> *You can hear the angels sing . . .*

A bellowing Kitty handed Lisa one of the coin bags. Lisa pulled the little tag away from where it was attached to the ribbon holding the bag closed and silently read: "A good name is more desirable than great riches; to be esteemed is better than silver or gold.—Proverbs 22:1."

> *When pastors' wives are happy,*
> *They are following Christ's way.*

Kitty had walked the circle of forty women, depositing a coin bag in each wife's hands, and now stood in the center of the circle for the last stanza.

> *And when pastors' wives are praying,*
> *They know God is saying, 'Yea!'"*

With "yea," Kitty punched her fist in the air. Lisa heard Jennifer, who was attempting to unravel and open her coin bag, snicker.

"Okay, ladies, now let's all sing our theme song together!" Kitty announced while she reset the CD player. "Follow along with me, and when we get to the final 'yea,' I really want to hear you shout it!"

Jennifer leaned toward Lisa's ear. "Is this a grown-ups' retreat or vacation Bible school?" she asked rhetorically.

Lisa shook her head and elbowed her.

While the group was fumbling their way through the song, Lisa saw Mimi snap her phone closed and go farther into the bunk room. A moment later she reappeared wearing her coat and holding her suitcase. She dropped it by the door and tiptoed toward Lisa and Jennifer.

"I have to go home," she said, crouching down and whispering between Lisa and Jennifer's heads. "Milo's throwing up and Mark's not sure what to do." Then she jutted her chin toward Kitty and smirked. "To be honest, if I stick around here much longer, I might be puking myself."

Lisa and Jennifer reached up and gave Mimi an arm-pat good-bye. Lisa saw her squeeze Felicia's shoulder as she moved quickly out of the door while Kitty had her back turned.

*Lucky dog,* Lisa thought. *Wish I still had some throwing-up babies at home to get me out of this.*

She glanced over at Jennifer, who was eagerly stuffing a couple of unwrapped chocolate coins in her mouth, and realized that no matter how bad the weekend got, she at least would have some quality time with her and Felicia.

After two rounds of her faux-rousing theme song, Kitty finally clicked off the CD player and stood at one end of the circle so she could see most of the women. "Now, ladies, please look at our theme Scripture on your net bag."

*Theme song and theme Scripture. Will there be a theme craft and a theme puppet show, too?*

Lisa would have loved to have seen what her mother would have thought of this "treat." She probably would have had a fit, she decided. Lisa secretly was glad her mother wasn't in attendance, although she should have been since she was also a pastor's wife in Southwest Ohio. But her mom and dad were in Indiana that week, leading a revival service for a friend's church.

Kitty allowed time for the women to read the Scripture, then said, "We want to have 'good names' at our churches, correct?" Some of the women nodded. Lisa sat still, unsure where Kitty was going with this. "In that case, I don't even want you to open those bags, ladies!" Kitty said that last statement with triumph. "No, instead I'm going to pass around my pot o'gold again"—she held up her crudely painted bucket—"and I want you to dump those coins right back in it!"

Lisa could hear Ricky's voice in her head, yelling at his sister, "Indian giver!" She wished she'd followed Jennifer's lead and opened her bag earlier. *A little sugar jolt would be good about now.*

Kitty handed the bucket to the first woman in the circle, who obediently tossed her coin bag in, as if the action was somehow fun. Lisa heard Jennifer make an *ugh* sound and peeked over to see her shaking her head and frantically trying to re-secure her bag as she scrunched down in her chair, munching a mouthful of chocolate.

Lisa nudged Felicia on the other side of her, pointed at Jennifer, and let out a giggle. "Kitty'll probably ask her to make it up with coins from her pocket," she whispered knowingly, causing Lisa to arch her head back in silent laughter.

But as she watched the bucket make its way around, Lisa felt a growing animosity inside. *I came here to get away from money talk and budget worries. Now the first thing we do is pass around coins? At this point I'd give up my "good name" to be able to pay the bills for six months straight.*

Lisa knew she should allow the Lord to handle her distress over the church's finances, but she was tired of those "give it to the Lord" platitudes her mom and everyone else had proffered.

*When is He going to give it to* me *instead?* she wondered glumly as she dropped her coin bag into the nearly full bucket.

# 25

# Peaceful Pines Christian Retreat Center

*Saturday, March 17*

*10:23 a.m.*

Jennifer leaned back and evaluated her creation. Learning to make a radish rosette wasn't really why she'd come to the retreat, but at least she was able to chat with Lisa and Felicia while she worked on it. The morning's session, "Culinary Creativity for Congregational Consumption," was Kitty's way of sharing her mastery of the kitchen so other PWs could wow their churches at potlucks and parsonage events. Or that's how Kitty had described it. To Jennifer, it was just one more opportunity for Kitty to make everyone else feel inadequate.

"It's too bad Mimi isn't here," said Lisa, curiously eyeing the "flower" she'd just made from butter. "She could have shown Kitty a thing or two about this stuff."

"To be honest," Felicia said quietly toward Lisa and Jennifer as she held out a lemon zester, "I really don't think I'll ever use this type of thing at my church. Our potlucks are more, well, potlucky. You know, fried chicken and tuna casserole. That sort of thing."

Jennifer remembered Felicia telling them about past potlucks at First

Baptist and how that meddling Nancy Borden had usurped Felicia's position at every turn. *Maybe a few radish rosettes and butter flowers would help her get a little more respect. But would she even want* that *kind of respect?*

Her thoughts were interrupted by Kitty's *clap-clap-clap* from the front of the room. "Ladies, let's take a little break. I don't know if it's being around all this food or what, but I have to admit my tummy's a little upset. Perhaps some fresh air would do us all good. Why don't you pour a cup of coffee—I put out some French vanilla creamer and cinnamon syrup—and stroll outside for a few minutes? When we come back in, I'll lead us in our theme song again and then Angela Arthur from my home church, the *largest* church in our county, is going to give us a little talk called 'Leading from the Passenger Seat.' "

The noise of everyone scooting their chairs and cleaning up the tables gave Felicia the chance to lean in to Lisa and Jennifer and whisper, "I'm guessing Angela's occupying that seat a lot these days to keep someone else from hopping in there."

All three grimaced sympathetically. They understood the embarrassment she must have endured over her husband's arrest. It was bad enough for their churches to know their every movement, but something like that brought scorn not only from the church but from the whole community.

"Let's grab that cup of coffee like Kitty suggested," Lisa said as she gathered their trash from the table and crunched it into a pile.

"Yeah, I think I have something in common with Kitty today—a sick gut." Jennifer rubbed her abdomen. "I haven't had any morning sickness yet so I don't know what that feels like. Maybe that's what this is." *I don't care if I'm sick for nine whole months as long as I get a baby at the end of it.*

"Or maybe it's that green eggs and ham Kitty served up this morning," Felicia said with a sour face. "Even though I knew it was just food coloring, something about green eggs on my plate made me want to vomit."

"Ugh, don't say that word!" Jennifer laughed.

The three waited their turn at the coffee urns, then stepped outside. For Ohio, it was a pleasant March day with sunshine and a light breeze.

"I think I smell spring," Lisa said.

*She's always so positive,* Jennifer thought. It was amazing, considering what she was going through with Callie and the church.

Jennifer took in a deep breath. "I'm really looking forward to spring, but not summer. What will it be like to be pregnant in the humidity?"

Lisa and Felicia nodded knowingly. "You'll survive," Felicia said. "It's a good excuse to gorge yourself on ice cream."

"Excuse me, Jennifer," Kitty said with a reprimanding tone as she *clip-clopped* toward them in her green-felt-covered high heels and mossy green pantsuit. "Could I speak to you in private?" She worded it as a question, but it felt more like a demand.

Feeling her face go from relaxed and amused to instantly stressed, Jennifer glanced at her friends before following Kitty away from the group. They walked down a wooded path until they were out of earshot and view from the others. Then, finally, Kitty stopped and turned to Jennifer.

"Every time I look at you this weekend all I can think about is seeing you at the park that day, holding hands with that man," Kitty said, all pretense of kindness and concern gone. "And in the spirit of Christian accountability, I want you to know *I* know what was going on."

*You do, huh?* "Yes, Kitty, I saw you, too," Jennifer responded patronizingly. She glanced over to see Lisa and Felicia standing back a distance, covertly spying on them. "We were praying, or getting ready to, at least. Not that it's any of your business, frankly."

Kitty drew herself tall. " 'Frankly,' it *is* my business. As the leader of the pastors' wives' support group, God has given me the authority to instruct wives in how they should go. So I'm going to tell your husband you are having an affair. Perhaps you can even resolve the issue without your church knowing. I'm sure my Norm would counsel you."

*Support group? Since when?* Jennifer wasn't sure if it was her nauseated state or what, but she felt an uncontrollable rage rising inside her for this haughty woman. She got in Kitty's face and raised her pointed finger to within an inch of Kitty's nose. "You listen to me," she barked, knowing those nearby could overhear. "If you tell Sam that secret, I'll tell Norm *your* secret!"

Kitty's face froze so fast that Jennifer wondered if a cup pressed to her chin would produce a stream of ice cubes. Jennifer backed away slightly, pleased to have one-upped the woman.

After making a quick recovery, Kitty uttered a guttural sound, then turned to walk away. She hadn't taken three steps when Angela came running toward her. But before Angela got close, Kitty waved her hand in a rebuff and called, "I'm going on a walk. Please take over."

Felicia and Lisa clearly were waiting for Jennifer to rejoin them and fill them in on what had transpired. She started to walk toward them, but then turned and took off after Kitty instead.

*She's not getting away with such a blatant accusation.*

# CHAPTER

# 26

# Peaceful Pines Christian Retreat Center

*Saturday, March 17*
*2:17 p.m.*

Sitting back in the circle after lunch, Felicia pondered that morning's face-off between Jennifer and Kitty. After they'd seen Jennifer run after Kitty, Felicia and Lisa had gone back into the retreat center, figuring Jennifer would join them soon enough. And although Felicia's mind was still partly on what she'd seen, Angela diverted her by offering a humble, thoughtful devotional on being prayerful helpmates to their pastor-husbands. Afterward, they all held hands and prayed. Felicia wondered if that same sweet spirit would have developed in the group had Kitty still been among them. But neither Kitty nor Jennifer turned up.

When the women took a short break, Felicia headed into the bunk room to get her toothbrush and saw Jennifer curled up on a bunk.

"Hey, girl, when did you get back?" she asked, crouching down next to Jennifer's lower berth.

"I snuck in while you guys were praying," Jennifer answered, rolling onto her side and propping herself on an elbow to face Felicia. "The smell of that lunch made me feel even worse, so I came in here for a nap."

Felicia shook her head. "You didn't miss much. You okay now?"

"Yeah, I think I'm all right. My stomach is better anyway. But I'm still pretty upset about that episode with Kitty." Jennifer scooted over so Felicia could sit on the edge of the bunk.

"What was that all about? I couldn't quite hear what you said, but I could pick up that you were angry."

Jennifer sighed. "Oh, it was about that whole Pastor Scott thing at the park last month when we were holding hands and praying."

Felicia's jaw dropped in surprise. She had a sinking feeling she knew where Jennifer was going with this story.

Jennifer nodded, apparently understanding that Felicia was getting it. "I knew when I saw her that day that I was going to pay somehow, some way. I guess today was the day. She said she was going to tell Sam I'm having an affair."

Felicia rolled her eyes and shook her head in disgust. "So what did you tell her?"

Jennifer lay her head back and closed her eyes. "Obviously I'm *not* having an affair, so I don't have to worry about that. But Sam doesn't know yet about Pastor Scott, and I'm not ready to tell him. . . . So I dropped the A-bomb. I told her if she tells my secret, I'll tell hers."

"Good for you!" Felicia knew that would have put Kitty in her place.

"But then after she left," Jennifer continued, "it occured to me that in my anger I hadn't denied the affair. So I ran after her to tell her it wasn't true, but when I got to the two trails, I wasn't sure which one she'd taken. I went down the base of the ravine—but I never found her, so I guess she took the upper trail."

"Well." Felicia squeezed Jennifer's arm in an encouraging embrace. "That should be the end of that."

"She just made me so angry that, for a second, I wanted to push the old bag down the ravine!"

"I hear you, sister. I've been there myself plenty of times where Kitty's concerned. Don't worry about it. Just get some rest and we'll talk more later."

Jennifer nodded and rolled onto her other side.

Later, when Jennifer rejoined the group, Felicia noticed that she wasn't her usual self. Instead of laughing and cracking jokes, Jennifer was sullen and edgy. As much as Felicia had looked forward to spending time with her Lulu's buddies, she began to feel as though Lisa were the only one she was really getting to enjoy, what with Mimi gone and Jennifer out of it.

But at least Kitty was nowhere to be seen. Angela said she thought she heard her come in the back door during their afternoon session—which was, again, so much more meaningful and warm without Kitty in the room—and assumed she was lying down since she'd said she was feeling sick earlier.

---

*4:07 p.m.*

*This feels good already,* Felicia thought as she picked up the pace a little and jogged toward the trail at the base of the ravine. With two large meals already—breakfast with the green eggs and ham, and then a lunch of corned beef and cabbage followed by Guinness cheesecake, in keeping with Kitty's Paddy's Day theme—she could practically feel the flab inflating her thighs.

Keeping pace along the trail, Felicia checked her watch. *Dinner's at five. I'd better hurry this up.* She sucked in the clean air. *This is so much better than running on that wretched treadmill at the gym.*

Slowing down for a turn at the river, at the base of the ravine, she slipped slightly, causing her ankle to bump a rock jutting out from the hillside. *Okay, maybe the treadmill is a good thing—at least I don't run into nature there,* she thought, stopping to pull down her sock and check the injury.

But as she propped up her foot, something caught her eye on the hillside just above where she'd stopped. *What in the . . . Kitty?*

Felicia forgot about her ankle and grabbed tree trunks and branches to hoist herself up the side of the hill where a green pantsuited body lay sprawled and still on a landing. The figure's feet were tucked underneath it as if the body had rolled into that position and stopped.

"Kitty? Kitty? Kitty!" she called in an increasingly loud voice as she catapulted toward the woman.

There was no answer.

Finally reaching her, Felicia knelt down and said in a pleading whisper, "Kitty?"

But it was no use. The combination of Kitty's open, set eyes and the gash in her head explained why they hadn't seen Kitty that afternoon. She was dead.

# CHAPTER 27

# Mimi

*Saturday, March 17*
*6:49 p.m.*

Mimi had returned home Friday night from the retreat as quickly as she could. She and Mark had spent the night and most of the morning holding Milo, cleaning up after him, and worrying about him. He hadn't been able to keep anything down. Mimi's prized comforter, doused. Her plants, covered. Even Buster got nailed. Not to mention several outfits both she and Mark had donned, along with bath towels to cover themselves.

She hadn't been able to get an appointment with their pediatrician—he was on a fishing trip in Florida—so by early afternoon, frantic and unwilling to wait any longer, she decided to take Milo to the Immediate Care center across town. Mark volunteered to stay home with the other kids.

*Immediate Care* was a misnomer, Mimi discovered. She sat with her screaming child in the crowded, sterile, white and beige waiting room for more than four hours. Between bouncing and rocking Milo to calm him—neither of which worked—she gave apologetic glances to the other patients also waiting to see a doctor.

Finally a nurse-practitioner called out "Milo Plaisance" and escorted Mimi and Milo back to the "inner sanctum" and a small, curtained examining room. Nurse Rachelle took Milo's temperature and announced astutely, "My, my, he isn't feeling too well, is he?"

"You *think*?!" Mimi wanted to yell at her but bit her tongue and smiled tightly—a practice she'd perfected as a pastor's wife.

Two minutes—*two minutes!*—later, Nurse Rachelle diagnosed Milo with a stomach flu and recommended Pedialyte. Mimi could only imagine what that medical bill was going to be. Mimi and Milo were soon on their way out the door, past the still crowded, sniffling, sneezing, coughing, achy waiting room, and on their way to Bryant's drugstore to pick up a bottle and then head home—to take a nap.

Mimi walked in the front door to the sound of the phone ringing.

"Mark?" she called out as she put down Milo, still in his carrier, next to the phone. No answer, and the phone was still ringing. She wondered quickly if he'd taken the kids to the church or if there was some emergency that had come up with one of the church members, even though he hadn't called her on her cell to alert her to anything. Finally she picked up on the fourth ring.

"Hello. The Plaisance residence," she said trying to sound professional, even though she was sure it seemed more weary than anything else. Mark dragged himself into the room, wearing a T-shirt and his lounging pants, and looking exhausted. He lifted his hand in greeting and slumped onto their couch.

"Mimi, it's Felicia." Her friend's voice sounded uptight.

"Hi. How's the retreat going?"

"Well . . . Mimi . . . Kitty's dead."

Although she held the phone to her ear, Mimi ignored the voice on the other end, instead focusing curiously on her husband, who was stretched out with the TV remote in his hand. Her mind was racing. *Where are the kids? Kids—oh, Milo. I've got to get some of that medicine in him pronto.*

"Mimi, are you there?"

"Um, yeah. Just a sec. Mark?" she said, covering the receiver and jiggling the small paper bag toward him. "Would you grab this and give it to Milo? And where are the kids?"

Mark slowly roused himself from the couch. "The Taylors took them. They're all watching some Disney movie or something at their house."

Mimi breathed a sigh of relief. The Taylors were a family from their church who had kids about the same age as Michaela and MJ. Mark must have called over and explained the situation with Milo.

Mimi spoke back into the receiver. "Sorry about that. What did you say?"

"Kitty's dead."

"Buster! Mark, the dog's leaving tracks all over the floor. Didn't you wipe off his paws?" It agitated Mimi that Mark would often let Buster run outside, then usher him into the house without a thought to the possible mess.

"Mim—"

"Aw, no! Buster! Mark! I'm on the phone, or I'd do it. Please hurry before he tracks everywhere."

"All right, all right," Mark said. "Buster! Go to the kitchen."

Mimi shook her head to clear it. "You'd think I live in a fraternity house the way this place is run. Lord only knows the condition of my children right now." She sighed loudly. "I'm sorry, Felicia. You were saying?"

There was silence on the other end.

"Felicia?"

"I'm here," the quiet voice replied. "There's been an accident . . . Kitty's dead."

Mimi was so exhausted, she thought she was hearing things. "Sorry, Felicia, I'm just back from the doctor and I haven't slept in two days. It sounds like you said—"

"Dead. Kitty Katt is gone."

"What do you mean she's dead? She was fine yesterday. Are you sure?"

Felicia exhaled over the phone. "Yes. We all noticed she was missing late this morning. I found her while I was out for a run. We're not sure what happened, but she was halfway down the ravine."

"You found her?"

"Mmm-hmmm."

"Oh, my." Mimi didn't know what else to say. It seemed so shocking, so unbelievable.

"The coroner and police are here now."

The word *police* got Mimi's attention. The reality of what Felicia was saying suddenly sank in.

"Oh, no." Mimi swallowed hard. "Do they know anything more?"

"Not yet. They've talked to us briefly, and they're going to be taking statements from everyone. But Mimi, Jennifer was the last one Kitty was seen with."

"Yeah?"

"And . . . they were arguing."

"I bet she feels awful."

Felicia paused. "There's more to it than that."

"What?" Then Mimi caught the subtlety of Felicia's statement. "The police think Jennifer, what, pushed her over the side?"

"I know. It's insane," Felicia whispered. "But the cop they have here is a real Barney Fife."

"Good grief, arguing doesn't mean Jennifer killed her! Come on, you and I both know that if arguing were a motive for killing Kitty, we'd all be guilty."

"Yeah. But Jennifer told me about the argument not too long after it happened. She also said, 'I seriously thought about pushing the old bag down the ravine.'"

Mimi was speechless. But then she thought about all the times Kitty had been so nasty to her and the others, spitting out venomous words while wearing that big, toothy grin. She had to admit, if she were in Jennifer's shoes, she might have said the same thing.

"We all know Jennifer didn't mean it," Mimi said defensively, pushing her hair behind her ear. She caught sight of Mark returning to the couch, looking curiously at her.

"What?" he mouthed with a face that told Mimi he was hoping beyond hope it wasn't some church matter he had to attend to.

She waved him off, causing instant relief to spread across his face. He returned to his TV remote.

Felicia continued, her voice quivering. "You know that. And I know that. And Lisa knows that. But Margie Henderson from Our Savior Presbyterian overheard Jennifer's comment and told that asinine cop as soon as he arrived."

Mimi sighed. *Just great.* Margie was a "Kitty follower": nice, but didn't use the brains God gave her and thought Kitty, with her singing and speaking ability, was the best thing since Gloria Gaither.

Tears welled up in Mimi's eyes. Tears for what Jennifer was going through. Tears of feeling guilty because her last thoughts about Kitty—before she died, of course—had been harsh. Tears of remorse for Norm's family—even though she hadn't particularly liked him, either.

"This is terrible."

"I know," Felicia said.

"Thanks for telling me."

"Keep Jennifer in your prayers, would you? It's been really stressful here. Be glad you got called away when you did."

"Yeah."

"Is Milo okay, by the way?"

"Yeah, he'll be okay. I took him to Immediate Care—which isn't immediate, by the way—and they say it's a stomach flu of some sort. I picked up some Pedialyte for him. That should help."

"Well, I should go now. They're not letting any of us leave. And they're monitoring our calls. I just wanted you to know what was going on."

"Oh, for goodness' sake. Well, take care of yourself and the others. Keep me posted on what happens, okay?"

Felicia promised she would, then hung up. Mimi leaned over and clutched the side of the phone table.

"What's up?" Mark asked casually.

"Kitty Katt's dead."

"Are you serious?" he said as he hopped off the couch and moved toward her, his relieved face twisting back into a knot of concern. She nodded and opened her arms to receive his comforting embrace. Instead he flipped through his datebook by the phone, found the number he was searching for, and picked up the phone to start dialing.

He stopped momentarily. "Did Norm go up there or is he here?"

"I . . . don't . . . know."

Before she had even finished answering, he was punching numbers.

"Norm?" Mark said into the phone as he lifted his hand for Mimi to be quiet. "This is Mark Plaisance. I just heard about Kitty. I'm so sorry . . ."

Mimi glanced down at Milo, who was busily throwing up again.

---

*10:51 p.m.*

Mimi slipped under the covers next to Mark and snuggled close to his warm body. She placed her hand on him, almost protectively, and whispered sadly, "Norm will never feel Kitty lying next to him again."

"I know." He reached for his Bible from the nightstand and flipped it open to Isaiah.

"Read to me," she said, hoping to find comfort in the pages.

" 'In that day he will remove the cloud of gloom, the shadow of death that hangs over the earth. He will swallow up death forever! The Sovereign Lord will wipe away all tears.' "

As he read aloud, Mimi's mind whirled through a replay of her day. She'd spent the past hours grieving, but not so much for Kitty. There was really no love lost between the two women. Of course, she felt bad about what had happened to Kitty. She may not have particularly liked the woman, but she certainly hadn't wished her dead.

Mimi did genuinely feel bad for Norm. Norm and Kitty had been perfect for each other, and Mimi knew that Norm was going to take this loss hard. Every time she thought about that, she would look at Mark and whisper some version of, "What would I do if I lost you?"

Guilt washed over her, too. Had she been too judgmental of Kitty? Maybe she should have tried to love her a little more. Tried to understand her. Maybe tried to befriend her. But the truth hurt: She just didn't like Kitty. Period. Not even death could change that.

But she did believe that Kitty loved God. Underneath all the mess that was Kitty's demeanor and attitude, Mimi really did believe that Kitty loved her Lord as best as she could. She knew Kitty loved being a pastor's wife.

*Am I ready to go?* she wondered. *When I stand in front of God, will he say, "You were a good wife and minister to your church. I'm proud of you"? Or do I get so caught up in life that I forget the calling Mark and I have to lead people to Jesus?*

Just then a picture of Officer McCarthy popped into her mind. Busted! Life felt so fragile. Why was she was wasting it on mistrust of Officer McCarthy? Her realization caught her and made her embarrassed, ashamed. *Why did I put so much energy into some foolish dislike of Kitty?*

"I'm so sorry I've been stupid." She whispered her prayer, knowing that, in Kitty's case, it was too late to change anything.

*Why can't life be simple?* she wondered. *Why does it have to be so complex?* Why couldn't she just deal with Milo, then once he was taken care of, move on to one of the other issues, such as Dan McCarthy and why she disliked him? But it just wasn't working out that way. It was every issue, pushing against her, demanding her time and attention. *What is that book? Men Are Like Waffles, Women Are Like Spaghetti?* That's exactly how she felt. One giant pile of mixed-up spaghetti. And it was coming to a head with Kitty's death.

# Peaceful Pines Christian Retreat Center

*Sunday, March 18*

*9:45 a.m.*

Their bags packed and stowed against the front wall, all the pastors' wives sat in the retreat center's folding chairs, placed in rows by the sheriff's department.

"No one is allowed to leave," Deputy Arnie Perry had declared when he'd arrived the night before. "We want to interview each and every one of you tomorrow at nine hundred hours."

So here they were, waiting their turn as if they'd been selected to audition for *American Idol*'s Randy, Paula, and Simon. But instead they were preparing to be interrogated by the small-town cop Lisa and Felicia had dubbed "Barney Fife" for his arrogant yet bumbling behavior.

A little levity was necessary to cut through the anxiety the women felt. When Felicia had arrived back at the retreat center and frantically announced her discovery the evening before, the room had been pandemonium as Angela called 911 on the camp phone and the others expressed their horror first in gasps and then in tears. Even Jennifer had teared up slightly. After the body was recovered and taken away and Deputy Perry explained that he would return in the morning to do a "full investigation" in daylight, the women spent two hours in prayer.

Except for Jennifer, who said she wasn't feeling well again and went to bed.

Felicia sensed that everyone wanted to go home to their families and get away from this catastrophe, but she also knew they were equally interested in speculating about how Kitty had died. Did an animal attack her? Did she jump? Did she simply stumble and fall over the edge? Maybe she was even pushed! But who would do such a thing?

After the prayer time the night before, Felicia had pulled Lisa aside. "Are you thinking what I'm thinking?" she'd asked, incredulous at her own thoughts that Jennifer might be involved.

Lisa ran a hand through her reddish-brown hair, then clicked open and closed a clasp holding the bangs she was growing out. "I couldn't help but think of that. And she's been acting so strange ever since. I can't believe it would be on purpose, though. Do you think maybe it was an accident and she's afraid to say anything?"

The two had made an unspoken pact not to discuss the possibility any further. If their friend were involved in such a horrible crime, surely she would confess it. If not to them, at least to the police.

Felicia thought again of Jennifer's last words: "I thought about pushing the old bag down the ravine." Felicia shook her head, as much to clear her thoughts as to deny there could be any connection. *Just a coincidence.*

Now sitting next to Lisa and Jennifer, who still seemed sullen and ill, she breathed in deeply, wondering when this was going to be over.

"Felicia Morrison. I mean, Lopez-Morrison."

The sound of her name from Arnie/Barney made Felicia jump.

"Good luck," Lisa said as Felicia stood. "Don't let 'im wear ya down."

Felicia rolled her eyes at Lisa, smiled weakly to Jennifer, and then turned and followed the deputy's leading arm into the bunk room where they had slept. Some of the beds were pushed to one side with a makeshift desk and two chairs taking their place.

"Please sit down," he said.

Felicia sat neatly, her hands in her lap.

"What is your name, for the record?"

Felicia surveyed the room. There was no tape recorder. "What do you mean, 'for the record'? What record? You just said my name when you called me in."

Deputy Perry looked frustrated. "That's just procedure, ma'am. Your name for the record?"

*The sooner I answer, the sooner I leave.* "Felicia Lopez-Morrison."

"And Mrs. Morrison, I mean Mrs. Lopez-Morrison, what relation are you to the decedent?"

*Relation?* "Uh, fellow pastor's wife?"

The deputy nodded as if that were a perfectly normal relation and wrote it on his yellow legal pad. "And what were you doing at 1600 hours on March 17?"

"I was out jogging when I—"

"And what were you wearing during this jog, ma'am?"

*Why would that matter?* "Uh, I don't re . . . oh, yes, I was wearing powder blue running shorts and a UCLA sweatshirt."

"When you came upon the body, what did you see?"

Felicia explained how she first caught a glimpse of Kitty while inspecting her injured foot. "The green pantsuit made her blend in at first."

Perry nodded and took notes. "Did you try to revive Mrs. Katt?"

Felicia narrowed her eyes. "Well, of course not. She was dead."

"And how did you know that, ma'am? Are you a health-care professional?"

*Am I on* Candid Camera? "Uh, no," she said sternly, "but she wasn't breathing and her eyes were fixed."

The deputy nodded and continued to scribble on his pad. "What did you do then?"

"I ran back and told the others and we called 911. Then you came."

Felicia peeked around his arm to see what he was writing. She saw him scribble, "Deputy Perry arrived at 1700 hours to take control of the crime scene."

"Is there anything else you want to tell me?" he said, finally lifting his head. "Did Mrs. Katt have any known enemies or people who would want her dead?"

*Everyone!* "Not to my knowledge. She wasn't the most well-liked person, but I don't think anyone here killed her, if that's what you're asking."

Deputy Perry pursed his lips and bounced his pencil against them. "So you think she was murdered, then?"

Felicia glanced away and then back again. "No, I was responding to your question."

"Why would you bring up murder if you didn't think it was a possibility?"

Smiling sweetly, Felicia said through gritted teeth, "Everything's a possibility, Deputy Perry. I've seen enough episodes of *CSI* to know that. It's also possible that Kitty simply *fell.*"

The deputy stared at her as if he were trying to see into her brain. "One of the other women I talked with told me she saw Mrs. Katt fighting earlier that day with a Jen—"

"Jennifer Shores, yes. But Jen—"

"So you saw this altercation?"

"I wouldn't exactly call it an 'altercation.'"

"What would you call it then?"

Felicia crossed her legs and leaned forward. "I wouldn't call it anything other than a little spat, Deputy. Now, are we finished here?"

Deputy Perry tore the page on which he'd been writing from his pad and slid it into a waiting folder. "You're dismissed. Please take your luggage and leave without conversing with the other suspects."

"Suspects?"

Deputy Perry turned sheepish. "I mean, witnesses."

Felicia went back into the main room. All of the women eyed her expectantly, as if she might burst out with an "I'm going to Hollywood!" declaration followed by the flourish of a yellow slip of paper.

Instead, she silently found her roller bag, then turned to Lisa, who gave her a halfhearted, slightly puzzled wave, which she returned. Scanning the room, Felicia's eyes landed on Jennifer, who was now in the corner, looking miserable and staring at the floor.

Walking out the door, Felicia turned and looked around the retreat center one more time. The welcome banner had been taken down, but the shamrocks still glistened on the walls. *I guess Kitty didn't have the luck of the Irish after all,* she thought despite herself.

Tossing her suitcase in the trunk of the BMW, Felicia flinched as she thought about Jennifer and Kitty arguing and then Jennifer's strange conduct since then.

*Oh, Jen, sweet Jen. I hope you have a good story for Barney Fife. Otherwise, you're going to have a lot more to worry about than a hot, humid summer.*

# Felicia

*Sunday, March 18*

*12:04 p.m.*

Felicia, eager to be home, pulled her cobalt blue sports car in the driveway. While she was driving back from the retreat—*what a misnomer,* she thought—she'd called Dave on her cell phone and filled him in on the weekend's turn of events. Now she was looking forward to seeing Nicholas, taking a long bath, and having a nice dinner.

She got out of the car and went around back to get her bag from the trunk. When Felicia pulled the trunk lid down, she saw Nicholas waving enthusiastically to her from the living room window.

*Ah, he missed me, too,* she thought lovingly.

But when she opened the door, it wasn't Nicholas she saw. It was the big ball of fur in his arms.

"Mom, look!" he said from behind the cat. Just then the black-and-orange tabby jumped down and took off running toward the family room.

Felicia was stunned. "Nicholas, where did you get that cat? Did you bring it in from outside?"

The thought of a stray cat walking around her house—on her furniture, the beds, even in their closets—made Felicia shiver.

"No, Mom, Becky—"

"Becky gave him the cat." Dave appeared from the bedroom hallway. "I told him it was okay."

Felicia shot Dave a "You should have consulted me first" look, then leaned down to give Nicholas a hug.

"What's the cat's name?" she asked.

"Bengal!" Nicholas answered triumphantly, then ran off to find his new pet.

"He wanted to name him 'Pooter' because he breaks wind so much," Dave laughed as he came toward Felicia to hug her. "But I convinced him that the cat's black-and-orange stripes meant he was a bengal, like the Bengals."

Felicia hugged him warily. "Yeah, I get the connection. Why did Becky give him the cat? Didn't she want it?"

"He's from her brother-in-law's farm. Evidently they found him out in the barn one day. They have no idea where he came from. But Nicholas took to him immediately. So when I went to pick him up at Becky's, she pulled me aside and asked what I thought about bringing the cat home. I didn't think you'd mind."

"But there is no way we can have a cat in this house, Dave. There's no place for a box."

"I put the box in the bathtub in the guest bathroom. Nobody ever uses that tub anyway."

Felicia wasn't sure if it was her low threshold for stress after the weekend or what, but she knew she was not going to have a cat in her house—and especially not taking over a bathtub for its toilet!

She began pulling her suitcase toward the bedroom, stopping briefly to inspect the litter box in the bathroom tub.

Dave followed her. "You know, Becky said Nicholas didn't try to bite her or Eli."

Felicia threw her suitcase on the bed, then threw herself down next to it. "I just don't get it. He goes over there and he's a little angel, then he comes back here and—"

Felicia held her thought as Bengal came tearing into the bedroom, followed closely by Nicholas. When the cat jumped up on the bed and started to bolt across Felicia, she grabbed it. Walking briskly toward the guest bathroom, she set the cat inside, then shut the door.

"Mom, what are you doing?" Nicholas shrieked. "We were having fun."

"Nicholas, we are not going to have a cat in this house. I don't like them, and we are gone too much to take care of it. And you're too young for a pet anyway."

Nicholas looked at Felicia with tears in his eyes. She reached out and touched his arm so she could pull him close and talk with him, but he leaned over and bit her hand, causing her to lose her grip.

As he darted for his bedroom, he yelled, "I'm not too little. I'm *four*! Four is big!"

She turned to see Dave with his eyes fixed on her as if she'd just drawn and quartered the cat right there in the hallway. "Well, Dave," she started out defensively, "I get a vote here and I don't want that cat in our home."

But she knew she'd overreacted. She could hear Nicholas's miserable sobs coming from his bedroom. Dave didn't say anything. He merely turned and walked back out to the family room.

Felicia slid down the wall and sat on the hallway floor with her knees tucked under her chin. She was exhausted. The whole weekend—a time she'd been looking forward to for relaxation and renewal—had added even more muck to her giant stressball of a life. It wasn't the cat itself that was the problem. It was the idea of one more responsibility, one more new thing to handle.

*Wasn't I about four when we got Poppins?* she reminded herself. The collie, named for her and her sisters' favorite movie at the time—*Mary Poppins*—was the girls' only pet until she died when Felicia was a sophomore in high school. *I guess Nicholas can handle a cat at his age, too, then. And at least cats are more self-sufficient. No waking up in the middle of the night to let them outside for a bathroom break.*

She pulled herself up off the floor. *But we have to find another place for that litter box. I'm not about to tell our houseguests they can't use the bathtub because the cat is relieving himself in it.*

Felicia moved quietly into Nicholas's room. His loud crying had subsided into pathetic hiccups. "Hey, my boy," she said gently, sitting on the edge of his bed. He scooted his body toward the wall to avoid her touch. "If that cat means that much to you, I guess I can find a way to love him, too."

Nicholas swiftly jumped up into a sitting position, his cried-out eyes bright with hope. "Really?"

"Really. But I want you to promise that you will help feed him and clean his box. A pet is a lot of responsibility. Think you can do that?"

He nodded rapidly. "Can I go let him out of the bathroom now?"

Felicia smiled, then kissed Nicholas's forehead. "Yes, you may let Bengal out of potty prison."

Nicholas jumped off the bed.

*Well, at least someone is happy and satisfied today,* she thought as she walked to the family room to see Dave.

He eyed her cautiously as she scooted in next to him on the sofa.

"All's well that ends well," she said, laying her head on his shoulder.

Dave set down the newspaper and put his arm around her. "Oh, so you can give in, Miss Cat Hater?"

"I don't hate them. It's just—"

"One more thing. Right?"

"Exactly!"

Felicia felt Dave's chest move in a silent laugh. "Well, I guess you could say on a day the community lost a Katt, our house gained one."

"Dave!" Felicia soft-punched him in the stomach. "What a terrible thing to say!"

Then she chuckled—she couldn't help it. He was right.

# CHAPTER 30

# Jennifer

*Sunday, March 18*

*1:23 p.m.*

Jennifer was reaching headfirst into the backseat to haul out her suitcase when she heard the front screen door click and then slam, followed by Sam's sneaker-clad feet clipping down the sidewalk until he was next to her.

"Hey, let me get that," he said, tugging gently at her waist to pull her out of the car.

She obediently reversed herself, gladly accepting a kiss and one-armed hug from Sam as he reached for the small bag with the other arm.

Tossing her keys in her purse, Jennifer headed for the house, Sam behind her.

"So how was the retreat?" The hope in his voice momentarily made Jennifer even more aware of the strange contrast in how the weekend had turned out. She'd expected to return home refreshed, but instead she was nauseated and still reeling in shock from Kitty's death.

As they walked into the house, Jennifer ignored Sam's question. Her abdomen had been grumbling all the way home from Peaceful Pines Christian

Retreat Center, and she was eager to get to the bathroom. *Maybe whatever this is has finally pushed its way through,* she thought, wondering if it was the wilted salad on Friday night that had made her sick or those nasty green eggs the previous morning. Whatever the cause, it was a doozy. She hadn't even felt like hanging out with Lisa and Felicia, the real reason why she'd gone on the retreat in the first place.

But before she could dart away, Sam grabbed her arm and turned her around. "Honey, how was the retreat? Is something wrong?" he said, his simple inquiry now spiked with urgency. "Is it something with the baby?"

Jennifer looked him in the eye, knowing what she was about to say would either bring alarm or laughter. "I'm just a murder suspect, that's all."

"Whaaat?" Sam had the mixed expression of suspense and humor Jennifer expected.

Although hearing it gave her a bit of mental relief, she now really felt the pressure to get to a toilet. "I'll fill you in when I get back," she said, half-pointing to the bathroom.

Closing the bathroom door, she noticed that Sam had wiped down the sink and mirrors. *Hope he stays this helpful once the baby's . . .*

Her thoughts were interrupted as she pulled down her panties and saw blood spots in the crotch. *How didn't I notice . . . ?*

A sharp pain caused Jennifer to reach out and grab the vanity from her seated position. She felt a flood of liquid drop involuntarily from her into the commode.

"Oh, no!" she whimpered.

Then gradually louder, as the impact of what had happened set in, her voice catapulted from a plea to a shriek. "Oh, no! Nooooo! Saaaaaam!"

———

*3:25 p.m.*

Even with a pillow over her head and her body curled in a tight ball on the bed, Jennifer could hear Sam and Dr. O'Boyle talking in hushed tones in the living room. Although it was a Sunday, Dr. O'Boyle had offered to examine Jennifer at home when Sam had called and explained the situation.

*How ironic. Here I am, in the fetal position, with no fetus left inside me.* The thought made her now two-hour-long cry continue with fervor.

The familiar click of the screen door told her the doctor had left. Moments later, she sensed Sam's presence behind her in the bedroom doorway.

"Can I get you anything? Some water maybe? Or—"

"How about a uterus that works?" Her voice was muffled under the pillow, but even she was surprised at her sarcasm.

She felt Sam ease himself onto the bed, stretching out next to her and wrapping his arms around her. The reminder of his unconditional love brought another rise in her tears.

"Jen, Dr. O'Boyle says we can try again in just a few weeks, as soon as you heal." He nuzzled the back of her neck and kissed her.

She tossed the pillow off her head and rolled quickly to face him. "But Sam, we've been trying for ten years. Ten *years*! What if this was just a fluke? What if this was it?"

Sam stared at her blankly. She could tell he was balancing what he should say next. Meanwhile, she felt a shift inside her—as if someone had turned off the water hose and lit the furnace.

Before Sam could speak, she sat up in bed and punched the pillow next to her. "How could he? How could God let me get so excited about finally being a mother, then take it away?"

Sam pulled up and turned toward her, cupping her face in his hands. "Jen," he said sternly, "you have to believe that God brings good from everything. Even this. When Emily died, I couldn't understand how God could possibly bring something good from that. But then I met you, and I knew." He dropped his hands from her face.

Jennifer thought about what had happened to Emily, Sam's first wife. Even though it was fifteen years ago, Jennifer knew Emily's death—she was killed by a drunk driver on her way home from choir practice—was probably something he'd never really get over, even though he continued to put on a good front.

The warmth of anger bubbled inside her. "Sam, God didn't kill Emily so you could meet me. I mean, come on. What kind of benevolent father would do that?"

"You know I don't believe that way, Jen. I meant that no matter how bad things seem, God can bring good from it."

Sam's sudden turn toward theology made Jennifer wonder if he thought she would leave the church again because of this miscarriage. Her little "vacation," as he'd called it last year (in fact, she had been questioning her faith because of her inability to conceive a baby), had hurt Sam, especially because she had been so unsupportive of him and his pastoral responsibilities. He clearly had some residual fears about her doing a repeat performance.

Then she remembered Father Scott's words from last fall: "You have let your life become a testament to selfishness." She hadn't even considered Sam's feelings about all of this, just her own. And here he was, not only a grieving father, but also a husband worried about his wife's health and faith, and a pastor trying to counsel one of his sheep.

She watched him now. She could tell he was bracing for her next jab. The sea of concern on his face made her own bundle of emotions even out a bit.

Jennifer reached toward him, her hands around his face this time. "I don't understand what good purpose there could be for losing this baby, but I want you to know I am not giving up on us or on God. We're a team." She let go of his face. "And this isn't just about me. You lost a baby today, too." She put her head on his shoulder just before the tears came again.

But the drops she felt on her blouse weren't just hers.

# First Presbyterian Church

*Friday, March 23*

*10:42 a.m.*

Mimi and Mark walked silently into the formal mahogany narthex of Norm and Kitty Katt's church, First Presbyterian—the largest church in the region, as Kitty had always reminded them.

It was still difficult for Mimi to believe that Kitty was gone. Kitty had always seemed larger than life, as though nothing could stop her. But, obviously, something had: a treacherous slide down a ravine.

A crowd was milling around the open casket—the last opportunity to say good-bye before they closed it and moved it into the sanctuary for the funeral service.

Mimi and Mark had stopped by the funeral home on Wednesday evening to pay their respects, so Mimi wasn't particularly interested in viewing the body again—although it was impossible to get into the sanctuary without passing Kitty one more time.

As they stepped closer, dodging the townspeople who'd come out to support Norm (or to gawk, as the case may be), Mimi glanced over at the coffin. The area resembled a florist shop, with dozens of floral arrangements (all yellow—surprise, surprise!). Some people had even sent ferns and other plants with yellow ribbons tied around them.

But it was the body that amazed her—just as it had at the funeral home. Kitty still wore that tight-lipped grin, as though she were pleased with the turnout. Mimi could just imagine Kitty bragging about it to St. Peter. Kitty's jet bottle-black hair puffed in a bouffant hairdo straight out of the 1980s, and her slightly bloated body took on the appearance of a Marshmallow Peep—her outfit was canary yellow; even her caked-on makeup had a yellow cast to it. And of course, there was the pose: Instead of her arms lying straight down at her sides, they were bent at the elbow, with her hands on her chest, proudly displaying ruby red nails that appeared freshly manicured, and rings that covered almost every finger. But the best part was that the hands were showcasing the largest rhinestone cross necklace Mimi had ever seen (as though she were a model presenting a prize on *The Price Is Right*).

Mimi kept thinking, *Gaudy,* then berated herself for thinking unkindly of the dead.

"Doesn't she look beautiful?" a woman whispered behind her.

"She would have been proud," whispered another voice.

Mimi tugged Mark's sleeve. "I've never seen jewelry on a body before. I thought they didn't do that, for fear of grave robbers or something."

Mark nodded. "I asked Norm about that at the funeral home. He told me it was in her will that she wanted to be buried with all her rings and her cross necklace. He said the necklace was especially important, because it would show people how dedicated to Jesus she was."

Mimi snorted, then quickly covered her mouth and pretended to cough.

"Now, now," Mark said, although his voice gave away the fact that he thought it was pretty ridiculous, too. "Oh, there's Norm. I'll be right back." He left Mimi standing by the casket as he walked to Kitty's husband to offer his sympathies again.

"Her nails look nice," a familiar voice whispered in Mimi's ear.

Mimi smiled and turned to see Felicia standing behind her. "Hey, you, good to see you."

"You too. Did you see the police hovering outside? Have you heard any more about how she died or the investigation? Who they're looking at?"

Mimi shook her head. "No. Have they tried to question you anymore?"

"I had a detective call and ask me exactly the same questions they did that day. But then they started to ask a lot of questions about Jennifer: How long had I known her? Was she experiencing unusual stress? Did she have any mental illness in her past? Stuff like that."

*Unusual stress? Hmmm, well, I guess being obsessed with having a baby could fall into that category.*

"And they asked about that argument she and Kitty had," Felicia continued, cutting into Mimi's thoughts. "I would never, *never* believe that Jennifer is capable of that."

*I don't know, though. Could I believe that?* Mimi sighed. "What if she did it, but didn't *mean* to? What if she was angry enough that she pushed Kitty, and Kitty slipped?"

"What if it was an accident, you mean?" Felicia nodded.

"Right."

"But she'd admit that. Wouldn't she?"

Mimi shrugged and felt someone in the large crowd inadvertently bump her shoulder. She realized she needed to move out of detective mode and back into funeral mode—even if the former was more interesting.

"How's Milo?" Felicia asked, apparently thinking the same thing.

"Much better, thank God. I've never seen so much vomit and diarrhea come out of one kid."

Felicia laughed.

"Where's Dave?"

"Parking the car. I can't believe how many people are here. The parking lot's packed and the cars are lined all the way down the street. I even saw the lieutenant governor as I was walking in."

Mimi's eyes widened. She knew Kitty had often bragged about her state-wide connections, but she was surprised those boasts were actually true.

Mark walked back over and nodded to Felicia.

"Mark, you remember Felicia Lopez-Morrison? Dave's wife, from over at First Baptist?"

"Of course." Mark shook Felicia's hand. "Nice to see you again. Where's Dave?"

"Parking the car. I'm sure he'll be here in a moment."

"Tell him I said hello, if I don't get a chance." Then turning to Mimi, Mark said, "We should go in. The service is going to start pretty soon and we want to make sure we get a seat."

Mimi nodded and waved to Felicia, mouthing the words, *We'll talk later.*

Mark and Mimi entered the very formal, cathedral-like sanctuary through the immense mahogany center doors. Huge panels of stained glass covered the windows on both sides, depicting various scenes from the life of Christ—from his birth in the manger to his baptism in the Jordan River to his crucifixion. The high ceilings held a dozen or so glowing chandeliers. At the front of the sanctuary was a large cross sitting below the organ pipes.

It was certainly a beautiful church, Mimi had to admit. As they walked down the center aisle toward a seat, Mimi was surprised by the "celebrities" who were in attendance: Gene Walker, Red River's mayor; almost everyone on the town's council; and other prominent people from the state. Mimi brightened when she spied Lisa sitting with Joel on the other side of the church. She wanted to wave but thought better of it, not sure it would be appropriate. *This is a funeral, not a social party,* she reminded herself. She stole one more glance to see if she could locate Jennifer. *Not here. What could keep her away from this pageant? . . . Maybe the cops have her detained outside. Or . . . maybe she fled the state!*

*Oh, stop it, Mimi. You're being ridiculous. Jennifer isn't responsible for this.* Mimi glanced again around the church.

They settled into a wooden, lightly padded pew about halfway to the front, and Mimi opened the funeral service program. It was six pages long. Three pages expounded upon Kitty's life. *Hmmm, no mention of a son named Seth,* Mimi noted. Two pages made up the order of service, including hymns, testimonials, Scripture readings, and four homilies. The last page of the program was—*Good grief, I can't believe it!*—advertisements from local businesses offering their condolences. *Are they going to take up an offering, too?*

She nudged Mark and pointed to the ads. Mark took one look and shook his head in disbelief. *Even in death . . .* she wouldn't let her mind finish the thought. *Be nice, Mimi,* she scolded herself.

At five minutes to eleven, the funeral director and a few assistants rolled a now-closed casket down the center aisle, turned it at the front of the church so it sat perpendicular to the aisle, and centered it. Another assistant placed a large flower arrangement of yellow roses across the top right side of the casket, and on the left, near where Kitty's head would be, she placed a photograph of Kitty and Norm. Next to that, sitting between the roses and the photo, she positioned a pair of yellow high heels, placed with the toes touching, facing the congregation.

Mimi forced herself not to roll her eyes.

*Let me guess,* she thought impishly, *she planned out her own funeral, right down to the smallest detail.*

---

*11:58 a.m.*

Mimi stifled a yawn and fidgeted slightly in the warm sanctuary, then checked her watch. It had been almost an hour and they were only three-quarters of the way through the funeral service. *When is this thing going to be over?* Mimi wondered, agitated, and yawned again.

They'd finally come to the part of the service that Mimi liked to refer to as "open mike." This was an opportunity for anyone in the congregation to say a few words or to share a story or a memory of the dearly departed. A few talked about how kind Kitty was and how devoted she was to her husband and church. Many people talked about how much she loved being a pastor's wife. *Well, that's definitely true,* Mimi knew. Kitty thrived on her position of honor and wore it like a crown jewel.

A few others read Scripture verses. Then a woman who appeared to be in her early fifties strode to the platform, her plump body nearly bursting out of her knock-off designer tangerine skirt suit as her hose-clad thighs spoke to each another in swishes. Mimi thought she recognized her as one of Kitty's adoring minions from last year's July Fourth picnic. Once at the podium, the woman reached up a hand to smooth her shellacked hair, just as Mimi had seen Kitty do a zillion times. Then she tearfully read a poem she said she'd written—rhyming, no less—about how much Kitty would be missed:

> *Kitty Katt,*
> *oh, Kitty Katt.*
> *You were so much and all that.*
> *We loved you in life,*
> *and that is no trife-*
> *eling thing.*
> *You will be missed*
> *But now you have kissed*
> *The face of our God.*
> *You have a new bod-*
> *y. Oh, Kitty Katt,*
> *sweet, Kitty Katt.*
> *May your days be blessed*
> *We'll try not to obsess*
> *Over missing you.*
> *That's what we will do.*

Mimi shut her eyes and furrowed her brow. She hoped her expression would appear to any onlooker as if she were trying to hold in her grieving. This was awful. *Well, at least she's sincere.*

The woman ended her presentation by saying, "I've made copies of this poem, if anybody would like one. They're on the back table."

Mimi couldn't help herself. She glanced across the room to see if she could catch the eye of one of the PWs. Sure enough, she noticed Felicia watching her. Felicia winked.

Suddenly Mimi sat up straight as she watched a grungy thirty-something-year-old man walk to the casket and put what appeared to be a photo on top. He touched the shoes almost lovingly, then turned and walked back to the microphone.

It was Seth, the son Kitty had given up for adoption when she was sixteen and with whom she'd only recently renewed a relationship. As far as Mimi knew, there were only five people who knew about Seth, and one of those was lying in that closed casket. He looked exactly as he had every other time Mimi had seen him. His clothes were wrinkled, as though they'd been crumpled in a ball for a week. His shoulder-length hair was greasy, and his face sported stubble that resembled smudges of dirt. Or maybe that *was* dirt. Mimi couldn't really tell. And she wasn't sure she needed to know anyway.

Seth awkwardly stuttered out his words, as though he felt compelled to say something but was extremely uncomfortable being in the spotlight. "Katherine Katt . . ." Cough. Cleared throat. "Um, sorry. Um, Mah—Katherine . . . Katherine, Kitty, I mean, was a good woman. She gave me a life and made love . . . I mean, made *me* love again. She taught me to feel things I didn't know I could. She made me care about myself . . ."

While he was stammering through his obviously impromptu soliloquy, Mimi could hear the murmurs and whispers all around her. She was fairly certain they were all wondering the same thing: *Who is that filthy young man? Why would he be involved with Kitty?* And *how exactly was he involved with her?*

Mimi stole another glance over at Felicia, whose wide-eyed expression matched Mimi's. Felicia simply mouthed what Mimi was already feeling: *Oh, no.*

# Lisa

*Saturday, March 24*

*10:10 a.m.*

"Hang on, I'm coming already!" Lisa yelled at the ringing phone, as if the person on the line could hear her. She dumped a load of towels into the washer and sped toward the kitchen to pick up the line.

"Hello?" Lisa answered breathlessly into the phone.

"Lisa?" It was Felicia.

Lisa breathed loudly and felt her tone soften immediately. "Hey, Felicia!"

"Hi. Listen, I don't want to keep you," Felicia said in a let's-get-down-to-business tone, "but something's been bothering me and I just wanted to know if you noticed it, too."

"Okay. What is it?"

Felicia paused. "Did you see Jennifer yesterday at Kitty's funeral?"

Lisa thought back over the day. She couldn't remember. But then again, she wasn't really paying too much attention. The thing had felt more like a circus act. "Huh. Now that you mention it, I didn't. I saw you, of course. And I saw Mimi. But, no, you're right. I didn't see Jennifer at all."

"I didn't either." Felicia paused again, as if letting her announcement sink in.

Lisa half-laughed. "Come on," she said, "you don't think she skipped it because . . ." She let her words trail off, almost afraid where they might go.

"I don't, Lisa. She's our friend and we've been through so much together. But I'll tell you, her actions have been very suspect."

"I know. But there's got to be an explanation. There has to be. I can't believe Jennifer would intentionally . . ." Again, she allowed the words to drift.

Felicia sighed heavily. "Well, we'll see if she comes on Tuesday. Then maybe we should have a talk to get to the bottom of this."

"You're right. If she doesn't show up, maybe we should go to her," Lisa said.

"Yeah." Felicia paused again. "Okay, well, I just wanted to see if maybe I was being paranoid and missed something. I guess I'm not. See you Tuesday."

"Okay. Oh, Felicia," Lisa said before Felicia could hang up, "maybe we should double up on our prayers for her. Obviously, something's going on with her, even if it isn't about Kitty."

"You're right. I will."

Lisa hung up and stood holding the phone. *What is up with Jennifer?* She said a quick prayer for her and added, "And please let her show up on Tuesday, Lord. If she is hiding something, she's going to need her friends now more than ever."

But after another moment's thought, she grabbed her datebook from her purse, flipped to the phone numbers in the back, and began to dial Jennifer's number. She wasn't about to wait four days to find out what was happening with her friend.

# Jennifer

*Monday, March 26*
*12:15 p.m.*

Jennifer peered warily over her Olive Garden menu as her mother, Jo Jo, perused the one in her hands. She couldn't believe how well and fit her mother looked after so many years. Jennifer noticed that she could have used some makeup and her long, wavy, reddish hair needed a cut, but her gaudy chandelier earrings and Stevie Nicks style of flow-y blouse and skirt didn't seem as out-of-date now as they had eleven years ago.

*She seems to be focusing well and she's sitting still, not tapping or bouncing,* Jennifer ticked off, remembering the bipolar symptoms her mother had exhibited when Jennifer was growing up.

"Hmm . . . I'm thinking that soup, salad, and breadsticks sound good," said Jo Jo, glancing up from her menu before Jennifer had a chance to turn her eyes away. Catching Jennifer's gaze, she smiled and laid her menu on the table.

"It's going to take some time for you to get used to this me, isn't it?" she asked Jennifer, who had averted her eyes and was now pretending to study the menu before her.

Jo Jo was right, of course, but Jennifer didn't know how to answer such a loaded question delicately, so she returned to her mother's first topic. "Yeah, I think soup and salad would hit the spot."

*Salad.* Just saying the word brought the pain of the last week from Jennifer's gut—where she was trying to bury it—up to her throat again. *How could I have thought those pains were some kind of irritable bowel thing?* She couldn't help but beat herself up over it, even though Dr. O'Boyle had told her there was nothing she could have done differently to avoid the miscarriage.

"These things happen," he'd said. "The body does what it needs to do when something isn't right inside."

In her prayers that week, she had found herself bargaining with God for a baby—any baby, even a deformed one. "I can handle it," she told him pleadingly, even though she realized how futile her efforts were when she knew God's omniscience made him aware that she carried a great deal of insecurity about parenting. Her work at the shelter had helped her overcome some of that feeling, but she still wondered how the wounds of her upbringing would surface in her child rearing.

"Jennifer? Are you okay? You know, we can do this another time if you need to rest."

Jo Jo's words snapped Jennifer back to the current conversation. She had been staring blindly into a gigantic jar of colorful peppers on the wall next to their booth.

Jennifer squeezed her eyes closed and shot them open to clear her head. "No, no, that's okay. I needed to get out." She spied the unmarked car sitting in the parking lot—the same car that had been following her since the retreat. The same car that held the detective who had now questioned her three times about Kitty's death. She hadn't told him about her miscarriage. It was too painful to admit to anyone—*especially* some stranger, even if he *did* suspect her of murder. But she knew her crying and not attending the funeral certainly didn't bolster her claim of innocence. *It doesn't matter. Nothing matters. Let them think I'm guilty. My life can't get much worse than this.*

She hadn't even been able to take Lisa's call on Saturday or return it. She knew Lisa was probably just phoning out of concern, but she hadn't had the energy, not even for a friend. She'd purposely stayed home from church, too, the day before so Sam could inform the congregation about their loss without her having to deal with the sorrowful looks and back pats she was sure to receive. Not to mention that she didn't want that detective showing up and giving people even more reason to talk about her.

Sam told her that before he'd had a chance to share about the miscarriage, his associate, Derek, had announced from the pulpit that Lucy, whom Derek had married last summer, was pregnant. Rather than steal Derek's thunder—although Sam told Jennifer he did cringe inwardly when Derek said there would be two PKs terrorizing the church soon—Sam had decided to withhold their news.

"I don't know if I said this on the phone when you called me for lunch last week," said Jo Jo, "but I am really sorry for you and Sam. Now that we're talking again, I was hoping for a—"

An uneasiness made Jennifer squirm in her seat. She might be able to do lunch with her mother, but she was nowhere close to wanting to open her soul to her, especially about losing the baby and her inability to conceive.

"Yeah, yeah, we were, too. Now tell me about your new job." Jennifer didn't care if her interruption hurt her mother's feelings. She figured she had about three thousand up on her mother in that department.

Jennifer was on the alert for signs of deceit or embellishment in everything her mother said. As her mother described her job, Jennifer even questioned her, wanting some assurance that what she was telling her was true. She'd dealt with too many lies and had her hopes dashed too often in the past, so she was not going to be convinced easily that this Jo Jo was a long-term one. When Jennifer was a child, she'd seen her mother get briefly lucid and reliable when she took her medicine, only to have those hopes dashed when Jo Jo, for whatever reason, stopped.

The server arrived to take their orders, providing a break in the conversation. But after he left, Jennifer had another question, whose answer she thought would tell her everything she needed to know about her mother's latest plateau.

"Mother, I have to ask," she started hesitantly, "what brought on this decision in you to stay the course? I mean, you know there have been many times—"

Jo Jo was the interrupter this time. "Yes, and those are in the past," she said, nearly gritting her teeth, it appeared to Jennifer. Her mother's determination startled her. Then Jo Jo relaxed and sat back while the server arrived with their salad and breadsticks. "Besides, I have a new man in my life. I want to stay healthy for him. He's special."

Jennifer stiffened while her mother reached for the salad tongs and dropped a portion in Jennifer's bowl. *I knew it,* she thought smugly. *I'll bet he's "special." About as special as Monty, the one who scarred me with his emotional and physical outbursts.*

But as disgusted as Jennifer was with the catalyst for her mother's new life—she figured this too would pass, and once the guy dumped her, she'd be back to unmedicated bipolar swings—she didn't have the energy to discuss it further. Losing the baby had sucked all the fight out of her. So instead she pasted on what she figured was a somewhat authentic pastor's wife smile.

"Oh, that's nice. How's your salad? I could eat a hundred of these breadsticks."

# Felicia

*Monday, March 26*

*1:34 p.m.*

Felicia stared at her office wall, glad for a few minutes of silence. Delores was on vacation, so Felicia had one of the interns, Heather, sitting at Delores's desk just to field phone calls and handle visitors.

Fortunately, the phone had not rung much. Unfortunately, that was one more sign Felicia was not even close to reaching the $250,000 goal Ted had set for her to keep the office running. As much as she hoped the new bank client would solve her problems, she knew if it had, Ted would have said so by now. Besides, the bank could be serviced just as easily from Chicago as from Cincinnati.

*He wants me to go out there so he can convince me to go to Chicago,* she thought, reaching down to rub a bite spot on her leg—from Bengal this time, not Nicholas. She still hadn't told Dave about the trip, but she knew time was not on her side. Easter was less than two weeks away. Why go through the trauma of informing him about her trip when he was facing the busiest, most significant time of year for their church?

*I need to be here,* she assured herself. *And there is no way we're moving to Chicago, so why bother?*

Felicia picked up the phone and dialed Ted's private office number. She breathed a sigh of relief after the third ring, because she knew that meant the call was going to voice mail.

"Ted, this is Felicia," she began. "I'm going to need to cancel my trip out there next week."

She took a deep breath.

"You see, a friend has died, and it's a really difficult time with the funeral and all." She tried to sound as gloomy as she could. "I just don't think I have the strength to leave town right now."

*I probably just sank the last nail into my career coffin,* she thought as she hung up, still focused on the funeral theme. Even though Kitty's death had not impacted Felicia the way she'd let on to Ted, she did find herself thinking about Norm's heartbroken face at the service. As much as she disliked Kitty, she didn't want to see anyone suffering as Norm appeared to be. And Jennifer. The whole thing still unresolved with Jennifer was bothering Felicia. She wasn't at the funeral; no one had heard from her. *Will she even show up at Lulu's tomorrow?*

Felicia's mind jumped back to her work. She opened the yogurt container on her desk and scooped out a creamy spoonful. She felt a strange sense of joy over leaving that message for Ted. *There are always other jobs,* she assured herself, but deep down she knew she'd never find a position in the Cincinnati area that compared with the prestige and compensation she received from Brown & McGrory.

She reflected on living a different life, one that was simpler and less focused on material things and getting ahead. It was unfamiliar territory for her, at least in her adult life, but she knew Dave would support it.

*We'll probably have to start living on a budget,* she reasoned. *And no more shopping sprees at Macy's.*

The more Felicia thought about a less complicated life, the more she thought of Becky. As far as she knew, Becky worked only a few days a week cleaning houses. Then again, she didn't really know much about Becky except that her husband used to be a rabbi, and he worked at the tool and dye company now. And that she was like Supernanny when it came to

Nicholas—he never bit around Becky and Eli, but he always returned to it when he came home.

Felicia couldn't help but wonder about Eli and Becky's "real" story. She didn't know any rabbis, but she figured it was just as unusual for them to leave ministry as it was for Christian pastors.

Felicia set down her yogurt and spoon and picked up her phone handset again. If Ted had taught her anything at Brown & McGrory, it was to always go the personal route when she wanted to get information.

"Hello?" came the voice on the other end.

"Hi, Becky. It's Felicia. I was wondering if you and Eli could come to dinner."

# Lulu's Café

*Tuesday, March 27*
*12:09 p.m.*

Mimi glanced at her watch. "Almost ten after," she announced to Lisa and Felicia. Still no Jennifer.

The previous night, Lisa had finally spoken with Jennifer, then called Mimi and Felicia to let them know the truth: Jennifer had miscarried the baby. Mimi had felt terrible—here she was acting the judge and jury, really starting to believe that Jennifer had killed Kitty. Accidentally, of course. But still. *A miscarriage.* She knew how badly Jennifer wanted a child. *If only I could give her one of mine,* she'd thought—*mostly* facetiously—when Lisa told her.

"Bless her heart," Lisa said, playing with the edge of her menu. "This has to be devastating to her. She was so excited. The poor girl deserves to have some happiness after all those infertility treatments. And that whole thing with Kitty's death. No wonder she didn't show up at the funeral."

"But she did say she'd be here today, right?" Mimi asked, not sure if they should go ahead and order or wait. She wanted to wait—after all, it was the polite, respectful thing to do—but she was famished.

"I feel terrible that I actually allowed myself to suspect something," Felicia said. "What kind of friend does that?"

Lisa patted Felicia's hand. "Don't beat yourself up over it. It was an honest mistake. It happens."

Felicia nodded, but Mimi didn't think Felicia was buying it.

"How do we help her?" Felicia asked. "How do we encourage her? We all have kids. It just seems like our comments and concern would seem trite to her, since we already have what she wants, and we can't relate to what she's experiencing."

"We can be honest with her," Lisa said wisely. "That's all we can do. We can love her. We can pray with and for her."

Mimi glanced out the front window of the diner and saw Jennifer's silver Toyota Corolla pull up and park in front. "She's here." Mimi felt a measure of insecurity about Jennifer's arrival. She hoped Jennifer would accept what they had to offer her. She thought back to the time she had discovered she was pregnant with Milo. Jennifer hadn't taken the news of Mimi's surprise pregnancy too well.

The little bell hanging on Lulu's front door jingled as Jennifer entered. She was wearing an oversize red-and-gray Ohio State University sweatshirt and matching gray sweatpants. Her hair was pulled sloppily into a ponytail. Gracie, their waitress, looked up. "Some Jekyll and Hyde you are. Last time, all smiles. Today, doom and gloom. Whatever it is, it's not the end of the world, kiddo."

Mimi cringed when she heard Gracie. *Yes, it is to her,* she thought.

Once Jennifer was almost to their booth toward the back of the café, Lisa rose and embraced her. "We're so sorry, sweetie. We're so, so sorry." Felicia also stood and squeezed her shoulder, while Mimi remained in her seat, not wanting to cause too much of a spectacle to onlookers. She was fairly sure Jennifer wouldn't want that.

"Thanks, all of you," Jennifer said, dropping her purse on the seat and scooting in. "I appreciate your prayers and friendship." Her words sounded hollow, without emotion.

*She's probably cried herself dry.*

"Want to talk about it?" Felicia asked.

"No," Jennifer said and smiled tightly. The smile didn't cover the lack of feeling in her eyes, Mimi noticed. They appeared almost dead.

"We missed you at the funeral," Mimi said, hoping an animated account of the spectacle would cheer her up. She didn't want to push a topic where Jennifer wasn't ready to go. She knew it would probably take a while for her to discuss it, even with her friends.

Felicia laughed—a little forced, Mimi thought. "What a show. It had more acts than a Shakespearean tragedy."

Gracie approached the table, her pen and notepad at the ready. "Ready, ladies? It's not like you need to look over the menus. You probably have 'em memorized by now."

The women ordered quickly and sent their waitress on her way to tend to other patrons. Felicia started with her rendition of the service. "Oh, and I almost forgot. You'll get a kick out of this. So my boss, Ted, sends me a bouquet of flowers at work, with a note that says, 'You're in my thoughts as you grieve the passing of your friend.' My *friend*."

"How'd he know about Kitty?" Mimi asked, impressed by the thought.

Felicia chuckled. "I told him I couldn't go to LA right now because I'm still trying to get over the death of a friend. But it was just an excuse—I just didn't want to be gone over Easter, and he'd never understand someone wanting time off for a holiday."

Jennifer listened politely, but it didn't appear as if she were too interested. Mimi hoped her imitation of Kitty's hand display would perk her up. If that didn't work, there was the poem. *I should have gotten a copy.* She kicked herself for not thinking ahead, but then, she told herself, *How would I have known I'd need it?*

Finally, Lisa popped in with the kicker news about Seth. Mimi saw Jennifer's eyes finally flash with some life.

"Are you serious?" she asked, her voice sounding more like the old Jennifer. "He really showed up—and said *that*?"

"Oh, yeah." Felicia nodded and took a sip of her water.

Lisa shook her head soberly. "I still can't believe she's dead!"

"I know," said Jennifer. "I've had a detective questioning and following me around since the retreat. He doesn't even try to be subtle. He parks his car directly in front of my house! How are the detectives with you guys?"

The table grew quiet. Lisa cleared her throat. "We didn't actually have any detectives."

"What?" Jennifer's face flushed. She paused, clearly trying to process that discovery. "So you guys haven't been tailed?"

The three others shook their heads.

"Questioned? Were you even questioned again?" Jennifer asked.

Felicia perked up, as though trying to be helpful. "I was!"

"But as a possible suspect?" Jennifer pushed on.

"Well, no," Felicia said and started to fidget. "They asked me questions . . . about you."

"Well, that makes sense, then. I got a phone call last night from some state police detective."

"State police?" Mimi asked. "How did they get involved?"

Jennifer sighed. "Apparently, that Barney Fife of a police officer at the retreat messed up the initial investigation, so Norm asked the governor to get the big dogs involved. It was so straightforward, they were able to resolve it in a day. You saw the write-up in the paper this morning, didn't you?"

Immediately all three women chimed in, chattering over one another.

"What?" Lisa said. "With our budget problems, the paper was the first thing to go."

"Ha! Hardly. With four kids? I don't read the paper." Mimi laughed.

"I can barely make it through the *New York Times* anymore, let alone our rinky-dink paper," Felicia admitted.

Jennifer raised her hands in mock protest. "Okay, okay!" She pulled a rolled-up newspaper from her oversize purse, unfurled it, and plopped it on the table. "Well, I'm officially cleared."

Mimi breathed a loud sigh of relief. "I knew it all along."

The headline read: "Famous Pastor's Wife's Death Ruled an Accident."

Jennifer turned the paper toward her and began to read:

*Katherine Katt, beloved wife of Norm, pastor of First Presbyterian*
*Church of Red River, one of southwestern Ohio's largest churches,*
*passed away last week when she slipped and fell into a ravine, break-*
*ing her neck. She was at a pastors' wives' retreat. "We interviewed*
*dozens of suspects," lead investigator Arnie Perry told the* Red River
Chronicle *by phone late yesterday evening. . . .*

"Wait a minute," Felicia cut in. "Isn't Arnie Perry the Barney Fife guy?
Why would the paper quote him and not the state police?"

Jennifer shrugged.

"Well, this is the *Red River Chronicle*," Mimi joked. "The *finest* in
reporting."

"Shh," Lisa said. "Let Jennifer finish."

Jennifer continued reading.

*"But nothing led to any clear motive for anything other than an*
*accident," Perry stated. "Of course, finding that shoe helped."*

Felicia interrupted with a snort. "You think?"

Jennifer continued:

*Perry and his father, a retired detective, discovered one of the de-*
*ceased's shoes at the top of the ravine on a path. The heel was missing.*
*"It was a clear case of accidental death," Officer Perry confirmed.*
*"Mrs. Katt was walking when she slipped on a slippery place and*
*broke her heel. We figure that sent her tumbling to the ground."*

Jennifer glanced up from the report and around the table. The women
were all silent. Finally Felicia shifted in her seat, readjusting her napkin,
and said, "Jennifer, you don't blame yourself over what you thought about
wanting to push Kitty off the side of that trail, do you?"

Mimi saw Jennifer gulp and look down.

"Oh, sweetie!" Lisa said. "That was a coincidence. You didn't wish that upon her and that made it come true. It was an accident. Pure and simple. Please don't feel any guilt over that."

Mimi appreciated how well Lisa offered grace-filled, comforting words.

Jennifer nodded but seemed unsure. "I'm dealing with a lot of stuff right now," she whispered. "I'm just not ready to talk about any of it yet, if that's okay."

"Of course it is."

"I know this sounds terrible," Mimi half whispered, "but have any of you thought about . . ." She wasn't sure how to express herself without it sounding horrible.

"Whether she went to heaven?" Felicia offered.

Mimi nodded, wide-eyed. "Yes! I mean, the whole judgment thing. Standing before God's throne and giving an accounting for your life. Let's face it, she was a mean woman. I'm sure she had some good qualities . . . somewhere . . . and I don't want to judge her—I know that's not my place. And I certainly wouldn't want her to go to, well, you know. But I just keep thinking about it."

"What's the passage about the two women who argued?" Jennifer asked.

"The women the apostle Paul talks about?" Lisa suggested.

"Mmm-hmmm."

"I think you're thinking of the passage in Philippians 4," Lisa said, "where Paul pleads with Euodia and Syntyche to agree with each other. He says their names are written in the book of life."

"Yep, that's the one," Jennifer nodded. "I remember Sam preached a sermon on them a few years ago."

"The truth is that we don't know," Lisa said. "But we trust that God is a God of mercy and that he will judge with mercy."

"Even to those who showed no mercy?" Mimi asked.

"We don't know Kitty's heart," Lisa said. "We don't know the baggage she had that influenced her to act the way she did. But we do know that she showed Seth mercy. That she loved him—maybe not in the way we would have—but in, maybe, the only way she knew how."

This whole episode of Kitty's death and Mimi considering her own mortality had made Mimi concerned about her stance with God. She eyed each woman in turn, wondering if she should share about her feelings toward Phil. She knew these women and trusted them, but still, what if they threw back their heads in shock and told her she should be ashamed? What if they maybe even lost respect for her? A nervous twitter shook through her body as slight tremors moved her legs and feet and hands. Breathing in deeply, she knew what she had to do. Quietly, but still unsure, she said, "Can I tell you a secret?"

Felicia scooted to the edge of her seat and leaned forward. "Absolutely. I love secrets. The juicier, the better."

Mimi wasn't sure that made her feel better. How would Felicia react when she found out how juicy the secret really was—especially since last year Felicia had believed her own husband had been intimately involved with a woman from their church?

Lisa squinted her eyes. "Is this a secret like the 'I don't like to play the piano, I'd rather play the bagpipes' secret you told us last year?"

Mimi shook her head and pushed back her bob behind her ears. "No, this one really *is* juicy."

She watched Felicia sit back, eyes wide, while Jennifer rubbed her lips. This wasn't instilling confidence in her.

"Go ahead, hon," Lisa said comfortingly. "We're not going to judge you. We're your friends. Remember that."

Just then, Gracie appeared with their food. *Saved,* Mimi thought, trying to gather her courage for her announcement. After they got situated with everyone's order and said grace, Lisa revisited her response. "So that secret you wanted to share?"

Mimi paused to nibble on a French fry. Finally, when she couldn't hesitate any longer, she said, "Have you ever been attracted to someone . . . other than your husband?"

Felicia nodded. "You bet. In my line of work, I meet good-looking men all the time. It's actually a running joke between Dave and me. In fact, I was in a situation a few weeks ago with a guy on my flight to LA but . . . I realized my mistake."

Mimi was surprised to hear that from Felicia, but pleased, too. She plunged in, explaining her growing attraction to Phil. "Is this natural?" she asked when she'd finished. "Is my marriage in trouble? Am I a bad person?"

The women all gushed at once with offerings of consolation. "No way! You're not a bad person." "Of course, those things will happen." "Every woman has probably been in that situation."

Felicia pointed her salad fork toward Mimi for emphasis. "Chemistry is uncontrollable. There will be times when you'll feel things toward someone other than your spouse. That doesn't mean your marriage is in trouble. We know how much you love Mark. It's what you choose to *do* about those other feelings that really counts."

"I worked with a woman once," Jennifer said, "who ended up in an affair, though. It started just like you were saying. Simple, innocent, fun conversation. She lost everything."

Mimi shook her head. *It won't go that far. But then why am I so worried?*

"I'm not saying that's you!" Jennifer added. "I'm just saying, be careful. Is something missing from your relationship with Mark? You say no, but is that true?"

Mimi fidgeted with the napkin on her lap. "It's nothing big. It's just that we've had no time together since Milo came along. And that kid's worn me down, more than I thought he would. And Mark just treats me like a maid. There's no romance—unless you count him groping me while I wash the dishes. But almost all our conversations center around the kids. I miss the conversations we used to have about theology and culture."

Felicia nodded. "Been there!"

Mimi decided to confess it all. She might as well. She was already in pretty deep. "The truth is, I find this guy attractive—not just physically. He stimulates my mind and emotions. And I love that."

"Okay, here's a test," Felicia said. "When you know you're going to see him, do you get concerned about how you look? You know, what you're wearing, how your hair and makeup are fixed?"

Busted! Slowly, feeling ashamed, Mimi nodded.

Felicia shrugged and lifted her eyebrows as if to say, "And there you have it. Guilty."

"Okay, the next time you see him," Lisa said, "make sure you're in your grubbies, wearing no makeup—"

The women laughed.

"So treat him the way I do Mark?" Mimi said.

"Ouch." Jennifer crunched her face.

"You know what I mean."

"Have you told Mark how you're feeling?" Felicia asked, to which Mimi shook her head. "Honestly? And this is just my opinion, but I'd stay away from Mr. Principal and start focusing on Mark. If you miss having those deep conversations, why don't *you* start them?"

"I'm just so surprised by how strong the attraction is. You know me"— Mimi laughed, trying to cover her discomfort—"Miss Always-in-Control. This guy has thrown me for a loop. I mean, I'm not going to do anything, of course."

"Okay, I'm going to throw in a Bible verse," Lisa said, smiling. "I'm a pastor's wife; it's my job."

The women laughed again.

"So here goes: 'No temptation has seized you except what is common to man. And God is faithful; he will not let you be tempted beyond what you can bear . . . '"

As soon as Lisa started to quote the verse Mimi knew from 1 Corinthians, she, Jennifer, and Felicia joined in saying it together. "But when you are tempted, he will also provide a way out so that you can stand up under it."

"And he will, Mimi, you know that," Lisa added, with a wink.

"It's like I know it's not right, but I can't help myself. And that makes me feel so guilty."

"I was reading a book not too long ago by Philip Yancey," said Felicia. "*Rumors of Another World*, I think it was, in which he says that the presence of guilt is actually a gift to us. But he also says we're like magnets. We have two polar opposite ends—one that's attracted to and the other that's repelled by the same force. We can cut a magnet in half, thinking we can cut out that part of us that causes the attraction. But even having cut the magnet in half, we still end up with two parts that have that same polarity. Cut the magnet again and again and we have a smaller magnet, but still with that same polarity. His point was that the tendency to yield to an evil or bad thing and also to resist it infuses every part of our body. That tension is always there."

"Maybe that guilt is helping you know which polar side to stick to," Jennifer said.

"Guilt is a great gift of the Holy Spirit," Lisa said as she smiled and cut a strawberry with the side of her fork.

Mimi pushed her burger and fries around on her plate. "I just don't want to die and have to stand before God and explain myself. I don't want to do something I'll regret at the end of my life. Does that make sense?"

"Completely!" Felicia agreed. "Too many of us *don't* think about how our words and actions and even thoughts will come back to us when we die. The Bible says that every word we utter will be judged. I shiver when I think of how I've talked about people in our church." She shuddered to emphasize her words.

The front door jingled again, causing Mimi to look over. She gasped. "Hey, guys, don't look now, but guess who just walked in and is headed this way?"

Jennifer turned.

"I said don't look!" Mimi whispered through her teeth like a ventriloquist.

"Sorry." Jennifer turned back quickly.

"Um, hi." Seth stood uncomfortably beside their table, shifting from one foot to the other. He appeared to be wearing the same clothes he had on at the funeral. "I thought you would be here. You're always here on a Tuesday. My mom always made comments about it."

His statement made Mimi's skin crawl. *Figures.*

Lisa stood and grabbed a chair from a nearby table. "Sit down, Seth. How are you doing?"

He nodded but said nothing.

Felicia spoke up. "That was beautiful, what you said about Kitty the other day."

Again he nodded, but remained silent.

Mimi caught Lisa's eye. *Awkward!* she tried to communicate.

"You know, Seth," Jennifer said, "I'm really sorry about what happened to your mom."

"Me, too," he finally said, even though his voice was so quiet that Mimi had to lean in to hear. "I didn't think I'd miss her. But I do. She never gave up on me. My whole life I've pushed people away because they'd always leave. She told me when she met me a year ago that she wouldn't leave me. And she didn't. I mean, besides the whole death thing. And I treated her real bad."

"She loved you," Mimi said, fighting back a tear that welled up and surprised her. *Kitty did do some things like Christ. She wasn't perfect, but neither are any of us here. And neither am I.* Then a thought slammed through Mimi's brain. *With everything I volunteer for and with everything I do, can anyone really say the same about me that this man says about Kitty?*

"Seth," Lisa said, interrupting Mimi's indictment of herself, "everyone wondered who you were at the funeral. Wouldn't it be nice to introduce yourself—especially to her husband? Kitty would have liked that. She would have been so proud of you."

He tightened his lips and bounced his head slightly. It looked as if he were trying not to cry. "You think she would have?"

Mimi and the others immediately joined voices in agreement. "Of course she would have!" "Are you kidding? You bet." "Absolutely."

"Maybe. But I'm not interested in those people at that church. They didn't treat her well."

Mimi blinked. *What did I just hear?* "What do you mean?"

He shook his head, acting unsure of trusting them with her secret. Finally he said, "She didn't have any real friends. Every time she'd get close to somebody at the church, they'd betray her by talking about her behind her back. She acted like it didn't bother her, but I could tell it did."

"How could you tell?" Jennifer asked.

"'Cause I've felt that way, too. I'd just cover it up. She used to even watch you guys have lunch over here. She'd say, 'They're friends. They found each other. They're fortunate.'"

Now Mimi watched Lisa, Jennifer, and Felicia join her as all their jaws dropped. *Oh . . . my . . . goodness.*

"They never did anything for me—or for her—so why should I tell them who I am?" It took a moment for Mimi to realize he'd switched subjects on them.

"But what a testament to your mother, if you rose above all that. If you got serious about spiritual things—you know that was important to her." Mimi placed her napkin over her plate. She was finished eating. She had no more appetite.

"Yeah, I'm working on that. She gave me a Bible and told me to start reading in the Gospels, I think she called them. They're okay. Pretty interesting, especially the stuff Jesus says."

That seemed to break the tension in the group. They were back on familiar ground. Mimi nodded and smiled. "You keep reading. Make that commitment for your mother's sake. Don't give up on that, okay? Don't let her life—" Mimi choked a sob. "Don't let your mother's life or love or investment in you be wasted, Seth. You'll find exactly what you're looking for in that book. Besides giving you life, that's the best present she gave you. The book will teach you the difference between life and death. Honor her with it, will you?"

He sighed and tapped his rugged, dirty fingers on the table. "Yeah, I will. I should be going. I just wanted to talk to you guys."

Lisa grabbed his hand and squeezed. "You come over and join us any time you want, okay?" Mimi and the others agreed.

"Okay. Thanks." He knocked on the table as he said good-bye and started to leave.

"Hey, wait a minute," Jennifer said quickly. "Not to be disrespectful, but what was your mother's fascination with yellow?"

Seth's face was blank.

"You know," Mimi jumped in, sensing that Seth didn't understand the question, "how she wore yellow all the time—shoes, clothes, jewelry . . . ?"

"Oh." He nodded and Mimi watched a slight smile cross his face. It was the first time she'd seen any sense of joy. "She wore that for me."

"What do you mean?" Lisa asked, clearly intrigued.

"Remember that old song, 'Tie a Yellow Ribbon'?"

"'Round the old oak tree." Felicia finished the phrase. "Yeah?"

"She told me that song inspired her to keep looking for me. So she wore yellow to remind herself—and me—that she never gave up on me and that she loved me."

*Cheesy, but it works,* Mimi thought and smiled.

Seth raised a hand silently, then turned and left.

Mimi, Jennifer, Lisa, and Felicia sat quietly. They'd just had a divine encounter—and it was all thanks to the person they least expected it from: Kitty.

# Lisa

*Tuesday, March 27*
*8:13 p.m.*

"Why not?" Callie stood in the kitchen, her hands on her hips and her stringy hair dangling in her face, half covering her pink-rimmed glasses. "Everybody's going!"

"Not everybody." Ricky laughed, taking a large bite of a peanut-butter-and-jelly sandwich he'd made as a snack. "*You're* not."

"Ricky, stop it," Lisa said sternly, wiping off the counter by the sink, having finished the dinner dishes and cleaned up after their meal.

"Shut up, stupid!" Callie hissed at her brother.

"Callie, don't say that. Ricky, this isn't your conversation, so stay out of it."

"I'm just saying," Ricky said, undeterred.

*Why did I have children again?* "Out." Lisa pointed toward the living room. "This is a private conversation, and you don't need to be here."

"It's a dumb party anyway," Ricky said, emphasizing his point by swaggering out of the room. "They're all going to be drinking."

"Mom!" Callie said, trying to regain her ground.

But Lisa was holding firm. "No, Callie. I've already said no, and that's the final answer. And Ricky's right. You want to go to a party with no parents there and a bunch of teenagers getting into mischief. I wasn't exactly born yesterday, you know."

"All my friends are going. And we're not going to drink."

"I don't care who's going."

"But they all expect me to go."

"Yep. Don't care."

"Don't care about what?" Joel entered the kitchen and grabbed a glass from the cabinet closest to the refrigerator.

Reinforcements had arrived. Lisa motioned to Joel. "Why not ask *him* about going? I'll tell you what. Whatever he says will be the deciding answer."

Joel opened the refrigerator door and took out a two-liter bottle of generic cola. "What am I deciding?"

Callie's face registered defeat. Lisa knew Callie had approached her about the party because she hoped Lisa would take her side. But Joel? No way.

When Callie didn't say anything, Lisa spoke up. "Callie has asked to go to a friend's party on Friday night."

"Which friend?" Joel asked, pouring his drink.

"Kyle Bishop," Callie reluctantly answered.

"A boy?"

"It's a coed party!" Callie cried in defense.

"His parents going to be there?"

Lisa crossed her arms in triumph.

Callie waited a little too long to respond, giving away the truth: no parents.

"Nope. You're not going." Joel put away the cola and walked out of the room.

"Well, that's settled, then." Lisa folded the dishrag and placed it on the sink divider.

Callie stomped her foot like a five-year-old. "You never let me do anything! I hate you!" Then she turned and ran from the room. Lisa could hear her daughter storm up the stairs and slam her bedroom door. It was becoming as common a noise in the house as the phone ringing from yet another complaining church member.

And it was just as depressing.

# CHAPTER
# 37

# Felicia

"I really hope they like Mexican food," Felicia told Dave as she pulled the enchiladas from the wall oven.

He didn't respond, so she glanced over at him. Dave was sitting on the family room sofa, rubbing his head.

"Are you hoping a genie will pop out of there?" she asked, earning a half-smile and a roll of the eyes from Dave.

"If she looks like that one from that TV show, then yeah," Dave said quietly, eliciting a return eye-roll from Felicia. "No, I've got a pounding headache for some reason."

Felicia shoveled enchiladas from the pan onto a serving platter. "Hmmm . . . let me see if I can come up with a reason. Could it be that Easter is a week from Sunday? Or that you've been in meetings almost every night for the last two weeks? Or that you're feeling pressure to grow the church after that pastors' conference last month? Or—"

"Okay, Felicia, you've made your point," Dave said wearily. "Do we have any aspirin? I don't want to be hanging my head the whole time the Cohens are here."

"Look in my purse. It's over there by the door . . . in my briefcase."

Felicia turned back to her dinner preparations. She'd decided on a Mexican dinner because she figured that was the one meal she could excel at that Becky couldn't make herself.

The sound of paper snapping down on the counter made her spin back around.

"What is this?" Dave said with an accusatory tone. Felicia stared down at her Delta itinerary for the next week. She'd canceled the flight but had forgotten to throw away the paperwork.

"Felicia, this is Easter weekend, for goodness' sake," Dave boomed, not giving her a chance to respond. "There is absolutely no way you can go. No way. I'll call that Ted myself—"

"No, Dave, you don't understand," Felicia interjected, holding up a pot-holdered hand. "The trip is—"

"I don't care what the trip is, Felicia. You can't—"

*Ding-dong.*

Dave and Felicia went silent.

As if nothing had happened—a move they'd perfected as a pastor and wife—Felicia went back to plating food and Dave set down the aspirin bottle to bolt to the front door.

"Becky! Eli! Welcome!" Felicia heard him greeting their guests in a completely opposite tone to the one he'd been using with her seconds before. "Here, let me take your jackets."

*Why didn't he let me explain?* she wondered as she poured beans into a red ceramic bowl. *Does he always expect the worst in me or what? Now he's going to be harboring bad feelings all evening.*

Felicia joined the Cohens and Dave. As she shook Eli's hand—she'd never met him before but Dave had briefly when he'd picked up Nicholas—she took in his lumberjack frame and graying beard. She hadn't expected Eli to be so large when Becky was so petite. They were like cartoon-character opposites.

Becky handed her a covered casserole dish. "I wasn't sure if you knew we kept kosher," she said meekly. "So I brought food for us. I hope you don't think we wouldn't have liked your food. It's just that—"

"Oh." *So much for the Mexican dinner I came home early to make.* "Of course, Becky. I should have asked." Felicia took the dish from her. "I see it's still warm, so we can go straight to the table. Dinner's ready . . . for us, I guess. I mean, for all of us."

*Would the whole evening be this awkward?*

"Where's Nicholas?" Becky asked eagerly, surveying the room as if he might be hiding behind a chair.

Felicia bit her lip and eyed Dave. "That's kind of why we asked you to dinner tonight." She hesitated. "Well, in addition to me wanting to meet Eli, of course. We were hoping to find out what you do to get Nicholas to stop biting. So we sent him over to a friend's for the evening."

Felicia saw Becky give Eli a knowing glance as they walked toward the dining room. *Wonder what that's all about?*

The four of them gathered around the table. After the blessing, Felicia picked up the enchilada platter and handed it to Dave. Meanwhile, Becky handed her casserole dish to Eli.

"I hope Nicholas isn't too much of a nuisance to you when he's there," Felicia said to Eli, trying to break the ice.

Eli put his hand to his heart. "I love that kid!" he said warmly, instantly relaxing Felicia. Not only did he look different from Becky, Eli's personality was much more open and easy than hers. "With our kids grown and gone, it's so much fun to have a little guy around. You see life all over again when you see it through a child's eyes."

Felicia nodded. "He teaches us something new practically every day, doesn't he, Dave?"

Dave ignored her question and turned to Eli. "So tell me about New York, Eli. I hear you were in ministry there."

As they went on talking, Felicia made herself look at them but her thoughts were in another place. *I hope they didn't notice his slight directed at me.* If there was one thing she didn't want, it was for anyone to think her marriage was in trouble. They were a pastor and wife, after all—their marriage was supposed to be a model for others, even people outside their church. What kind of witness would they be if they couldn't exemplify a happy union?

When Felicia tuned back in, she noticed that the men were already swapping ministry war stories. *It's just like having another pastor and his wife over for dinner,* she thought as she listened to them talk shop. *Why should it surprise me that rabbis suffer as much as pastors from being put on a pedestal and run through the mill?*

She turned her eyes to Becky momentarily and saw the same faraway gaze that must have been emanating from her own face seconds ago. *Ah, the pastor's wife look,* she thought, amused. *Becky has that "I'm really interested in what you're saying" thing down pat.*

Felicia decided to try to guide the subject back to include her and Becky. "So when did you guys move here from New York?" she asked as soon as she caught a lull.

But before they could answer, Dave again turned to Eli without looking at Felicia. He was intent on talking shop. "How do you compete for members in New York when there are so many synagogues?" he asked.

*I give up,* Felicia thought. *He's clearly angry with me so he's going to keep steering this conversation back to the topics he knows drive me crazy—and leave me out.*

Once she was finished eating, Felicia set down her fork and noticed that Becky was done eating as well. She rose to take their plates into the kitchen.

Becky popped up, too. "Oh, let me help."

The two women glided into the kitchen, their husbands so deep in conversation they were oblivious to their departure.

Felicia took Becky's plate to rinse it, smiling gently at her but saying nothing.

"Felicia, I don't mean to pry, but I know you and Dave pretty well now. You two are usually so . . . in sync. Is something going on?"

Felicia reached down to open the dishwasher. "Why would you say that?" she responded nonchalantly.

Becky was quiet for a moment. "It's just . . . he seems to be overlooking you tonight or something."

Felicia placed the second plate in the dishwasher, then straightened up and gazed at Becky. Even at Bible study, Felicia couldn't be totally open with the women because they were members of her church. As much as they said they were there for her, she knew they really looked up to her and didn't want to hear about any problems in the pastor's family. That's why she was so thankful for the PWs, who stood by her no matter what.

But Becky . . . she seemed safe enough. She did have experience as a pastor's wife of sorts. And Felicia knew she wasn't involved in their local community, where she might spill Felicia's beans.

"Dave and I had a little fight right before you got here," Felicia confided.

Becky nodded in a knowing way. "Ah, yes. I thought I sensed the 'We're getting along even though we aren't' act from you two. Been there, done that."

Felicia smiled. As wonderful as the PWs were, it was nice to have someone in her own home who understood what it was like to be a minister's wife. She leaned back against the counter and told Becky about her office closing, Dave finding the ticket for her canceled trip, and the pressures they were under.

Becky listened intently. When Felicia was finished, Becky put a hand on her arm. "Let's go back to the table. I think Eli and I might have something to share with you that could help."

Felicia followed Becky back to the dining room. The men were deep in conversation, but as Becky passed by Eli, she tapped his arm, interrupting.

"Eli, I think we should share our story with the Morrisons," she said ominously as she eased into her chair.

Dave turned from Eli to Becky. "Eli was just telling me about the pressures you guys were under in New York. I have to admit, I never knew rabbis had the same kinds of problems as Christian pastors."

"Oh, our situation turned into more than a problem," Eli said, wiping his forehead with his napkin. "That's why we're here. We left New York because we couldn't take it anymore."

"If we hadn't, we would have lost everything, including our marriage," Becky said, reaching over to put her hand on Eli's.

Dave finally looked at Felicia—the first time since he'd found the airline itinerary earlier that evening. Evidently whatever he'd felt before had been washed over by this new revelation that cut a little too close to home.

Eli went on to explain how his synagogue's members grew increasingly less tolerant of his admonishments to maintain traditional thinking and observance and avoid liberal outlooks. Gradually his synagogue began losing members to the more liberal one just blocks away.

"When that happened, even the conservative members started pressuring me to back off, but I couldn't," Eli said, crossing his arms. "I was teaching lessons from the Torah the way my father had taught me and his father had taught him. I wasn't going to relax what I thought God was telling me to do just to please some folks who thought those teachings were too 'old-fashioned.'"

"But we didn't want to uproot the kids, and being a rabbi was all Eli knew, so we waited until Silas, our second, was off to college, then we packed up and moved here," said Becky, her eyes filling. "Thank God Eli's brother could get him that job at the plant. Otherwise I don't know what we would have done."

"Why didn't you just go to another synagogue?" Dave asked.

Eli and Becky looked at each other as if they were replaying a conversation about Dave's question in their heads.

Eli returned to Dave. "We decided we couldn't take that chance again. It was too painful the first time."

A thoughtful quietness settled heavily over the table full of dried dishes and half-empty platters.

Becky turned to Felicia. "So that's what I wanted to tell you."

Felicia was sympathetic with the Cohens but unsure how their experience related to hers.

Evidently Becky recognized her confusion. Clasping her hands, Becky took a deep breath. "You two have so much going for you, but you are under a lot of pressure. We left our synagogue because they wanted us to be people we couldn't be. You two aren't getting that so much from your church, but you do seem to get it from each other." Becky hesitated.

*I think this is the most I've ever heard Becky speak,* Felicia thought, intrigued. *Most people would infuriate me analyzing us like this, but she's different somehow.*

"I think what Becky wants to say is that you two need to find a way to reduce the stress in your lives—if not for yourselves, then for your little guy," Eli said.

Felicia looked at Dave. Finally they'd gotten to the original purpose of this dinner! A knot formed in her throat.

*Oh, not tears,* she thought, sensing that hot feeling that comes right before the flood. Dave didn't return her gaze, but his face went from neutral to angry to sad, as if his emotions were horses on a racetrack.

Becky seemed to sense their inability to speak. "I hope we haven't been too blunt here—"

"No, no." Felicia had finally found her voice, though much to her annoyance, it did crack a bit. "It's just difficult to hear that *our* behavior might be the cause of Nicholas's problems. Here I was thinking something was wrong with him, when instead . . ." Her voice drifted off.

Silence fell over the table again.

Dave cleared his throat. "Well, this is clearly something Felicia and I need to work on," he said, his jaw set determinedly but still not joining his eyes to hers. "But let's not drag down our dinner here with it. Why don't you get comfortable in the living room and I'll help Felicia get the dessert."

Felicia considered Dave curiously. Why was he trying to gloss over all this when the Cohens were being so vulnerable?

She caught Eli and Becky giving each other that knowing glance again as they obediently rose from the table. Felicia quietly picked up Eli's and Dave's plates and headed to the kitchen behind Dave.

"Why did you shut down that conversation?" she whispered angrily as soon as she knew the Cohens couldn't hear her. "They were only trying to help us."

Dave avoided her eyes as he pulled four coffee mugs from the cabinet. "I don't appreciate them telling us that we're making our kid into something bad," he said in a low voice while he poured coffee in the first cup.

Felicia watched him fill the others and start to carry them out of the kitchen. "But we asked them to, Dave. That was the reason we invited them over here in the first place."

He finally turned and allowed his eyes to meet hers, but she immediately wished he hadn't. His look was all business with not a hint of concern. "I'm done with this tonight, Felicia. We need to go entertain our guests." He didn't wait for an answer but instead left the kitchen balancing three mugs—leaving hers on the counter—in his agile football-player hands.

Felicia dazedly took the lid off the brownie pan and began cutting sections and topping them with ice cream, occasionally lifting her forearm to her face to catch the falling tears.

# 38

# Lisa

*Friday, March 30*

*11:31 p.m.*

Lisa was curled up on the couch next to Joel, snuggling and watching Jay Leno's opening monologue on *The Tonight Show.* They were alone in the house. Ricky was spending the night with his buddy Steve Markins, and Callie was having a sleepover with Theresa (Lisa had called Theresa's mother halfway through the evening to make sure they were, in fact, at Theresa's house). It felt wonderful to be alone as a couple. It happened so infrequently.

She and Joel started the evening by ordering pizza—what *they* wanted on it, thank you very much. It was loaded with onions, green peppers, mushrooms, and sausage. Then they drove to the local Baskin Robbins and each ordered a hot fudge sundae, extra fudge.

Afterward they stopped at the video store and rented *The Illusionist.* Both Felicia and Jennifer had gone on and on about what a great "date" movie it was. They were right. She and Joel both loved it.

Now the perfect ending to a great date night: Watch Leno and go to bed. In the morning, wake up and make love—with no worries about a child hearing. Ah, yes, it was perfect. A great respite from the troubles of their daughter and their church.

Lisa sighed contentedly and snuggled closer to her husband. Joel responded by tightening his arm around her in a warm embrace. She glanced up at him and caressed his face. He was so attractive to her. Sure, he was developing a bit of a paunchy gut. And his face showed creases across his forehead, and his hair was sprinkled with gray—attributable to Red River Assembly of God, she figured. But he was still just as wonderful as when she'd first met him way back when they were in youth group together.

"What?" Joel asked, as if afraid there was pizza sauce or something on his face.

"Nothing," Lisa said. "I'm just appreciating what a handsome man I have."

"Is that right?"

"That's right."

Joel's hand reached down and began to tickle Lisa. She squealed with delight and tried to tickle him back. They were both laughing easily and loudly when the doorbell rang.

Lisa felt Joel's body stiffen. They both glanced at the digital clock on the DVD player. *11:37* shone in bright numbers.

"Who in the world could that be?" she wondered aloud, afraid of the answer. Someone coming to their house this late could never be good.

Joel released Lisa and quietly walked to the front window to take a peek outside. He groaned. "There's a police car."

Lisa's stomach lurched as her motherly instincts kicked in. Somehow she knew this had to do with Callie. *The party. They snuck out after I called.*

Lisa followed close behind Joel as he walked heavily to the front door and opened it. Sure enough, there, standing beside the police officer, was their daughter, panic written across her face. Her hair was in typical form, stringy and hanging in her face. But her clothes were different. Lisa had never seen them before. *Theresa's?* she wondered. The dark brown shirt was a little too tight and a little too short, showing off Callie's navel and developing figure. Wide-eyed, Lisa blinked a few times to make sure the tiny belly-button ring she was seeing was actually there. Her jeans sat snugly on her hipbones. Way too low for a young girl.

"Mr. and Mrs. Barton?" the police officer said a bit gruffly. "Is this your daughter?"

"Yes." Joel opened the door wider to invite the officer inside, but the officer didn't move. Nor did he remove his hand from Callie's arm.

"This young lady has been getting into some trouble."

"At a party?" Lisa said it as a statement more than a question.

"Yes, ma'am," the officer said, glaring at Lisa as if he wondered why she would knowingly let her kid go to such an event. "The party got out of hand. No adults, loud music, and lots of underage drinking. The neighbors called to complain. She wanted me just to escort her to her friend's house, but as a parent myself, I didn't think you would appreciate not knowing what your daughter's been up to."

Joel turned from the policeman to Callie, his gaze shifting from concerned parent to stern disciplinarian, and back again. "Thank you for that. My wife and I appreciate your bringing her home."

"And here." The officer held out a pack of flavored Camel cigarettes. "She had these, too."

Joel accepted them and quietly looked down as he turned them over in his hands. Lisa knew that inside, he must be seething. If word of this got out, Callie would be successfully killing in one evening's work everything Joel had tried to do at their church and in the community to make a positive impact for Christianity.

Joel finally reached out to take Callie. Lisa watched the exchange take place from one authority figure to the next.

"Thank you again, Officer," Joel said. "We'll make sure this never happens again. Won't we?" Joel directed his last statement toward Callie, who simply nodded, looking like a puppy who'd been caught going through the garbage.

"Have a good evening," the officer said, then walked to his waiting car.

Lisa backed up to allow Joel and Callie to enter the house. The silence was deafening. As soon as Joel closed the door, he crushed the cigarette pack in his hand.

"Dad."

Joel's face tightened, then he turned and walked into the kitchen.

Callie turned ghost-white and swallowed hard as her father walked away. As if attempting to get somebody to listen to her defense, she said pleadingly, "Mom."

Straightening her shoulders and lifting her head, Lisa said softly, "I think you'd better go to your room."

Callie's eyes filled with tears, which she tried to brush away. She opened her mouth as if to offer an explanation, then closed it again and ran up the stairs. This time there was no slamming door.

Lisa stood in the center of the hallway and tried to even out her breathing. "God, I don't know what to do anymore," she whispered. "She's totally out of control. How do we get through to her?" She waited quietly, almost as if she expected to receive God's answer in an audible tone. But she was met only with more silence.

She could hear Joel pacing in the kitchen.

"What do we do now?" Lisa asked as she entered the kitchen.

Joel leaned over the counter with his head in his hands and sighed heavily. "I don't know. I keep trying to think of what I'd say if this were a church member's kid. What would I tell them?" He huffed. "I'd probably say something like, 'Get really serious about praying. Lay down the boundaries and make them clear. Give them tough love.' All things I've been doing. And none of them are working." He touched the smashed cigarette pack next to him on the counter. "None of them are working," he repeated, resigned. "I feel like such a failure."

"You're not a failure!" Lisa interjected sharply. "Everybody has these parenting issues. Even pastors' families." She paused, hoping her words were sinking in. "Let's ground her. We'll tell her if she wants to act like a baby, that's how we'll treat her. I'll drop her off at school and pick her up every day. We'll talk to Theresa's parents and see what they're doing. Maybe we should take her to see a counselor, someone who specializes in dealing with troubled teens."

"We have to do something. I don't know how much more of this I can take. Especially on top of all the trouble at church."

"I know, honey. Let's let her stew in this tonight, and we can talk to her in the morning."

# CHAPTER 39

# Felicia

Saturday, March 31

10:17 a.m.

Felicia pushed open the back door and walked into the quiet house. She'd just dropped off Nicholas for a play date at Trevor's, one of his friends from preschool. She hung her purse on a hook by the door, then slipped off her lime windbreaker and fit it over her purse on the same hook.

After the Cohens left on Thursday night, Felicia had tried in vain to talk with Dave, but he said his head was hurting again so he went to bed, leaving her to finish the dishes. Both Friday morning and evening he avoided her by being what she thought was overly occupied with Nicholas. She couldn't tell if that was in response to the Cohens' suggestion that they reduce the stress around their son or if he was simply avoiding interaction with her.

Felicia thought they could finally talk after she put Nicholas down to sleep last night, but when she returned to the family room, Dave was sprawled out on the sofa, snoring away.

Now that just the two of them were home—she could hear the *click-clack* of his fingers typing in the office—she thought they surely could resolve their stalemate.

"Dave," she said, appearing in the office doorway, "don't we need to talk?"

He looked up from the computer, but she could see he wasn't really focused on her. "Not now. I have to finish this sermon while Nicholas is gone. I promised him we'd throw the ball around out back when he gets home."

He dropped his eyes back to the computer, but Felicia stayed put. Her Bible study group had been discussing how to interpret the biblical mandate for a wife's submission. Felicia believed in the Bible's inerrancy, but she also knew God intended couples to be loving partners, not dictator and follower. Still, she was aware of her tendency to rule the roost, so she was trying to back off and let Dave lead—or at least feel as if he were.

But this time she'd had enough of the cold shoulder treatment. Leading was one thing. Avoiding was another.

"Hey," she said in an annoyed tone as she walked over and slid between Dave and the computer screen, half sitting on the desktop.

He pushed back the desk chair to give her space. "What?" His eyes narrowed.

Felicia furrowed her brow. "Do you want to give me a chance to explain? That's what."

Dave crossed his arms and glanced at the clock.

"Oh, give me a break, Dave," she said, following his eyes. "I know your sermon's already written. I saw it on the computer two days ago."

Caught, he avoided her. "I was . . . just tweaking it a bit."

Normally Felicia would have admonished him for fibbing, but she wanted to get to the bigger issue. "Dave, I'm not going to LA next week. That was an old itinerary you found in my purse. I'd canceled it, but I forgot to throw that copy away. You didn't give me a chance to explain Thursday."

"Oh." His eyes shot briefly to hers, then looked away again.

"Right, oh." She caught herself being a bit too smug and changed her tone. *Submission.* "But I have bigger news than that."

Dave met her eyes now. She scooted herself farther back on the desk so her feet were dangling. "They're closing the Cincinnati office. Ted wants me to head up Chicago—that's why he wanted me to go out to LA, to talk about it—but I told him no."

Softening, Dave unfurled his arms. "Was this before or after you signed National City?"

"At about the same time. I thought that account would be enough to keep Cincinnati open, but they said it could be serviced from Chicago. They're right."

Dave sat quietly for a minute, thinking.

Felicia started to playfully kick his knees with her toes. "Looks like you're getting that Martha Stewart wife you've always wanted," she said brightly, but the words caused a knot in her stomach.

Dave reached down and gently grabbed her left foot. "Why wouldn't you just look for another job? Surely someone else is looking for a go-getter like you."

Felicia's mind flashed to Randall from first class. "No, I don't think I could find the kind of job around here I have with Brown & McGrory. And I don't really want to take a step back."

She almost could see the wheels in Dave's head turning. "Well, we do have a pretty good savings built up," he said. "And if what Becky and Eli said about Nicholas is true, maybe it would be good for you to be around more. We'd save a lot in day care and babysitting. And gas, since you wouldn't be driving so much. I just never thought it was possible—that's why I got so angry the other night when they were here. It seemed like we were stuck between a rock and a hard place. But maybe the Lord is fixing it for us by setting up a situation where you can be home."

Felicia hadn't really allowed herself to think about being at home full-time. But now that Dave was on board with the idea, her thoughts spun like a top. She'd been working since she was sixteen. What did people do who stayed home?

She jumped off the desk. One part of her was relieved that the tension with Dave had dissipated, but she sensed another part filling with a new anxiety.

"Get back to that 'sermon,'" she said, planting a quick kiss on Dave's cheek before she zipped out of the room. "I've got a resignation letter to write."

But as she walked to the family room to grab her laptop, she felt a strange sense of dread. She loved her family and was eager for a more relaxed home life and a chance to nurture Nicholas more, but she'd worked so hard to get where she was professionally.

Pulling out her laptop, Felicia inadvertently unleashed a few stray business cards. One fell on her thigh:

FELICIA LOPEZ-MORRISON
SENIOR EXECUTIVE

She slipped her hand into the case and pulled out a pen. Crossing out Senior Executive, she wrote Wife and Mother below it.

She snickered at her impulsive creation, then *looked* at it again.

Airplanes coming to a screeching halt were all she could hear in her mind. One after another after another.

# Jennifer

Once again guiding her car down the familiar streets of her old neighborhood toward Jessica's apartment, Jennifer was deep in thought about the roller coaster of the last few weeks. First she was pregnant, then she reconnected with her mother, then she was suspected of murder, and now she wasn't pregnant anymore.

*It's times like these that I wonder how people make it without the Lord.*

She'd just gotten over daily crying jags about the miscarriage when Sam's careful announcement about it in the church newsletter caused a flood of cards and calls to their house, many from women who had never worked through their own emotions about their miscarriages. She'd found herself in the strange position of on-the-spot counseling about something she hadn't yet resolved for herself. As she was listening to these women's stories, she knew they were only trying to relate, and she did want to help, but it seemed cruel to her that they were refocusing her heartbreak on themselves.

One thing she did know for sure: she was not going to pursue pregnancy anymore, at least not in such proactive ways. "If it happens, it happens," she'd told Sam, but his look let her know that he, as usual, wasn't convinced by her pronouncement about letting go.

"We could always adopt," he'd said, but something in his tone made Jennifer think he wasn't making a suggestion as much as trying to offer an out.

And he wasn't the first one to mention the idea of adoption. Pastor Scott had made the same suggestion two months back when they had met on the walking path. And a few people at church had brought it up to Jennifer, as if she had never heard of the concept. As they were going on and on about it, she couldn't help but think, *If it's so great, why aren't you adopting?*

She winced as she remembered her nasty internal reaction, but she knew where her negativity about it came from. Her Aunt Jackie, her mother's sister, had adopted a boy and a girl as infants. Unlike Jo Jo, Jackie and her husband, Len, were loving parents, at least from what Jennifer saw (and envied). But as each of the kids reached eighteen, they found their birth mothers and never spoke to Jackie and Len again, leaving them utterly heartbroken.

"I think I'd rather never have a child than have that happen to me," she'd told Sam after sharing the story with him.

After parking her car in front of Jessica's building, Jennifer pulled a box from the backseat and hoisted it up the stairs to Jessica's second-floor apartment. Jessica's baby was due in a few weeks, so the shelter had gathered some infant supplies to help her prepare for the arrival.

"Hi, Jen. It's so nice to see you! I have good news!" Jessica was nearly bouncing up and down as she let Jennifer in the door.

Jennifer hoped Jessica's exuberance meant she had made better arrangements with family or friends to see her through the baby's birth. Although Jennifer had volunteered to be there when the baby was born, her miscarriage had changed her feelings about that.

"Great! Tell me!" Jennifer set the box on the floor, trying to match Jessica's upbeat mood. She noticed how difficult it was even to fake it, but she didn't want to discuss it with Jessica.

Jealously, Jennifer glanced down at Jessica's swollen belly protruding through the thin Baby on Board T-shirt. *That should be me.* Then she scolded herself for having that selfish thought.

Jessica shut the door and turned dramatically to face Jennifer. "Ronny and me are gettin' back together," she announced proudly, then lurched toward Jennifer for a hug.

Jennifer's arms were limp as her heart began beating faster. She gently pushed Jessica away. "But Jessica, I don't understand," she said, drawing her toward the couch, where they both sat. "How can you go back to him after what he did to you? And how could you risk your baby girl being there?"

Jessica sat back and tried to cross her legs but untwisted them when she couldn't get one leg over the other. *It's like she doesn't even know she's pregnant.*

"Well"—Jessica maintained her enthusiastic tone—"Ronny did the anger management program like the sheriff's department told him to. He's like a different man now, Jen, I swear."

Jennifer nodded. She wasn't sure how to respond. *Sure, he's different now. Just wait 'til you're back in his house again.*

"And as far as the baby goes . . . now, don't get mad at me." She checked Jennifer seemingly for assurance, but Jennifer's mind was tumbling so fast she felt her face go blank.

Jessica's gaze turned sorrowful for an instant, then reverted to happy. "I'm puttin' the baby up for adoption. Ronny said he ain't ready for no kids yet. We'll have 'em someday. But I'd rather have a husband and no kids right now than be stuck here in this tiny apartment with a cryin' baby and a stack of bills I can't pay."

Jennifer rapidly sucked in her breath in reaction to Jessica's "good news." Did Jessica really know what she was doing?

"Jessica," she said, her voice rising, "how can you choose this wife-beater over your own child? This is a *baby* growing inside you. You're going to regret it later, and there will be no going back."

Jessica got tears in her eyes. "We're moving to Montana as soon as the baby's borned," she said softly. "Ronny says we're gonna have a fresh start.

I think things will be different. I really do. And like I said, we'll have our kids later."

Jennifer stood to go. She knew if she stayed one more minute, she'd say something she'd regret. Instead she snapped into counselor mode.

"The shelter has contacts with a couple of adoption agencies," she said coldly. "I'll send someone by to bring you the paperwork."

And with that she turned, opened the door, stepped through it, and slammed it behind her.

# Felicia

*Friday, April 6*

*10:47 a.m.*

The ringing phone was just the "interruption" Felicia had been waiting for.

*I hope it's the office calling to ask me a question,* she thought as she pushed off the breakfast nook chair to answer it.

Instead she heard a prolonged silence, followed by a nasally voice asking, "May I please speak to the man or lady of the house?"

Disappointed, Felicia issued her standard "Please take us off your calling list" instruction and set the phone back in its cradle.

She turned back to the nook table and picked up her coffee cup. Glancing around, she felt a strange combination of accomplishment and disheartenment as she saw the empty sink, wiped counters, perfectly arranged pillows on the family room sofa, and Nicholas's toy box filled with the lid closed. After dropping Nicholas at Happy Times that morning—she'd removed him from day care but kept him enrolled in the preschool—she'd joyfully returned home to her new career as an at-home wife and mother.

But by ten, she'd done her Pilates tape, picked up the house, vacuumed, loaded the dishwasher, tossed some clothes in the washer, and showered. Now here she was . . . bored. And it wasn't even noon yet!

Felicia walked into the family room and picked up the TV remote. Seeing her laptop case still propped against the wall next to the back door made her pause. *It's like a dog, sitting by the door and waiting to be let out,* she thought with an emotional blend of amusement and sadness.

On Monday, she'd faxed her resignation letter to Ted. Minutes later he called, again pitching the Chicago office to her as if it were a new option. When she politely declined, he speculated she'd taken another job. When she explained she hadn't, he tried to encourage her to stay on at least until the Cincinnati office closed.

"Ted, I can't keep motivating myself and the staff when I know there is no future," she told him.

After a few more tries, Ted wished Felicia well, but his tone told her he really wished her anything but. She knew she'd let him down, and she felt awful about it. As a favor to him, she agreed to his request to keep the office closure to herself and simply announce her own departure. At first she'd balked at this idea, until he'd assured her that all of the Cincinnati staff would receive generous severance packages. She believed him.

Tuesday and Wednesday she kept Nicholas home from preschool as a treat for both of them. One day they drove down to the Cincinnati Zoo—a trek that felt automatic to her—and the other they went to the mall to get Nicholas's picture taken with the Easter Bunny. So this was the first day she'd really been home.

Alone.

With nothing to do.

She had just flipped on the TV—ironically, *The Martha Stewart Show* came on—when the phone rang again.

"Hello?"

"So how's my housewife doing?" Dave asked from the other end.

*You can only be as happy as you think you are.* "Great! I just finished house stuff, so I was going to relax for a while before I go get Nicholas."

"But that's not 'til three."

Felicia sighed inaudibly. She was trying to stay positive, but she knew Dave would never buy that she was "relaxing" for the next four hours. She never relaxed that much.

"Oh, well, I was only going to watch a little TV, then I was going to go get some groceries and swing by the dry cleaners," she said enthusiastically, but the tasks sounded hollow to her.

Dave didn't seem to notice. "That should keep you busy. I'll be looking forward to a great dinner then, I guess!"

Felicia wanted to be as excited as Dave was about her being home full-time—she kept reminding herself what a privilege it was that she didn't *have* to work—but she couldn't deny the emptiness she felt.

She didn't want Dave to suspect anything, though, so she put on her happy PR voice. "You bet you're going to have a great dinner tonight, mister." Then to add even more punch to her upbeat act she added, "And if you play your cards right, you might even get a little dessert, if you know what I mean."

Felicia was still smiling when she hung up, an outward appearance that defied her inner uncertainties. But at least she had a mission now: make a delicious meal for her family. There would be no warehouse club, ready-made chicken and boxed au gratin potatoes tonight!

Energized, she walked over to the bookshelf and pulled down a cookbook she'd received as a wedding gift. Thumbing through the pages, she pondered innocently, *What* do *people make for dinner when they have six hours to prepare?*

# 42

# Mimi

*Monday, April 9*
*2:31 p.m.*

"Hi," Phil Horvath said, holding open his office door and inviting Mimi in. "You're right on time."

"I try," Mimi said sweetly and smiled the best, prettiest, most genuine smile she'd exhibited in weeks.

Even though the topic of this meeting with Hemmings' principal was serious business—MJ and his friend Oscar had been caught sneaking into the girls' restroom on the second floor and setting off stink bombs—Mimi felt exhilarated about seeing Phil again. In fact, after Phil had called earlier to alert her to MJ's behavior and to invite her for a parent-principal conference, she had sifted through her closet until she came upon a thin, pink, billowy blouse that she'd often worn when she wanted to impress Mark. Fortunately, she could still fit into it, although it was a bit snug. Checking herself in the bathroom mirror, she'd smiled. *Not too shabby for a mother of four,* she thought, pleased. She had reached into the back of the bottom cabinet, below the sink, and found a curling iron she hadn't used in several years. *Let's see what this will do.*

After almost three-quarters of an hour, she took another look in the mirror. Her makeup made her face look fresh and even mostly covered the Samsonites under her eyes from lack of rest. Her blond bob curled up slightly at the ends, almost in a smile that said, *Finally, you're paying attention to us!*

Her blouse showed a whisper of cleavage, nothing obvious, but hinted at desire. And her black Dockers fit nicely, sitting perfectly on her hips and thighs—thanks to the girdle she was wearing.

She told herself this attempt at appearing civilized wasn't for Phil Horvath's benefit; it was her opportunity to pamper herself and feel like a woman again, rather than an exhausted mother of four.

She'd dropped off Megan and Milo at the church with Mark, who hadn't even noticed her effort.

Now, entering Phil's office, Mimi scanned the diplomas and various photos hanging on the wall. She spied a picture of a young Phil standing next to Boomer Esiason, a legendary Cincinnati Bengals player. And another photograph of Phil standing beside astronaut and former senator John Glenn. No family photos, though, Mimi noticed.

"Wow, you look fantastic," Phil said, shutting the door behind them, leaving them in privacy.

"Thank you." She smiled again. She felt goofy, but hoped it didn't show. She wanted to appear calm, confident, womanly.

Lightly he took her arm and directed her toward a seat across from his desk.

"I'm sorry this couldn't be a more friendly visit," she started, unsure of what to say and beginning to feel awkward about them being alone.

"Me, too." He settled into his bulky but comfortable-looking office chair, and stared at her. And stared. The dimple in his right cheek displayed itself prominently.

Mimi tucked her hair behind her ear and crossed her legs. *He really is nice-looking. I love that dimple.* "I don't know where MJ could have gotten ahold of stink bombs. We don't let him play with those things."

Her statement seemed to rouse Phil back to the topic at hand. "Well,

237

apparently Oscar visited his father in Indiana and got them there. He talked MJ into setting them off in the girls' restroom."

"I doubt MJ took much convincing," Mimi said disapprovingly. This felt almost like a game. Of course she was concerned about what her son had done, but at the same time, she enjoyed having somebody appreciate her appearance. Plus, they were still in that safe zone—it was his office at school! What could possibly happen there?

Phil laughed. "Yes, that's true. MJ is, well, special that way."

"So, how are you going to punish him?"

"I gave him a week's worth of afterschool detention. He'll do some projects around the school—clean up the playground, wash the desks, that sort of thing."

Mimi watched Phil push back the chair and walk toward her. He sat on the front edge of his desk across from Mimi but close enough that she could smell his cologne. It was a wonderful, citrusy scent.

Mark wouldn't wear cologne. He had sensitive skin that broke out when he tried it.

Mimi felt Phil's eyes taking her in, especially the bodice of her blouse. *Okay, maybe that's not so good,* she thought as she tried to shift nonchalantly in her seat in order to cover anything that might be showing.

"MJ really isn't a bad kid," Phil said. "He's rambunctious, to be sure. But he's just all boy. He's lucky to have a mother like you." He quietly and almost without notice moved into the seat next to Mimi and touched her hand. "A beautiful mother. A woman who probably doesn't get nearly enough credit for being who she is."

He spoke so gently, so kindly, almost in a whisper. It was seductive and hypnotic, and she could only nod. *Yes, he's right.* He was close enough now that she could see the slight creases on his temple and around his eyes. Those eyes. *They look so deep, like they could go all the way to his soul.*

"Have I told you how much I appreciate everything you do for the school?" he said. "For me?"

She felt breathless, as if his words had disrupted her ability to think clearly. "Mr. Horvath, you don't have—"

"Phil."

"Phil," she whispered. She thought his first name all the time, but she'd never said it aloud. Now it felt so natural falling from her mouth. She admired his lips. They were full and soft. Mark's were chapped and thin.

She was safe, she kept telling herself, justifying their behavior. *Nothing will happen here. . . . Nothing will . . .*

"You're so beautiful," Phil whispered back and moved closer.

*Beautiful.* Mark hadn't called her that in forever, she thought. She knew Phil's words were inappropriate, but she couldn't stop how they were making her feel. She didn't *want* to stop that.

"My wife is going to her sister's again next weekend. I'm going to be here doing some work around the building. Maybe you could join me?" The invitation sounded wonderful. And she was sure it was innocent. They'd paint something or fix a broken desk or . . . something.

They locked eyes. She nodded slightly, feeling unable or unwilling to say no. Anything he wanted felt okay to her. If he asked, she would agree.

She felt him squeeze her hand, and he moved his mouth toward her. *He's going to kiss me,* she thought, partly excited, partly horrified. *My kids are upstairs! I can't do this. But what would it hurt? It's only a kiss . . .*

She willed her mind to shut out her rational thought and began to meet him halfway.

*BBrrrrrrnnnnnnggggg!*

The bell announcing the end of the school day rang out the alarm.

Jerking back to her senses, she immediately pulled away and they both stood.

"I should get my kids—"

"Yes, I need to do a few end-of-the-day things," Phil agreed. "Thank you for stopping by. I look forward to seeing you again soon." He opened the door and politely held out his hand for a handshake.

She took it, feeling confused and shaken.

# Lulu's Café

Jennifer was the first to arrive at Lulu's, so she waved a greeting at Gracie, who was standing behind the front counter, wiping it down, and grabbed their usual booth, toward the back, next to a window, with a view of the side street.

It was a beautiful spring day. Balmy, so she'd worn only a light jacket, which she wasn't even sure she'd need. The clouds had a snowy-white, puffy look, so billowy—almost as though they were puffed up with pride at how grand the day was turning out to be.

Jennifer wished her mood could match that of nature's. But between her miscarriage, Jo Jo's reentry into her life, and Jessica's announcement, she wasn't sure she was able to muster that much joy.

Out of the corner of her eye, she caught Lisa and Felicia both pulling into parking spaces on the street in front of the café. She watched as they got out of their cars and hugged each other. Felicia was dressed in a burgundy running suit. *That's weird. Wonder why she didn't go to work today?* Jennifer thought. She knew Felicia always came to lunch straight from her office, so she was always dressed in business suits. She spotted them hugging another time, seemingly excited about something, then walking arm in arm into the diner.

Jennifer noticed their faces lit up when they saw Jennifer, which made her feel warm inside. *At least I have my friends. They think I'm okay.* The thought brought some comfort to her.

"What are you wearing?" Jennifer called out to Felicia, once she and Lisa drew closer to the booth.

Felicia's face broke into the widest smile Jennifer had ever seen. Her olive complexion shone and she looked younger and peppier than she had in a long time. "I quit my job!" she announced and did a little hip shake in celebration.

"What?" Jennifer's mouth dropped. She could understand Lisa being thrilled—Lisa didn't work. But Felicia was Jennifer's "working class" partner. Was everyone *abandoning* her? "Wow, Felicia, what happened?"

Lisa lifted her hand in protest. "No. Not yet. We have to wait for Mimi."

Her name had barely been uttered when Mimi burst through the door and nearly ran to the booth. "Okay, you guys are not going to believe this!" Mimi gushed, barely able to control her giggles as she plopped next to Lisa and across from Jennifer and Felicia.

"What?" Jennifer asked, wondering what could possibly be so funny.

"So you know Easter is like the biggest Sunday of the year, besides Christmas, and we do this huge church service—pull out all the bells and whistles. And everything has to be perfect. Mark's tense for, like, weeks beforehand."

"Yeah?" Felicia shoved her menu to the edge of the table.

"Okay, so our choir has this big number right before the sermon. They're singing 'He Is Alive.' "

"Oh, yeah!" Lisa broke in. "I know that song. That's a great one."

Jennifer laughed. "The point, Mimi, the point." She could tell this was going to be a good story—she just hated it when people drew things out.

Mimi was undeterred. "Well, only in the bulletin—which Mark proofread about a hundred times before Sunday—printed right there, larger than life, it declared that the choir was singing, 'He Is Alvie.'"

The women hooted. "Are you kidding?"

Mimi cackled. "Before the choir sang, the choir director went to the podium and announced, 'God is many things. Creator, Healer, Savior. However, he is *not* "Alvie," as the bulletin suggests.'"

They doubled over again in squeals of laughter. "Poor Mark!" Lisa said between giggles. "What did he do?"

"He turned fire-engine red. You could see his face flush from the neck up. Like he had an elevator riding up his face to the penthouse!" Mimi snorted, which put her into another round of giggles. "Needless to say, he didn't appreciate it too much when I told him it was a great lesson in humility."

"Oh, no!" Lisa said with her typical compassion. "I bet not." And she good-naturedly laughed again.

"What are you gals going on about this time?" Gracie had arrived at their table, surprising them with a round of beverages. "Well, I know what you all get every time you're in here. Unless you're going to throw me a curve this time, I just saved myself the extra steps and brought it all without asking."

"We appreciate that, Gracie," Lisa said, taking her iced tea. "You know us too well."

After the drinks were handed out, Gracie put her tray on a table beside their booth and pulled out her notepad and pen. "Since I'm here, why don't you save me a few more steps and just order?" She sounded gruff, but that was Gracie's way. The PWs had discovered that underneath her hardened exterior was a warm, special lady. Although Gracie wasn't a follower of Jesus, Jennifer knew she and the others were going to keep working on her and praying for her.

"Okay, I'll start." Mimi said lightly. "Hamburger with mayo and pickles. Fries, of course. And what's the soup today?"

"Chicken and rice or beef vegetable."

"I'll try the beef vegeta—"

Gracie shook her head slightly and grimaced.

"Chicken with rice," Mimi finished, smiling and handing Gracie her menu.

"Wise choice. Next?" Gracie said, waiting for Lisa.

They went around the table, ordering their usual. Lisa went with the tuna salad and fruit; Felicia got the chicken Caesar salad.

Jennifer sighed. "Oh, I don't know, Gracie. I'll just take the chicken strips deluxe plate." *It's not like I have to worry about eating healthy for a baby.*

As soon as Gracie left, Jennifer turned back toward Felicia. "Okay, so tell us your news."

"What news?" Mimi asked, taking a sip of her milk.

Jennifer pinched at Felicia's outfit.

"Hey!" Mimi said, obviously picking up on the clue. "Where are your work clothes?"

Felicia lit up again. "I quit."

"What?" Mimi slammed down her glass, splashing some of the milk over the side. "Oh!" She grabbed a napkin to clean up the spill. "When? Why?"

Felicia laughed and began to tell her story about the Cincinnati branch closing and how she didn't want to move to Chicago. So she quit.

"Talk about a new life! You're in for a treat," Lisa said.

"The only thing is, what do you *do* all day?" Felicia asked. "I'm afraid I'm going to be bored, bored, bored."

Jennifer noticed both women stiffen slightly, as though they took offense at her comments.

"Believe me," Mimi started, sounding a little put out, "you'll find plenty to keep you busy. For starters, your child will have you running constantly. And you'll be learning how to take care of a home. You'll become *domesticated.*"

Was that a dig? Jennifer wondered, surprised that Mimi would make a comment about what they all already knew about Felicia—great professional, not-so-hot housewife.

"I know, but how much time does that take, really?" Felicia evidently hadn't noticed.

Lisa laughed. "You'll see!"

*Always the peacemaker,* Jennifer thought. She was probably trying to make sure Felicia *didn't* get the dig.

"I decided the first thing I was going to do was really learn how to cook—more than enchiladas and heating up frozen pizzas," Felicia said, laughing. "So I bought a Julia Child cookbook."

Jennifer felt as if she were gazing into a mirror. She knew Lisa and Mimi were mimicking exactly what Jennifer was doing—raising her eyebrows. Except they looked more appalled and aghast. Jennifer just thought it was funny.

"Julia Child?" Jennifer finally asked. "Why not Rachael Ray?"

Felicia slurped the last of her Diet Coke and raised her glass for Gracie to notice. Then she shrugged. "That doesn't seem interesting enough. You know, Rachael Ray does all those quickie meals for busy working women. Since I have all this time now—"

Mimi choked on her milk. "Sorry," she said, wiping her mouth with her napkin.

Lisa touched Mimi's arm, but gave Felicia a look that seemed to suggest that Felicia was in for a treat. "Well, you know, Felicia . . . it *might* be a good idea to get a basic cookbook. I have a few I'll loan you. Then you can work your way up to Julia Child."

Felicia smiled. "Hey, how tough can it be, really? I ran a public relations office; I'm used to challenges. This should be a piece of cake."

Mimi cringed, her face turning red. "Well, *I* think—"

"Hey, Lisa, how did Callie enjoy her spring break with your folks?" Now it was Jennifer's turn to be the peacemaker.

Lisa chuckled. Jennifer could tell Lisa knew what she was trying to do.

"Well, we'll see if it has any lasting effects. I'm not so sure it was everything we wanted it to be for her. But we certainly enjoyed the peaceful house. We walk around on eggshells with that girl. She's so moody. But Joel and I got to go out to a movie and we took Ricky bowling. That was fun. I talked with my mom during the week. She told me she gave her lots of chores, took her to visit the homeless women's shelter in downtown Cincinnati (and, of course, made that a lesson time), and gave her several lectures on the importance of her role as a pastor's kid. It was probably the same lecture she gave me when I was growing up: 'You have a responsibility to be a role model to this church. They expect you to be serious in your walk with the Lord. They're watching you.' Stuff like that."

Jennifer winced. "Do you really think that's the best idea? I mean, she's probably already feeling the heat. Now you're giving her more?"

"We didn't send her there for the brainwashing. I think, more than anything, we sent her there so she'd see how bad she *doesn't* have it at home."

"Reverse psychology," Felicia said, nodding.

Gracie arrived with their plates of food and began passing them out.

"Hey, Gracie," Felicia said, taking her salad from Gracie's outstretched hand. "What can we pray for you for today?"

"That you'll give me a big fat tip."

"So you want a miracle?" Jennifer played along, and Gracie threw back her head and laughed. "You girls are something else. Let me know if you need anything."

Felicia volunteered to bless their food. Then the women dug in.

Rather than having them ask, Jennifer decided to plunge in with everything that had been happening to her. She finally felt like talking and opening up again. "Well," she started, with a half-eaten fry in her mouth, "I guess you're wondering what's been going on with me."

"It's about time, girly!" Mimi said, dipping her own fry into a puddle of ketchup on the edge of her plate.

"Sam wants us to try again." She popped another fry into her mouth, hoping she sounded nonchalant and casual about the whole miscarriage/baby thing. "But I don't know. What if I keep miscarrying?"

The women were silent, all eating and listening. The distraction of eating gave her more confidence.

"I just don't think I can go through that again. So I decided I'm not going to—at least not in any extraordinary way. It's just not meant to be, I guess. And anyway, it's probably better. Maybe it's God's way of keeping me from passing along the crazy genes from my mother."

Mimi narrowed her eyes slightly. Jennifer couldn't tell if her friend was bothered by the comment or simply trying to process what Jennifer meant.

"I didn't tell you last time, because I had so many emotions flying around, running into each other, I couldn't handle talking about my mother, either. But I reconnected with her."

"Really?" Lisa wiped her hands on her napkin. "You haven't seen her in what, ten years?"

"Eleven. But I thought, with the baby and all—this was when I was still pregnant—I figured it would be good to try to see if things could be different. But . . ."

"That's great news, Jen. How did it go?" Felicia asked.

Jennifer sighed. "I don't know. She's taking her medicine, so she says. And she seems to be okay."

"But?" Mimi asked.

"But she's done this kind of thing before. She gets herself together. And it works for a little while, then she's back to her crazy self again. There's no way I'm letting that back into my life."

"People do change, Jen," Lisa said.

"Not her."

"You don't know that for sure. You said yourself—it's been eleven years. Don't you think she may have really made some good changes? Gotten herself together?"

"I want to believe that, but—"

"Don't judge her too harshly yet," Felicia said. "Give her time. Give her a chance."

Jennifer nodded and dipped a chicken strip into the barbecue sauce. "Yeah, you're right." But deep down, she wasn't so confident. She'd seen the warning signs, the manic behavior, and wondered how it was going to affect her this time, now that she'd reopened a door with her mother that she'd closed long ago. *Did I do the right thing?* She didn't want to think about it, so she changed the subject.

"Oh, remember that girl, Jessica, I told you about? The pregnant one from the shelter? Husband's a wife-beater? Well, when I went to see her last, she informed me that she and Hubby are getting back together. But since he doesn't want any kids yet, she's going to give up her baby. No remorse. No hard feelings. Nothing. Just straight, 'This is how it is.' And she was actually excited about it! I wasn't too nice to her. Got pretty snippy, actually. The way she's willing to throw away this baby! She didn't even care. Anyway, I can't get my mind off what's going to happen to that child."

"There are plenty of couples looking for a white baby," said Felicia. "I hate to say it that way; it sounds so racist. But it's true. Just think how happy she'll make some family."

"I know. Maybe I'm just in complete amazement at how Jessica can be so cavalier about the whole thing. But I'm sure her husband's going to beat her again, so at least the baby won't be part of that."

"Speaking of giving up for adoption," Mimi cut in. She nodded toward the front of the diner. Jennifer turned to look. Across the street, she could see Seth walk out of his apartment building and trudge down the sidewalk, away from them.

"Wonder where he's going?" Mimi said what Jennifer was thinking.

"See? That's what I mean," Jennifer said, turning back in her seat. "Kitty gave up Seth when she was sixteen, assuming that the family he was given to would love him. But look what happened to him. His family didn't love him; they beat him. And all of those foster homes he went to after that didn't work out much better."

"But that's not a typical story, Jennifer, and you know that." Mimi placed her napkin on her now-empty plate. "That baby will be fine."

"That reminds me," said Lisa, laying the last of her sandwich back on her plate. "After Seth talked to us the last time, I really got to thinking about Kitty. Not that she did it right, but at least she tried to connect the pastors' wives so they'd have one another for support. Well, I keep thinking that maybe we should take the mantel of her work and continue it."

"What?" Felicia said, mouth dropping.

"It would be our way to honor her."

Mimi pursed her lips. Jennifer could tell she wasn't crazy about the idea. "I don't know. Mark's already after me about being overcommitted."

"Just think and pray about it, okay? We could do it right, where the wives would actually enjoy it."

"Only if we get to keep the shamrock outfit," Jennifer said, unable to keep a straight face.

Felicia groaned. "And no one's allowed to die at any of the retreats we do, right?"

Mimi laughed. "And no sick babies! I missed out on everything!"

Lisa rolled her eyes. "Just promise me you'll seriously pray about it. Look at how much *we've* benefited from one another's friendship. Kitty wanted that. She just didn't know how to do it. You figure all those other women have to be dying—*not* literally!" she said when Felicia started to laugh. "You know what I mean. We were lonely. You have to figure all those other women are, too."

"You're right. We do need to do something." Jennifer surprised herself by agreeing so quickly.

"Just promise you'll think seriously about it, okay? We can discuss it more in detail and make plans next time."

Jennifer felt lighter. It was a good idea, and it could actually give her something else worthwhile to focus on. She nodded. "I promise."

# Lisa

"Thank you for seeing me, Mrs. Bentz," Lisa said as she accepted a finger sandwich of ham and cheddar.

"Always a pleasure, dear." The ninety-year-old woman took the tray filled with the sandwiches and placed it in the center of her glass table.

They were sitting in Mrs. Bentz's sunroom off the back of her house. The room was floor-to-ceiling windows that opened to a pleasant view of the backyard and Mrs. Bentz's flower garden.

Lisa could see the yard had signs of new life poking out of the ground. Tulips and daffodils were rising up, almost in worship, so thrilled to be alive. The room had a pleasant feel to it, warm and comfortable.

The last time Lisa visited Mrs. Bentz in her home had been when she and Joel were struggling with their marriage. This saint and founding member of their church had invited her over to give her some motherly advice on relationships. Their conversation had actually saved Lisa's marriage. She was now hoping Bonnie Bentz could do the same for her child.

"What brings you here this afternoon?" Mrs. Bentz said, pouring each of them a cup of steaming hot tea.

Lisa considered the lovely, soft-spoken woman who had the wisdom of Solomon. Her cheeks were painted rosy with a circle on each of pink rouge, and her lips had a soft covering of light pink lipstick. Her pure white hair was coiffed neatly, as if she'd just come from the hairdresser's.

But it was her inner beauty that most attracted Lisa. It was rare to be able to be vulnerable with a church member. Lisa knew too many pastors and their families who had tried to, only to be betrayed and hurt even worse. But Bonnie Bentz was different. She had a gift of mercy and hospitality—and the wisdom to keep confidences. She was genuine.

Still, Lisa wondered if this time it was too much. Would Mrs. Bentz think she and Joel were total failures?

As if reading her mind, Mrs. Bentz chuckled slightly. "This visit wouldn't, by any chance, have to do with a certain young lady?"

A crack from somewhere deep within her broke open, and Lisa began to cry. She gingerly held her ham-and-cheddar finger sandwich and let the tears flow.

Mrs. Bentz didn't say a word—just nodded and smiled sweetly. After a few moments, she walked across the room to a small end table and picked up a box of tissues to give to Lisa. Grateful, Lisa took one, then rethinking her choice, pulled several more from the box.

"We don't know what to do," Lisa finally croaked out.

"Tell me about what's going on. You can leave out the part about wearing the tattered jeans to church. I already know that."

Lisa caught a slight smile cross Mrs. Bentz's face, which in turn made her attempt to smile. She took a deep breath and told her everything—Callie's attitude, her mouthiness, her refusal to attend church, her poor grades, her smoking and drinking, her police escort. When Lisa had finally run out of stories, she sat back in her seat and breathed in deeply. Her throat felt raw and achy, so she sipped her now-cold tea. Still, it soothed all the way down her throat.

"You've had a rough road, haven't you? Between your daughter and some they'll-go-unnamed church members who have been causing trouble, you've got your hands full. Is your marriage okay now?"

"Yes, that's the one thing I'm not concerned about!" Lisa half-laughed, half-cried.

"I pray for you and your family every day," Mrs. Bentz went on. "It's tough being in the ministry today. The pressures on you young folks; I can't even imagine." She offered Lisa a pinwheel cookie from a plate next to her on the table.

"My Charlie and I had our share of adolescent angst, especially with Sally, our youngest. They can be so melodramatic at that age, especially the girls. You'd think life was coming to an end, they've been so wronged." She chuckled again.

Lisa nodded vigorously. "I know!"

"Some of what Callie is going through is normal. All those hormones she's trying to deal with. That part she'll grow out of. Give her a few more years and a little more maturity. But I suspect part of this may be something more profound." Mrs. Bentz paused to sip her tea. "I'm an old woman who finished her parenting long ago. But I know about relationships. In my many, many years as a Christian, I've had a lot of pastors. And I've seen a lot of their children rebel and struggle. Not all. But many. They all handle that calling differently. Some better than others. Pastors' families all feel the pressure to be perfect, to meet the expectations of God and community and church. But many of them also pile the pressure onto themselves. I remember one pastor's wife—I won't tell you which one—who told her son that he wasn't allowed to doubt about God. He had to be there every week in the front row of the choir, supporting his father, because 'That's what everybody expects.' The last I heard"—she looked up at the ceiling as if trying to recall some old memory—"he'd left Christianity altogether. He's working for some atheist organization now. A shame."

Lisa gulped. What a reminder. She knew those stories too, and she didn't want Callie to leave her faith because her dad was a pastor. But she didn't know how to protect her, either.

"Your dad is a pastor. You grew up in that environment," Mrs. Bentz continued. "Is it possible you've forgotten the intense pressure a kid is under because you've been trying to deal with your own pressures being a pastor's wife?"

Tears sprang to Lisa's eyes again.

"I'm not saying that to judge you. For heaven's sake, you have a lot on your plate! You can't be expected to be and do everything. And I'm not blaming you, either. Let me be clear about that. But have you ever spent the day with Callie and just been straight-out honest with her? Have you ever asked her pointed questions about what she's feeling? Have you ever told her the struggles you're having and how you long to protect and nurture her, but maybe you're not sure what she needs? Have you made it safe for her to open up to you?"

Lisa wanted to say she had, but she knew the truth. She hadn't. Both she and Joel had taken a reactive stance with their daughter rather than a proactive one. Slowly Lisa shook her head, deeply ashamed.

"Honey, don't be so hard on yourself," Mrs. Bentz said, leaning over to pat Lisa's hand. "No one is a perfect parent. I don't care who you are, we all struggle with it. That's nothing to be ashamed of."

"I know," Lisa said, sobbing. "It's just that I keep thinking that because we're the pastor's family, we *should* be doing everything right."

"That's a load of hooey. Don't you let guilt or those false thoughts or accusations plague you. That's from the Evil One." Mrs. Bentz's face went from kind and motherly to determined warrior.

"It's so hard."

"I know it, dear. That's why we were created for community. The apostle Paul tells us in Galatians to bear each other's burdens. We weren't meant to carry them alone. Not even pastors' families."

Lisa was again amazed at this woman's insight and gracious manner. "You're right," Lisa said simply. "I'll try that. I'll try just to talk with her honestly."

"You'll be supported in prayer. How about I pray for you right now? Would that be okay?"

"Of course."

Mrs. Bentz rose slowly from her seat and motioned for Lisa to stay where she was. She walked behind Lisa and placed her hands on Lisa's shoulders. The bony, aged hands felt light to the touch, but as Mrs. Bentz began to pray, those hands seemed to have electricity flowing through them.

"Our heavenly Father," she began, her voice strong and clear. "We come to you because you are a Father who is trustworthy and good. You are our Creator and Redeemer. You specialize in healing broken, hurting relationships. We praise you, God, for how you've placed each of us in family, in community, and how you grow and strengthen our character through those vehicles. I bring to you my precious sister in Christ, who is hurting over a broken relationship with her daughter. Give her the wisdom to love unconditionally, the discernment to speak truth gently, the knowledge to hear her daughter's heart, not just the words she speaks.

"And we lift up young Callie. What a precious girl, so sensitive and kind. She's lost her way right now, and she needs your hand to clearly guide her back to the warm embrace of your love. Help her know she can find that love in her parents. Help her recall your goodness and mercy, that she would remember you and look to you for peace, rather than trying to seek it through the dead-end road of rebellion.

"I give you this family, who love you, Lord, who seek to serve and honor you through their lives and work. May you be glorified and may they praise you every step of the way, even when the way looks dark and bleak. May they know that you are working even now—even in your silence. May they find joy and peace in the journey. In Christ's name. Amen."

Lisa immediately felt as if a huge weight had been lifted from her. *Why did I wait so long to come to her?* "Thank you, Mrs. Bentz. You're a dear saint. I don't know what I would do without you."

"You're sweet." Mrs. Bentz reached to pat Lisa's cheek. "Would you like to walk some in my garden?"

# 45

# Jennifer

*Thursday, April 12*
*11:36 a.m.*

"I cannot get this baby off my mind. And I don't get it—it's not like Jessica is the first birth mom I've worked with at the shelter who put her baby up for adoption. We do a few every year. And I've never felt like this with any of those."

Jennifer sensed the release of pouring out to Father Scott everything she'd been feeling over the last week, but with it came the discomfort of not knowing where the turmoil would end. She glanced at her watch. She had to be back at the church office by noon. Even though they'd ended their counseling sessions last year—at his request, to help her stop focusing so much on herself and start focusing on others—she'd wanted to stop by to update him on what was going on in her life after they'd last talked in the park, and try to gain some clarity.

Father Scott, sitting across from her in his burgundy leather chair, was quiet for a moment, as was his way, then smiled slightly. "I think the Holy Spirit might be knocking on your heart's door," he said, leaning back.

"I've thought of that." Jennifer nodded. "But what? Do you think the

Lord wants me to talk her out of it? To maybe offer to have her live with us or something so she can keep her baby?"

Another minute or two passed as Father Scott observed her. She'd always noticed his little breaks in conversation allowed her to gear down her emotions instead of revving higher and higher, but she never could seem to put that into practice on her own. She wondered if they taught that method in priest school or if he was just slow to answer and that's how it worked out.

"Jen, have you considered this baby for yourself? Since you told me you're not going to pursue any more extraordinary fertility treatments, which I applaud by the way, perhaps adoption is the answer for you."

Before he could even finish, Jennifer was vigorously shaking her head. "No. No way. Not after what my aunt and uncle went through." She related that story to him, then ended with, "And besides, I don't think Sam would be up for it, either."

Again, a few minutes passed, and Jennifer pulled back her sleeve and looked again at her watch. *Good thing I can just dart across the street.* She knew Sam, who was busy leading a pre-marriage counseling session, would be looking for her to go to lunch at the stroke of noon and would have no idea where to find her. Certainly not in a counseling session of her own at the Catholic church across the street! She'd thought about telling Sam about her sessions, but kept putting it off until finally, she decided not to for fear he'd think she was still unhappy at church. It was just easier this way.

Father Scott sat forward again, which Jennifer knew was a sign he had something profound to say. She braced herself. "About your aunt and uncle, I think we can say that was an anomaly. I've known hundreds of adoptive families who never had an experience like that."

Jennifer was skeptical, but deep down she knew he was right. She'd seen many adoptions herself through women who came to the shelter. It was never easy on the birth mothers, but most of them knew it was the right thing for their babies, and they let go when they knew their babies were safe in loving homes.

"And from what you've told me about Sam, I think at this point he'd probably be open to anything that would make you happy."

Jennifer felt her uncertainty about Sam's feelings give way to agreement with Father Scott's assessment. As usual, Jennifer had come to Father Scott with what felt to her like deeply held convictions, only to have him swiftly bring out her real feelings, which were hiding underneath.

"But all that aside, here's the concept I think you can relate to most," he continued. "Remember when we talked about your not having a father and how much it meant to you to find out about our heavenly Father?"

Jennifer nodded. Those counseling sessions with Father Scott nearly a year ago had really connected her Christian commitment with the longings of her heart.

Father Scott smiled slightly again and nearly whispered, "When you asked God to come into your heart and life, he adopted you as one of his own. You are adopted and loved through God's grace and power, Jen."

She felt the tears welling up.

He continued with what she knew was coming. "And how wonderful would it be to model the love and grace of God by adopting a child—a helpless baby, as our Lord was when he came to us—and show that unwanted baby the same grace and unconditional love our Father has shown us?"

Jennifer felt something like a *ping* inside her. The turmoil was instantly gone. She knew what she had to do, and she wasn't going to waste any time in doing it.

---

*12:02 p.m.*

After dashing back to the office and telling Sam she needed to go help Jessica with something—not a lie, she reasoned—Jennifer hopped in her car and headed straight for Mel's Mufflers, hoping she could catch Jessica on her lunch break.

Walking in the shop's door, Jennifer saw two mechanics leaning on the chest-high counter, with Jessica holding court from a tall stool behind the cash register, telling some animated—and clearly off-color, from the language Jennifer briefly heard—story. Judging from the way they were looking at Jessica, Jennifer knew Jessica had been right about their intentions. She saw one staring straight at Jessica's pregnancy-enhanced breasts, which were made more obvious by the tight tank top she was wearing underneath an open blouse.

*Like vultures waiting to prey once the coast is clear.*

"Jennifer!" Jessica called as soon as she saw her. She jumped off the stool and waddled around the counter to greet her. The two mechanics, clearly perturbed at the interruption, each shot Jennifer a "Why are *you* here" look and skulked back to the garage.

The two women hugged. "What's up? Did you come to bring me more stuff?" Jessica asked.

*Is a selfish personality hereditary?* "I thought I'd take you to lunch," Jennifer said.

Jessica wasted no time darting behind the counter to grab her purse. She came back around, then returned, punching the button on the loudspeaker and announcing flatly, "I'm going to lunch."

After settling in at the Hardee's across the street, Jennifer was eager to get right to the subject at hand, but she didn't want to scare off Jessica. "So, how are you feeling?" she started out.

"Oh, I'm excited. Me and Ronny have our movin' truck rented and ready to go. He's got two interviews already set up for next month in Billings with the police and the sheriff's."

*No mention of the baby.*

Jennifer had hoped for a segue, but at the absence of one she devised her own. "So you'll be leaving right away then? I mean, soon after you deliver?"

Jessica sucked on her soda straw, as if she needed time to snap into another world. "Pretty much. Ronny says he can even pick me up at the hospital in the U-Haul if I want him to." She chuckled. "But he said to make sure I'm not leakin' or anything 'cause he don't want no smelly woman next to him all the way to Montana."

Jennifer couldn't believe the crassness of what she was hearing. If she thought Jessica should keep that baby before, she was even more sure now that giving the child up was certainly the best thing for that child. And God forbid those two conceive again!

"Listen, Jessica. I wanted to talk with you about the adoption."

Jessica nodded as she dipped a fry in ketchup. "Yeah, you said someone would come by with papers. Did you bring them?"

Jennifer hesitated. "Well, no. I wanted to talk with you first." She stopped again, took a sip of her Diet Coke, and crumpled her cheeseburger wrapper. "We've talked before about how Sam and I have had trouble having a baby."

"Oh, the miscarriage and all, mmm-hmmm." Jessica *looked* truly empathetic, which surprised Jennifer. *Maybe there is hope for this girl.*

"Well, ever since you said you wanted to put your baby up for adoption, I've been overcome with thoughts about it." Jennifer decided to leave the spirituality out of her speech and cut to the chase. "And I decided that maybe I've been so bothered because I—I mean 'we'—feel like we should adopt your baby." *Sam had better go along with this since I just committed him.*

Jessica's eyes widened, but Jennifer couldn't tell if it was a joyful kind of surprise or a more negative reaction. Finally she spoke. "I woulda never thought you'd want a baby from someone . . . like him," she said, her eyes returning to normal.

Jennifer smiled. She sensed Jessica's openness to the idea already, which relaxed her a bit. She hadn't known what she'd do if Jessica got angry or offended at Jennifer's suggestion. "I'm not worried about that," she said. "This baby would be raised in a loving home and church. A lot of mistakes we make as adults are because we never had that kind of love as kids."

Evaluating her with curious eyes, Jessica said, "Are you sure you can love a baby that comes from people . . . like us? I mean, like him? Not everyone could."

*Wow, she realizes their behavior is wrong. Wonder why she can so easily judge herself, yet isn't willing to change?* "Of course we can. It's not the baby's fault where she comes from." Jennifer bit her lip at that last statement. It hadn't come out the way she'd intended.

Fortunately, the bluntness made Jessica laugh. "Well, isn't that the truth? You just tell her that her mama was doin' the best she could at the time she was made and that I'm sorry for anything bad that comes her way because of me bein' so dumb about things."

Jennifer had the wide eyes this time. "Does that mean you will allow us to adopt her then?"

Jessica stared at her fries spread around her tray and pushed them around with a finger. "Better you than some stranger, I s'pose," she said, not raising her eyes. Then her head snapped up suddenly, her eyes narrowed, and she said with an accusatory tone, "But you'd better not try to back out once she's here. I mean, once we sign those papers, it's a done deal, right? I can't be tellin' Ronny and all only to have you bring her back 'cause you don't want her no more."

Jessica's insecurity about the adoption startled Jennifer. Here she was concerned about Jessica changing her mind when Jessica's only misgiving seemed to be Jennifer changing hers.

"Jessica, you have nothing to worry about. That girl isn't going anywhere once we have her in our arms."

After they finished eating, the two made their way back to the muffler shop, where they agreed that Jennifer would call before she brought Sam over so they could all sign the papers.

As Jennifer climbed into her car, she finally allowed the decisions of that simple lunch to sink in. *I'm going to be a mother! Sam and I are going to be parents! Oh, Sam . . . I completely forgot about him. Here I am making plans and he doesn't even know!* The rest of the way back to the office, she plotted how she would tell Sam he was going to be a dad . . . in just two weeks.

# 46

# Mimi

*Saturday, April 14*

*2:25 p.m.*

Mimi stood in her underwear and examined herself in her bedroom's full-length mirror. Finally Milo had gone to sleep, and at last she'd had an opportunity to take a shower. *I forgot how much I took cleanliness for granted,* she thought wryly. The pooch that had replaced her once-flat (okay, almost-flat) stomach seemed to want to take up permanent residence on her body. She'd been able to get rid of most of her post-pregnancy weight with each of her other children. But not this one. With this one her body seemed to cling to her post-pregnancy "Milo mass" like a burr clings to dog fur.

Mimi had taken to wearing oversize sweaters—not that she particularly liked them. She just couldn't fit into any of her pre-pregnancy clothes (not even the ones that were post-pregnancy for the other children) and the sweaters seemed more convenient. Fortunately, she thought, they also deceived anyone looking at her because they made her look thinner than she actually was.

She knew to be patient—that she'd only been *not* pregnant for four months, but still . . .

Turning to the side, she eyed her profile critically. Her breasts were larger than her normal petite ones, thanks to Milo. *Okay, that's not so bad,* she thought. *Of course, they're sagging more.* That, she knew, was thanks to aging and the four little milk-guzzling children she'd breastfed as infants.

Next, the stomach. Straightening her shoulders, she sucked in her abdomen to make it as flat as possible and held it, along with her breath. The flabby skin was hanging out, as if it were giving her a raspberry.

"Hey, whatcha doin'?" Mark's voice surprised Mimi, causing her to gasp and her stomach to return to its previous spongy, stretch-marked condition.

"Nothing." Mimi quickly stepped across the room to their bed, where her sweater and stretch khakis were neatly laid out.

Mark followed her and put his arms around her. "Since you're almost there, why not let me help you remove the rest and we can—"

"Oh, no, you don't."

Mark nuzzled her neck while his hand moved up her body. "And the kids are with the Taylors for the afternoon . . ."

"No, Mark," she said as she wiggled away from him. "I mean it. I'm not in the mood."

She watched him sigh and shrug. "Well, you can't blame a guy for trying." He gazed at her hungrily, and she sucked in her stomach in hopes that he wouldn't notice her bulge.

Mimi was grateful to the Taylors, who'd offered to take the kids for the afternoon so Mimi could rest and get caught up on her housework. They'd been such a help to her over the last several months.

The sounds of Milo waking from his nap blared through the tiny intercom sitting on the nightstand next to Mimi's side of the bed.

They studied each other silently. Mimi knew in the art of negotiation that the first to speak was the loser. Apparently, Mark knew that too, because he also remained quiet.

She cocked her head in the direction of Milo's room down the hall. Mark nodded but didn't move. Milo's cries were growing louder. Mimi pursed her lips and pointed at her semi-clothed body.

The standoff continued as Mark again nodded silently. Now she was growing frustrated and stamped her foot to let him know. He simply grinned and folded his arms.

"Mark Plaisance, get in there and check on your son!"

With great flair, Mark dug into his jeans pocket, pulled out a pair of spongy green earplugs, and smiled. "I think these little babies *will* come in handy," he said, popping them into his ears and striding from the room.

Milo's crying jags had been so disruptive to the family that Mimi had finally purchased earplugs in bulk and left pairs easily accessible in every room. She'd also often wanted to pass them out to church members and to strangers when they were at church or anywhere in town during Milo's "episodes," as she and Mark were now calling them. She'd envisioned painting "I'm" on one plug and "Sorry" on the other to help make her apology and embarrassment complete.

Through the intercom, Mimi could hear Mark in the nursery tending to their baby. Grateful for his assistance, even if they did each try to "pass the buck," she glanced at herself again in the mirror across the room. Dismayed, she picked up her sweater.

Throughout the house, the echoes of the doorbell chime rang out. She glanced down at herself and at the sweater she was holding. *Great.*

Used to receiving unannounced visitors—this was the pastor's house, after all—she yelled to Mark to get the door.

"I can't get it; I've got Milo. You get it," his response came.

"I can't get it; I'm not dressed," was her yelled reply.

"Well, get dressed. I'm in the middle of changing a diaper."

Mimi threw on her sweater and grabbed her khakis, trying to pull her legs through them while heading toward the stairs.

The doorbell chimed again. "Oh, hold your horses," she muttered, zipping up her pants.

She swung open the door to find Phil standing in front of her. Her surprise must have registered clearly on her face, because Phil lifted his shoulders slightly and chuckled awkwardly.

"Mr. . . . . I mean, Phil. Um, it's good to see you. Come in." She opened the door wider so he could enter. "Can I get you a cup of coffee or tea or something?"

He shook his head. "Sorry to disturb you at home, Mimi," he said, walking in and removing his Cincinnati Reds cap. His hair was sticking up everywhere, looking as if it was charged with enough electricity to power all of southwest Ohio. He glanced upward as Milo's bloodcurdling screams drifted down the stairs.

"Mark's with him," she said casually, so used to the sound that she didn't recognize that it might be alarming to someone new to what had become their House of Horror.

"I just received these and I wanted to drop one off to you personally." He handed her a small book.

"Thank you," she said, feeling confused over why he'd give her a book. "Sure I can't get you something?"

His hands were wrapped around the hat with which he was now fidgeting.

Mimi narrowed her eyes at Phil, trying to figure out why he was acting so strangely. He shifted his eyes from her to the present he'd given her.

Finally she glanced down at it.

*School's Out*
*How to Educate Your Children at Home*
*to Make Their School Lives Successful*
*Phil W. Horvath*

She read the words again. *Phil W. Horvath.* "Did you write this?" she asked, surprised that he'd never mentioned anything about writing a book.

He lifted his eyebrows and smiled.

"Phil, that's great! I'm so proud of you. But why didn't you ever say anything?"

"I don't know. I guess I wanted it to be a surprise."

"Well, it is. Really, this is wonderful. I hope it sells millions of copies." She gave him a quick hug.

"Me, too. Well, I can't stay. I just wanted to drop that off while you were at home. You get a free copy. I'm making everyone else in the PTA buy their own."

"I'm honored. Thank you."

He nodded and shoved his cap back over his tousled hair. "I'll see you next week at PTA?"

"You bet. Thanks again." She showed him out, closed the door, and ran her hand over the book's cover. The letters were embossed and bumped out.

Standing with her back to the door, she opened the book and caught something written in ink on the opening page.

> *To Mimi,*
> *A mother who does so many things well.*
> *A leader who steps up in times of need.*
> *But mostly, a woman of great character and beauty.*
> *I'm proud to know you.*
> *Phil Horvath*

His name was scribbled so she could make out only the *P* and the *H*. But she smiled at his kind words. *Character. Beauty.*

"Who was it?" Mark called from the top of the steps.

Mimi snapped shut the book and headed upstairs. "Phil Horvath. He brought me a copy of a book he wrote."

"That's nice," Mark said, clearly disengaged and war-worn from his episode with Milo, who'd calmed down to crying only every few beats, as if he were playing a timpani and hitting it to the music.

Clutching the book, she started to walk into their bedroom, then turned back to Mark. He was holding Milo and standing in the hallway, wearing the blue jeans she bought him for Christmas and a plain gray T-shirt. He looked so manly holding their child. They shared so much between them—

children, a deep love for God, and a commitment to the call to pastoring. He wasn't perfect and could, frankly, get on her nerves plenty. But she loved him. He was quietly cooing and bouncing Milo, when he caught her eye and smiled.

She returned the smile. "Hey. Thanks for helping out with Milo. I appreciate it."

"No problem. He's definitely a handful, though, isn't he?"

"I think he's going to give MJ a run for his money."

"The gratitude statement becomes, 'Thank God Milo is one and not twins.'"

Mimi sighed contentedly. "Have I told you today that I love you?"

"Nope. I love you, too."

She stared at the book with Phil's name on it. "You know, we haven't talked about adult stuff in a long time. How about I make some coffee and we go downstairs and talk? No agenda, just nice, fun conversation."

"Would that also, by any chance, include a detour to, say, the bedroom?"

"No. But you get points for trying." She leaned over Milo and kissed Mark's cheek, then strode over to her bedside table, dropped the book inside the drawer, and headed downstairs.

# 47

# Felicia

Thursday, April 19
2:43 p.m.

Felicia peered into the pot on the stove as she stirred. *So this is vichyssoise,* she thought, wondering if Dave and Nicholas would be more impressed if she didn't tell them it was really just potato-and-leek soup. Then again, they might not eat it if she didn't reveal its simple ingredients.

After a few days of nothingness, Felicia had decided to throw herself into being a homemaker, much as she had her PR career. So instead of continuing with the few dishes she knew how to make from her mother's kitchen, she'd bought Julia Child's *Mastering the Art of French Cooking.* She was almost through the soups chapter, which meant she'd soon enter into sauces.

The strange sense of glee she felt at completing one chapter of a cookbook gave her hope that she would soon acclimate to being at home and not having a career. She couldn't help but wonder, however, what would happen once she graduated from Julia's printed cooking school. Should she learn to knit? Or perhaps take some of those Home Depot courses on tiling and upholstery?

The soup finished, she turned the stove down to let it simmer, then pulled her jacket off the hook by the door to go get Nicholas. But before she could put it on, the phone rang.

"Felicia!" said a singsong voice. It was Ted.

*Why is he calling?* "Hi, Ted," she said hesitantly. "What's up?"

"First, tell me how you're liking that homebody thing," he asked, but it wasn't really a question with a desired response.

Felicia rolled her eyes, thankful camera phones hadn't become mainstream. "It's fine, Ted. I'm learning all kinds of new things." *Why did I say that? Please don't ask what kinds of "new things" I meant.*

Ted chuckled, giving Felicia a dull feeling in her stomach. Just in the last few days she had begun feeling the emotional separation between her career and her new situation. Now hearing his voice brought back the flood of apprehension she'd started to overcome.

He seemed to hear her silent plea. "Well, I won't ask what those 'new things' are, even though I'm sure they are quite interesting," he said smugly, making her hold the phone in front of her and stick out her tongue at it.

She put it back to her ear just in time to hear him continue. "Listen, Felicia, we have a situation I'm wondering if you could help with."

Felicia again sighed internally. As much as she'd wanted a call like this those first few days after she'd quit, and now did get a tiny surge of importance, she really didn't want to be an unpaid consultant. "What's that, Ted? You know I gave all my notes and files to Maureen before I left. She should be able to—"

He interrupted as if he hadn't heard her. "We got a call from National City Bank. They said they're pulling the account unless you are brought in to handle it."

Felicia's mind ran wild. Was Dave involved in this? Maybe he was sick of Julia's soups. How could she go back to work now, after everything was settled? "Oh, Ted, I'm sorry to hear that," she said with resolve, "but I'm still not moving to Chicago—"

"I'm not calling to pitch *that* again," he said, sounding annoyed at his unsuccessful effort. "This account is too important for us to lose. And to be perfectly frank, we've heard from a couple of other accounts there who were, shall we say, highly perturbed to hear about your leaving Brown & McGrory."

Where was he going with this?

She kept quiet and let him talk. "So here's what I'm proposing. You have a decent-size house there with an office, right?"

"Mmm-hmmm," Felicia answered, trying to anticipate what he would say next.

"Good. We want to bring you back to handle these accounts from home. Once Cincinnati is closed, you can use the Chicago office for administrative support, but realistically you will be a one-person shop there in—"

Felicia's head was whirling so fast at this offer that she missed his awkward pause at first. "Oh, Red River," she said.

She could hear Ted smile, as he said, "Mmm . . . Red River. So Brown & McGrory would have offices in LA, New York, Chicago, Dallas, and . . . Red River, Ohio. Isn't that . . . quaint?"

Felicia was too busy sorting through the impact of Ted's proposal to hear his second question, which wasn't really a question. Could working from home give her the challenge she needed . . . with time to learn sauces?

# Lisa

*Thursday, April 19*

*9:17 p.m.*

The last eight days had passed without much success talking with Callie. Every time Lisa tried, Callie just shut down, making Lisa feel even more miserable as a parent. She had such resolve when she visited Mrs. Bentz. Where had it gone?

Lisa knew she needed to be intentional, but there was a part of her that was afraid of failure. *What if it blows up in my face? What if she won't talk?*

Lisa was thinking in front of the television, trying to strategize how to start the conversation, when Joel walked through the back door. She hopped up and ran to the kitchen to greet him. "How'd the meeting go?" She noticed his face was beet red—either from the chilly night or from the board meeting—the "face-off," as she'd taken to calling those gatherings lately.

"Yeah, great," he said, dropping his jacket onto the kitchen counter. "Really super."

"Uh-oh. Do you still have a job?" She kissed him lightly. His lips felt cold.

"Huh." He half snorted. "Barely." He stepped back and ran his fingers through his hair. "They cut my salary almost in half. Said the budget wasn't able to support me and all the bills."

A heavy breath pushed from Lisa's mouth. "You've got to be kidding. I know they've been threatening it for several months. Half?"

"That's not even the worst part. They seemed to take delight in doing it. They went on and on about how they knew this was the last resort, and how terrible they felt about it, and how I should maybe be doing a bit more to 'drum up' tithes. 'Drum up.' Like it's a religious telethon we're running."

"Did you look around and say, 'Well, if everybody on this board would actually tithe'?"

"No, but I sure wanted to."

"So what are we going to do?" Lisa thought this may finally be the time to bring up her getting a job. She'd been after him to agree to it, and he'd always said no. He wanted her home. Now he might view things differently.

"Well, on the way home, I stopped by Ryland's Hardware and picked up an application."

"What? You can't—" Lisa started but turned when she heard the fleeting sound of her daughter's footsteps running from the room. Callie must have entered and heard part of their conversation. Joel's pinched face betrayed his anguish. It was one thing for a wife to know her husband was struggling to support his family. It was another thing entirely for a child to know it.

"Do you want to talk to her?" Lisa asked tentatively. She already knew the answer was no.

Joel shook his head sadly. "No, maybe you'd better. My mind isn't clear right now."

*Neither is mine,* Lisa thought as she leaned in to kiss her husband again. "We'll get through this. God will provide."

Joel nodded but seemed unsure.

Lisa tried to measure her breathing as she walked upstairs toward Callie's bedroom and tapped on the closed door.

There was no answer. Lisa was now used to being ignored by her daughter.

"Callie?" Lisa said softly. "Please open up."

"Why?" Lisa heard Callie say from the other side of the door. "There's nothing to talk about."

"Well, I could maybe help clarify whatever you heard."

Suddenly the door flung open to reveal Callie's red, tear-stained cheeks. "I heard everything perfectly. That stupid church is gypping Dad and now he has to work two jobs, while those church people go home to a nice house and nice clothes. Did I hear *that* about right?" She spat out the words as if they were venom.

Lisa slid through the door before closing it, and past Callie, hoping Callie would calm down more if they were in the same room. If, for no other reason, she didn't want Ricky to hear what was going on.

"It's complicated, Callie."

"No, it's not, Mom. Why are you defending them? They're horrible, and they treat Dad like dirt."

*At least she's talking to me now*, Lisa thought as she tried to figure out how to answer her daughter respectfully.

"Sweetie, I'm not defending them. What they're doing isn't right. But us getting upset about it won't help your dad's position. He needs us to support him."

"Well, why doesn't he just leave and get a regular job, where at least they'd treat him better and pay him?"

"I wish it *were* that simple."

"Fine, whatever," Callie said coldly. She turned from Lisa and picked up her book bag from the corner, where she'd obviously thrown it after school. "I have homework."

Lisa didn't move, hoping that Callie wouldn't shut her out again, hoping that if she hesitated long enough, Callie would talk to her, open up more. *Yell, scream, hit me, anything, just don't shut me out*, Lisa thought desperately.

Putting one hand on her hip, Callie raised her eyebrows as if to say, "Leave now."

Lisa stood slowly. At the door, she turned. "If you want to talk more about this—"

"I don't."

"Well." Lisa surveyed the pink-and-white bedroom. She and Callie had had so much fun picking the colors to paint the room and decorate it. She missed those easy days with her daughter. Her eyes fell on Callie, who was now pulling her books from her bag and scattering them across her bed. She bit the inside of her lip to keep from tearing up. This young woman before her was hurting, and Lisa felt helpless to do anything about it. "Good night, then."

She didn't wait for Callie *not* to answer.

Outside Callie's door she paused, trying to decide if she should run into her own bedroom, fling herself onto the bed and have a good cry, or if she should go downstairs and see how Joel was holding up, and cry. It seemed that tears were going to be part of whatever equation she was working.

*God, you worked a miracle when you saved my marriage. Would you work one now?*

For a brief moment she thought about barging back into Callie's room and having that talk that Mrs. Bentz had recommended. But she knew with all the emotions full tilt, this would not be the best time. She needed to wait until Callie calmed down some.

Right now she needed to go back down and comfort Joel.

# 49

# Mimi

*Monday, April 23*
*1:25 p.m.*

Mimi couldn't wait to get out of the house and over to Hemmings. The morning had been a nightmare! Megan had found where Mimi and Mark had stashed the leftover candy from her Easter basket and had gotten into it. By the time she was finished, she was bouncing off the wall, jumping around and on and off the furniture. She'd finger-painted on the wall leading upstairs, and had broken Mimi's prized crystal vase that had been a wedding present. Mimi had yelled and threatened to spank Megan, but it didn't seem to help. Megan's sugar high had developed a mind of its own.

Milo, feeling full-out cranky, was upset that he wasn't receiving Mimi's full attention. He'd also shot a straight stream into Mimi's left eye as she tried to change his diaper.

When Mimi had called Mark to remind him that he needed to be back at the house so she could go to the PTA meeting, he'd balked, saying he had to stay at the church because he was expecting an important phone call from the bishop. "Fine," she'd told him over the phone. "I'll just bring the kids over to you, then, shall I?" Which is exactly what she did, hardly slowing down to drop them off.

"Serenity now. Serenity now. Serenity now," she repeated as she drove to the school. The one bright spot was that she could get away and be among adults—even if they did talk almost exclusively about their children. *At least I don't have to check their hands and wipe their noses.*

As she walked toward the school's front door, she noticed Phil Horvath standing there—almost as if he were waiting for her to arrive. She knew that was ridiculous, but it did seem that every time she arrived, he was there to greet her and escort her to the gymnasium for the meeting.

He winked as he held the door for her. "Hello, there."

"Hi." She smiled. There was that feeling again—that tingling, electric jitter starting in her stomach and flowing through her body. It felt nice. With a hair flip, she breezed by him.

"No cookies today?"

"Nope," she answered. "Didn't have time between diaper changes and trying to catch Megan in her sugar-induced adventure time."

"Too bad. I had a taste for those chocolate chippers."

"Next time."

*Good. Okay, he's not really interested in me. He just likes my food. I'm safe.*

She kept insisting to herself that there was nothing inappropriate about their friendship, and that she'd be vain to think that Phil shared the same attraction.

"I started to read your book and I really—"

"Mr. Horvath!" Gloria Redkins scurried over to their little cluster. "We're having some problems with the lights in the gym. They kept blinking, and now they've totally gone out."

Phil immediately walked past Gloria toward the gym. "Hi, Mimi!" Gloria said over her shoulder.

For a moment, Mimi felt put out that she'd been interrupted, just as she was going to compliment Phil. But then she realized this was probably better anyway, so she followed slowly behind.

*2:15 p.m.*

The PTA meeting had to be moved to the library, with extra chairs (the adult ones) brought in. Mimi found herself sitting directly across from Phil, which made her happy because they could joke and talk more during the meeting.

She was feeling safer. After all, they were in public. Nothing was going on. But she could still feel special.

While everyone else was getting settled, Mimi and Phil chatted privately about a few of the parents and what was going on at the school. Neutral, safe ground. Finally she said, "Earlier I was trying to tell you that I'd read your book. It was really good. Thanks!"

His face lit up. "Good! I'm glad you liked it. I can't even get my wife to read it," he whispered. "You were a model I kept thinking about as I was writing."

She felt warm inside at his words. "That's a nice thing to say."

"Okay, everybody," Gloria, the PTA president, began. "Thanks for your flexibility. And sorry about the last-minute change. We had some trouble with the lights in the gym. But hopefully this will work out just as well for us."

Gloria talked, and then the secretary, Judy, read the minutes from the last meeting. Mimi was drifting mentally, thinking about how Megan must be passed out on a pew in a sugar-shocked coma by this point. Her eyes wandered around the room until they landed on Phil, whose warm blue-gray eyes were focused on her. They brimmed with tenderness. She shifted away, thinking maybe she'd imagined his look.

But as she allowed herself to glance back at him, she noticed he was smiling *at* her, a smile that seemed to reveal bemusement, indulgence, and affection. She read his face as filled with fondness—a fondness that should not have been there.

Mimi shot her eyes back to the speaker and unconsciously pushed her hair behind her ears as rational shock and panic set in. His gaze shattered her denial. *I was right! He is interested! I know the kiss thing was unexpected, but still . . . Why doesn't Mark look at me like that anymore?*

She could feel her face growing warm. *It's probably bright red right now.* She bit her bottom lip and averted her eyes—anywhere but toward Phil. She was determined not to look at him for the rest of the meeting, which was going to prove tricky, since he was seated in the direction of Gloria, who had now moved into talking about their financial reports.

*Okay, God, what do I do now?* she prayed frantically. As much as she tried, she couldn't focus on the meeting and just prayed for it to be over as quickly as possible. *Why can't Mark call and tell me Milo's got diarrhea or something?*

She'd never felt so self-conscious—and so wrong. She knew she had no business flirting with danger as she'd done. She'd really meant no harm.

*Why did I explain away the kiss?* she kept wondering. *Why didn't I stop? What is wrong with me?*

Finally, after what seemed forever, Gloria ended the meeting and Mimi wasted no time rushing over to talk to her, hoping that if she procrastinated with Gloria long enough, Phil would be called away to other duties.

# Lulu's Café

*Tuesday, April 24*
*12:01 p.m.*

"And there is Miss All-or-Nothing," Gracie said to Jennifer from behind the counter as Jennifer breezed into the diner, Felicia right behind her. "Looks like today is an 'All.' "

Felicia gave Gracie a wave.

"And hello there to you," Gracie acknowledged. "Whatever happened to those fancy suits and shoes you used to wear? I miss the Princess Di effect around here."

"In the back of the closet, but not too far back," Felicia answered cryptically, giving Jennifer a little nudge to where Lisa and Mimi were waiting.

"Hurry up and get over to the table because I want to hear what all that smiling's about with you," Felicia said to Jennifer's back.

Jennifer plopped down next to Lisa while Felicia scooted into Mimi's bench. Greetings all around were followed by Felicia's impatient, "Okay, Jennifer, spill the beans."

"Yeah, something's up with you," Mimi agreed. "I can see it all over your face."

Jennifer laughed. "I know, I've never been too good at hiding my feelings. Not such a great trait for a pastor's wife, is it?"

Felicia play-kicked her under the table. "You're killing us with the suspense. Speak!"

Pushing her menu to the end of the table, Jennifer said, "I'm going to be a mom—for sure this time."

The others looked at her curiously. Mimi broke the silence. "Wow, after all those years of trying and you guys are pregnant again that—"

"Nope, not pregnant." Jennifer shook her head. "Remember I was telling you about Jessica and how I couldn't get her baby out of my mind?"

The others nodded.

"I went to talk with Pastor Scott about it, and he made me realize that God had placed that child on my heart for a reason," she explained. They all watched Gracie set their drinks on the table but Jennifer still held court. "So without even telling Sam, I went to see Jessica that day and asked her if we could adopt the baby. And she said yes!"

Jennifer sat back and looked from Lisa to Mimi to Felicia. They appeared stunned.

"You did that without even asking Sam first?" Lisa said with astonishment. Jennifer knew Lisa did not have that kind of decision-making leeway in her marriage. Of course, she knew she didn't really have that either—even though she'd taken it.

When Jennifer nodded, Mimi and Felicia's eyes widened even further. "But I have to admit, after I met with Jessica, I went back to Sam and kind of slow-played it on him. I didn't tell him I'd already asked Jessica. Instead I asked him to pray about the possibility and let me know because I figured if he was really against it I could go back and tell Jessica things had changed."

"That would have been awful," Lisa said as she stirred her iced tea.

"Yeah, but I just knew in my soul that God didn't give me those feelings only to have Sam have different ones," Jennifer explained. "And I was right. It took him about a week, but Sam agreed that God was leading us to this child. As a matter of fact, we're meeting with Jessica tomorrow to sign the papers."

Hearing the finality of it all, the other women seemed to make the transition from skepticism to joyful acceptance. "Hey, then, that's great. Congratulations," said Felicia, reaching across to grab Jennifer's forearm gently.

"You're going to be a mommy!" Lisa gave Jennifer a half hug.

Mimi smiled at them. "And you won't even have to work out afterward to get rid of the pooch," she joked, rubbing her abdomen.

"Oh, I still need the exercise." Jennifer laughed. She pretended to pinch an inch on her torso.

Felicia turned serious. "Is there any chance Sam might back out once he meets Jessica? I remember you saying she's quite the redneck. Will that affect his decision?"

Jennifer felt sheepish. "I sort of skirted that issue. I used a bit of reverse psychology and said people aren't as much a product of their biology as they are their environment. Look at me, for instance."

"And Callie," Lisa chimed. "Here we are providing her a perfect PK existence and she has the audacity to act out on us!"

The table erupted with laughter. Jennifer knew it was one of those inexplicable stereotypes that PKs should be perfect angels, when in fact many ended up rebelling.

Gracie stopped by and waved her arm around the table, not even uttering a word. All of the women nodded their unspoken "I'll have the usual" sign.

"So are you nervous about the whole thing?" Mimi asked.

Jennifer thought for a second. She'd been so busy preparing the nursery and getting the house ready for their new arrival that she hadn't had time to get anxious. "I think when you're following the Lord's path, things just come easier," she reflected. "When I look back on our infertility struggles, all I see is a big bundle of negativity—toward Sam, toward the church, and toward God. But now, even though we're facing some uncertainties with this baby, I feel a calm and peace about her."

"So it's a girl then?" Mimi smiled. "Maybe someday we can hook her up with Milo." She hesitated. "That is, if he ever lightens up. I swear, that kid has finally seemed to grow out of the colic, but he's still as irritable and touchy as ever. I guarantee you he didn't get that from *me!*" She pointed at herself and chuckled.

"I wonder that about Nicholas, too," Felicia joked. "He certainly didn't get that biting from my side of the family." *But where did he get it? And why doesn't he do it around Becky and Eli?*

Thoughts of Becky spurred Felicia to tell her news. "Ted offered me a job working from home," she announced to a chorus of surprised *ohs*. "Much to his chagrin, I might add. But the National City Bank guy was going to pull out if I didn't stay on."

"What power you have, my friend," Lisa said, elbowing her lightly.

"Yeah, well, I'm not sure Dave thinks so. He hasn't been real supportive," Felicia said, perplexed. "Maybe he thought he finally had the housewife he'd always wanted and now everything's changing again. I don't know. One minute he's saying he thinks it's the best of both worlds, and the next he's asking me if I'm sure it's what I want to do. I'm getting mixed signals from him."

"Men," Mimi said, shaking her head. "Can't live with 'em, can't ship 'em back to their mothers."

All four women hooted with laughter.

Later, their meals finished, the PWs were wrapping up their lunch conversation when a thought occurred to Felicia. "Hey, Jen," she asked, "what are you going to name the baby?"

Jennifer shrugged. "We haven't come up with anything yet. At first we talked about giving her 'Emily' as a middle name to honor Sam's first wife, but then we decided that would be too creepy."

*Uh, yeah,* Felicia thought, but she didn't say anything. It was common in Mexican culture for families to name their babies after dead people—even dead children—but she found the whole thing unpalatable.

"You guys have any suggestions?" Jennifer asked.

Mimi made a straight face. "How about 'Katie,' you know, in honor of Kitty?" After a beat, she smiled, bringing relief around the table.

"I do have a bit of a different take on Kitty these days after everything that's happened, but not enough to name my baby after her," Jennifer said. "And I wonder what she would have said about me adopting a baby, since she adopted out Seth."

"Ooo, that reminds me," Lisa said. "You know how we talked last time about rejuvenating the Southwest Ohio Pastors' Wives Fellowship?" The others nodded. "What if we set a date for some time this summer and just see who shows up? Once the word gets out that there's new leadership, maybe more women will want to join."

Felicia could nearly see Mimi's mind whirling. "I'll plan it!" she said excitedly.

"Mimi . . . ," Jennifer cautioned, "I'm speaking as a friend here. You know how you're always going on about taking on too much. Are you sure you want to do this, and that you have the time and energy?"

Mimi paused. "Well, it's not like I'd be doing it by myself. Trust me, you'll all have roles to play."

"What about Lisa leading it?" Jennifer suggested.

"What?" Lisa looked surprised. "Why me?"

"Because it was originally your idea."

Lisa paused, as if trying to decide how she felt about that. Finally she smiled. "What if we take turns? I'll lead the first one, then we can rotate each time."

Jennifer clapped her hands. "Brilliant! That's a great idea."

Felicia smiled reassuringly, but inside she wasn't so confident. She'd met Lisa, Jennifer, and Mimi at one of those meetings, but that was the only blessing she'd received at the gathering. They all blamed Kitty, of course, but what if it was more than that? With them rotating leadership responsibility, Felicia wouldn't be able to bow out at will if she didn't like the meeting. And now that she'd be working from home, it would be difficult to beg off due to the travel distance.

*Things can't always stay the same,* she told herself, *and we don't get to pick and choose which ones do and which ones don't.*

# CHAPTER

# 51

# Felicia

Wednesday, April 25
9:22 a.m.

Finished with her fax, Felicia closed the top on the combination fax/copier/scanner and shuffled back to her desk, her feet snuggled into hot pink furry slippers.

Easing herself into her new, gray microfiber chair, she rolled forward and stretched out her legs under her new desk. Everything was new around her—even the job to some degree. While she was working on familiar accounts, the home setting provided a different atmosphere that rendered her part executive and part secretary.

And part mommy. Even though she had returned to work, Felicia was reticent to put Nicholas back in day care. She was home, after all. Why should she ship off her son for someone else to watch?

Just as she clicked on her e-mail, Felicia heard a crash from the other side of the house. Jumping up, she toppled her coffee cup, sending brown liquid across the paper she'd just faxed.

Letting out a little squeal as she saw the spill, she quickly threw some tissues across it and sped off to find Nicholas. After breakfast, she'd left him happily playing with his Legos in the family room.

Dashing into the kitchen, where she thought the noise was coming from, she found him.

"Nicholas!" she said, stopping and putting her hands on her hips. "What on earth?"

The kitchen floor was strewn with cans—some still rolling—and boxes from the cabinets above. Bengal pranced through sniffing a few boxes. Nicholas was standing in the middle of the mess with an expression of restrained panic. His big eyes told Felicia he was trying to decide if his punishment would be worse if he made up a story or if he told the truth.

"What is that in your hand?" she asked, reaching down and pulling his chubby arm forward. A plastic spatula fell from his grip onto the floor.

"I . . . I was trying to get the Twinkies."

Felicia looked up into the top cabinet. She had indeed hidden a box of Twinkies behind some canned vegetables. If she left them out, she knew Nicholas would eat them all day since she wasn't able to watch him constantly. All the talk about obese kids had made her more conscious of what Nicholas was putting in his mouth these days.

But she had to laugh at his tenacity. "Good grief, kiddo, you really wanted a treat, didn't you?"

His face melted from fear into a hesitant smile. "Sorry, Mama."

She reached down and cupped his chin. "That's okay, my boy. Just ask next time because you could have gotten hurt climbing up on the counter like that. Now, help Mommy clean this up."

Nicholas crouched down to pick up the cans of beans and peaches while Felicia stood tall and took them from him to place back in the cabinet. As he worked, he began to sing one of his Sunday school songs in Spanish, as Felicia had taught him.

*I've got my own little Julio Iglesias,* she thought, amused at the mini-stereotype before her. But Nicholas's joyful rendition of "This Little Light of Mine" touched her heart.

The phone—the ever-ringing phone—interrupted their production line.

Felicia stepped over the cans to reach the receiver, catching her left foot on the last one and causing her to trip just as she was grasping the receiver.

"Hello?" she panted, righting herself. Nicholas, clearly figuring himself relieved from duty, bounced by on his way back to the family room.

"Oh, hi, Felicia," said the woman's voice. "It's Margaret Teneman from the church."

*I don't have time for a casual chitchat.* "Oh, hi, Margaret. Are you looking for Pastor Dave?"

"No, no. I was looking for you. Pastor mentioned that you are home now. How nice it must be to have more time for Nicholas."

Felicia gazed at the grocery store littering her kitchen floor. "Oh, yes. But you know I am still wor—"

Margaret interrupted. "And more time for the church, too, I'm guessing?"

Felicia bristled at the implication that she hadn't been spending enough time with the church previously. But her words did not reflect her worry. "Yes, but even though I'm home I'm still wor—"

"Great! That's why I'm calling." Interrupted again! *Why doesn't anyone ever let me finish a sentence?* "You know the mother-daughter banquet is coming up in a few weeks and I'm the director. We wouldn't have asked before because we knew you were too busy, but now that you're home, we were wondering if you could be the emcee that day."

Emcee? How tough could that be? "Sure, Margaret. I'd be delighted."

"Great! Oh, I should probably tell you that the emcee is responsible for doing the program."

*Crash.* Nicholas was punting a giant tower of Legos he'd made while Bengal darted from the room. Blocks were flying through the air and ping-ponging around the family room furniture. *I've got to get back to work.* "Program? What does that entail?"

Felicia knew the silence on the other end didn't bode well for her. "Well . . . it's whatever you want it to be. You can talk, or you can bring in a speaker. There can be music, prayer—" Margaret's voice drifted off.

*Why are they saddling me with this so close to the date?* Felicia thought, but as usual she didn't dare share how she felt. "Um, sure, okay. I'll see what I can do."

After Margaret gave Felicia a few details about the event, they hung up, but Felicia stood staring at the wall for a minute. Yesterday, Annette Laramie from the Benevolence Committee had called with the same "now that you're home" line as Margaret, wondering if Felicia could help make food for funerals and new moms. She hadn't been able to say no—visions of pot-stirring with one hand and laptop typing with the other filling her head—and now here she was taking on yet another responsibility.

*How do they even know I'm working from home?* she pondered. And then it hit her—Annette and Margaret's husbands were both elders. Had Dave told the elders that Felicia was now home and ready and waiting for church work?

She scooped the phone back up, anger spiking inside her, and hit speed dial for the church. Before she could hear Linda answer, Nicholas was at Felicia's feet.

"Mom!"

"Not now Nicholas. Linda?"

"Mom!" Nicholas said more earnestly.

Felicia heard a chuckle from the other end. "Oh, hi, Felicia. Sounds like you've got your hands full there. Then again, I guess you're used to that after working in such a high-pressure career."

*I'm still working there,* she thought, frustrated, but didn't change her tone. "Mmm-hmmm. May I speak to Pastor Dave?"

While Linda was transferring her, Felicia finally glanced down to see what Nicholas needed. He was holding out his hand. Blood!

"Hey, *amor,* how's it going?" Dave said when he picked up.

"Oh, Nicholas!" Felicia wedged the phone between her ear and shoulder and quickly pulled him to the kitchen sink.

"Hello?" Dave asked, concern in his voice.

Felicia threw open the cold water tap and forced Nicholas's bleeding finger under it, half lifting him off the floor. "Did you tell the elders that I am just sitting around here waiting for people to call me to help them?"

Her tone was accusatory, but at that moment with a bleeding child, a desk full of work, and a growing list of church activities, she was in no mood to beat around the bush.

"Felicia, what is going on there?"

She wrapped Nicholas's finger in a paper towel and held pressure on it to stop the bleeding. "What is going on here? Well, it's nine thirty and I'm standing in a kitchen where more food is on the floor than in the cabinets. I am holding my child's bleeding finger in one hand, and in the other I am holding a phone that keeps ringing with people wanting me to help at church 'now that I'm at home.' Meanwhile, I have two projects to finish today for work, but I can't seem to stay in my office for more than ten minutes at a time."

Felicia huffed at Dave's silence.

"Do you want me to come home?"

She did, but she knew that wasn't the answer.

Then the solution popped into her head like one of Nicholas's Legos sailing through the air. Letting go of Nicholas's finger, she slipped a Band-Aid from the box on the counter—she'd put boxes all around the house because of the biting—and secured it around the small wound.

"No, no. It just occurred to me what to do."

"Good!" Dave sounded relieved, but she was a little perturbed that he didn't even ask her about her idea. "I've got someone coming in for counseling so—"

"Wait, you didn't answer my question." She sensed he was being purposely evasive.

"You mean about helping more at church?" he asked. "No, I just asked for prayer at the elders meeting that our new home situation would work well and be pleasing to the Lord."

Felicia studied the mess around her. Was this "pleasing to the Lord"? Was her attitude?

"Dave, I've gotta go. I need to get back to work."

After they ended their call, Felicia didn't put down the phone. Instead she dialed a now-familiar number, a sprout of peace growing inside as she knew she was doing exactly what would please the Lord—and allow her to get back to work.

# CHAPTER 59

# Jennifer

*Wednesday, April 25*

*6:16 p.m.*

Jennifer reached over and grabbed Sam's hand as she watched Jessica turn toward the small kitchen in her apartment. She saw Sam's pastor face disappear in Jessica's absence, as if a movie camera had been turned off.

"Is that cigarette smoke I smell?" he whispered to Jennifer, grave concern on his face.

"Not from her. From Ronny, her hus—"

"Here we go," Jessica said, reentering the room with two cans of off-brand diet soda. "But are you sure y'all don't want a beer?"

Jennifer felt electricity zip through Sam's hand at her question. They both shook their heads.

"Hmmmph." Jessica lowered herself onto the couch. "Man, I can't wait to have a beer as soon as—"

"Jessica, you haven't been drinking during your pregnancy, have you? Or smo—"

Sam stopped his questioning at Jennifer's sharp hand squeeze. Before

Jessica could answer, Jennifer let go of his hand and picked up a snapshot from the coffee table.

"Oh, so this is you and Ron?" she asked, trying casually to slide the photo to Sam. He'd asked what Ron looked like, and Jennifer had realized she didn't even know. What she saw in the picture didn't surprise her—a paunchy sandy-blond guy with a two-day beard wearing a *Beer. The Breakfast of Champions* T-shirt while flipping his middle finger at the camera. *Except for the hair color, he really isn't all that different from Sam in looks.* This small surprise of a connection pleased Jennifer.

Jessica craned her neck to see the photo, then said as if she were apologizing, "That's him all right. I took that when we were on vacation down in Florida at the NASCAR race. He doesn't like havin' his picture taken."

"I see that." Sam questioned Jennifer with his eyes as he handed the picture back to her.

"I told him until we're together again for good I needed something of him here, so he brought me that." Jessica gingerly took the photo back and laid it aside on the coffee table, then looked eagerly at Jennifer.

*Is his leftover cigarette smoke not enough of a reminder?*

Sensing her cue, Jennifer pulled out of her thoughts and snapped open the manila envelope on her lap.

"Okay, Jessica, here is everything," she said, sliding out stapled documents and laying them on the coffee table. "The attorney put little sticky arrows everywhere you need to sign."

Jessica started to pick up the pen Jennifer had set next to the paperwork, then pulled her hand back and put it on her blossomed tummy. "Oh, there she goes again."

She motioned for Jennifer to come over and put her hand where the baby was kicking. "Wow, she's some mover," said Jennifer, envious that she wasn't able to feel that in her own body. The concept that this child was hers—or almost, anyway—was still difficult for her to grasp fully.

Jessica signaled for Sam to come over. "Don't you wanna feel your baby?"

Jennifer saw Sam slowly rise from his chair, a shadow of confusion on his face. "Sure," he said, then hesitantly put his hand where Jennifer's had been.

His surprised reaction when the baby kicked again—he jumped back as if he'd touched a hot stove—made both women laugh.

"Does that hurt? I mean, when she punches out like that?" he asked.

*Wish I could answer that question.* Jennifer felt a guilty pang at her jealousy. She *was* going to be a mother after all, but she couldn't help but wonder what the actual pregnancy felt like.

Jessica shook her head. "Nah, but I think she's ready to get out of there." She snickered. "And I'm ready to have her out!"

Jennifer and Sam returned to their chairs, an air of discomfort between them. She'd warned Sam about Jessica's odd sense of detachment from the baby, but seeing it for himself had clearly surprised him.

"Just remember, the baby doesn't come pre-programmed with the awful attitudes of its mother," she'd told him in the car on the way over.

Jessica picked up the pen again and began quickly looking for the arrows and signing her name on the sheaf of papers before her.

"That one says we are under no—" Jennifer tried to explain the first document but Jessica signed it and moved on to the next one before she had a chance to finish.

"Jessica, don't you want to know what you're signing?" Jennifer asked softly as she reached out to grasp Jessica's forearm and stop her from continuing. *Does she understand the finality of her actions?* "This is basically a closed adoption. After the baby is born, we are under no further obligation to you—to communicate with you or allow you to visit the baby or anything."

Jennifer let go of Jessica's arm and, like a pinball machine that had momentarily had its plug pulled, Jessica flew back into action, not even looking up. "Guys, I know this is your baby once it's borned. I ain't stupid."

The way Sam drew in his breath let Jennifer knew he was stifling a laugh at Jessica's comment.

*He'll be testing this kid from the day she arrives to make sure she isn't somehow taking after her birth parents.*

Jessica kept signing. A strange silence blanketed the room.

"Jessica . . . ," Sam started.

Jennifer again shot him a look to hush, but he ignored her. *He can't help himself. It's the pastor/counselor.*

"About your extended families. Do you or Ron have anything . . . we should know about?"

Jessica looked up, confused. "Whaddya mean our 'extended families'? You mean our parents and such?" She snickered again. "You got nuthin' to worry about there, Sam. I ain't seen my daddy since I was about three, and my momma ran off with some truck driver when I was sixteen. And believe you me, Ronny's momma and daddy wouldn't want anything to do with *this* baby."

Jessica returned to signing, giving Jennifer ample opportunity to stop Sam's questioning with a wide-eyed "I told you not to ask questions" stare.

She could tell he wanted to reword his question—he was worried about health issues in their family lines, not if they would want the baby—but he sat back quietly.

Jennifer, worried that his line of questioning might turn Jessica's decision, shook her head at him, as if to say, "Jessica wouldn't know if there were any problems. She can barely get along herself."

Finally Jessica finished signing. Seeming pleased with her accomplishment—and slightly relieved, Jennifer thought—she fit the papers back into the manila envelope and presented it to Jennifer, who along with Sam, stood to leave.

"Well, that's that," Jessica said glibly.

"Shouldn't we get Ron's signature too?" Jennifer asked.

"No," Jessica answered glumly. "He doesn't want anything to do with this baby."

Jennifer cringed as she sensed Sam opening his mouth again. "Listen, Jessica, we really appreciate—"

Jessica play-pushed them toward the door. "Now, I don't want to hear none of that. We have a deal here and that's all it is. Like I just sold you a car or somethin'."

Sam turned toward Jennifer as if for permission to say more. She linked her fingers in his, pulled him toward the open door, and said over her shoulder before he could add anything, "We'll see you at the hospital then. Give us a call when you're on your way. And please call us if you need anything between now and then."

"Yep, I've got all your numbers," Jessica called cheerfully. "Now go put together that baby bed or whatever it was you said you gotta do."

As they walked down the stairs from Jessica's apartment, Sam began to spill out to Jennifer all of his impressions of the situation. Feeling as if someone were watching her, Jennifer stopped when they got to the landing and glanced back toward the front window of Jessica's apartment.

There she was, rubbing her belly with one hand—and using the other to swipe the tears rolling down her face.

Jennifer started to wave, but as soon as Jessica caught her looking up, the curtains closed and she was gone.

*Tough on the outside, soft on the inside. If that's how this baby turns out, she'll be just like her mom. Both of them.*

# Lisa

*Thursday, April 26*

*7:25 a.m.*

Lisa was sipping her coffee when Callie entered the kitchen, book bag in hand, ready to go. She was used to the routine by now: Lisa was her official chauffeur to and from school.

"Ready?" Lisa asked, already knowing the answer but not able to think of anything else to say. She was nervous today.

"Yeah."

"Good. Let's go." Lisa grabbed her purse and keys and opened the door for Callie. They both quietly walked to the car and got in. Just like every other morning.

Lisa pulled out of the driveway and took the familiar three-mile route to the school. Only, once they arrived, Lisa didn't slow down. She caught Callie's confused expression when Lisa drove by the drop-off spot.

"You missed it," Callie said with disdain.

"Oh, didn't I tell you?" Lisa tried to sound nonchalant. "You're not going today. I called the school and told them you weren't coming in. We're going to Cincy for a day of shopping and food." That was something Lisa and Callie used to do every month or so; it was their mother-daughter bonding time.

"What?"

"Yeah, I didn't think you'd mind," Lisa continued. "Plus, we need to find you a dress for the school dance next month."

"But . . . I didn't think I was allowed to go."

"Who told you that?"

Callie scrunched her face in confusion. "I'm grounded."

"Oh, that." Lisa felt energized now that she'd caught Callie off-guard.

Callie was silent for a moment, as if trying to figure everything out.

Lisa broke into her thoughts. "Unless, of course, you don't want to go. I can turn around . . ."

Callie started to say no, then stopped short. The mean look reappeared. "We can't afford to go shopping, remember? Dad's pay was cut in half."

"Well, I'm sure we'll be able to work out something. You don't need to worry about that. And anyway, we aren't using cash—we've got all those gift cards the people from church gave us last Christmas. Remember?"

They drove on, going back and forth in their cat-and-mouse game until thirty minutes later when Lisa pulled into a Bob Evans, Callie and Lisa's favorite breakfast joint.

"This okay?" Lisa asked, trying to sound innocent, but loving every minute that her daughter was talking.

"I guess."

*Ha! I do believe this could be working!*

———

*1:24 p.m.*

Lisa and Callie had spent the morning under a truce. It was almost tension-free as they laughed and tried on clothes and tried to outdo each other finding the best sales. But underneath it, the anxiety of Callie's choices still weighed heavily on Lisa. She was hoping the day's outing would loosen up Callie enough so she'd feel comfortable talking openly about what was going on. But Lisa was careful not to talk about anything that would put Callie in a mood.

"You hungry?" Lisa said as they were walking through the Kenwood Towne Centre, loaded with bags of goodies for their family.

"Yeah, I could eat."

"I was thinking—now hear me out—that we could get some sandwiches and go to a park or something. Maybe find some ducks to feed?"

Callie paused, then seemed to brighten. "That sounds good." Lisa knew Callie loved feeding ducks. She always laughed at the noises they made and the way they waddled everywhere.

They drove around until they found a Jimmy John's sandwich shop, grabbed some turkey sandwiches, chips, and two Diet Cokes, and then headed off in search of a pond or lake with ducks. It seemed the perfect day to be outdoors— it was in the sixties and sunny—so they could sit outside and talk for a while.

After about a half hour of wandering around, they finally found a little pond with a picnic area. They gathered the food and drinks and made their way to the pond. Since it was lunchtime on a school day, no one was around to bother them. Perfect.

Lisa picked a picnic table that was out in the sun so they wouldn't get too cold.

Lisa said a prayer of blessing over their food and they dug in.

*God, you have to help me here. Help me not screw this up.*

"I owe you an apology," Lisa started casually.

Again, Lisa was pleased to see she'd caught her daughter off-guard.

"For what?"

"Well, you've had a rough road and I really haven't been there for you. Your dad and I have been so absorbed in dealing with the church and trying to please everyone there that we've left you to fend for yourself."

Callie was silent as she continued to eat, but Lisa could tell that she was keenly listening, so she kept talking. "You didn't sign up to be a pastor's kid. You didn't ask for all the pressure—and I know you feel it. And I know it's tough for you to watch your dad get criticized by people in the church. It hurts and it's not fair."

Callie took a swig of her Diet Coke and looked down, but Lisa could see tears welling up in her eyes.

"I'm so sorry you have to go through this. Your dad and I both want to protect you from all of it, but we can't."

"God could," she whispered.

"You feel like he's let you down?"

She nodded.

"It's okay to feel that way. Sometimes I feel that way, like God is silent. Like we're doing all this work for him and *this* is what we get? Sometimes I wonder where he's gone and why he doesn't make our lives easier. But the reality is that we can't blame him. He's not at fault here."

"But he's letting Tom and the others do this to Dad. Why doesn't he get them? Why doesn't he do something so they'll stop? Why does he allow them to cut Dad's pay?" Callie's tears fell from her cheeks onto her shirt.

"Oh, sweetie." How could she possibly answer Callie when she wasn't even sure of the reason herself? So she decided to be honest. "I don't know. I don't understand those things myself. But one thing I do know is that God and the church are different. We can be angry at church people because they do hurtful things. But God doesn't. He gives us all free will. So those people can treat us badly. God gives them the free will, the choice to do that. But he also gives you the choice to react badly. And if I believe God is just, which I do, then I have to believe that he sees what's going on and he will make things right. Maybe not in the time or the ways we want, but it will be the right and perfect time and way."

She paused to see if Callie was accepting what she said.

"I just want to be normal," Callie cried.

"You are!"

"Everyone at school makes comments all the time about how I'm little Miss Goody-Goody because my dad's a pastor."

"Yeah, I got that, too, when I was growing up."

"What did you do?" Callie asked, seeming to be genuinely interested.

"I decided to wear it like a badge. Of course, I knew if I tried to prove them wrong, my mom would kill me."

Callie laughed. "Good ol' Grandma."

Lisa laughed, too. "But it hurt. It hurt every time I felt somebody watching what I did. I felt the pressure to be perfect, to be good and moral and righteous. And you know what? It just made me angry inside, because I just wanted to be me and didn't feel I could."

"I feel that way, too."

"Of course, I never did the drinking . . . or smoking."

Callie bit the inside of her cheek. "Yeah, I didn't really do it that much. The smoking just made me cough. And I didn't like the taste of beer. It was really nasty! How do people drink that stuff?"

Lisa shrugged and took a chip. "Can we make a deal?"

Callie nodded.

"Whatever you're feeling or going through, don't shut us out. Your dad and I may not like to hear it, but we love you and we promise to listen. We might not be able to fix it, but we're here for you and we'll work together. Okay? But you have to *talk* to us."

"Yeah, okay."

"And if you want to wear jeans to church, you can. Not the raggedy, faded torn ones. The nice ones."

"Really?" Callie's hazel eyes grew wide.

"Really. But let me break that to your dad before you try it, okay?" Lisa laughed. "Your dad and I are much more interested in what's going on in here." She pointed at her heart. "And here." She pointed to her head. "Than in what you're wearing. Although we do need to have a serious conversation about the belly-button ring."

Her daughter smiled slyly. "At least it wasn't my tongue."

Lisa held up her hand. "Don't even go there."

They both laughed and Lisa reached across and grabbed Callie's hand. "I love you. I don't tell you that nearly enough. But I do. And there's not a day that goes by when I don't pray for you and love you even more than the previous day. And that will never change."

"I love you, too, Mom."

Lisa stretched across and pushed Callie's hair from her face and tucked it behind her ears. "You're such a beautiful girl."

"I know," Callie interjected mockingly. "I should keep my hair out of my face so everyone can see how pretty I am."

"That's right, baby girl."

"Hey, Mom? Does this mean I'm not grounded anymore?"

"Yes. But it still means you have to be nice to your brother."

"Aw, man. Are you sure he's not adopted?"

"Quite sure. Sorry, you're both blood-related. I can fix or change many things; that's not one of them. Now how about we feed those ducks?"

# Mimi

*Saturday, April 28*
*9:32 a.m.*

Mimi splashed her sponge into the sudsy water and scrubbed the kitchen floor. She was getting better, she told herself. She'd only rearranged the cans in the food pantry and scrubbed the floor twice this time. In stressful times, Mimi had a habit of *over*cleaning.

She'd put the kids to work cleaning their rooms and had placed Milo in his crib so he could sleep—finally! Mark was in his office in the back of the house, putting the finishing touches on his message and the Sunday service.

Dressed in her regular cleaning outfit—blue jeans and the Cincinnati Reds T-shirt the kids had given her one year for Christmas, she wiped her wet hands on her jeans and scratched her forehead. She knew she had to tell Mark. But she kept battling that little demon on her shoulder, who whispered in her ear, *Why make trouble? It's really no big deal. And it's not as if he's ever going to find out anyway. You did nothing wrong.*

But on the other shoulder she could imagine her three PW friends sitting, wearing angels' wings. *It's the right thing to do. Secrets only control you when they're secret—not when they're out in the open. Confess it. He'll forgive you.*

*Those blasted friends of mine. Why do they have to be right?* she thought as she dunked the sponge back into the water bucket.

Finally, the angels won out and she stood, taking the bucket outside and dumping it, before walking to Mark's office.

What bothered her even more than what could have happened with Phil was that she'd lost control. That never happened with Mimi. She was a woman who prided herself on being in control. *What's happened to me?* she berated herself.

Mark was busily scanning a concordance. She stood for a moment in the doorway, watching him.

He deserved better than what she was giving him.

"Hey," he said finally, not looking up. "I see you there."

"Got a minute?" She really hated these confessionals.

"What's up?" He regarded her with mild interest. *Why can't you gaze at me longingly, like Phil?* Her thought caught her by surprise and she swallowed hard.

"Isn't today a workday at the school?" he said.

She nodded. "I didn't want to go."

"What?" He half laughed. "Are you sick or something? The infamous Mimi Plaisance not follow through on her volunteer projects? This must really be something good." He leaned back in his chair and wove his fingers together.

Mimi's eyes grew wide at his mocking tone. "Why would you say that? I thought you might actually be glad I *am* home."

"It's a joke, Mims. Relax."

For some reason, his comment set her off.

"Never mind." Mimi turned on her heel. "Forget it."

———

*1:36 p.m.*

"You ready to talk about what's bothering you?" Mark leaned against their bedroom door as Mimi was finishing up changing the sheets on their bed.

"I'm a little busy being the maid at the moment." Mimi couldn't help flinging out the comment.

Mark exhaled loudly and walked to the other side of the bed, across from her. "Does this have anything to do with the book you've been hiding in your drawer?" He nodded toward her bedside table.

Mimi's eyes widened as she quickly turned away.

"I'm a man, Mims, but I'm not stupid."

Silence. Mimi focused on tucking in the comforter.

"So does he have the hots for my woman?"

"And would that be so difficult to believe? Is it so unlikely that some-body else could find me attractive?" She rushed on defensively before Mark could respond. "No, really. I feel taken for granted. I'm your wife, nurse-maid, mother to your children. Can't I possibly be sexy or attractive to someone of the opposite sex? Or have I totally lost that?"

Mark surprised Mimi by laughing. "Not at all. You're hot—even as a mom and a maid."

"Mark," Mimi said, exasperated.

"Sorry. Okay, talk to me."

Mimi considered him skeptically. *It would be so much easier for you to let it slide. Especially now.* She saw her friends floating around with their little angel wings again. Shrugging almost in defeat, she sat on the edge of the bed and inhaled sharply. "First of all, nothing happened."

"I know."

"Mark, would you let me fini—what do you mean 'You know'?"

"Mimi, it's not in your personality to cheat on your husband."

"Ha!" She stood quickly. "That's where you're wrong! I *could* cheat—and I had the opportunity." She mentally kicked herself. This was certainly not the way she wanted to tell her husband.

"But did you?"

"Why are you being so smug and self-assured? Aren't you the least bit concerned?"

"About what? That you're human? That you have an attraction to another man? I would be insane to think that you turn off those feelings just because you're married."

"And that doesn't *bother* you?" she asked aghast. "It drives me crazy when I know women are attracted to you."

"That's where trust comes in. You trust me because I've never given you reason not to."

His words made her feel miserable and hot tears burned her eyes. "Stop being so cocky!"

He lifted his hands in defense. "Okay. I'm sorry. I take you for granted. Shoot me for that."

"That's just it. You *do* take me for granted."

"Mimi, wait. I saw what he wrote to you in his book."

"Why didn't you say anything?"

"Because I wanted to see what you'd do."

"I—"

He held up his hand to stop her. "You don't have to explain. I know you haven't done anything physically inappropriate. Maybe you did in your mind. Maybe you thought a whole lot about it. Honestly, that's between you and God—and you need to make that right."

Mimi started to explain, but Mark held up his hand. "I was pretty ticked when I read that inscription to you. And I spent some time raging in my mind against you and Phil and just about everybody else. But in the last few weeks, God's convicted me to keep quiet and just pray. Pray for you—that God would bless and encourage you. And as I've been praying for you, God showed me something about me."

Mimi watched Mark shift and fidget uncomfortably, as if *he* were about to cry. "To be honest, I've let you down as a husband. I know that. I should have treated you with more respect and honor. I should have understood that you need some mental stimulation—not just a physical grab every once in a while. I haven't truly understood what having four kids has taken out of you. I've treated you more as a mother and less as my beautiful, prized wife. I've neglected you. And I'm sorry."

"No, Mark—" Mimi tried to interrupt, but he shook his head.

It felt as if all thoughts of Phil Horvath were melting away like the Wicked Witch after she'd gotten doused with that bucket of water. Mimi still knew he was attractive. And she knew she'd probably always feel a chemistry with Phil. But she *loved* Mark. She was committed to Mark.

His voice became a little quivery as he continued. "You know what? Before a few weeks ago, I never even prayed consistently for you. Isn't that something? Here I am, a pastor who preaches the importance of praying with and for each other, and the most important person in my life gets nothing from me. I'm really ashamed of myself. I need your forgiveness, and I want you to know that I've committed to God to pray for you every day."

Mimi didn't know what to say. Here she was the one who needed forgiveness for straying mentally—and almost physically!—and he offered her grace and asked for his *own* forgiveness. He never ceased to amaze her.

"I'm sorry, Mark. When Phil called me about MJ's stink bomb exhibition, we almost kissed. If it hadn't been for the school bell. . . . And then at this last PTA meeting, I saw him look at me the way you used to—and it terrified me. I knew I was enjoying the attention of someone who appreciated me, but I realized it could go somewhere I didn't want to go. I wanted to go to those places with you. But I've felt so tired and . . . lonely."

"Promise me something." Mark knelt in front of her and took her hands tenderly. "No secrets."

Mimi wiped her tearstained cheeks and nodded. "I really do love you, Mark. And I love our family. I would never want to hurt us. If I walked away from you, that would destroy me. And you. And our kids. And our church. And I'm not about to do that."

"A lot of pastors and their wives do, though. They do allow their personal problems to destroy everybody."

"I know, and I don't want to be one of them."

Mark took Mimi's left hand and looked at it. He turned her ring around several times.

"How about I go with you to the PTA meetings and work days?"

She smiled widely; it was wonderful to smile so genuinely again at her husband. "I would love to have my husband there."

"Done."

He stood and kissed her—a long, sweet kiss. And those thin, chapped lips felt wonderful.

"Thank you," she whispered.

Mark kissed her forehead.

"Really, I mean it. Thank you for being such a good husband and for listening to God. And for forgiving me."

"Maybe we should celebrate." He raised his eyebrows and motioned toward the bed.

She rolled her eyes playfully. "Oh, all right. But you better not get me pregnant again, mister."

"I'll call the Taylors and see if they can take the kids," Mark said excitedly as he raced toward the phone.

# Jennifer

*Monday, April 30*
*9:32 a.m.*

The delivery room was in chaos. One nurse scurried around hooking up machines while another held Jessica's screaming head and tried to soothe her. Meanwhile, a doctor rolled on a stool into place below her spread legs.

*It's almost like he should be wearing a catcher's mitt,* Jennifer thought, amused, then chastised herself for making fun when Jessica was clearly in so much pain. Watching from a distance across the room, Jennifer felt out of place. Jessica had told her on the way to the hospital that she was okay with Jennifer being in the delivery room but she didn't want her at the bedside.

"I need to just get this over with on my own," she'd told Jennifer.

Another high-pitched wail from Jessica made Jennifer cringe. It was just like the ones she'd heard in the car to the hospital. When Jennifer's cell phone had gone off an hour earlier, all she'd heard when she answered was, "My car won't start! My car won't start!"

Once Jennifer figured out Jessica was in labor, she'd tried to get her to call 911.

But Jessica wouldn't hear of it. "Just come and get me!" she'd cried. "I ain't goin' in no ambulance."

Alarmed, Jennifer had grabbed her purse and run for her car. On the way, she'd called Sam, who was already at the office, and told him to meet her at the hospital.

*Wonder if he's here yet.* Sam had been firm that he didn't want to be in the delivery room. After losing Emily, which he was told about in a hospital emergency room, he didn't even like going to hospitals for pastoral visits. The drama of childbirth by a virtual stranger was more than he could take, he'd said.

"Here she comes! I see the head!" the obstetrician called jubilantly. Jennifer checked her watch. *I thought first babies were supposed to take a long time. We haven't even been here thirty minutes!*

One of the nurses came over and put her arm around Jennifer. "Come watch your baby being born, Mrs. Shores."

Jennifer followed obediently, the overwhelming emotions inside her finally breaking through the barrier she'd built as she'd watched from afar—both physically and emotionally.

"One more push!" The doctor patted Jessica's legs as if to instruct her.

Another deep groan from Jessica and the baby emerged. Again, as if playing sports, the doctor handed off the baby to one of the nurses as he busied himself cleaning up Jessica. There was so much activity that Jennifer couldn't get a good look at the baby, but she could hear her first cry.

"Would you like to cut the cord?" the nurse asked.

Jennifer moved around the doctor to where the nurse held the baby, eager to lay eyes on her daughter.

But what she saw made her gasp. "Jessica!" She looked from the baby to her sweaty mother, still breathing hard from the strain. "You didn't tell me you got pregnant from your *affair!*"

The room went dead silent except for Jessica's loud breaths. An expression as if she'd been caught crept across her face. "You can't give her back!" she yelled between huffs. "You can't! You said you wouldn't!"

Jennifer scanned the room, wondering what to do. She silently scolded herself for that poorly timed outburst. The doctor returned to his work, shaking his head. One nurse turned away, obviously trying to stifle a laugh at the scene. Meanwhile, the baby, still attached to Jessica, was squirming in the other nurse's arms.

"Mrs. Shores," she asked impatiently, "are you going to cut this baby's cord or should I do it? We need to get her cleaned and in a blanket."

Jennifer took the instrument from the nurse and allowed herself to really observe the baby for the first time. Her head held a crown of curly black hair, and her skin had a mocha hue. She was clearly the product of Jessica's encounter with Jamal, the African-American cop who used to work with Ron.

Once Jennifer cut the cord, the nurse whisked the baby away to a side table. Jennifer remained by the bed.

"I'm sorry," Jessica said quietly, her breath returning to normal. "I should have told you. But I wasn't totally sure it was Jamal's. I was hoping . . ."

Jennifer observed her, a spent wisp of a woman whose desperate eyes told Jennifer she didn't mean harm. Jennifer remembered looking up at those same eyes—eyes that spoke to Jennifer's heart—a week ago from the stairs at Jessica's apartment.

She reached down and patted Jessica's hand. "I know you just wanted the best for her."

Tears came to Jessica's eyes but before Jennifer could say anything else, the nurse reappeared, a tightly wrapped bundle in her arms. "Jessica, would you like to hold your baby?"

Jessica's lips tightened into a determined line as she turned her shaking head away from the nurse and waved off her offer.

"It's okay if you want to." Jennifer leaned across Jessica and patted her shoulder, but she didn't turn back.

"No, take her away," she said, her voice muffled from the pillow where she'd buried her face.

Jennifer pulled herself straight again just as the nurse began to hand her the baby instead. Wanting to protect Jessica from further grief,

Jennifer silently motioned for the nurse to join her outside the delivery room.

Once the door was closed behind them, Jennifer finally felt like she could be herself. She let out a little squeal as the nurse carefully emptied her arms into Jennifer's.

"Not what you expected, I take it?" the nurse said as Jennifer smiled into the small unwrapped area where the baby's face peeked out. The warmth of that tiny body next to hers made her toes tingle.

Jennifer thought about the nurse's question. Sure, the baby's race was unexpected, but before the birth, she had worried about bonding with the baby. Now that she held her, she was overwhelmed with an indelible and fierce love for this little squirming life—and she knew her previous anxious expectations were completely unfounded.

She didn't look up as she answered, "Oh, not at all."

Excusing herself from the nurse, Jennifer crept toward the waiting room, where she knew Sam would be by now. As she walked, she gingerly pulled the blanket flap over the baby's face.

Sam beamed and jumped up as he saw Jennifer approaching. "Is she okay? Ten fingers and ten toes?" he asked, excitedly holding out his arms.

Jennifer pulled back. "Sam, there's something I need to tell you first."

The corners of his mouth went flat and a quick paleness overtook his ruddy face.

"What . . . did something go wrong? Is she sick?"

Jennifer tried to smile reassuringly. She knew Sam would be as okay with the baby's race as she was after the quick adjustment, but she wanted to ease him into it. So while she was still holding the baby in her arms, she pulled back the flap to reveal their daughter.

Sam peeked in and looked questioningly at Jennifer. "She's . . . black? How did that happen?"

The others in the waiting room—a couple of waiting grandparents— chuckled at Sam's discovery.

Jennifer ignored his question—there would be time for explanations later—and just shrugged and smiled as she handed him the baby.

# A MATTER OF WIFE & DEATH

As he cuddled her into his chest, Jennifer watched the same transformation take place that she'd just experienced in the hallway. With every moment he took in the baby, she could see drops of disconcertedness vanish from his face.

Finally he reached his lips down to kiss her tiny cheek. "Hello, Carys Samantha Shores. Welcome to the world."

# CHAPTER

# 56

# Mimi

Mimi was in the kitchen cutting vegetables for the casserole she was preparing to take over to Jennifer's house. Jennifer had called late Monday evening to announce her daughter's arrival. Mimi knew Jennifer would have her hands full with a newborn—Mimi knew that situation only too well!—so she decided to whip up a meal to take over. They'd also decided to cancel that week's Lulu's get-together, since it would be too much on Jennifer.

Mimi started to slice and dice a large carrot when the doorbell rang. She grabbed a dishtowel laying next to the cutting board and walked toward the door. Through the window she could spy two people—one in a uniform.

*That's odd.*

Suddenly anxious, she pushed her hair behind her ears, threw the dishtowel on the table next to the phone in the hallway, and opened the door a crack. Sure enough, there stood Officer Dan McCarthy in his uniform blues and hat, standing stiff and solemn. His grasp was on the other man's

310

arm. Mimi examined the scruffy, gray-bearded man in a wrinkled shirt and black pants. And immediately she felt eight years old again, peering through the crack of the basement door at her father being handcuffed and escorted out of the house. It had been almost a decade since the last time she'd seen him. He'd left town to follow a woman out to the West Coast. He had found true love, he'd told Mimi's family, plus he was going to strike it rich panning for gold.

"Mimi!"

"Dad." *Great.*

"Mrs. Plaisance," Dan cut in with his most professional, strict tone. "I take it you know this man?"

She opened her mouth to speak, then shut it again, and simply nodded. A huge lump settled in her throat. A lump that she wanted to pull out and fling at her father.

"He claimed he knew you and begged me to bring him here rather than take him to jail."

*Take him! Don't let me stop you.* "Drinking?" She didn't know to whom she should address the question, which felt more like a statement.

"I picked him up on Randall doing twenty." On Randall Road, the speed limit was fifty-five.

"Thank you, Officer McCarthy." She opened the door wider to let the men pass. "I assume you took his car?"

"We're impounding it, yes, ma'am."

She pursed her lips and stared at the man she grudgingly called "Father," then sighed. She didn't need Dan to see her feelings.

"Can I get you a lemonade or tea or something?"

Her father piped up. "I'd like a lemon—"

"*Officer* McCarthy?" she cut in as she tried to smile.

"No, thank you, I need to be on my way. Are you willing to keep an eye on him?"

*Do I have to?* "Of course." She turned to really look at her father for the first time. He was old and worn out and thinner than she'd remembered. His eyes were the normal bloodshot, but there was a sadness there she had never noticed before. "Have a seat in the living room," she told her dad, her tone void of compassion. "And don't touch anything. I'll be back in a minute."

"I'll still be able to hear you talking about me!" he said, almost paranoid.

Mimi escorted Dan to the front porch. "This is a surprise. Thanks for bringing him over here."

Dan nodded. "Please don't take offense at this, Mimi. But it's sort of nice to see you have a messed-up family, too."

Mimi cringed inside. *Thanks so much for reminding me.* "I'll see you on Sunday?"

"Wouldn't miss it. Give me a call if you need anything," he said and nodded toward the door.

"I will."

She stood on the porch until Dan's squad car drove around the corner and disappeared. Exhaling and pushing her hands through her hair, she slowly opened the door and wondered what new adventure she was in for. *It's always something.*

She walked past the living room and noticed her father had already found the TV remote and was surfing the channels. "Stay there, Dad. I'll be right back."

"I'll take that lemonade any time."

"I'll get right on it."

"Unless, of course, you've got a cold one laying around somewhere." He chuckled, obviously pleased with his little joke. "I prefer Budweiser."

Shifting back her shoulders, she marched past the kitchen to Mark's office and dialed the church. When Mark picked up, she breathed hard into the receiver. "Mark, you need to come home. Dad's here."

"Uh-oh," Mark said, sounding as frustrated as Mimi felt.

"I get the feeling he thinks he's staying. Honestly, if it's not one thing with this family, it's another."

"I'll be right home."

Mimi started to hang up when she heard Mark's "Hey!" calling back to her. She placed the receiver back to her ear.

"Just breathe, babe. It'll be okay. We'll get through this together. And don't forget, I love you."

Despite herself, she smiled, and knew somehow, some way, he was right. It *was* going to be okay.

*Well, I guess Jennifer's casserole is gonna have to wait. I'm not leaving Dad alone here—and I'm sure not taking him with me.*

# 57

# Jennifer

*Wednesday, May 2*
*2:27 p.m.*

Jennifer had just fed and put a sleeping Carys in her crib when she came into the living room and saw Jo Jo through the front window, bounding up the driveway with several shopping bags clutched in each hand.

*What is she doing here* now?

Sam's parents, eager to see Carys, were driving up from West Virginia and set to arrive in a few hours. So he'd have time to spend with them, Sam had gone into the office to wrap up Sunday's sermon and tend to any other odds and ends. Meanwhile, Jennifer hoped to tidy the house, change the sheets in the guest bedroom, and get a roast in the oven.

But here was Jo Jo.

Jennifer opened the door. "Mother! You're kind of early, aren't you?"

Jo Jo didn't stop to answer her, instead pushing by with her packages and dropping them in the center of the living room floor.

"Whew," she huffed, ignoring Jennifer's question. "I wasn't sure if I could get those in here by myself or not."

Jo Jo stood with her hands on her hips, her eyes darting around the room. Jennifer could feel a wave of electricity emanating from her.

"Where's that grandbaby of mine?" Jo Jo asked.

"She's sleeping, but we can sneak in and take a peek if you want," Jennifer answered, but she couldn't take her eyes off Jo Jo. *Something isn't right here.* "Mother, when I called you last night, I said to come at five tonight for dinner. Remember, Sam's parents are getting here today?"

Jo Jo nodded but didn't say anything. *Her eyes look weird. Like she's in another world.*

"So then . . . did you just decide to come on your own now for a reason? And where did you get all this stuff?"

Jo Jo rolled her eyes at Jennifer, as if Jennifer were the one who was acting peculiar. "I figured you might need some help with the baby while you were getting ready. But if you want me to go—"

"No, no." Jennifer felt bad for making her mother feel unwanted. After all the years they'd been at odds, the last thing she wanted to do was create another wall between them. "I just . . . I need to get this place in shape before Dad . . . I mean . . . *Dale* and Patty get here." Jennifer hadn't told Jo Jo yet that she called Sam's parents "Mom and Dad." She wasn't sure how she was going to explain it without hurting her feelings.

Jo Jo dropped her hands and gave Jennifer a mock salute. "Sergeant Jo Jo, ready for duty, ma'am."

As she observed her mother's high spirits, Jennifer felt a strange recognition wiggling out of some deep place where she had buried it. *She's too motivated, too restless. And why isn't she at work?*

"Mother, did you take the afternoon off?" She was afraid to hear the answer.

A silly smile crept across Jo Jo's face. "Eh, those places decided they can keep their own books."

*Oh, here we go.* "So you're unemployed?" She turned to the pile of bags. "And yet you went out and bought all this stuff?"

Jo Jo looked exasperated. "Hey, a little shopping therapy is good. It's just a few things anyway."

It was more than a "few" things. The store names on the bags told Jennifer these were no cheap purchases.

Suddenly, it all clicked in and that inkling of an old emotional response came full force into Jennifer's mind. It was as if she were fourteen again, with a mother who was more like a child than a parent. That sense of responsibility she'd carried around when she was growing up came roaring back into her brain like a freight train, the final impact like a thud on her body.

"Mother, I hate to ask this, but are you taking your meds?"

Jo Jo tsked and turned away. When she looked back at Jennifer, almost into her eyes but not quite, Jennifer knew what was coming.

"I'm sick of those things," Jo Jo said. "They don't let me *feel*. I want to know what it's like to feel sad and feel joy. That medicine just makes me feel nothing." Her arms flailed about while she was speaking, as if she were beckoning the feelings to come in.

*You're sick all right.* "Mother, you know you need to take them. It's the only thing—"

Jo Jo waved her off. "I'm good, sweetie. I'm good. Trust me."

*Trust. Right.*

Jennifer eyed the clock. Sam's parents would be there in two hours. *I can't do anything about this now. Might as well take advantage of Manic Mother while I can.*

"We'll need to talk about this later," Jennifer said, stepping over the bags. Jo Jo appeared relieved that the inquisition was being put on hold. "If you're really here to help, let's get moving."

Jo Jo turned in front of Jennifer and did a little fake march toward the kitchen.

*Why did I call her and get this relationship started again?* Jennifer wondered as she followed behind. *This should be such a happy time, and now I'm going to have to start worrying about her again. I should have just left well enough alone!*

Jo Jo turned quickly and put her hands on Jennifer's shoulders, as if she could hear Jennifer's thoughts and wanted to divert them. "Hey, I forgot to say—welcome to motherhood, baby girl! You're going to make a great one!"

Jennifer accepted Jo Jo's hug, but she wondered if Jo Jo could feel the anxiety rumbling through her body. *A great mother. Yeah, for Carys* and *for you.*

# CHAPTER
# 58

# Felicia

*Wednesday, May 2*

*4:35 p.m.*

Dave carried two stem glasses with apple juice in them out the back door and onto the deck. Felicia, following behind him, toted a plate of cheese, crackers, pickles, and olives. They eased into the green Adirondack chairs and dove into their snack as they surveyed their blossoming backyard.

"This is some weather for early May, isn't it?" Dave asked, unbuttoning his dress shirt cuffs and rolling up the sleeves. He had finished his day early, so when he got home at 4:30 he persuaded Felicia to close up shop and relax with him.

Felicia finished chewing her bite of Triscuit with provolone. "Love it. I could do without winter, but there is something really special about spring coming, all the new life."

New life. Yes, she was experiencing that in spades. On her day of panic last week, she'd called Becky, who was eager to help. They decided that Becky would keep Nicholas at her house from nine to five on Mondays and Wednesdays, then on Tuesdays and Thursdays she would pick him up after preschool at two and care for him until five. Fridays would be family days with Dave and Felicia both taking off work to be with their son.

Dave took a sip of apple juice—a nonalcoholic substitute that gave them an excuse to pull out the fancy crystal wine goblets they'd gotten as a Christmas present from Ted a few years ago—then set his glass on the plastic table between them and reached for Felicia's hand.

"*Amor*," he asked, "are you sure this 'new life' is what you want?"

Felicia heard the beginnings of screeching airplanes in her head. She'd suspected Dave didn't like her working from home, but she hadn't brought it up for fear of an argument. That old insecurity about his need for a homemaker rose inside her.

She pulled her hand away is if to reach for her juice, then stopped abruptly. "If you don't want me working from home, just say so, Dave. Don't ask me if it's what *I* want just so you can tell me what you want." The warm afternoon was chilled by her tone.

Dave shifted in his chair to face her better, the mini-picnic in front of them suddenly forgotten. "No, it's just that you seemed so happy not working, I thought maybe you decided to work from home because you were worried about money or something."

Felicia shook her head. How could their thinking still be so far apart after nearly eight years of marriage? "Actually, I was sort of pretending to like being home," she said quietly. "But really I was bored out of my mind. I thought maybe it would go away after a while. But I can't help it, Dave. As much as I love taking care of Nicholas and our home, I really do have a passion for my career."

Felicia reached for her glass and took a sip. As she did, she spied Dave over the top of the rim. He wore an amused look. "I gotta say, I don't miss the freaky soups," he said sheepishly.

Dave's comment nearly made Felicia spew juice across the table as she burst out laughing, but she swallowed quickly instead. "Me neither," she said. "Can you imagine what we might have endured if I'd made it to Julia's chapter on eggs?"

He reached across for her hand, and this time she interwined her fingers with his. "Why do we still have these misunderstandings?" she asked lovingly. "Do you think we'll ever know each other so well that we'll just know what the other is thinking, and we'll be right?"

"Yeah, when we're about eighty-five, and then we'll die," Dave said with a chuckle.

"Oh, something to look forward to!" Felicia smiled and reached for another cracker with her free hand. "All those years of work on our marriage, only to have it perfected in heaven anyway!"

As Dave lifted his hand to grab an olive, Felicia noticed a Band-Aid on his forearm. "Did the vampire kid get ya?" she asked, jutting her chin so his eyes would follow hers to the bandage.

"No, I—"

Without finishing his sentence, Dave turned to look at Felicia. Almost simultaneously, their mouths dropped in surprise as their hands released from each other.

"Have you—"

"No!" she responded with astonishment. She knew his question without hearing it. The irony of the moment after just complaining about their lack of understanding was not lost on her.

"Me neither!" he said.

"How long, do you think?" she asked, continuing a conversation only they could understand.

"Wow, I'd say around Easter or so."

The timeline established, they let their eyes move away from each other and sat in silent bewilderment.

Felicia spoke first. "What do you think . . . did he just grow out of it?"

Dave sighed and looked away. When his face turned back to Felicia, she could see the slightest glistening of tears in his eyes. "No, *amor*, I think we were the ones who had to grow a little this time. Even though the last several weeks have been hard for us to get used to, it's what Nicholas really needed. I've never seen that boy smile so much."

Felicia nodded. She knew Dave was right, but she hadn't put two and two together until he pointed it out. As usual she'd been organizing and planning so much she'd forgotten to recognize the results of working from home. And the blessings. It had been weeks since Nicholas had thrown a crying fit . . . outbursts that were almost daily when she was working in Cincinnati.

And, on a much more trivial level, she was saving a ton of money on pantyhose!

The sound of a car pulling in the driveway triggered them to gulp down the rest of their juice and scoot their chairs back. Just as they were standing up, Nicholas appeared from around the corner of the house, his face flushed with excitement. Becky followed behind him.

"Dad, Mama," he said running up to them, "I got to groom the horse today!"

As Felicia reached down to hug him, her eyes met Becky's. "Thank you," she mouthed, but her gratitude was more than just simple appreciation. And she knew Becky's smile and wave before she turned and left were more heartfelt than just a casually unspoken good-bye.

With Nicholas still chattering about his day, the three of them walked closely together into the house. Dave reached around to tuck an arm across Felicia's waist and they gazed at each other.

"It's nice to all be home, isn't it?" he whispered in her ear so Nicholas wouldn't feel interrupted.

Felicia smiled in agreement and put her head on his shoulder. *Yes, it certainly is.*

# 59

# Jennifer

*Sunday, May 6*

*10:15 a.m.*

Hoisting the baby carrier out of the car, Jennifer saw that Carys was awake. *I hope she doesn't cry during the service. Maybe Sam was right. Maybe I should put her in the nursery until . . .*

"I'll grab the diaper bag," Patty called cheerfully from the other side of the car. Jennifer appreciated having Sam's mom with her, especially on this first day at church with the baby. Although Patty was about as wide as she was tall and not someone who would turn heads, her confidence was extremely attractive, Jennifer thought. She always had something good to say, and she knew how to make people laugh. She sort of reminded Jennifer of that Southern lady on the cooking channel, the one who uses prepared mixes (which Jennifer thought was the best kind of cooking!).

In comparison to Patty's rosy cheeks and reddish hair, Sam's dad, Dale, was a complete opposite—tall and thin with dark hair, and he hardly spoke a word. Dale and Patty were an unmatched set, but their love and appreciation for each other was always apparent in the way they looked at or touched each other. Jennifer enjoyed being around them because she saw some of each of them in Sam, and they made her feel special and loved—that's why she called them "Mom" and "Dad."

Patty came over with the diaper bag and saw Carys with her eyes open. "There's my pretty little girl," she cooed. "Are you going to be quiet for Mommy during church?"

"It seems like every baby cries when she's being dedicated, doesn't it? I see Sunday school must be out," Jennifer said as they walked to the church door, where Dale was waiting. He had gone with Sam to Sunday school while the women stayed behind to get ready. Jennifer had realized already that getting herself showered and dressed was nothing compared to preparing Carys for the day, so she knew she'd need that extra time. And she did.

"Eh, there's times I'd like to cry out during church, too, when that pastor of ours is going on for forty minutes," Patty said, laughing. "But I'm sure I won't feel that way today with my Sam preaching and our little Carys being dedicated. Lots to keep my attention."

"I'm so glad you're here," Jennifer said with a sigh of relief, smiling at Patty as they reached the door.

Before they went in, she glanced back at the parking lot. When her mother had heard them talking at dinner the other night about the dedication, she'd said she wanted to come. Then later she'd said she would bring her "guy," too. Jennifer had tried subtly to discourage it—she didn't need the circus of her mother and whatever man she was dragging along on what she anticipated to be a stressful day—but then Patty had spoken up.

"Jo Jo, I think it would be wonderful to have all the grandparents there," she'd said. "We can all sit together."

With such a gracious invitation, Jennifer couldn't deny her mother the right to join them. Besides, how awful was it that she wanted to bar her mother from coming to church, where she might learn about the Lord? Though Jennifer knew it was selfish, she couldn't help it. With her mother off her meds, it was like living with a time bomb, ticking away.

Once they were inside, Dale silently took the carrier from Jennifer and held it while Jennifer pulled Carys out and into her arms. "Would you like to hold her, Grandpa?" she asked.

He shook his head shyly. "I'll be the keeper of this—" he glanced at Patty, apparently searching for the right word for the carrier but Jennifer noticed that she was already engaged in conversation with someone else. " . . . of this while you carry her. Just let me know if you need it back."

She didn't have the baby out two seconds before a gaggle of older ladies—gathered together talking after Sunday school—spied her and darted over. Jennifer felt a surge of apprehension. Because Dale and Patty had been visiting, no one had been over yet to see Carys. Or more precisely, to see Carys's race.

"There's that new PK," one called.

"Oh, let's see her!" squealed another.

When they got close enough, Jennifer tilted the baby toward them and smiled, watching their eyes for a reaction.

The moment of uncomfortable silence confirmed everything Jennifer had dreaded.

"Oh . . . what beautiful . . . skin . . . she has." Bitsy Underwood was the first of the four women to find her words.

"Well, isn't it nice that you adopted a needy child," Lana Maxter added approvingly. "That's our pastor and his wife," she said, catching her three friends' eyes and nodding. "Always setting a good example for the rest of us."

Jennifer wasn't sure what to think. On the one hand they seemed accepting, but on the other they seemed to be trying too hard. Should she explain that they didn't *know* she was biracial until she was born? She didn't want them to think she and Sam had been intentionally altruistic.

Patty walked over at just the right time. "Now, I'll bet one of you ladies would love to hold her, wouldn't you? We older gals can't help ourselves around newborns—built-in grandmas, we are."

Patty gently took Carys from Jennifer and handed her to Bitsy, who looked surprised to be chosen. "Isn't she precious?" Patty asked encouragingly.

Jennifer had to laugh inside. Patty was totally working these women in an effort to expose and do away with their church-lady opinions. She wished she could be more like her.

"Hey, that's my grandbaby you're holding." Jo Jo strode up to Bitsy, bracelets jangling on both wrists and long skirt snapping on her cowboy boots. She practically snatched Carys from her.

"Mother!" Jennifer said in a muffled shout, glancing around quickly to see who noticed the scene besides those in it. "You shouldn't just—"

"Hello, baby girl," Jo Jo said into the blanket, ignoring Jennifer. But Jo Jo's soothing voice did nothing to erase the sudden jolt Carys must have felt when Jo Jo grabbed her. She started to cry.

As Bitsy, Lana, and the others backed away, Jennifer gingerly took Carys from Jo Jo. "What's wrong with you?" she spat over Carys's crying. "Why would you walk in here and make a scene like that?"

Before she could answer, Patty put a hand on each of their backs. "Ladies, we should probably head in to church now. Don't want to be late!"

Jennifer knew her face was full of rage so she turned from her mother and Patty, took a deep breath, pulled on her pastor's wife's mask, and walked toward the sanctuary. *Oh, Lord, please just let Mother sit quietly during this service. And help me not to have anger in my heart toward her—even though right now I want to smack the living daylights out of her.*

---

*11:58 p.m.*

Jennifer was never so glad to hear the organ recessional. Everything had gone fine during the service—Carys had slept like an angel the whole time, even during her dedication, and Jo Jo had been a model grandmother, although Jennifer had noticed her fidgeting hands and legs. Still, as Jennifer stood at the front of the sanctuary holding Carys during the dedication, and looked around at the congregation, she didn't get a sense of acceptance.

Doubt gnawed at her. *Am I a failure in their eyes because I couldn't produce a baby naturally?* She knew it was an unlikely premise, but she couldn't help what she felt.

And it wasn't over yet. The Women's Guild had provided a cake and punch, as was tradition for baby dedications, so everyone was invited to the fellowship hall after the service.

*Will this day ever be over?* Jennifer wondered as she smiled and nodded at people while she quickly walked toward the hall, Carys asleep in her arms. *Do you think they can tell I just want to get out of here and go home?*

She could hear Jo Jo chattering away behind her and wondered whom she was talking to but didn't dare turn to look. *Please don't let her say anything embarrassing.*

Patty came up beside her. "Honey, if you need to freshen up before this little party, I can take Carys for you."

"Oh, thanks, Mom. I *could* use a quick break." Jennifer slipped away toward the rest rooms, figuring she'd have to wait awhile, but when she got there she had it to herself. *Thank you, Lord.* She figured if every good thing came from God, even an empty rest room during a stressful day qualified.

With her business finished, Jennifer headed back toward the fellowship hall. She noticed the church seemed strangely quiet and empty, except for a couple kids bouncing a ball to each other in the narthex. *Where is everyone?* she wondered. Then it hit her: They've gone home. They grabbed their cake and left so they wouldn't have to make small talk about . . .

Her mind stopped completely as she opened the door to the hall. There, sitting quietly and now staring at her, was practically the whole congregation. Sam stood at the front, bouncing Carys, and smiling. A large table was decorated with pink streamers and a giant cake that read, "Congratulations, Sam and Jennifer!" Next to the table was a pile—more like a mountain—of gifts wrapped in every shade of pink possible with bows and ribbons fluttering off them.

"Well, we didn't mean for this to be a surprise party, but from the look on your face, it looks like it is," said Derek, coming over to escort a gaping-mouthed Jennifer to her family. The room erupted with applause.

"I . . . I don't know what to say." Jennifer linked her arm in Sam's when she reached him and allowed herself to look around the room. Whatever negative feelings she'd thought she sensed from the congregation during the baby's dedication were gone.

Jennifer's mind raced. *Did I allow my insecurities to cloud the love they were trying to show me? Have I been doing that all along?*

"Let's have a word of prayer, and then we can get this party started," Derek said, bowing his head.

As she was closing her eyes, Jennifer remembered that she hadn't seen her mother in the crowd, so she lifted her head halfway and peered across the room. She finally found her in the back, whispering animatedly—and, what looked from a distance at least, flirtatiously—to Dexter Ridgley, a recent widower. It suddenly occurred to her that with everything going on, she hadn't noticed the absence of Jo Jo's boyfriend. *He probably balked at going to church. Monty never would have set foot in a church.*

After the prayer, Sam showed off the baby while people mingled and ate cake. Jennifer was sharing war stories about caring for an infant with some other moms when Jo Jo came rushing over, her arms full of jewelry clinking like a gypsy's.

"Jen, Jen." She pulled breathlessly at Jennifer's shirtsleeve like a little kid.

Jennifer didn't want the others to hear what her nutty mother might say, so she excused herself and drew her mother to a quiet corner.

"What?" she asked with slight exasperation.

"That Dexter, I like him!"

*What is this, seventh grade?*

"Mother, he just lost his wife a couple months ago. Shouldn't you—"

Jo Jo wasn't interested in Jennifer's caution. "I'm going to ask him out for a drink."

Jennifer started shaking her head.

"Jen, it's just a little drink," Jo Jo said a bit too loudly.

Jennifer grabbed Jo Jo's arm to try to knock some sense into her. "Mother, we don't invite people for drinks here," she said through clenched teeth. "If you must ask him out, tell him you want to have a cup of coffee or something."

Jo Jo regarded Jennifer as if she didn't know what she was talking about. "Coffee? Please, that's no fun!"

She turned away, but before Jennifer could follow her, Sam walked over with Carys. "I think someone needs a little change from her mama," he said, holding her out.

But Jennifer's mind was still on Jo Jo as she watched her zip through the crowd and back to Dexter, her intended conquest. "Yes, she does. She sure does."

Turning back to Sam, she was struck by his cherubic grin. His round face seemed to glow with pride and joy as he looked from Carys to her and back again. He moved the baby into one arm and opened his other arm for her to join him. It was as though they were inside a bubble, with all of the activity around them on the outside.

As they huddled together, Jennifer realized that even though they had been taking care of Carys since her birth, with so much going on it wasn't until this actual second that she fully absorbed her new status. She was a mom. Sam was a dad. They were a family. Finally!

The thought made her let out a long, contented breath.

Sam turned his head to place a soft kiss on Jennifer's cheek. "I have to admit, this all happened so fast that I wasn't totally convinced we were doing the right thing with this adoption. But, wow, I couldn't imagine her being any more beautiful than if she'd come from us. I'm far and away in love with this little imp already."

"It's like a fairy tale, isn't it?" Jennifer whispered, then pulled away and started to take Carys from him. "Okay, Daddy, time to get the princess cleaned up. This is her party, after all."

Carys started to whimper as they transferred her, then erupted into a full-blown cry. At the same time, Marian Bell, the church's Nervous Nelly, whizzed up seemingly from nowhere and clutched Sam's forearm. "Pastor," she whined, "the youth have taken some of the cake outside and are throwing it at each other. Some of it even got on the stained-glass window. Can you do something to make them stop?"

Sam obediently followed Marian, leaving Jennifer holding a crying Carys. The sudden jolt from tranquility to chaos, which in the past might have infuriated Jennifer, this time made her laugh. She trundled Carys in the crook of her left arm and hoisted the black pleather diaper bag with her right hand. "Back to reality," she said to the unaware baby, then darted toward the bathroom, happy that her dreams and her reality had finally merged into one bliss.

# Lulu's Café

*Tuesday, May 8*
*11:54 a.m.*

Lisa stepped back and examined her "masterpiece." She appreciated that Gracie and Lulu's owner, Lester, agreed that the PWs could commandeer the back of the diner for an "un" baby shower.

Lisa moved forward to adjust the giant cardboard pink stork that almost touched the ceiling. It held a wrapped bundle, supposedly the baby, with the words WELCOME CARYS SHORES! written across it.

On a table next to their usual booth, Lisa arranged several neatly wrapped packages, all decorated with baby gift wrap, except one that was bundled in a pink baby blanket.

Lisa loved doing this type of thing—especially for Jennifer, who'd waited so long to become a mother. Lisa thought back to when her own children were babies. What a wonderful time—no rebelliousness to deal with in babies.

But she was glad her children were okay. Ricky was the same ornery, lovable kid. And now Callie appeared to be back on track—at least almost back on. She still had her moody occasions, when she just went loopy. But those times usually coincided with her period, so while Joel still didn't get it, Lisa was there with a large Hershey chocolate bar, a can of Cherry Diet Pepsi, and a heating pad.

She was also pleased that the spring break Callie had spent with Grandma Jenkins weeks ago had actually turned out better than she'd anticipated. A few days before, Callie had entered the kitchen when Lisa was making dinner and had said, out of the blue, "You really had it tough, too, being a preacher's kid, didn't you?"

It was a connection. Lisa had almost cried all over the taco casserole she was making.

Now Lisa turned to see if anybody else had arrived yet. Felicia, dressed in jeans and a white button-down pressed shirt, was pulling bags of presents out of the backseat of her BMW. Lisa was proud of Felicia, even though for a few weeks the whole "adjusting to being a homemaker" deal had been wearing a little thin. But Felicia had managed and now the combination of working *and* being at home had done her a world of good—Lisa had seen the change. More relaxed, happier, calmer. Lisa smiled when she thought about the surprise present she and Mimi had gotten for Felicia. Knowing that Lisa and Joel were running tight financially, Mimi had said she'd pay for most of it if Lisa would pick it up. Lisa glanced at the single present, poking out from behind the stork. *Boy, will she ever be surprised!* she thought delightedly.

Mimi wasn't too far behind Felicia, carrying her own bags of presents and goodies. "I have to go back out," Mimi said, dropping the presents on the table and scurrying back toward the door. "The cake."

Lisa and Felicia busied themselves arranging the new arrival of gifts and chatting about how excited they were to see Jennifer's face and to finally meet Baby Carys.

"It's an unusual name, isn't it?" Lisa asked.

"Mmm-hmmm." Felicia said, pushing a bow back on one of her gifts. It had apparently fallen off in transit.

Lisa saw Mimi standing outside the door, trying to get somebody's attention. Her arms were filled as she balanced a large cake. Putting down one of the ribbons she was messing with, Lisa started to race to the door but stopped when she noticed Gracie walking over.

"I'm coming," Gracie announced. "Hold your horses."

"Thanks," Lisa heard Mimi say. "I wanted to get this in before Jennifer gets here."

"Is she bringing the baby?" Gracie asked, moving a few chairs out of Mimi's way.

"Yes, but with a new baby, that girl will be lucky to make it by one o'clock!" Lisa laughed.

Arriving at a table next to the gift table, Mimi gently lowered the cake box. "Can we take a look?" Lisa asked, eager to see what kind of cake Mimi had baked. Mimi gingerly lifted the lid for Lisa and Felicia to peer in. It was the brightest purple Lisa thought she'd ever seen.

Felicia burst out laughing and high-fived Mimi.

"What is it?" Lisa asked, confused.

"Barney!" Mimi said proudly. "The purple dinosaur is going to become Jennifer's best friend. Trust me."

Felicia poked Mimi. "Close it up. She just pulled in."

Lisa glanced at her watch. *12:16.* "Not bad! She's almost on time."

They finished the final touches, then stood waiting for Jennifer to enter.

After a few minutes, Felicia said, "Maybe we should go help her? She's probably not used to the routine yet."

Just then, Lisa saw Jennifer heft two bags onto her shoulder, pick up the baby carrier, and start for the door. Again, Gracie was there to greet her.

The door jingled, announcing the arrival of their new guest.

"Thanks, Gracie!" Jennifer said, sounding happier than Lisa had ever heard her.

They all descended on her. "Good grief! Do you have enough stuff?" Felicia asked at the sight of a very loaded-down Jennifer.

Mimi grabbed two oversize diaper bags, while Lisa took the baby carrier.

"We started buying when I was PG, and then when Sam's parents heard, they sent boxes of stuff from West Virginia, and then the church had a surprise shower for me."

"Do you realize you don't need to travel with every single thing they all gave you?" Mimi laughed, placing the bags next to their booth.

"Well, we're having a shower for you, too, but this stuff might not be as, um, useful, shall we say." Lisa placed the baby carrier on top of their booth.

"I see that!" Jennifer laughed and pointed at the stork. "This is great! Thank you so much."

"We haven't even done anything yet," said Mimi. "Hold off on that thanksgiving until you see what we've gotten you."

Jennifer laughed again and hugged each one of them.

"Well, let's see this beautiful baby," Mimi said, starting to lift the carrier's top. "That story you told about Sam's reaction when he first saw her was hilarious!"

Lisa laughed at the memory. Right after the baby was born, Jennifer had called Lisa and the others to tell them how everything had gone—and to share the surprise of the baby's skin tone.

"She's gorgeous!" Felicia cooed at Carys, as Mimi unhooked the carrier latches and lifted the little girl out.

"What a precious little one," Mimi said, holding her close.

Lisa saw Jennifer smiling, and asked, "How are you doing?"

"I've never been so happy," Jennifer said. "So *exhausted,* but so happy. I had no idea how much work she would be!"

Her friends laughed in understanding.

"Now, why the name *Carys?*" Lisa asked. "It's such an unusual name. I've never heard it before."

"It's Welsh for *love.*"

"Perfect," Mimi said, passing the baby to Felicia.

"Let me see who's causing all this commotion in our restaurant," Gracie said loudly, walking over. Lisa saw her eyes widen slightly, obviously surprised at Carys's race but not wanting to say anything about it out loud. "She's beautiful. You're going to love that baby as if she were your own flesh and blood, you just watch."

"I already do, Gracie! I can't believe how God knits your heart so quickly to a baby. I wish I could have carried her in my belly for nine months, but I'm going to make up that time bonding with her!"

"And Jessica?" Lisa asked, wondering about the birth mother.

"Took off for Montana as soon as she was released from the hospital. Didn't leave a forwarding address or anything."

"Did you have any trouble getting the *real* birth father's signature for the adoption?" Mimi asked.

"Our attorney handled it for us, but he said the guy signed with no problem," Jennifer answered, appearing relieved.

"Well, let's order," Felicia said, sitting down. "I'm starving! I haven't had a decent meal in ages."

"How is that cooking coming along?" Mimi asked Felicia, quickly winking at Lisa. Lisa dodged behind the stork and grabbed the present.

"Well, let's just say Julia and I have a healthy respect for each other, but we're no longer spending time together."

"Here." Lisa pushed the plain wrapped gift toward Felicia. "This is for you. A little gift from Mimi and me."

"What's this?" Lisa could tell Felicia was taken completely off-guard. "The shower isn't for *me*."

"We know," Mimi said. "Just open it."

Felicia excitedly tore into the wrapping and stopped, then she threw back her head and howled. "Thanks a lot, guys!" She held up her prize: *Cooking the Basics with Betty Crocker*. "I'll make sure to bring something special from one of these recipes when we have our first pastors' wives' get-together next month."

"This isn't so much for you as it is for Dave and Nicholas's sake." Mimi ducked as Felicia crumpled her napkin and lobbed it at her.

*The pastors' wives' get-together next month.* Lisa was excited to think about it. She was so glad they'd all agreed to take charge of it. For the first few times, they decided to trade off leading it. Lisa was responsible for the first month, so she'd made phone calls and sent out personal invitations to all the pastors' wives' in the region, encouraging them to attend a potluck—hey, it was still a church function!—and bring their favorite dish. After the meal, Lisa was going to simply open up about her own experience of trying to be a good wife, mother, pastor's wife, and Christian, and how often she felt as if she were failing. She believed that if she shared her own struggles, it would help the other women open up as well. She knew it had for the PWs here in Cheeksville. She only hoped that the wives would find it a great experience and that they would forge a support network and encourage one another.

"Hey, guess what?" Felicia broke into Lisa's thought. "I've been asked to emcee the Mother's Day event at church this Sunday. I found an associate's wife from a Baptist church down in Paducah. I guess she's started a speaking and singing ministry, in which she shares her testimony about how she had several abortions when she was younger and how that affected her life, because she's now unable to have children. So her message is that we are all God's daughters. And the best part is that all I have to do is open, pray, and close."

"Good practice for when you lead the PW meetings," Mimi said.

"Also, I'm thinking about inviting Becky, too. Would that be okay? Since she's sort of a PW, too."

Lisa remembered Felicia telling them about Becky and her husband, the rabbi.

Felicia continued. "She's been such a good influence on Nicholas as a loving, attentive adult. But she told me that he's been a great influence on her, too. That him needing her has helped her through not being a PW—or actually, an *R*W—anymore."

"Of course she's welcome." Lisa thought it would be a good opportunity to meet her, since she'd heard such good things about this mysterious woman.

"Hey, I just thought of something," Jennifer announced. "I beat Lucy at becoming a mom. Ha!"

Lisa knew that Lucy was the associate pastor's pregnant wife at Jennifer's church. They laughed. "It's shallow, I know, but work with me here."

Felicia cocked her head toward Mimi. "Not to bring down this par*tay*, but Mimi, what's the update on Mr. Principal. Did you tell Mark?"

Mimi bit her lip, then nodded. "It wasn't as bad as I thought it would be. He actually asked me for forgiveness first. I couldn't believe it. He said he had neglected me. I should have been the one begging for forgiveness." She paused and stared at her lap. "There was . . . an opportunity. I almost kissed him."

"Mark?" Jennifer asked, shaking a rattle at Carys, who was cooing happily.

"No. Phil," Mimi said quietly. "And I *wanted* to. I was in his office, alone with him—"

"First mistake," Felicia said.

Mimi only nodded in agreement. "And he—"

"But you didn't do it, right?" It was Felicia interrupting again.

"No. The school bell rang. But, honestly, I shudder to think of what might have happened if it hadn't. But there's something else."

"Oh, boy," Felicia groaned.

"No, no, it's nothing like that," Mimi's protest matched her huge eyes. "It's my dad, the drunk. He's in town and staying at my house. And it looks like he's staying who knows how long."

"What's he doing here?" Lisa asked.

Mimi sighed. "The cops dropped him on my doorstep and he doesn't have anywhere else to go. It looks like we're stuck. And Mark is *not* happy."

"It doesn't sound like you're jumping up and down with joy, either," Felicia said.

"If it's not one thing, it's another," Mimi said, as if trying to be overly confident. "I'll manage. Hey, what's one more 'kid' in the sea of what I already have?"

"This is a lesson I've learned," Jennifer said as she put down the rattle and looked directly at Mimi. "We can't do it on our own. That's why we need the Holy Spirit to guide us. Maybe this is a lesson to remind you that *he* needs to be captain of your ship, to use a cliché."

Lisa was impressed. Jennifer had changed, had somehow deepened. She remembered sitting across from Jennifer less than a year before when

Jennifer has been ready to walk completely away from her faith. Now here she sat, sharing spiritual insight.

"I wish I could say that Phil's no longer attractive to me—but that's not true. He is. I'm just praying that the attraction moves from emotional longing to a healthy respect."

"Even PWs can fall prey," Lisa chimed in. "So, if you think you are standing firm, be careful that you don't fall!"

Felicia and Mimi both added, "Paul."

Lisa laughed. "Yep. From 1 Corinthians."

"We can't afford to be naive—or stupid," Mimi said. "Affairs happen— even to pastors and their wives. And they can happen to *us* if we don't guard our hearts and our lives. That's why I'm so glad I have you three. You wouldn't put up with it!"

"You're right about that one!" Felicia squeezed Mimi's arm.

"Okay, enough with the serious talk," Jennifer broke in. "Let's open my presents!"

Lisa hopped up, pleased that they were going back to a lighter subject on this celebratory day. Mimi appeared relieved, too.

Lisa began to transfer the gifts to the booth so Jennifer didn't have to get up.

"Aw, you shouldn't have," Jennifer said, placing her hands on her heart. "But I'm so glad you did!" She tore into the first package. "It's a . . . what in the world?"

Felicia laughed as she reached over and took the item. "It's a baby. Look—you pull her apart and you can use all the pieces. There's a washcloth—that's the baby's arm."

"Okay, that's disgusting. I have to dissect a baby to use the items? You're a sick woman, Felicia."

"Thank you! Here, open this one next."

Jennifer picked up what looked like a small book and unwrapped it. "*Hugs for Moms,*" she read, then looked at Lisa. "From you?"

Lisa smiled. "It's for when you need a hug and we're not around."

"Thank you," Jennifer said. "I'll take one now."

Lisa leaned over and gave her friend a squeeze, then whispered in her ear, "You're going to make a wonderful mother—and you have all of us praying for you every day."

"And I'm going to need it. My mother's coming to church now—"

Lisa, Felicia, and Mimi cooed in excitement.

"That's great!" Lisa started to say, but Jennifer quickly lifted a hand that stopped her.

"Yeah, not so fast. For a normal mother, yes, it's a good thing. But my mom has started back into her Marilyn Monroe mode where's she trying to woo everything that wears pants. I don't get her. She told me she's dating a guy, but she keeps flirting with all the single men at church."

Mimi narrowed her eyes.

"It's part of the bipolar thing," Jennifer explained.

"Oh!" Mimi nodded.

"She seems normal, but then she does this off-the-wall stuff. You never know what she's going to say or do—but you can bet that it's going to drive *you* crazy."

Felicia laughed. "Kind of like being a pastor's wife! You never know what your congregation's going to say or do, but you know you'll have to make the best of it."

"Well, then, we'll pray for the new mother and *her* mother." Lisa noticed her words brought tears to Jennifer. She reached over and grasped Jennifer's hand. "Oh, sweetie, it'll be okay. You've got us to help you through the mommy phase."

"Both of them!" Felicia smiled tenderly.

Jennifer squeezed Lisa's hand, then let go so she could wipe her eyes. "That means a lot. Thank you again."

Lisa nodded and handed her the next gift.

As Jennifer continued to open the presents, she piled up quite a stash.

Airport worker earplugs. Two pairs—one for her and one for Sam.

A plastic hand. "You'll need an extra hand," Mimi explained.

Nose plugs. They all laughed as Mimi said, "This one requires no explanation."

And a breast pump. "I've read some studies that say you can produce milk, even if you haven't had a baby," Mimi offered helpfully.

"I have to tell you," Jennifer said after she'd opened and laughed at the final gift. "One of the most surprising gifts for me was when I discovered that not all church people are bad. I mean, I had judged them because I guess I thought they were busy judging me, and in the process, I never allowed them to love me. I know I need to give them a chance—especially now that I'm going to need babysitters!"

Lisa gazed at her friends—three pastors' wives, all from different denominations, but all in this thing called "life and ministry" together. They needed each other—just as surely as they needed God and their husbands. She was truly blessed.

"I have a gift for you, too," Gracie said, sneaking up behind Lisa. She dipped into her apron pocket and pulled out an envelope. "It's not much, but I know pastors don't make too much money. So here. This is to start the little one's college fund."

Jennifer opened it, pulled out a twenty and a five, and got choked up. "Gracie, you didn't have to do this."

"I know," Gracie said gruffly. "I wanted to. Someone needs to think about these things."

"Bless you for this," Jennifer said softly.

"Well, now, don't get all worked up over it. And don't think this lets you out of giving me a tip today." She patted Jennifer on the head and lumbered back toward the counter.

"I'm so blessed." Jennifer wiped away a rebel tear that had escaped and trickled down her cheek.

"We all are," Mimi said and grabbed Felicia's and Lisa's hands. "Here's to friends who love God and their husbands and one another. May we go through life experiencing and appreciating the kind of joy we have right now."

"And especially when that joy seems distant," Felicia joined in, "may we be ever mindful of the giver of all good and perfect gifts, Jesus Christ. May he continue to lead us through the valleys of darkness and into his reward of eternal life, both now and always."

"Knowing that he's there with us, when we feel his presence and when we don't," Jennifer added, smiling.

"Amen," Lisa said. *May it be so.*

Lisa squeezed Mimi's and Jennifer's hands, then let go.

"How about some of that cake?" Felicia asked. "I'm in the mood for dinosaurs!"

Lisa laughed out loud. "You said it, my friend. Let's celebrate!"

# About the Authors

*Ginger Kolbaba* is editor of *Marriage Partnership* magazine, a publication of Christianity Today International, and author of numerous books, including *Surprised by Remarriage: A Guide to the Happily Even After* (Revell). She lives with her husband, Scott, in the Chicago suburbs. Visit Ginger at www.gingerkolbaba.com.

*Christy Scannell* is a freelance writer and editor. She and her husband, Rich, a newspaper editor, live in Southern California. Visit Christy at www.christyscannell.com.

# Welcome to
# *Lulu's Café...*

## where secrets
## are the daily special!

This sassy novel follows the lives of four pastors' wives who each have a distinctive desperation: Jennifer is desperate for faith, Felicia for fulfillment, Lisa for love, and Mimi for peace.

These "desperate four" are from different denominations, and none has close friends within her church, so they secretly connect with each other for a monthly lunch at Lulu's Café. An up-close and personal look at the behind-closed-doors lives of pastors' wives, filled with humor, romance, mystery, suspense, and the Lord's grace.

After reading this remarkable tale, every woman will come to the same realization: "I am not alone."

Ginger Kolbaba & Christy Scannell

# DESPERATE
# PASTORS' WIVES

*A Novel*

SECRETS FROM
LULU'S CAFE
SERIES

◆ HOWARD BOOKS
A DIVISION OF SIMON & SCHUSTER

*Coming Soon . . . Book 3*
*The Secrets of Lulu's Café series*

Spring has sprung in Red River, Ohio, but as the daffodils pop from the ground, so do the problems for the PWs, who need each other now more than ever.

Mimi thought Milo was the Plaisance household's last new addition—until her dad came calling.

Tormented by a childhood spent in shame, she fears what effect his drinking will have on her family, not to mention what the church will say. Where does a daughter's responsibility end?

A daughter who knows she's had enough is Jennifer. Her mother, Jo Jo, continues to whirl around in manic highs and depressive lows. But just when Jennifer is ready to distance herself from her again, a shocking new discovery makes her reconsider what it is to be a parent.

Meanwhile, Felicia's family visits from L.A., along with lots of baggage—emotional, that is. Once secrets are revealed, all but Felicia and Dave refuse to talk to each other. How can Felicia end the deafening silence, heal her family's wounds, and get them on a plane so she can get back to work?

Lisa is a woman ready to fly—away from the church that is splitting as she and Joel watch helplessly. Watching church members slap one another with cruelties, Lisa is just about to give up when a surprising source inspires her next step.

Despite their trials behind closed doors, the PWs build on their Lulu's support group by taking over the Southwest Ohio Pastors' Wives Fellowship. All is well until Ally, a new pastor's wife, decides to make the PWs her personal mentors, with hilarious results.

Out-of-control parents, stunning disclosures, estranged families, a demanding newcomer, and one mutinous church—you will laugh and cry with the PWs as they face yet more joys and heartaches in this third book of the Secrets from Lulu's Cafe series.